"A LORA LEIGH NOVEL IS AL[WAYS...]
—Fresh Fic[tion]

P R A I [...   ]EDS

"Anoth[...   ] Highly
charge[...   ] *Fiction*

"Incred[...   ]d seriously h[...   ]"

Books

"Delive[...   ]he ride
into th[...   ]dy for
more."   *Reviews*

"It is p[...   ]viewed*

"Wick[...   ]u begging fo[...   ]*mance*

"Erotic[...   ]*Junkies*

"Hea[...   ]*views*

"Lei[...   ]man-
tic p[...   ]*views*

"Lei[...   ]*ritics*

"No[...   ]xplo-
sivel[...   ]*eams*

"Siz[...   ]*Today*

"Lora Leigh doesn't disappoint when it comes to sexiness, intrigue and an added little bit of humor." *—Bitten by Love Reviews*

OVERCOME

LORA LEIGH

BERKLEY BOOKS, NEW YORK

THE BERKLEY PUBLISHING GROUP
Published by the Penguin Group
Penguin Group (USA) LLC
375 Hudson Street, New York, New York 10014

USA • Canada • UK • Ireland • Australia • New Zealand • India • South Africa • China

penguin.com

A Penguin Random House Company

This book is an original publication of The Berkley Publishing Group.

Library of Congress Cataloging-in-Publication Data

Leigh, Lora.
Overcome / Lora Leigh.
pages ; cm
ISBN 978-0-425-27773-7 (softcover)
1. Paranormal romance stories. I. Title.
PS3612.E357O94 2015
813'.6—dc23
2014041341

PUBLISHING HISTORY
Berkley trade paperback edition / February 2015

PRINTED IN THE UNITED STATES OF AMERICA

10 9 8 7 6 5 4 3 2 1

Cover art by S. Mirogue.
Cover design by Rita Frangie.

· CONTENTS ·

The
Breed Next Door

◆ ◆ ◆

✦ P R O L O G U E ✦

"You were created. Created to give your lives to the Genetics Council at any time deemed appropriate. You are animals. Nothing more. You have no sire. You have no bitch mother. You have only us. And we will decide if you are strong enough to live or die."

The dream was merciless, stark in the memory of who and what he was as he watched the scientist point out the procedure that had created him.

The genetic enhancement of an unknown sperm and ova. The fertilization, the development before it was ever placed within a human womb. And finally, the death of the vessels that had carried each Feline Breed babe to term.

Nothing was hidden from the immature creatures. They sat on the floor of their cells and watched the graphic video daily. They saw it nightly in their dreams.

"You are not human. No matter your appearance. You are an animal. A creation. A tool. A tool for our use. Never imagine you will ever be anything different . . ."

Tarek tossed within the nightmare, years of blood and death passing by him. The lashes of the whip biting into his back, his chest. Hours of torture because he had not killed savagely enough or because he had shown mercy. The pain of knowing that the dream of freedom might be no more than a fantasy, quickly lost to death.

He came awake in a rush, the blood pounding through his veins, sweat dampening his flesh as the horrors he had fought so long to distance himself from returned.

Breathing roughly, he rose from the bed, pulling on a pair of boxer briefs before leaving the bedroom.

He inhaled deeply as he left the room, his brain automatically processing the scents of the house, sifting through them, searching for anomalies. There were none. His territory was uncorrupted, as secure now as it had been when he settled into his bed.

He rubbed his hand over the ache in his chest, the almost ever-present remembrance of that last beating, and the whip running with a current of electricity that sent agony resonating through his body.

He was created, not born.

Those words echoed through his mind as he opened the back door and stepped onto the porch. *Created to kill. Not human . . .*

He stared into the bleak emptiness of the late-fall Arkansas night as he let the memories wash over him. Fighting them only made it worse, only made the nightmares worse.

You will never know love. Animals do not love, so before you ever imagine this is a benefit due you, forget it!

The Trainers had been quick to destroy any flicker of hope before it drew breath, took form, or hinted at an end to their tortured suffering. The psychological training had been brutal.

You are nothing. You are a four-legged beast walking on two. Never forget that . . .

Your ability to speak does not mean you have permission to do so . . .

He stared into the star-studded night.

God does not exist for you. God creates His children. He does not adopt animals . . .

The final destruction. A silent snarl curved his lips as he glared into the brilliance of a sky he had never been meant to see.

"Who does adopt us then?" he snarled to the God he had been taught had no time for him or for his kind. "Who does?"

◆ CHAPTER 1 ◆

Wasn't there some kind of law that said a man wasn't allowed to look that damned good? Especially the tight, hard bodies who persisted in mangling a perfectly good lawn at the wrong time of the year.

Lyra Mason was certain there had to be such a law. Especially when said male, Tarek Jordan, committed the unpardonable sin of whacking down her prized Irish roses.

"Are you crazy?" She ran out the front door, yelling at the top of her lungs, waving him away from the beautiful hedge that was finally managing to achieve reasonable height.

That was, before he attacked it with the Weed Eater he was wielding like a sword.

"Stop it. Dammit. Those are my roses," she wailed as she sprinted across her front lawn, skidded around the front of her car, and nearly slipped and broke her neck on the strip of lush green grass in front of him.

At least he paused.

He lowered the Weed Eater, tipped his dark glasses down that arrogant nose of his, and stared back at her as though she was the one committing some heinous act.

"Turn it off," she screamed, making a slicing motion across her throat. "Now. Turn it off."

Irritation and excitement simmered in her blood, heated her face, and left her trembling before him. He might be bigger than she was, but she had been maneuvering big, brawny men all her life. He would be child's play next to her brothers. Maybe.

He cut the motor, lifted a brow, and flashed all that bare, glorious muscle across his chest and shoulders. As though that was going to save him. She didn't think so.

The man had lived next door to her for almost six months and never failed to totally infuriate her at least once a week. And she wasn't even going to admit exactly how much she enjoyed razzing his ass every chance she got.

"Those are my roses!" She felt like crying as she rushed to the broken, ravaged branches of the four-foot-high hedge. "Do you have any idea how long it took me to get them to grow? Have you lost your mind? Why are you attacking my roses?"

He lifted one hand from the steel shaft of the Weed Eater and scratched his chin thoughtfully.

"Roses, huh?"

Oh God, his voice had that husky little edge. Dark. Deep. The kind of voice a woman longed to hear in the darkness of the night. The voice that tempted her in dreams so damned sexual she flushed just thinking about them.

Damn him.

He tilted his head to the side, staring at her roses for long moments behind the lenses of his dark glasses.

"I can't believe you did this." She flicked him a disgusted glance as she hunched in front of the prize bush and began inspecting the damage. "You've lived here six months, Tarek. Surely it occurred to you that if I wanted them cut down I would have done it myself."

Some men just needed a leash. This was obviously one of them. But he was fun—even if he was unaware of it. It just wouldn't do for him to know how often she went out of her way to come down on him.

"Sorry, Lyra. I thought perhaps the job was too large for you. It looked like a mess to me."

She stared up at him in shocked surprise as he said the blasphemous words. Only a man would consider roses a mess. It was a damned good thing she liked that helpless male look he gave her each time he messed up.

She could only shake her head. How long did the man have to live beside her before he learned to leave her side of the yard alone? He needed a keeper. She considered volunteering for the job. "You should have to have a license to use one of those. I bet you would have failed the test if you did."

A grin quirked his lips. She loved that little crooked grin, almost shy, with just a hint of wickedness. It made her wet. And she didn't like that, either.

Her eyes narrowed as she ignored the chill in the early winter air, her lips thinning in true irritation this time.

He was obviously ignoring the chill. He didn't even have on a shirt. It was barely forty degrees, and he was using a Weed Eater like it was June and the weeds were striking a campaign to take over. That or he just didn't like her roses.

"Look, just take your little power tool to the other side of your property. There are no neighbors there. No roses to mangle." She gave him a shooing motion with her hand. "Go on. You're grounded from this side of the yard. I don't want you here."

A frown edged between his golden-brown brows as they lowered ominously and his eyelids narrowed. What made men think that look actually worked on her? She almost laughed at the thought.

Fine, he was dangerous. He was getting ticked. He was bigger and stronger than she was. Who gave a damn?

"Don't you give me that look," she snorted in disgust. "You should know by now it doesn't work on me. It will only piss me off worse. Now go away."

He glanced around, appearing to measure some invisible line between where he was to his own house several yards away.

"I believe I'm on my own property," he informed her coolly.

"Oh, are you?" She stood carefully to her feet, staring over the edge of her pitifully cropped rosebush to where his feet were planted. Boy, he really should have known better than that. "Go read your deed, Einstein. I read mine. My roses are planted exactly six feet from the property line. From oak to oak." She point out the oak tree at the front of the street, then the one at the edge of the forest beyond. "Oak to oak. My brothers ran a line and marked it real carefully just for dumb little ol' me," she mocked him sweetly. "That puts you on my property. Get back on your own side."

She would have chuckled if it weren't so important to maintain the appearance of ire. If she was going to survive living next to a walking, talking advertisement for sex, then some boundaries would have to be established.

He cocked his hip, crossing his arms over his chest as the heavy Weed Eater dangled from the harness that crossed over his back.

He was wearing boots. Scarred, well-worn leather boots. She noticed that instantly, just as she noticed the long, powerful legs above them. And a bulge . . . Nope, not going there.

"Your side of the property is as much a mess as your bush is," he grunted. "When do you cut your grass?"

"When it's time," she snapped, pulling herself to her full height of five feet, three and three-quarters inches. "And it's not time in the middle of winter when it's not even *growing*."

Okay, so she barely topped his chest. So what?

"I would get in the mood if I were you." He used that superior male tone that never failed to grate on her nerves. "I have a nice ride-on lawnmower. I could cut it for you."

Her eyes widened in horror. He was staring back at her now with a crooked grin, a hopeful look on his face. She sneaked a look around his shoulder, stared at his grass, then shuddered in dismay.

"No." She shook her head fervently. This could be getting out of hand. "No, thank you. You hacked at yours just fine. Leave mine alone."

"I beg your pardon." He threw his shoulders back and drew up in offended male pride as he propped his hands on his hips.

He did it so well, too. Every time he messed up something he pulled that arrogance crap on her. He should have known it wasn't going to work.

"And so you should," she retorted, propping her hands on her hips as she glared back at him. "You hacked your grass. Worse, you hacked it in the winter. There's no symmetry in the cut, and you set your blade too low. You'll be lucky to have grass come summer. You just killed it all."

He turned and stared back at his lawn. When he turned back to her, cool arrogance marked his features.

"The lawn is perfect."

He had to be kidding.

"Look," she breathed out roughly. "Just stick to mangling your own property, okay? Leave mine alone. Remember the line—oak to oak—and stay on your side of it."

He propped his hands on his hips again. The move drew her eyes back to the sweat-dampened perfection of that golden male chest.

It should be illegal.

"You are not being neighborly," he announced coolly, almost ruining her self-control and bringing a smile of pure fun to her lips. "I was told when I bought the house that everyone on this block was friendly, but you have been consistently rude. I believe I was lied to."

He sounded shocked. Actually, he was mocking her, and she really didn't like it. Well, maybe she did a little bit, but she wasn't going to let him know it.

She refused to allow her lips to twitch at the sight of the laughter in his gaze. He very rarely smiled, but sometimes, every now and then, she could make his eyes smile.

"That Realtor would have told you the sun rose in the west and the moon was made of cheese if it would assure him a sale." She smiled mockingly. "He sold to me first, so he knew I wasn't nice. I guess he neglected to inform you of that fact."

Actually, she had gotten along quite well with the real estate agent. He was a very nice gentleman who had assured her that the homes on this block would only be sold to a specific type of person. So, evidently, he had lied to her, too, because the man standing across from her was not respectable, nor was he family-oriented. He was a sex god, and she was within a second of worshipping at his strong, male feet. She was so weak.

He was a rose assassin, she reminded herself firmly, and she was going to kick his ass if he attacked any more of her precious plants. Better yet, she would call her brothers and cry. Then they would kick his ass.

No, that wouldn't do, she hastily amended. They would run him off. That wasn't what she wanted at all.

"Perhaps I should discuss this with him." He tipped his glasses down his nose once again, staring at her over the rim. "At least he was right about the view."

His gaze roved over her from her heels to the tip of her head as his golden-brown eyes twinkled with laughter—at her expense, of course. As though she didn't know she was too homey. A little too normal-looking. She wasn't the sexy, siren type, and she had no desire to be. That didn't mean he had to make fun of her.

It was perfectly acceptable for her to toy with him. Having him turn the tables did not amuse her in the least.

"That was not amusing," she informed him coldly, wishing she could hide behind something now.

The ratty jeans she wore hung low on her hips, not because of fashion, but more because they were a bit too loose. The T-shirt she wore fit a bit better, but it was almost too snug. But she was cleaning house, not auditioning for Fashions R Us.

"I wasn't trying to be amusing." His grin was wicked, sensual. "I was being honest."

He was trying to get out of trouble. She knew that look for what it was. It wasn't the first time he had pulled it on her.

"I have three older brothers," she informed him coolly. "I know all the tricks, mister . . ."

"Jordan. Tarek Jordan," he reminded smoothly.

As though she didn't already know his name. She had known his name from the first day he had moved in to his house with the honkin' Harley he had ridden across her front lawn.

Damn, that Harley had really looked good, but he had looked even better sitting on it.

"Mister," she repeated, "you are not putting anything over on me, so don't think you are. Now keep your damned machines away from my property and away from me, or I might have to show you how they are used and hurt all that male pride you seem to have so much of." She shooed him again. "Go on. On your own property now. And leave my roses alone."

His eyes narrowed on her again. This time, his expression changed as well. It became . . . predatory. Not dangerous. Not threatening. But it wasn't a comfortable expression, either. It was an expression that assured her that an abundance of male testosterone was getting ready to kick in. And he did male testosterone really well. He got all snarky and snarly and downright ill-tempered as he glared at her, his voice edging into dangerously rough as he growled at her and attempted to berate her.

She refused to back down.

"Don't look at me like that, either. I told you. I have three brothers. You do not intimidate me."

His brow arched. Slowly.

"It was very nice to see you today, Lyra." He finally nodded cordially. "Perhaps next time, you won't be in such a bad mood."

"Yeah. Sometime when you're not mangling the looks of the block would be nice," she snorted as she turned away from him. "Geez, only I could get stuck with a neighbor with absolutely no landscaping grace. How the hell do I manage it?"

She stomped away, certain now that she should never have let her father talk her into this particular house.

"It's close to the family," she mocked, rolling her eyes. "The price is perfect," she mocked her eldest brother. "Yeah. Right. And the neighbors suck . . ."

◆   ◆   ◆

Tarek watched her go, hearing her mocking little voice all the way to the porch as she stomped up the sidewalk. Finally, the front door slammed with an edge of violence that would have caused any other man to flinch. Breeds didn't flinch.

He glanced down at the Weed Eater hanging from his shoulders and breathed in deeply before turning to glance back at the lawn.

The cut of the grass was fine, he assured himself, barely managing not to wince. Fine, it might not look so great, but he had fun cutting it. Hell, he even had fun using the Weed Eater. At least, until Ms. Don't-Attack-My-Roses came storming out from her house.

As though he wasn't well aware that all the female fury was more feigned than true anger. He could smell her heat, her arousal, and her excitement. She wasn't hiding nearly as much as she thought she was.

He chuckled and glanced back at the two-story brick-and-glass home. It suited her. Nice and regal on the outside, but with depth. Lots and lots of depth. He could see it in her wide blue eyes, in the pouty softness of her lips.

She was a wildcat, though. Well, she was as fiery as a wildcat anyway. He cleared his throat, scratched at his chest thoughtfully, then hefted the Weed Eater off his shoulders and headed back to the little metal shed behind his own house.

He liked his house better, he told himself. The rough wood two-story with the wraparound porch was . . . comfortable. It was roomy and natural, with open rooms and a sense of freedom. There was something about the house that soothed him, that eased the nightmares that often haunted him.

He hadn't been looking for a home when he gave in to the Realtor's suggestion to check out the house. He had been looking for a rental, nothing more. But as they pulled into the driveway, the fresh scent of a summer rainfall still lingering in the air, blending with the smell of fresh-baked bread wafting from the neighboring house, he had known, in that moment, this was his.

This house, too large for him alone, the yard begging for sheltering trees and bushes and the laughter of children echoing with it, called to him. Six months later, this home he hadn't known he wanted still soothed the rough edges of his soul.

He pulled open the door to the shed, pausing before stepping into the close confines of the little building to store the Weed Eater. He was going to have to replace the shed with a larger one. Each time he stepped into the darkness, he felt as though it was closing in on him, trapping him. Caging him in.

There was something different, though. He paused as he stepped from it, staring back into the interior as he considered it thoughtfully.

He hadn't smelled the usual mustiness of the building. For once, the smell of damp earth hadn't sent his stomach roiling with memories. It was because his senses were still filled with the soft scent of coffee, fresh-baked bread, and a warm, sweet female.

Lyra Mason.

He turned and stared back at her house, rubbing at his chest, barely feeling the almost imperceptible scars that crisscrossed his flesh there.

Coffee and fresh-baked bread.

He had never eaten fresh-baked bread. He had only smelled it drifting from her house in the past months. It had taken him forever to figure out what that smell was. And coffee was, unfortunately, a weakness of his. And she had both.

He wondered if she could make better coffee than he did.

Hell, of course she could. He grunted as he turned away and stalked to his back door. Jerking it open, he stepped into the house, stopping to pull off his boots before padding across the smooth, cream-colored tiles.

The kitchen was made for someone other than him.

He still hadn't managed to figure out the stove. Thankfully, there was a microwave or he would have starved to death.

He moved to the coffeepot with every intention of fixing some before he paused and grimaced. He could still smell the scent of Lyra's coffee.

His lip lifted in a snarl as a growl rumbled from his throat. He wanted some of her coffee. It smelled much better than his. And he wanted some of that fresh-baked bread.

Not that she was likely to give him any. He had cut her precious bush, so she would, of course, have to punish him. This was the way the world worked. He had learned that at the labs from an early age.

Well, he had known it. The scars that marred his chest and back were proof that it was a lesson he had never really fully learned.

He propped his hands on his hips and glared at Lyra's house. He was a Lion Breed. A fully grown male trained to kill in a hundred different ways. His specialty was with the rifle. He could pick off a man a half-mile away with some of the weapons he had hidden in his bedroom.

He had excelled in his training, learned all the labs had to teach him, then fought daily to escape. His chance had finally come with the attacks mounted on the Breed labs seven years before.

Since then, he had been attempting to learn how to live in a world that still didn't fully trust the animal DNA that was a part of him.

Not that anyone in the little city of Fayetteville, Arkansas, knew who or what he was. Only those at Sanctuary, the main Breed compound, knew the truth about him. They were his family and his employers.

He dropped his arms from his chest and propped his hands on his hips.

He couldn't get the smell of that coffee or that bread out of his mind. That woman would drive him crazy—she was too sensual, too completely earthy. But the smell of that coffee . . . He sighed at the thought.

He shook his head, ignoring the feel of his overly long hair against his shoulders. It was time to cut it, but damned if he could find the time. The job he had been sent here to do was taking almost every waking moment. Except for the time he had taken to cut the grass.

And the time he was going to take now to see if he could repair the crime of cutting that dumb bush and getting a cup of Lyra's coffee.

A taste of the woman would come soon enough.

◆ CHAPTER 2 ◆

Bread lined the counter of Lyra's perfect, beautiful kitchen. Fresh white bread, banana nut bread, and her father's favorite cinnamon rolls. A fresh cup of coffee sat at her elbow, and a recipe book spread out on the table in front of her as she attempted to find the directions for the étouffée she wanted to try.

The cookbook was no more than several hundred pages, some handwritten, some typewritten, and others printed from the computer and bound haphazardly over the years. Her mother had started it, and now Lyra added her own recipes to it as well as using those already present.

The soft tunes of a new country band were playing on the stereo in the living room, and her foot was swaying in a cheerful rhythm along with the music.

"Do you actually like that music?"

A shocked squeak of fear erupted from her throat as she jumped from her chair, sending it flying against the wall as she nearly threw the coffee cup across the room.

And there he stood.

Her nemesis.

The man had to have been placed here just to torment and torture her. There was no other answer for it.

"What did you do?" She turned and jerked the chair from where it had fallen against the wall, snapping it back in place before turning and propping her hands on her hips.

He was here. And acting just a little bit too awkward to suit her. He had to have messed up something again.

He stood just inside the doorway, freshly showered and looking too damned roughly male for any woman's peace of mind. If he were conventionally good-looking, she could have ignored him. But he wasn't. His face was roughly hewn, with sharp angles, high cheekbones, and sensual, eatable lips.

A man shouldn't have eatable lips. It was too distracting to those women who didn't have a hope in hell of getting a taste.

"I didn't do anything." He ran his hand along the back of his neck, turning to look outside the door as though in confusion before returning his gaze to her. "I came to apologize."

He didn't look apologetic.

He looked like he wanted something.

He rubbed at his neck again, his hand moving beneath the fall of overly long, light-brown hair, the cut defining and emphasizing the harsh planes and angles of his face.

Of course he wanted something. All men did. And she doubted very seriously it had anything to do with her body. Which was really just too bad. She could think of a lot of things that tough male body of his would be good for.

Unfortunately, men like him—tough, buff, and bad—generally never looked her way.

"To apologize?" She caught the half-hidden, longing look he cast to the counter and the cooling bread there.

"Yes. To apologize." He nodded ever so slightly, his expression just a shade more calculating than she would have liked.

She firmed her lips, very damned well aware that he was not there to apologize. He was wasting her time, as well as his, by lying to her.

He wanted her bread. She could see it in his eyes.

"Fine." She shrugged dismissively. What else could she do? "Stay the hell away from my plants, and I'll forgive you. You can go now."

He shifted, drawing attention to his wide chest and the crisp white shirt he wore. He had changed clothes in addition to showering. He wore form-hugging jeans with the white shirt tucked in neatly. A leather belt circled his lean hips, and the ever-present boots were on his feet, though these looked a little better than the previous pair.

His gaze drifted to the bread once again.

It figured. And the hungry, desperate gleam in his eyes was just about her undoing. Just about. She was not going to let him sweet-talk her out of it, she assured herself.

She stared back at him coolly as her hand clenched on the back of the chair. He was not going to eat her bread. That bread was gold where her father and brothers were concerned, and she desperately needed the points it would earn her. It was the only way she was going to get her pretty wooden shed built, and she knew it.

He glanced back at her, this time not even bothering to hide the cool calculation in his gaze.

"We could make a deal, you and I," he finally suggested, his voice firm, almost bargaining.

Uh-huh. She just bet they could.

"Really?" She let go of the chair and leaned against the counter as she watched him with a skeptical look. "How so?"

Oh boy, she just couldn't wait to hear this one. It was going to have to be good. She knew men, and she knew he had obviously been preparing the coming speech carefully.

But she was intrigued. Few men bothered to be straightforward or even partially honest when they wanted something. At least he wasn't pulling out the charm and pretending to be overcome with attraction for her to get what he wanted.

"However you wish," he finally stated firmly. "Tell me what I would have to do to get a loaf of that bread and a cup of coffee."

She stared back at him in shock.

She wasn't used to such straightforward, fully mercenary tactics from anyone. Let alone a man.

She watched him thoughtfully.

He wanted the bread; she wanted a shed. Okay, maybe they could trade. Not what she had expected, but she was willing to roll with the opportunity being presented.

"Can you use a hammer any better than you can a Weed Eater?"

She needed that shed.

His lips thinned. He glanced at the bread again with a faint expression of regret.

"I could lie to you and say yes." He tilted his head and offered her a tentative smile. "I'm very tempted to do so."

Great. He couldn't use a hammer, either.

She stared back at the muscular condition of his finely honed body. A man didn't look like that as a result of the gym. It was natural muscle and grace, not the heavy, packed-on appearance guys got from the gym. But if he couldn't cut his own lawn or swing a hammer, how the hell did he manage it?

She shook her head. Obviously nature really, really liked him, because Tarek Jordan was so not an outdoor sort of person.

"Let me guess. You're really good on the computer?" She sighed at the thought. Why did she attract the techies instead of the real men?

"Well, I am actually." He offered her a hopeful smile. "Does yours need work?"

At least he was honest—in some things. She guessed that deserved some compensation, though she fully admitted she was just too nice sometimes.

"Look, promise to keep your machines away from my property line, and I'll give you some coffee and a slice of bread," she offered.

"Just a slice?" His expression fell, rather like a child whose favorite treat had been jerked from his hands.

Men.

She looked over at the counter. Hell, she had baked too much anyway.

"Fine. A loaf."

"Of each kind?" Hope sprang in those golden eyes, and for a moment it made her wonder . . . No, of course he had eaten fresh-baked bread. Hadn't everyone? But there was a curious glimmer of vulnerability there. One she hadn't expected.

She glanced at the counter again. She had four loaves of each kind and plenty of the cinnamon rolls. It wasn't like she didn't have enough.

"Come on in." She turned to get an extra coffee cup when she stopped and stared at him in surprise.

He was taking his boots off? He did it naturally, toeing at the heels until the leather slid from his feet, and then pulling them off to sit them neatly at the door.

His socks were white. A pure, pretty white against the dark maroon of her ceramic tiles as he walked to the table.

He waited expectantly.

What the hell was he? An alien? No man she knew had white socks. And they sure as hell didn't care if they took their shoes off at the door, no matter how grimy or muddy they often were. Her brothers were the worst.

She poured the coffee and set it in front of him before turning to get the sugar and creamer from the counter. As she turned back, she frowned as she watched him take a long sip of the dark liquid.

Ecstasy transformed his face.

The expression on his face made her thighs clench as her sex spasmed in interest. Which only pissed her off. She was not going to get any more turned on by this man than she already was. She was doing perfectly fine without a man in her life right now. She did not, repeat, *did not* need the complication.

But if that was how the man looked when he had sex, then her virginity could be in serious danger. Strangely predatory, savage, filled with pleasure, his face carried a primal, intense look of satisfaction and growing hunger.

For a moment, her chest tightened in surprising disappointment. She wanted him to look at her like that, not at her bread.

Just her luck. Someone else to harass her for her bread instead of for her body. Not that she wanted him to harass her for her body, but it would be nice if someone would.

Taking out a bread knife, she sliced into a loaf of the banana nut bread and then into the white bread. The white bread was still warm enough to melt the fresh, creamy butter she spread atop it.

Fine. Maybe she could bribe him into hiring someone to cut and trim his lawn so he would leave hers alone. Stranger things had happened.

◆   ◆   ◆

The coffee was rich, dark, and exquisite. The bread fairly melted in his mouth. But that wasn't what was keeping his dick painfully engorged as he savored the treats. It was the smell of this woman, hot and sweet and aroused.

That arousal was killing him. It wasn't intense and overwhelming, but curious and warm. Almost tentative. He savored the smell of it more than he savored the bread and coffee he was trying to stay focused on.

"So what do you do on the computer?" She was cleaning the loaf pans she had used to bake the bread, carefully washing and drying them at the sink.

He glanced at the slender line of her back, the taut curves of her rear, and shifted restlessly in his chair. His hard-on was killing him.

He hadn't meant to give her the impression he worked mainly on the computer, but he guessed it was better than telling the truth.

"Mostly investigations and research." He shrugged, telling as much of the truth as possible. He hated the thought of lying to her. Which was strange. He was living a lie, and he knew it. He had been since his creation. So why should it bother him now?

"Criminal or financial?" She picked up the coffeepot and walked to the table, filling his cup with the last of the heated liquid.

He frowned at the question as he watched the way the soft, midnight silk of her hair fell forward, tempting his fingers. It looked soft, warm. Like everything he had believed a woman should be.

She wasn't hard, trained to kill, or living her own nightmares, as many of the Feline Breed women were. She was feisty and independent but also soft, exquisite.

"More along the lines of missing persons," he finally answered. "A little bit of everything, though."

He nearly choked on that one. He was, quite simply, a bounty hunter and an assassin. His present assignment was the search for one of the escaped Trainers who had murdered countless Feline Breeds while they were held in captivity.

The assignment was starting to take second place to the woman in front of him, though.

Damn that coffee was good, but if she didn't get the scent of that soft, heated warmth simmering in her pussy across the room and away from him, then they were going to have problems.

He could feel the growing sexual need tightening his abdomen and pounding in his brain. He wanted to shake his head, push the scent away from him in an attempt to make sense of it. He had never known a reaction so intense, so immediate to any woman.

From his first glimpse of her outraged expression when he committed the supreme sin of riding his Harley over her lawn, she had captivated him.

She wasn't frightened of him or intimidated by him. She didn't watch him like a piece of meat or an animal that could attack at any moment. She watched him with equal parts frustration, innocence, and hunger.

And if he didn't get the hell away from her, he was going to commit another sin. He was going to show her just how damned bad he did want that curvy little body of hers.

"I guess I should be going." He rose to his feet quickly, finishing off his coffee before taking the cup and his empty saucer to the sink where she was working.

She stared up at him in astonishment as he rinsed them quickly before sitting them in the warm, sudsy water in front of her.

He stared down at her, caught for a moment in the depths of her incredible sapphire eyes. They gleamed. Little pinpoints of brilliant light seemed to fill the dark color, like stars on a blue velvet background. Incredible.

"Thank you." He finally forced the words past his lips. "For the coffee and the bread."

She swallowed tightly. The scent of her wrapped around him—a nervous, uncertain smell of arousal that had his chest filling with a sudden, animalistic growl.

He throttled the sound firmly, clenching his teeth as he backed away from her.

"You're welcome." She cleared her throat after the words came out with a husky, sexy tone of nervousness.

Dammit, he didn't have time for such complications. He had a job to do. One that didn't include a woman he knew would run screaming from him if she had any idea of who and what he was.

She had wrapped the loaves and set them out on the counter by the door for him. He jerked his boots on quickly and picked up the bread, opening the door before turning back to her.

"If you need any help." He shrugged fatalistically. "If there's anything I can do for you . . ." He let the words trail off.

What could he do for her besides complicate her life and make her regret ever meeting him? There was little.

"Just stay away from my yard with your gadgets." Her eyes glowed with humor. "At least until you learn how to use them."

The woman evidently had no respect for a man's pride. A grin tilted his lips.

"I promise."

He turned and left the house, regretfully, hating it. There was a warmth within the walls of her home that didn't exist within his own, and it left him feeling unaccountably saddened to leave. What was it about her, about her house, that his suddenly seemed so lacking?

He shook his head, pushed his free hand into his jeans pocket, and made his way across her neatly trimmed backyard to his own less-than-pristine lawn. And his less-than-content life.

A cold winter rain fell, not quite ice, but close enough to chill Tarek's flesh as he stood in the shadows of his porch late that night.

He wasn't certain what had awakened him. But something had. He had come instantly alert, his senses rioting, the tiny, almost imperceptible hairs raising along his body as he slid from the bed and dressed quietly.

Now he stood within the concealing darkness, staring around the backyard, his eyes probing the night as his unique vision aided him in seeing through the moonless night.

In his hand he carried a powerful ultralight submachine pistol. It rested at the side of his leg as his opposite thigh held the weight of the lethal knife tucked securely in the scabbard he had strapped there.

The hairs along the back of his neck prickled, warning him that he wasn't alone in the darkness. His eyes scanned his yard and then turned to Lyra's.

Her upstairs lights were on; every few minutes he could see her pace past her bedroom window. She needed heavier curtains. Something hardened in his chest, became heavy at the thought that whatever stalked the darkness could be a threat to her.

His jaw tightened as he lifted his head, drawing in the scents surrounding him, and quickly, automatically separating them.

Something was out there; he knew it, and he should be able to smell it. It made no sense that the answers he sought weren't on the air around him.

He could smell the scent of Lyra's brothers. They had shown up that evening, carrying bread when they left. Damn their hides. He had considered mugging them for one insane minute.

He could smell the lumber they brought, sitting in her backyard, and the smell of charcoal on the air from the steaks they had grilled for dinner. But there was no scent of an intruder.

He flexed his shoulders, knowing the rain could be distilling the smell, knowing he was going to have to venture into it and hating the thought.

He moved silently from the porch, careful to stay in the shadow of the small trees he had taken the time to have planted before he moved in. Most were firs of some type, evergreens that never lost their concealing foliage. They were spaced at just the right distance to provide the concealment he needed as he made his way along the perimeters of his property.

There.

He stopped at the far corner, lifting his head to breathe in roughly, feeling the rain against his face, the ice forming in the sodden length of his hair. But there was the scent he was searching for, and it was on Lyra's property.

He turned his head, and his eyes narrowed, searching for movement that wasn't there, yet the scent of it was nearly overpowering.

Where are you, bastard? he growled silently as he made his way to the stack of lumber, using it to conceal himself from the back of the house, allowing him a clear view of her back porch as he thumbed the safety off on the powerful weapon he carried.

Icy rain ran in rivulets down his hair, his arms, soaking the flannel shirt and jeans he wore. He pushed the chill and the feel of wet fabric out of his mind. He had trained in worse conditions than this for years.

He breathed in again, sifting through the scents until he could determine where this one was coming from. The wind was blowing in from the west, moving across the house and through the small valley the housing development was situated in.

The scent was definitely at the back of the house. It was too clear, too thick with menace to have been diluted by the shrubbery in the front yard.

The moonless night left the yard nearly pitch-black, but the DNA that made him an abomination also made him capable of seeing much more clearly than the enemy stalking the night with him.

It wasn't a Breed. He could smell a Breed a mile away. But neither was it a harmless threat. He could feel the menace in the air, growing thicker by the moment.

Moving from the concealment of the stack of lumber, he edged his way closer to the house. Even more important than locating the threat was keeping Lyra in the house and safe. She was so damned feisty, if she even thought anyone was in her backyard she would be out there demanding answers and ignoring the danger.

He moved around the little wooden arch that held the bench swing, carefully sidestepped the beginnings of a flowerbed he had seen her working in days before, and slid along the fence that separated her property from her neighbor on the other side.

He could feel the intruder. The itch along the back of his neck was growing more insistent by the moment. He paused, bending low beside an evergreen bush as he scanned the area again.

And there he was. Crouched at the side of the house and working his way to the porch. Dressed entirely in black, the bastard might have escaped notice if Tarek hadn't caught the movement of the whites of his eyes.

He was good.

Tarek watched as he made his way to the electrical box at the side of the house. Too damned good. Tarek watched as a penlight focused a minute sliver of light as the intruder worked.

When he was finished, Tarek bet his incisors the security system had somehow been canceled. The lights were still on, and not even a flicker of power had been interrupted. But there was an edge of satisfaction in the way the black-clad figure now made his way to the back door.

It wasn't happening.

Tarek moved quickly, raising his gun, aiming, only to curse virulently as the figure turned, jerked, and raised his own weapon.

Tarek rolled as he heard the whistle of the silenced weapon. Expecting, foolishly perhaps, for the assailant to turn and run, he came to his knees, aiming again, only to be slammed back to the wet grass as the gun was kicked from his hand.

He rolled to the side and jumped to his feet. His leg flew out to connect with a jaw, and he heard the grunt of pain as the other man went backward, flailing for balance.

Tarek whipped his knife from its sheath, prepared now as the other man came at him. He kicked the gun from his hand, turned, and delivered a power kick to his solar plexus, snarling as he flipped around to see the bastard coming for him again, armed with a knife as well.

At the same time, the back porch light flared, blinding him for one precious second as the assailant made his move. Pain seared his shoulder as the knife found its mark before he could jump back.

A gunshot blasted through the night. The sound of the powerful shotgun made both men pause, breathing roughly before the assailant turned and ran.

"Like hell," Tarek snarled as he rushed after him, his feet sliding in the muck beneath his feet before he found traction and sprinted behind him.

He almost had him, dammit. He was within inches of throwing himself against the other man and bringing him down when another silent shot whistled past his head, causing him to duck and throw himself to the side instead.

The sound of a vehicle roaring down the street shattered the night. Tires screamed as the car slammed to a stop, voices raised demandingly, then it peeled from the front of the house as Tarek raced to get a glimpse of it.

"Fuck! Fuck!" His curse filled the night as the black sedan, no plates of course, roared away.

The assailant was well trained and obviously came with backup. The suspicion that it was the Trainer he was searching for filled his mind. But why go after Lyra? The man was smart enough, well trained enough that he could never have mistaken which house to attack.

On the heels of that suspicion came the knowledge that he, the hunter, could very well become the hunted. And it looked as though Lyra had been drawn into the middle of the war playing out between the Council and their now-free creations.

"The police are on their way," Lyra screamed from the back door. "Tarek, are you okay?"

At least she was still in the house.

A growl vibrated through his chest as he turned and ran back to the yard, locating the knife and illegal machine gun from the now-muddy yard.

The back door was open, and there she stood, dressed in a long gown and matching robe, holding that fucking shotgun like it could protect her.

He snapped his teeth together as he heard the sirens roaring in the distance and stomped to the house.

"Do not mention me, do you understand?" he ordered as he stopped in front of her, staring into her wide, shocked eyes as she blinked up at him.

"Do you understand me, Lyra?" he hissed impatiently. "Do not mention me. After they leave, I'll come back. Do you understand?"

He reached out to grip her arm, pulling back at the sight of the blood trickling to his hand. Fuck, his shoulder burned.

"You're hurt." She swallowed tightly.

The sirens were getting closer.

"Lyra." He bent close, breathing in her scent, her fear. "Did you hear me?"

"Yes. Why?" Her breasts were rising and falling roughly, her pale features emphasizing her large, dark eyes.

"I'll explain later. I promise." He grimaced painfully. "As soon as they leave, I'll be back. I swear, Lyra. But don't tell them what happened."

His cover was shot to hell if she even hinted at him. The police would converge on his house, and he would be forced to tell them exactly who he was. Good-bye assignment, good-bye Trainer.

She nodded slowly, glancing back into the house as the sound of the sirens echoed around them.

He nodded fiercely before turning and disappearing into the night. The cut to his shoulder wasn't life-threatening, but it was deep. He was going to have to take care of that first.

He disappeared into his house as the police units whipped onto the street and skidded to a stop outside Lyra's house. He locked the door quickly, taking precious seconds to pull off his boots before moving through the dark house.

What the hell was going on?

He stripped off his clothes in the laundry room, dropping the cold, soggy clothing into the washer before taking a clean towel from the cabinet and wrapping it around his arm. Damned blood was going to stain everything.

He strode quickly upstairs, moving through his bedroom to the bathroom where he could take care of the wound to his shoulder.

As he cleaned and carefully stitched the wound, he sifted through the earlier events, trying to make sense of them.

Why had someone attempted to break in to Lyra's house when it was clear she was home? Burglars waited until their victims were in bed, most likely asleep, or gone. They didn't break in while lights blazed through the house, and they sure as hell didn't hang around after they were clearly caught.

And they weren't as well trained as Lyra's burglar had obviously been. That wasn't an attempted robbery. It was a hit. Why would anyone want to kill Lyra, unless it was to get to him? A warning? And if it was that damned Trainer, how the hell had he learned Tarek was tracking him?

He smeared gauze with a powerful antiseptic before laying it over the stitched wound and taping it securely in place.

Then he dressed and waited. He stood at his bedroom window, watching, waiting, as the police talked to Lyra, wondering how well she would heed his earlier warning. Praying she would. Knowing it might be better for both of them if she didn't.

He was a Breed.

Lyra answered the questions the police asked, filled out and signed a report, and waited impatiently for them to leave.

Thank God she hadn't called her brothers before jerking that shotgun up and racing to the back door. She hadn't even thought of it. She had watched through her bedroom window as the moon broke past a cloud, shining clearly on the figures struggling in her backyard. She had recognized Tarek immediately.

Tarek Jordan was a Breed.

She had seen it in the fierce glow of his amber eyes as the light had shined into them, in the overly long incisors when he had snarled his furious orders on the back porch.

It made sense.

She should have suspected it from the beginning.

He had lived in the house beside her for months. His obvious discomfort in doing things most people did every day of their lives should have clued her in. The haunted shadows in his eyes.

His inability to cut grass should have told her something immediately. All men knew at least the rudiments of cutting grass.

The joy he found in a freshly made cup of coffee and homemade bread. As though he had never known it.

She had thought him a computer geek. That wasn't a computer geek fighting in her backyard. That had reminded her of her brothers, practicing the tae kwon do they had learned in the military. He had reminded her of an animal, snarling, his growl echoing through the yard as he fought with the attempted burglar.

She should have known.

She had followed every news story, every report of the Breeds, just as her brothers had joined in several of the missions years before to rescue them. They had told her the tales of the ragged, savage men and women they had transferred from the labs to the Feline Breed home base, Sanctuary.

Men near death, tortured, scarred, but with the eyes of killers. Men who were slowly being fashioned into animals—killing machines and nothing more.

"There's nothing else we can do, Ms. Mason," the officer taking her statement announced as she signed the appropriate line. "We've called your security company, and they'll be out here tomorrow to repair the system."

"Thank you, Officer Roberts." She smiled politely as she handed the papers back to him, wishing they would just leave.

"We'll be going now." He nodded respectfully.

It was about time.

She escorted them to the door, closing and locking it before pushing her feet into a pair of sneakers and waiting impatiently for them to pull from the drive.

The minute their taillights headed down the street, she grabbed her keys, threw open the door, and slipped onto the porch. Closing it quickly, she sprinted through the rain toward Tarek's.

She wanted answers *now*. Not whenever he decided to show.

A frightened scream tore from her lips as she passed one of the thick evergreen trees in his yard and was caught from behind as another hand clamped over her mouth.

A hard arm wrapped around her waist, heated, muscular, nearly picking her from her feet as he began to move quickly to the house.

"How did I know you would do something so stupid?" His voice was a hard, dangerous growl in her ear as he pushed her through the living room door and slammed it shut. "I told you to stay put, Lyra."

He released her quickly, throwing the bolts closed on the door before punching in the code to the security pad beside it.

"You were too slow," she snapped. "What the hell was going on tonight?"

She turned on him fiercely, with every intention of blasting him over the previous hours' events. Her eyes widened, though, as she caught sight of his pale face and the bloodstained bandage.

"Are you okay?" She reached out, her fingers touching the hard, sun-bronzed flesh just beneath the bandage.

"I'll live," he grunted. "And stop trying to distract me. I told you to stay put."

His eyes glittered a menacing gold in the dim light of the heavily curtained living room.

"I don't obey orders so well." She licked her dry lips nervously. "And I was tired of waiting."

"The police had barely left, Lyra." He pushed his fingers through his damp hair with rough impatience. "I was on my way."

His voice gentled, though not by much as he stared down at her. For a moment, his expression softened and then turned fierce once again.

"You would drive a grown man to drink," he finally growled before turning to stalk through the house. "Come on, I need coffee."

"Do you know how to fix it?" She followed him quickly, the question falling from her lips before she could stop it.

"Hell no. But I'm fucking desperate," he snarled impatiently, his voice rough.

"Then don't touch that coffeepot, because I want some, too."

She moved quickly in front of him before coming to a dead stop in the middle of the immaculate kitchen.

"Fine, go for it." He moved past her to the door where the tiles shone damply, the smell of disinfectant heavy in the air.

"What are you doing?" She was almost afraid to touch anything. It was almost sterile-clean.

"Blood." He grunted. "I don't want it staining the tiles."

He knelt on the floor, a heavy towel in his hands as he mopped at the puddle of cleaner he had poured on the floor.

Her brothers, bless their hearts, would have waited for her to try to clean it. She doubted they cleaned anything besides their weapons, at any time. The slobs.

"Do you ever cook in this kitchen?" she questioned him nervously as she moved to the cabinet and the coffeemaker sitting there.

"I'd need to know how to first," he grunted, working at the floor with single-minded intensity. "I'll figure it out eventually."

She searched the cabinets until she found the bag of pre-ground coffee and two mugs.

The term *bare cupboards* definitely applied to this man.

"What do you eat?" The silence was stifling as he rose to his feet to watch her measure the coffee into a filter with narrowed eyes.

"I eat," he finally growled as he moved through the kitchen into a short hall.

Seconds later she heard water running in the sink and then a heavier flow, as though into a washer.

He moved back into the kitchen a minute later as she was checking the refrigerator.

Cheese. Baloney. Ham. Yuck.

"Not all of us are gourmets," he grunted, moving to the cabinet over the stove and pulling down the bread she had given him that afternoon.

There was no sign of the cinnamon rolls. Half a loaf of white bread was left and perhaps a third of the banana nut bread.

She checked the freezer and then sighed. He had to be starving. A body that big took energy.

"What happened tonight?" she asked as she moved back to the coffeemaker and poured two mugs of the dark brew.

"Someone tried to break in to your house, and I caught him." He shrugged, his voice cool as he took his mug from her.

"Yeah." She believed that one. "Fine. I'll just go home then and call my daddy and my three ex–Special Forces brothers and let them know what happened. Shouldn't hurt, if that was all it was."

He paused, his gaze slicing back to her for a long moment before he lowered the mug.

She didn't think anything could take his mind off that coffee.

"Ex–SF, huh?" He breathed out roughly, shaking his head with weary acceptance.

"Yes, they are." She nodded mockingly. "They retired about five years ago. They were even part of the Breed rescues that took place just after the main Pride announced their existence."

His expression stilled and grew cold and distant.

"I know you're a Breed, Tarek." She wasn't playing games with him. She hated it when they were played with her. "Tell me what's going on."

He grimaced tightly before picking up his mug and moving to the kitchen table as though putting distance between them. She followed him.

He turned his head, watching as she leaned against the counter across from him and waited. Other than appliances, the kitchen was bare. No disorder. No clutter or decoration. The living room had been the same as she remembered. As though he had yet to decide who he was enough to mark his home with those things that defined him. Unless . . .

"Did you buy the house?" she asked him then.

Surprise crossed his features. "It's mine." He nodded before sipping at his coffee. "What does that have to do with anything?"

Nothing, except the thought of him leaving bothered her. Fine, he had no interest in her outside of her bread and her coffee, but she liked him. At least he wasn't boring.

"Nothing." She finally shrugged. Thankfully, she was wearing her thick flannel robe rather than one of her thinner ones, the ones that would have shown her hard nipples clearly and made it impossible to hide her response from him.

That was what pissed her off so bad about him. He was the one man in years who had actually interested her, and he seemed totally oblivious to her as a woman.

It sucked.

"You haven't told me what happened tonight yet," she finally reminded him. "I've been pretty patient, Tarek."

He grunted at that statement. "Yeah, I saw that while you were running through the rain."

He inhaled deeply, grimaced, and shifted restlessly in his chair. His hand rubbed at his arm, just below the bandage, as though to rub away the ache.

She ached for him, for that wound. The sight of his blood earlier had weakened her knees and filled her with a fear she hadn't expected. He had been hurt. While she dealt with the police and filing that stupid report, all she could think about was how severely he could have been wounded.

"I don't know," he finally answered, staring at her directly. "I knew someone was out there. I followed him. I caught him messing with the electric box and attempting to get to the back door when I tried to stop him." He pushed his fingers through his hair again, feathering the dark gold strands back from his face. "I don't believe he was after your TV set, though."

She didn't like the sound of that.

"The security company said the alarm couldn't be dismantled in the electrical box. That it has a backup . . ."

"It can be done." He shrugged heavily. "Your system is residential. It has its drawbacks. I'll get you a new one tomorrow."

"I didn't ask you to do anything." She was growing sick of this cat-and-mouse game of his. "I want to know what the hell was going on. Any burglar worth his salt would have run when he was noticed. This guy didn't run. Why?"

"I don't know. I was hoping you would." That wasn't a lie.

He stared at her, his unusual eyes darker, heavy-lidded . . . She swallowed tightly. That was not lust glittering in the golden depths. Men like him didn't get turned on for frumpy little accountants.

She drew in a deep, uneven breath, flickering her tongue over her dry lips nervously. He followed the movement, his gaze heating.

Okay. This was odd enough. She could understand being hotter than hell herself, but now he was? Why? Did he have a flannel fetish or something?

"Fine. It was no big deal then." She crossed her arms over her breasts just to be certain he couldn't see her nipples pushing against the cloth. "I'll just go home . . ."

"Not tonight." His voice was darker, deeper. "It's not safe as long as your system is down. You can stay here or call your brothers. It's up to you."

"I can take care of myself." She drew herself up stiffly as she faced him.

He rose from the table, suddenly appearing stronger, broader, fiercer as he scowled down at her.

"I said, you could stay here or call your brothers. I did not give you any other choices." A growl echoed in his voice as his eyes seemed to glow with arrogant intent.

"I didn't ask you for choices, Tarek." She wasn't about to bow down submissively to him, either. "I don't need a keeper."

His jaw tightened furiously, his lips thinning as he glared at her.

And that really shouldn't have turned her on further. But it did. She could feel the moisture gathering, pooling, spilling along the sensitive folds between her thighs. Her breasts felt heavier, swollen, too sensitive.

And he wasn't exactly uninterested anymore.

Her gaze flickered down, her face flushing heatedly before she jerked it back up. He was filling out those jeans like it was nobody's business.

And he hadn't missed the direction of her look, either.

"Don't tempt me, Lyra," he suddenly warned her, his voice rasping over her sensitive nerve endings. "My control is shot for the night. Either call your brothers or march your sweet ass upstairs to my spare room, or you're going to find yourself flat on your back in my bed. Your choice. The only ones left. Make it."

✦ CHAPTER 5 ✦

He was nearly shaking with the need to touch her. Tarek stared down at her pixie features, the blood pumping so hard and so fast through his veins it was nearly painful. His cock was a torturous ache between his legs, the glands at the side of his tongue swollen and throbbing.

His hard-on made sense. The rush of blood was explainable. The tongue was an enigma, and the taste of spice in his mouth confusing. The only thing that did make sense was the need to kiss Lyra.

She had tormented him for months. Tempted him. Laughed at him and mocked him with a gentle, feminine warmth that shouldn't have touched him as deeply as it had.

The smell of her arousal was killing him. It was hot, liquid sweet, and he was dying to lap at the soft cream he knew was spilling from her pussy. It would be hot, frothy with her growing need, and as rich as sunrise.

"Hell of a choice." Her arms tightened over her breasts.

He knew what she was hiding. The lush curves of her breasts, her swollen nipples.

"Make it fast if you don't mind," he growled. The erection was killing him. "Because the scent of your arousal is making me insane, Lyra. Pretty soon, I'm going to make the choice for you."

A whimper escaped her lips as her eyes widened in horror. In shame? He frowned as she paled and then flushed furiously, her eyes brightening as though with tears.

"What?" He caught her shoulders as she moved to turn from him, turning her back to face him, knowing that touching her was the biggest mistake he could make.

"You smell me?" She trembled, embarrassment bringing tears to her eyes as she struggled against him.

He sighed wearily. Dammit, he was too tired, too hungry for the taste of her to watch every damn word he said and every move he made. He wasn't exactly the social sort, and the "rules of polite society" wasn't a class he had found the time to take.

"Lyra." He breathed out roughly, his hand lifting to her cheek, marveling at the silken texture of her flesh. "I'm an animal," he whispered softly. "My sense of smell is so highly advanced that I can detect any scent. Especially the sweet, soft heat coming from you. It's like forcing a starving man to stand before a banquet and not taste the riches."

She blinked up at him, swallowing tightly, her gaze suspicious, softening only slightly as his thumb smoothed over her lips.

He wanted to say more, but the silken curves held his attention, mesmerized him.

His tongue throbbed as the glands spilled more of the spicy taste into his mouth. The blood pumped harder through his veins as his control slipped further.

He lifted his hands from her shoulders carefully.

"The bedroom is upstairs, third door on the landing. Get away from me, Lyra. Now. Before I lose all control."

She frowned back at him.

"I don't like the way you make decisions for me, Tarek," she snapped furiously. But, thank God, she began to back carefully away from him. "It's annoying."

"I'm certain it is." The smell of her still wrapped around him, tormented him. "We can discuss it tomorrow over coffee. Now go to bed."

She sniffed in disdain, glaring back at him as she reached the doorway.

"This tendency to boss me around best not become a habit," she warned him again. "Otherwise, I might disabuse you of the idea that you can get away with it. Count yourself lucky I'm letting you off the hook and escaping. Otherwise, you'd be one molested kitty, Jordan."

He could do nothing but stare at her disappearing back in shock as she muttered the heated words. Molested kitty? He groaned at the phrase. Good Lord, the woman was going to make him completely insane.

He sighed in relief, forcing himself to let her go before pulling the cell phone from its holder at his side and pressing the calling pad impatiently.

"Jonas." Jonas Wyatt, head of Feline Enforcer Affairs at Sanctuary, answered on the first ring.

"We have a problem," Tarek said quietly. "I think I encountered our Trainer tonight. Unfortunately, it wasn't me he was after."

He couldn't get the scent of the assailant out of his mind. It was too damned close to the smell of the clothing, admittedly from years before, that the bastard had worn. Not exact, but damned close.

"Explain." Jonas was a man of few words, which was one of the reasons Tarek liked working for him.

"He was breaking into the neighbor's house. Lyra Mason, she's the sister to three . . ."

"Special Forces agents." Jonas finished for him. "Grant, Marshal, and Tyree Mason. They headed the force that took down some of the main Breed labs."

Tarek closed his eyes, pinching the bridge of his nose in irritation. "Did you know she lived here when I bought this house?" he questioned him.

"I knew *of* her. I hadn't run a full investigation because I saw no reason to." He could almost see Jonas shrug with the words. "Twenty-four, accountant, lives modestly, a nice little nest egg but nothing substantial. Medical records show a virgin, with all the normal childhood ailments and no police record. I didn't have time to go deeper and had no reason to. Why?"

Tarek shook his head. "No reason. I might need to come in soon, though; I think I need a checkup or something." He ran the sides of his tongue over his teeth, feeling a soft warmth spill into his mouth.

"What's wrong?" Jonas was sounding concerned now. About damned time.

"I don't know." He moved to the small foyer that led to the stairs. "Those damned glands at the side of my tongue. They're inflamed and doing funky shit. I swear I taste cinnamon."

Silence filled the line.

"Where's the girl?" Jonas asked then. "The Mason girl."

Tarek frowned at the question.

"My guest room. Her security system was breached."

"Hell!" Jonas breathed roughly. "Have you fucked her?"

A growl rose in his throat. "That's none of your damned business now is it, Jonas?" he asked silkily, dangerously. "Don't overstep your place, buddy."

"Can it, Tarek," he snorted. "And listen close. This is straight from the old scientist who treats the main Pride members. The swollen glands contain a special hormone. That spice filling your mouth, buddy, is an aphrodisiac. Lyra Mason is your mate."

Tarek laughed. Damn, he hadn't taken Jonas for a comedian.

"Fine. Whatever." He grunted. "Now tell me the truth."

He was going to kill Jonas for playing fucking games with him. He wasn't in the mood.

"No shit, Tarek." Jonas sounded much too serious. "It's kept very quiet. A complete ban on the information unless a couple appears to be mating. One of the best-kept secrets in the world."

Heat rushed to his head, and then to his dick.

"What do you mean, 'She's my mate'?" Could that account for the almost obsessive lust that had developed in the past months? The patience with her that he would never have had with anyone else? The growing, clawing hunger that kept his cock hard, his senses inflamed?

"Biological, chemical, whatever you want to call it," Jonas snorted. "If you kiss her, it causes the hormone to affect her even more than you. Mating Heat. Complete sexual abandon from now until forever. You poor bastard." There was an edge of envy in his voice, though.

Complete sexual abandon? From now until forever? His mate?

"She's mine," he whispered.

"Yep. That's what the doc says. Somehow, nature picked your perfect woman for you. Have fun."

"Have fun?"

Jonas chuckled. "Tarek, you sound dazed, buddy."

He gazed up at the stairs before closing his eyes and shaking his head miserably. He had a feeling Lyra was really going to have a reason to be pissed now.

"Shit," he breathed out roughly. "This is not a good time for this, Jonas. I don't have time for sexual abandon or some kind of fucked-up aphrodisiac. Get the cure out here."

Jonas laughed at that.

"I'll bring the latest attempt at contraception instead," he informed him. "Tell her what the hell is going on, and before you take her, be sure she takes the little pink pill. It's worked so far. Their best guess is that the Mating Heat is nature's way of ensuring the success of the species. Because without this pill, conception of the first child occurs quickly. They sure do make some pretty babies, though."

Babies? Tarek swallowed hard. The thought of Lyra carrying his baby did things to him he couldn't explain.

"Just get me some help out here," he snapped, attempting to cover the emotional response suddenly surging through him. "I'm telling you, Jonas, it's getting dangerous here."

"That goes without saying," Jonas agreed. "I'll head out there myself with Braden and cover you. Let me know how she takes it."

Tarek grunted at that one.

"The information. Not that." He laughed, entirely too amused to suit Tarek. Then his voice sobered. "She's a good woman from what I learned, Tarek. You could have done worse."

"She could have done much better," he said. "You say it's permanent?"

"Like a drug," Jonas said, his voice quieter now. "There are only a few mated couples so far. They're still doing tests, trying to find answers. But so far, it's permanent."

He was fucked. He would have to tell her the truth. If she had a brain in her head, she would run as fast and as far from him as possible. And he would be stuck, obsessed—hell, in love with a woman he knew he had no right to, and no chance of touching.

⋆ C H A P T E R 6 ⋆

The next morning dawned cold, the rain still falling in a listless, icy drizzle along the windowpanes. Every curtain in the house—thick, heavy, rubber-backed curtains—was closed tightly, and the atmosphere between Lyra and Tarek was decidedly tense.

Breakfast consisted of rich, strong coffee and the mound of sausage biscuits Tarek had nuked in the microwave. She had managed to choke down two. God, how did he stand that stuff? Then she sat, finishing her coffee, watching as he consumed the rest.

He was too quiet. Brooding. His expression savagely relentless as the silence became thick enough to cut with a knife. She could almost see it distorting the air around them.

"I have to go home," she announced as she rose to her feet and took her cup over to the sink. "The security company should be around soon . . ."

"I canceled the call." His response had her turning back to him slowly. "My people will be here in a few hours to replace the system entirely."

She stared back at him silently for long moments. This wasn't the lazy, often-cautious man she had come to know. He was still, prepared, his body tense. Still sexy as hell, but the caution had been replaced by a dangerous sense of expectation.

"Really?" she finally answered, crossing her arms over her breasts. "And I gave permission for this, when?"

When he raised his eyes to hers, she shivered, a tremor racing up her spine at the intense lust, the pure, driving hunger she saw in those eyes.

She could feel her vagina weeping. The juices were fairly dripping from the hidden flesh. And he could smell it. She watched him inhale slowly, as though savoring the scent of her.

"Pervert," she snapped, frowning as sensuality fully marked his expression. "Fine, you make me hot. You can smell it. Now it's time for me to go home. Thanks for saving the night and all that."

She turned for the door.

"Touch that doorknob, and you'll regret it."

Her hand was within an inch of gripping it when she drew back slowly at the sound of his voice. She turned, swallowing tightly at the savage expression on his face as he lifted his cup and finished his coffee slowly.

"Tarek, you're going to piss me off," she warned him, suddenly wary. "The silent He-Man crap doesn't get it with me."

He leaned back in his chair, watching her with predatory interest. She had seen glimpses of this side of him, but it had never been focused entirely on her. It had her body tightening, adrenaline and excitement rushing through her.

She was sick. That was all there was to it.

He scratched at his chest slowly.

"Amazing things, genetics," he finally stated with a forced calm that made her think of the eye of a hurricane. This was not going to be good.

"Really?" She lifted a brow, standing close to the door as she arched her brow mockingly.

"Really." He nodded. "All kinds of little things start cropping up, surprising the hell out of you, reminding you that Fate does get the final laugh on all our asses."

Oh, this just wasn't going to be good at all.

She moved closer. The bleak, haunted shadows in his eyes had her chest tightening in fear.

"What's wrong?"

He stared back at her silently for long, tense moments.

"I'm debating something," he finally growled, his voice deepening, roughening as his gaze pinned hers. "I've debated all night."

Why did she have this bad feeling he was debating something that she really wasn't going to be pleased with?

"Yeah?" She inserted mild curiosity into her tone when every bone and muscle of her body was trained on what was coming next.

"Yeah." He nodded slowly, his gaze drifting over her body with lustful intent. "You've made me crazy for months. I'll be damned if I haven't stood by, amused, curious, letting you razz on me every chance you've had."

Yeah, that one had bothered her, too. He never got pissed. Surely he wasn't getting pissed now?

"What, you want an apology?" she asked him, incredulous. "A little late, Tarek."

"I couldn't figure out why." He shook his head slowly. "Then, the strangest thing happened. The more I smelled the sweet heat flowing from your pussy, the more I denied myself a taste of it, the more I started noticing a few changes."

She flushed heatedly at the explicit language, furiously chiding herself silently over her breathless reaction to it.

He rose from the chair as she watched him warily.

"Changes?" She swallowed tightly as she glimpsed the more-than-healthy bulge between his thighs.

"These little glands along my tongue swelling. The taste of spice filling my mouth. The hunger for you growing by the day until I could almost taste your kiss. And I wanted your kiss bad, Lyra. So bad it was killing me. I wanted to push my tongue in your mouth and make you taste it, too. Make you as crazy for me as I was for you."

He stepped closer.

Lyra was breathing roughly, her hands knotted in the front of her robe as she watched him advance on her.

"Are you sick or something?" She had to force the words from her mouth.

A mocking, bitter smile twisted his lips.

"Or something," he agreed as he towered over her and then stepped slowly behind her.

She was not going to run from him, no matter how weird he acted.

"Would you like to know what's wrong with me, Lyra?" He bent close, his breath whispering over her ear as he spoke.

A shiver raced up her spine as her nipples tightened further, rasping against her gown, almost making her moan at the pleasure of the action.

"No." She had a feeling she was certain she didn't want to know.

"There's this nasty little hormone filling my mouth." That growl was deeper now, more animalistic. "It's an aphrodisiac, Lyra. Caused only when a male Feline Breed hungers for his mate. Do you know what's going to happen if I kiss you?"

Her knees weakened. A hormonal aphrodisiac? Something to make her hornier? She didn't think so.

"What?" She couldn't hold back the gasping whisper.

"If I kiss you, it goes into Mating Heat. Complete sexual abandon until you've passed ovulation. Do you know you're preparing to ovulate? That my body is reacting to it? That my cock is so damned hard, my balls so tight with the need to fuck you that it's like an open wound in my gut? All because you're ovulating. My mate. My woman."

Her eyes widened in horror at the words he whispered at her ear.

"You're crazy." She jerked away from him, turning on him furiously. "That's not possible."

The curve of his lips was bleak.

"You would think, wouldn't you?" He moved to the counter, picking up a small oval disc that he slapped on the kitchen island. "This will stop conception. Nothing can stop the heat. Now, my problem is, I'm ready to rip that gown off your body and throw you to the damn floor where I can fuck you until we're both screaming. Until you're as wild for me, as crazy for me, as I am for you. Or you can run out of that door right now, as fast as you can run, and find someplace, any place, to hide until I can find enough control to keep from hunting you down and taking you like the animal I am. Make your choice now, baby, and make it fast. Because this kitty is all out of patience."

Make a choice? He wanted her to make a choice?

She stared back at him, eyes wide, trying to force her brain past the shock to actually make a decision as to whether or not she was still sleeping. Because this had to be some kind of screwed-up nightmare. That was all there was to it.

"Let me get this straight." She edged farther back from him, simply because she was becoming so wet her panties felt damp and his eyes were getting darker. "Your tongue has glands. That have a hormonal aphrodisiac in them?"

He nodded as he advanced on her. He didn't say a word, just nodded his head as he inhaled deeply. She trembled at the knowledge that he was actually smelling her.

"If you kiss me, we go into heat?"

"You go into heat." He smiled, a tight, hard curve of his lips that denoted way more male intent than she was comfortable with.

She cleared her throat. "What do you do?"

"I put out the flames."

She moved back.

Okay. She was retreating. So fucking what? He was stalking her across the room like the damned Lion he was. And the closer he got, the hotter she got.

"Tarek . . ." She jerked in surprise as her back came up against the wall, staring up at him in shock as he stopped, only inches from her, his hand lifting.

He touched her. The backs of his fingers brushed against her throat before trailing down to her collarbone, his eyes tracking each movement his hand made as her breasts began to swell and throb.

"You're running out of time." His guttural whisper had her womb clenching furiously, the breath locking in her chest.

This was a side of Tarek she wasn't accustomed to. A side she knew should not be turning her on as it was. He had barely touched her. In nearly six months of confrontations, arguments, and snapping debates, he had never touched her, never kissed her, and she was going up in flames for him.

She could feel it in every cell of her body, every hard pulse of blood through her veins.

"How long does it last?" she finally asked. "The heat stuff?"

His eyes narrowed as his head lowered. He was going to kiss her, she knew he was. But he didn't. His lips moved to her neck, burning a heated caress to the sensitive flesh where her shoulder and neck met. There, his lips opened, his tongue stroking her skin a second before the incisors scraped against it.

Her hands flew to his arms, her hands gripping his wrists as her knees weakened.

"It lasts forever." Bleak, bitter pain filled his voice. "From now until forever, Lyra. Always mine."

He bit her. Not hard enough to break the skin or to cause her undue pain. But he bit, his teeth clenching in the tender muscle as she arched on her tiptoes, a sizzling bolt of electric pleasure pulling a strangled cry from her lips.

Her clit pulsed, her vagina wept, her nipples became so hard, so tight, they were a near violent ache as a lethargic weakness left her gasping rather than fighting for freedom.

"Always?" She should have been alarmed. Always was not supposed to be in her vocabulary. She had no desire to be under a man's thumb, just under this man's body.

His lips moved back up her neck, his tongue licking at her flesh as a rumbling growl broke from his chest.

"Just a taste," he whispered as he reached her lips, his arms lowering from the braced position against the wall beside her head. "Stay very still, baby. I just need a taste."

His lips ghosted over hers as she stared back at him, her gaze locked with his, seeing the hunger, the aching, soul-deep need he had kept hidden beneath lowered lashes or behind mocking humor.

But now it was laid bare to her, as clear, as desperate as the aching hunger for him that pulsed low in her stomach.

She trembled as she felt his hands at the front of her robe, his lips, nipping at hers, parting them, retreating, only to come back for more as she held on to his wrists with a death grip.

The buttons on her robe gave way, the edges falling apart as they both breathed harshly, the silence of the kitchen broken only by their gasps of pleasure.

"You're so wet. I can smell how wet you are. How sweet," he whispered as he stared back at her, his fingers working on the buttons of her gown. "Like the fragrance of summer, heating me, reminding me of life, of living."

His words shook her to her core.

"Do you know what the smell of your sweet pussy does to me?" He smoothed her gown apart, the cool air brushing against her naked breasts as she whimpered in an arousal so sharp, so desperate, she wondered if she would survive it. "It makes me hungry, Lyra. Hungry to take you, to hear you screaming beneath me as I bury every inch of my cock as deep inside you as possible."

She cried out sharply, unable to contain the sound. Could a

woman orgasm from words alone? His explicit language was driving her over the edge, earthy and lustful, filled with a desire no man had ever shown her before.

He grimaced, showing the incisors at the side of his mouth as his gaze moved to the rapid rise and fall of her breasts.

"Look how pretty." He took her hand from his wrist, spread her fingers, and then wrapped it around the lush mound.

She stared back at him in shock, her eyes flickering to where she cupped her own flesh, her hand surrounded by his.

"Feed it to me," he whispered then, his voice wicked, filled with lust. "I want to taste it."

She shuddered, a whimper escaping her throat at the pure eroticism of what he was doing to her.

His hand moved back hers. "Give it to me, Lyra. Press that pretty, hard nipple into my mouth."

She couldn't believe she was doing it. That she was lifting her breast, leaning forward as he bent his knees, lowering himself to allow the straining nub to pass his lips.

He licked it first.

"Oh God, Tarek." She was shaking like a leaf, pinpoints of explosive pleasure detonating through her body.

He licked it again, his tongue, rasping roughly, like wet velvet gliding over the sensitive tip.

Then he growled. A hard, savage sound as his lips opened, parted, to envelop the hard point into the wild, wet heat of his mouth.

She climaxed.

Lyra's hands shot to his head, her fingers tangling in the rough strands of his hair as something exploded deep within her womb. Pleasure rushed through her sex, drenching her, spilling to her thighs as she lost her breath.

He hadn't even kissed her yet.

His head rose from her nipple, his hands lifting, pulling hers from his hair as he settled them against her sides.

He laid his against her shoulders, smoothing the unbuttoned gown and robe slowly from her arms as she shook before him.

Lyra swallowed tightly, small whimpers passing her lips as she stood naked before him. Naked—she never wore underwear beneath her gowns—while he was fully clothed, watching her with glowing gold eyes, his expression predatory, savage.

"Sweet little virgin," he whispered, his gaze moving down her body, finally coming to rest on the bare, slick folds between her thighs. "Naughty little baby." His eyes moved back to hers. "Imagine how my tongue is going to feel there. Sliding through all that hot, sweet syrup. Will you come for me again, Lyra? Will you cry for me again?"

He took her hand, moving it to the snap of his jeans as he watched her with savage eyes.

"Make your choice now, Lyra. Accept me."

Good Lord, what was she supposed to do about him? She was standing there naked in front of him, and he still could not reason out that she had already accepted him? Even with all the weird Breed mating stuff, she couldn't imagine not accepting him.

"Kiss me," she demanded roughly, her fingers moving to the metal snaps of his jeans, releasing them slowly, the hard heat of his erection beneath making the task difficult.

"God." He snarled the prayer as he shuddered against her, his hands gripping her hips as his eyes clenched shut for long seconds.

"Kiss me, Tarek," she whispered, reaching for him, her lips brushing his as his head lowered, his eyes blazing with hunger, pain, and need as he watched her. "Make me crazier."

The front of his jeans parted beneath her trembling fingers, the hard, generous width of his erection rising from the material, flushed and desperate as she glanced down nervously.

She licked her lips.

"I hope you know what to do with it." She finally swallowed tightly. "Because I don't have a clue."

And he didn't bother with explanations.

In that second his head lowered, his lips slanting over hers as his tongue licked and then pressed demandingly between her lips.

Immediately the taste of spice exploded in her mouth. Heat surrounded her, whipped through her mind, then cell by cell began to invade her body.

She thought the clawing, driving hunger for his touch, his kiss, couldn't get worse.

She was wrong.

Exploding fingers of sensation began to tear through her nerve endings. Her womb clenched, knotted. The already aching flesh between her thighs began to burn with a spasming, violent need.

She screamed into his kiss, rising on her tiptoes for more, pressing against him, trying to sink into the heat emanating from beneath his clothing.

He tore his lips from hers, his breathing rough, harsh as she tried to claw up his body and capture his lips again.

"That fucking pill." His voice was animalistic, rough, hungry.

"No. Kiss me again." She pulled his hair, dragging his head back down until his lips covered hers again, a groan tearing from his throat as her tongue pushed between his lips.

It was wildfire. It was destructive. She could feel the flames licking over her body, pinpoints of electricity sensitizing her flesh. And pleasure—the pleasure was overwhelming.

She felt him pick her up. Lifting her from her feet as she lifted her legs, bending them to clasp his hips as the fiery hot length of his erection suddenly seared the folds of her cunt.

He was moving. Walking. Sweet heaven, how was he walking?

He pulled his lips back again, his movements jerky as he braced her rear on the kitchen island and jerked open the small plastic container.

He pushed the pill between her lips.

"Swallow it," he growled. "Now, Lyra."

He was moving against her, his cock sliding in the juices of her sex as he stared down at her fiercely, raking the tender bud of her clit, sending spasms of sensation ripping through her belly.

She swallowed the pill before her gaze dropped to her thighs.

She whimpered.

"Do it," she whispered, watching the bloated head of his cock part her and then slide up, raking against her clit.

"Damn," his voice was filled with lust, with a strengthening demand as his fingers caught in her hair, pulling her head back to force her gaze to his. "I told you. I'm eating that sweet pussy first."

"I can't wait, Tarek," she whimpered, her hands pulling at his shirt, amazed as the buttons tore free, revealing his golden chest. "Now. I need it now."

"You can wait."

But he wasn't about to.

Her eyes widened as he pushed her back, spreading her thighs as he lifted her legs and buried his head between them.

The first swipe of his tongue through the sensitive slit of her cunt had her screaming. He licked at her, lapping at the juices spilling from her vagina as he groaned against her flesh.

She had never imagined such agonizing pleasure. She writhed beneath him, twisting, bucking against his mouth as he circled her clit, only to move lower to lap at her again.

He nibbled at the sensitive lips, parted her, and then suddenly, astonishingly, drove his tongue inside her. She exploded in a firestorm of blazing pleasure as his tongue fucked inside her with hard, blistering strokes. Her muscles clenched, shuddered, and more heated liquid spilled to his greedy lips.

And still, it wasn't enough.

She was gasping, tears dampening her face as she shuddered a final time, staring up at him as he straightened between her thighs.

"Tarek?" She sobbed his name beseechingly. "I need more."

She was exhausted, but the fire burning in her womb was never-ending.

"Shh, baby." He lifted her quickly in his arms. "I refuse to take you on the kitchen counter, Lyra. I won't do it."

He stumbled as her legs wrapped around him, clasping his hips tight, her clit rubbing against the shaft of his cock as he began to carry her to the stairs.

"I won't make it upstairs." She was riding the thick wedge, the agonizing pleasure ripping through her mind.

If she could just get the right position. Just a little higher . . .

She felt the thickly crested head part her, lodge against the tender opening before his first step onto the stairs forced it inside her.

He stumbled, growling, one arm locked around her as he braced his hand to the wall, breathing harshly.

"Not like this," he breathed roughly. "Oh God, Lyra. Not like this. Not your first time . . ."

Regret, remorse. She saw it in his expression, heard it in his voice. But stretching her entrance wide, teasing her, tempting her, was the head of the instrument she needed to relieve the agonizing lust claw-ing at her pussy.

She shifted in his embrace, feeling him slip farther inside her before coming to a halt against the proof of her virginity.

"Baby . . ." He whispered the endearment against her ear as he struggled up another step.

Each move pulled his cock back, pushed it in, and stroked her no more than inches inside the gripping muscles of her cunt, sending shudders wracking through her body at the exquisite pleasure.

He was killing her.

"I'm sorry." He stopped, bending, placing her rear at the edge of the step as he knelt in front of her. "God, Lyra. I'm sorry."

She had no more than a second's warning before his hips flexed and then pushed forward, driving his thick, hot erection to the very depths of her hungry, gripping pussy.

Shocking, blistering. The sudden penetration had her arching as the pleasure/pain of his abrupt entrance sizzled across her nerve endings. Overfilled, stretched tight, she could feel his cock throbbing inside her, setting flames to her ultra-sensitive depths.

Lyra's head fell back against an upper step, her legs lifting, clasping his back tightly as he began to drive inside her.

It was unlike anything she could have imagined. She could feel him pushing the tender muscles apart, stroking delicate tissue, and sending almost unbearable pleasure whipping through her system.

She held on to him, feeling his lips at her neck, his incisors scraping over her flesh as the pressure began to build inside her womb, the pleasure coalescing, tightening with each desperate lunge of his cock inside the snug depths of her cunt.

She could barely feel the hard wood of the step beneath her. All she felt was Tarek, heavy, hot, wide, overfilling her, making her take more, thrusting inside in an ever-increasing tempo until she felt the world dissolve around her.

Then she felt more.

Her eyes widened, staring in dazed shock at the ceiling above her as, simultaneously, his teeth bit into her shoulder, holding her still for something so incredibly unreal, she was certain she had to be imagining it.

He slammed in deep, his body tightening as she felt an additional erection, an extension swelling from beneath the hood of his cock, locking him inside her, caressing a bundle of nerves high inside her pussy, and sending her rushing past ecstasy into rapture. The heat of his semen filled her, pulse after violent pulse echoing in the flexing depths as he growled harshly at her neck.

He was locked inside her. The extension holding him in place sent cataclysms of sensation exploding through her over and over again.

When it finally eased, when the hard pulsing jets of his release and the violent shudders of her own eased, her eyes closed in exhaustion.

She had thought no arousal could be worse than what she had known before his kiss. She was rapidly learning just how wrong she was.

• C H A P T E R 8 •

You are not human . . . You may look in the mirror and declare your humanity. You may tell yourself that looks are all that matter. They do not. You are animals. Created in a lab, a man-made creation, and you will serve the men who made you. You are animal. Our tools. Nothing more . . .

Tarek stared at the ceiling as he held Lyra in his arms, her head on his chest, her body draped over his. She was like a kitten, determined to get as close as possible in her sleep, curling around him with a sigh before she had relaxed into exhaustion several hours before.

He wasn't human. That had been driven irrevocably home on the stairs, his body covering hers, as it betrayed his sense of humanity. His belief in himself as a man, not an animal.

A barb.

He closed his eyes as bitterness swamped him.

He pushed back the shudder of pure lust at the memory of the sensations.

Dear God, the pleasure. It had been unlike anything he could have anticipated. The extension had been highly sensitive, pulsing, throbbing in orgasmic delight as he poured his semen into her.

He breathed in roughly, grimacing at the erection he still sported. He had a feeling he would never get enough of the feel of her silken cunt, with or without the Mating Heat.

His hand smoothed over her hair, his fingers tangling in the soft strands as he relished the feel of her lying against him.

She was warm. Precious. She was a gift he had never imagined he would ever have.

And she liked him. He knew she felt at least some affection for him, though perhaps not as much as he felt for her. Hell, he had fallen in love with her during the first few months he had known her. He had known it was love. Known the possessiveness, the joy, the sheer delight he found in her could be nothing else.

He wanted to clutch her to him, tighten his arms around her and hold the world at bay forever. But he knew, realistically, it wasn't possible. He could only hold her for now and see how she reacted when she awakened.

And that part terrified him.

Would she be disgusted?

Hell, of course she would. What sane, reasonable woman could so easily accept something so animalistic? So outside the bounds of what she knew was human?

He felt her shift against him and restrained his growl of impatient lust as her leg slid over his thigh, her knee nearly touching the taut flesh of his scrotum.

Sweet Lord, she made him hot. And he wasn't blaming it on the Mating Heat. He had known what she would do to him from his first confrontation with her.

She sighed against his chest, a soft little sound that clenched his heart as her hand smoothed over his chest and then back again.

He stilled, his breath nearly suspending as she repeated the action, her body tensing.

"What happened to you?" Her fingers picked up the nearly invisible line of scars that crisscrossed his chest.

"Training." He hoped she would leave it alone. Prayed she would let it go.

"What kind of training?" She leaned up enough to open drowsy eyes, though her gaze was as sharp as ever.

He was willing to bet she drove her father insane. She was too curious, too independent, and too set on having the answers she demanded.

"Simply training, Lyra," he finally answered her. "At times, I was not the perfect little soldier I should have been."

He heard the bitterness that laced his voice, wincing at the sound of it.

Her fingers moved over the abrasive scars once again as her gaze flickered to his. A gaze filling with anger. Making her angry had not been his intention. He wanted only to shelter her from what he had known during those years. There was no reason for her to know the brutality, the mercilessness of those who created him.

"I hope they're dead." Her snarl surprised him, as did the bloodthirsty fury in those beautiful eyes as she stared back at him. "Whoever did this, I hope you killed him."

He had. But it wasn't something he was proud of.

He was proud of this small sign of protectiveness from her, though. She was angry on his behalf, not with him.

"It's over. That's all that matters." He touched her cheek, amazed at her, just as he had been from the first moment he had seen her.

She snorted at that, a completely unladylike sound that didn't really surprise him as her expression conveyed her disagreement with him.

"I need a shower." She finally shifted from him, her moves hesitant.

"I'll show you the shower and get you one of my shirts to wear." He moved from the bed before turning back and lifting her into his arms.

She gripped his shoulders, staring up at him in surprise.

"You're tender." And she was as light as a feather. "Perhaps try a bath to relieve the soreness. I have some Epsom salts in the cabinet that will make you feel better."

Jonas had suggested hot baths rather than showers to help ease the soreness as well as the building heat for a small respite.

He knew the scent of her and could detect the change as she moved further through the ovulation process. The pill she had taken would do nothing to stop the heat, only the end result of the ovulation process. There would be no egg, no conception. He ignored the small flare of regret at the thought of it.

"I'm hungry, too," she informed him. "And I don't want any of those nasty biscuits, either. I want some real food."

He set her down in the bathroom, staring down at her in confusion. "Such as?"

"I'll call Liu's. She'll have one of her boys deliver." She stared around the large bathroom before looking back at him pointedly.

An invitation to leave. That one was hard not to miss. But not yet.

"Let me know what you want, I'll have a friend pick it up for us," he suggested instead. "For the time being, I would prefer not to let anyone I don't know into the house."

A small tremor raced through her body as she glanced away from him for a moment and breathed in heavily.

"Fine. I can understand that. As long as I get my Chinese fix."

He listened carefully to the dishes she wanted ordered, restraining his smile. It was enough to feed an army. It was a damned good thing he had a near-perfect memory.

"Bathe. I'll call Jonas and have the food picked up. By the time you're finished, it should be here."

He could smell the heat building in her and wanted her to have the time to enjoy the food.

"Thanks. Now go away." She waved him away with a delicate gesture of her fingers. "I don't need you in here right now."

His lips quirked at her irritated expression, but he did as she asked. And he prayed. Prayed she had forgiven him for the animal he was, rather than the man he knew she needed.

◆   ◆   ◆

"I need to go to the house for some clothes and stuff." Lyra found her gown and robe in the washroom, folded neatly on the top of the dryer after they had consumed the delivered Chinese food.

Her hunger was sated, but that was all. The steadily rising lust building in her body was about to make her crazy.

It tingled in her breasts and spasmed in her vagina. And she ached for his kiss—literally. She was certain no drug could be as addictive as his kiss was.

"You can't leave the house yet, Lyra." His voice brooked no refusal.

Okay, a man could be really sexy when he was being dominant, especially this man. But she just wasn't in the mood for it. She wanted to be fucked, but she would be damned if she was going to ask him for it. And because she knew he could smell her arousal, she knew he was very well aware of the hunger building within her.

She turned carefully, clutching the folded material to her breasts.

"Too bad. I need clean clothes and time to think . . ."

A bitter smile twisted his lips as a raging pain reflected in his gaze.

"The time for thinking was before you decided to take my kiss."

She shook her head against the anger in his voice.

"Not about this," she informed him fiercely. "I have to decide things, Tarek. This has changed my life, you know it and I know it. There are other things involved than just you and I and this Mating Heat, or whatever you call it."

Heat? Try inferno. It was killing her.

"Then take care of it on the phone." There was no give in him. Good Lord, why hadn't she heeded the warnings of his complete male stubbornness that she had glimpsed over the months? He looked about as immovable as a boulder.

"I need clothes. My laptop . . ."

"You won't have time to wear clothes, or to work . . ." He advanced on her, his eyes lowering over the lust gleaming in his gaze. "You'll be lucky to have time to eat."

Her stomach clenched at the growl in his voice as he reached out, taking the gown and robe from her before setting them back on the washer.

"I want to take you in the bed this time." His fingers tangled in her hair as he dragged her head back, his head lowering as though for a kiss.

As though she were that easy.

She didn't care how hot she was or how much the arousal was becoming painful. She was not just going to bow down and accept whatever. She might not be a Breed with a clear appreciation of this Mating Heat stuff, but she still had a mind of her own.

Before he could stop her, she twisted away from him, moving through the doorway and stalking through the kitchen to the foyer. She wasn't going to attempt the back door. But she might have a chance of getting to her own house before he stopped her through the front yard. Icy rain and all.

"Lyra. Where the hell do you think you're going?"

He moved ahead of her before she could reach the door, staring back at her broodingly as she restrained the urge to kick him.

"To my own house," she reminded him. "Remember? Clothes? Laptop?"

"No." The rough growl sent shivers up her spine and spasms attacking her vagina. Damn him. A man should never have a voice so inherently sexy.

"Tarek, you are under the impression this Mating Heat of yours somehow gives you rights you do not have." She pointed her finger into his chest, pushing back at the stubborn male muscle that wouldn't budge an inch.

Savage intensity tightened his expression, giving him a dangerous, predatory look.

"You are my mate. It's my place to protect you." He fairly snarled the words, lifting his lip to display those wickedly white incisors.

"It's daylight, Tarek," she pointed out as though speaking to a young child. Sometimes, men responded to nothing else. "I'm safe, sweetheart. I'm just gonna walk across the lawn."

"You will not." He stepped toward her.

And of course, she retreated.

The look on his face assured her that he was done ignoring her arousal and now ready to do something about it. Of course, the erection straining beneath the loose fit of his sweatpants pretty much assured her of that on its own.

"Tarek, these strongman tactics are going to piss me off," she bit out, irritation surging through her. "I don't like it."

"So?" His lips tilting in a mocking smile. "Tell me, *mate*, how will you stop it?"

Cool male confidence marked his features.

"I'm really going to hurt you," she muttered, frustration surging through her because she knew there wasn't really a damned thing she could do.

She could call her brothers.

But that wouldn't really be fair. Would it?

No, she decided, this one she had to handle on her own.

She backed up again as he moved closer, her eyes narrowing on him.

"I am not ready to have sex with you yet," she stated imperiously as she tried to escape into the living room.

He smiled. A wicked, sensual smile that had her pussy weeping. Damn him.

"Aren't you?" He stalked her through the large room, her gaze moving around the heavy furniture, taking in the clean masculine lines and nearly clinical sterility of the room. There wasn't even a picture.

"No. I'm not."

Oh but she was. It was beating through her veins and pounding in her chest. Her breasts were tight with the need for it, her pussy clenching in hunger.

He stopped as she edged around the heavy cherrywood coffee table, watching him warily.

"You make me want to smile," he whispered then, his eyes filled with warmth, with longing. "Even as stubborn as you can be, you make me want to smile."

Her heart melted. Now, dammit, how was she supposed to stand her ground when he said things like that?

"Now is not the time to be nice, Tarek," she snapped, infuriated at him.

"But I want to be nice to you." He used that whiskey-rough voice like a caress, and it was much too effective for Lyra's peace of mind. "I want to be very nice to you, Lyra. I want to lay you down on that couch, spread your pretty legs, and show you just how nice I can be to you. Wouldn't you like that, baby?"

The heat in the room jumped a hundred degrees. She could feel perspiration gathering between her breasts and along her forehead, and hunger tearing her apart.

She didn't run as he made his way around the table. She watched him, wondering what the hell had happened to her willpower, her strength, her determination to not let this man get around her so easily.

But he did. Not with his words. Or his intent. It was the longing in his eyes, the vulnerability, the joy that sparkled there as she faced him.

"I'm really going to get mad at you one of these days," she warned him as he stepped closer, surrounding her, his hand moving beneath her hair to cup her neck. "And don't bite me again, either. That's just too freaky."

She could feel the wound pulsing, achingly sensitive.

"You complain about the bite, but not the barb?" The casual tone of his voice was not reflected in the tenseness of his body.

"Yeah, well." She cleared her throat nervously. "The barb I can forgive you for. That bite is going to get your ass kicked if my brothers see it, though. I'd prefer to keep you in one piece."

He stared down at her thoughtfully.

"I think you enjoyed the barb." He lowered his head, his tongue rasping over the small wound from his bite. "And I think you liked the bite, too, Lyra."

She shivered as his tongue rasped over it, sending currents of pleasure whipping through her.

"Maybe," she gasped in pleasure, standing still, her hands at her sides, curled into fists to keep from touching him, to keep from disturbing the emotion she could feel weaving around her.

"Come here, baby." He pulled her into his arms, leaving her no other choice but to lift her own, her hands moving to his neck, to his glorious mane of hair. "Let's see how much you like both."

His head lowered, his lips covered hers, and she was lost. She knew she was lost. Taken in a firestorm of sensual heat as the delicately flavored hormone began to surge through her already prepared senses.

She moaned into his kiss, her lips parting, accepting his tongue, drawing on it as a savage growl vibrated in his throat.

Her nails bit into his shoulders, scraped the flesh, caressing him in turn as his hands gripped her buttocks and lifted her against his thighs.

She was aware of him moving her, laying her back on the cushions of the overstuffed couch as he moved over her.

He pushed the shirt over her breasts, but neither of them could break the kiss long enough to tear it off. But somehow he had removed his sweats.

She could feel his cock, hard and heavy against her thigh as his hands roved over her sensitized body. They moaned, the sounds of their pleasure mixing, merging as he lifted her to him, the broad crest of his erection pressing against the slick, readied entrance to her spasming pussy.

"Lyra . . ." His harsh, graveled voice pierced her heart as he tore his lips from hers, raising his head to stare down at her with eyes that seemed to melt with emotion.

Oh God, she loved him. Everything about him. Every portion of him.

"Now," she whispered as he paused. "Love me, Tarek . . . Please . . ."

He grimaced, his lips pulled back from his teeth in a savage snarl as he stared down at her in surprise.

"Don't you know, Lyra?" His smile was bittersweet. "Don't you know just how much I do love you?"

She would have smacked him, or at least yelled at him for saying it with such hopeless pain. But he chose that moment to begin pushing into her, stretching her snug muscles as he worked his cock inside her.

Fiery, agonizing heat filled her. The pleasure was lightning fast, flaring through every portion of her body as he rocked against her.

She felt him, inch by inch, sinking into her, just as he had taken her heart. Bit by bit, forcing her wide, searing her with not just the pleasure, but the sheer gentleness he used.

"I would die for you," he whispered against her ear, hiding his expression against her neck as she convulsed around him, her hands locking in his hair. "Don't you know, Lyra, I live for you now. For now and for always."

He surged through the final depths of her aching sex, pushing in fiercely before retreating with the same agonizing pace he had used to enter her.

"Tarek." She bit his ear. He was making her wild, setting her heart aflame, sending her body into quaking shudders of pleasure. "Just live for me," she gasped. "Oh God." He thrust into her quickly, retreated slowly, stealing her breath, her thoughts.

"Oh baby, I'm not nearly finished with you." His voice was so dark, so velvet-rough it nearly sent her into climax. Her womb convulsed; her breath caught in her throat as her clit swelled in nearing ecstasy.

He leaned back, his knees pressing into the couch as he draped her legs over his thighs. His hands free, he lifted her against him, holding her to his chest as he stared into her shocked face.

"Take off the shirt."

His cock throbbed inside her. Her pussy was sucking at him with rapturous greed, and he was worried about her shirt?

"Now." His voice hardened, his gaze turning stubborn. "I won't give you what you need, Lyra, until you do."

Her hands lowered from his neck, gripping the shirt and struggling to jerk it over her head as one hand gripped her buttock and lifted her several inches from the thick wedge of his cock. Then he released her, thrusting hard and deep inside her again as she whimpered in delirious need.

The shirt cleared her head, though she struggled to force it from her arms. Finally it was gone, her hands moving to his shoulders again, her legs tightening around his hips as she fought to force him to move inside her.

"Tarek, I'm going to skin you alive if you keep torturing me." She knew the pitiful whimper in her voice didn't exactly carry the threat well. But he should know her well enough to know she would keep her word. Maybe.

He chuckled.

"Hold on. We're going to the bed."

"The bed?" Her eyes widened in horror as he moved easily from the couch.

She shuddered as his cock shifted with each movement.

"I heard that last time," her strangled gasp nearly became a mewl of rapture as his cock began to fuck in and out of her with each step. "Those steps . . ." She moaned at the sensation of his movements inside her. "Aren't so comfortable."

"We'll make it." He sounded too confident. Too determined.

Sweet Lord, he was going to kill her.

She swore he would. She knew he would.

"Oh God. Tarek. Tarek, I can't stand it." She was screaming his name as he began to take the steps with a heavy, quick stride.

His cock slammed inside her, taking her breath before retreating, rocking in, thrusting forcibly, then rocking inside her again.

Her nails dug into his shoulders, gasping, desperate cries fell from her lips as she tightened her legs around his hips and fought to hang on.

The first orgasm ripped through her on the sixth step. On the twelfth she was shuddering, jerking in his arms as the second stole her breath and her mind.

She was only barely aware of him actually making it to the bed, laying her back, and gripping her hips as he began to fuck her into a third, destructive climax.

She arched, her breath leaving her body in a rush as she felt his release tear through him then. The barb swelled forcibly from beneath the head of his cock, pressing into the delicate bundle of nerves that no man would have reached otherwise. It throbbed, caressed, and sent her flying into an orgasm that had no beginning and no end. It only had Tarek, holding her, his teeth scraping the wound he had left earlier before his teeth locked on it once again and dark oblivion overtook her.

"I love you. Oh God, Tarek, I love you . . ." Velvet darkness enclosed her as the words whispered free, her heart expanding as her soul seemed to lift, shudder, and open to accept a part of him that she knew even death could never steal.

". . . I'm just tired, Dad. I had dinner out with a friend last night, and I have all this work backed up. I just think it would be best if you and the boys come over after all this rain lets up. You know how they mess up my kitchen when it's wet outside . . ."

Tarek listened to Lyra spin a song and dance to her father later the next evening that even he wouldn't have believed from her.

His sensual, sexual little mate was giving her father excuses that even he, who had no experience with parents, would never have tried.

What was it that made her think that delicate, sweet little voice was fooling anyone?

You're crazy! he mouthed slowly, ignoring her as she waved him away with a graceful little flip of her hand.

After two days of sex that should have killed him, in positions he hadn't tried in all his sexual lifetime, he was even prone to be fairly prejudiced in her favor. But the sweet, candy-coated innocent tone had him rolling his eyes at her before giving her a fierce frown.

What? she mouthed back, shooting him an irritated glance before turning her attention back to the call she had made to her family.

Considering the fact her brothers were Special Forces, he doubted their father was dimwitted. Yet here was his independent, feisty mate, reclining naked in his bed with nothing but a sheet to cover her, weaving an excuse that had him wincing painfully.

Her silken hair was tangled around her flushed face, her blue eyes gleaming with irritation, and she had the nerve to sit there and attempt to put her father off in such a way.

She was tired. She didn't feel like cooking. Her brothers made messes . . .

Give him a break. Hell, give him strength because he had a feeling the full fury of a father plus his sons would arrive on her doorstep, fouling the careful setup Braden had there to catch the Trainer.

"Yes, Dad, I know how irked they get when they have to wait to do things, but my yard looks like a swamp right now, and they couldn't do anything even if they wanted to. They just want a free meal, and I'm busy."

She was pouting. Seriously pouting. What happened to the independent "do it my way or no way" woman he knew? He shook his head, pushing his fingers through his hair as he tried to think of ways to fix this before her family became his headache.

There was no stopping her. He sliced his hand across his throat, frowning at her warningly. To no effect. All he got was a glare in return.

That glare effectively hardened his cock. All she had to do was think about opposing him, and that stubborn flesh rose to rigid life. Dammit. She was wearing him out.

But what a way to go.

He would have grinned at the thought if she hadn't chosen that moment to tell *daddy,* in that sweet innocent tone, that she was going to work all evening.

It was enough to make him groan silently.

"Yes, Dad, I promise I'm being careful and locking the doors and windows at night." The promise was made in an almost automatic tone. "I promise, the only wild animals I'll let in are the four-legged variety. Not that I've seen any lately." She grinned cheekily at her words as she winked at Tarek.

Insane woman! He snarled silently, mouthing the words to her as she rolled her eyes at him. Who did she think was believing this?

"This isn't bread-baking day," she yawned after the muted sound of her father's deep voice stopped speaking. "Besides, I'm busy. They can wait another day or two." She nestled deeper in the pillows, frowning as he watched her with almost morbid fascination.

She was actually convinced she was pulling this off. He could see it in her face. In her father's tone of voice, he heard another story. Not that he could hear the words, just the alert tone, the almost military crispness.

She was going to get him killed. His training was excellent, but three Special Forces of the caliber that had helped free the Breeds from the Council Trainers and soldiers wouldn't be in any way easy to defeat. Especially considering he couldn't exactly kill his mate's family.

"Yes, Dad, I promise to rest, and I'll call you tomorrow," she answered in a placating tone that was so sickeningly sweet, it had him wondering if his dinner was going to stay down.

He made a note to never be taken in by that tone of voice himself.

When she finally hung up the phone, he glared at her sternly.

"I hope you are not convinced that you pulled that off," he growled furiously. "We will now have your entire family ripping the neighborhood apart looking for you."

"Don't be silly." She laughed at his prediction. "They'll come here first. I don't think they entirely trust you. Something about not being able to find enough background information." She wiggled her finely arched brows suggestively. "Have you been a bad boy, Tarek? Hiding records and such?"

She shimmied beneath the sheet, bracing her hands on the mattress as she leaned closer to him, her eyes dancing with shimmering lights of amusement as she gave him a suggestive little smile.

"Should I spank you for being bad now?"

His brows snapped into a frown. He was ignoring the ache in his cock. He needed a shower and food or he was going to collapse in exhaustion.

"You, I will spank later." He pointed his finger at her with determined emphasis. "Someone needs to teach you better than to play such obvious games with men who know you much too well."

"Yeah. Right." She had the nerve to laugh at him. "I didn't lie to him. He can see straight through my lies. Everything I said was the truth . . ."

"In a roundabout way," he grunted.

"How do you think I managed to get out of his house?" She plopped back against the pillow, the sheet falling away from her breasts and their hard, tempting nipples. "But you can punish me now if you want to."

She was becoming much too confident in her ability to drive him completely insane.

Finally he just threw up his hands as he rose from the bed and stalked to the bathroom door. If he was going to have to fight her brothers, he didn't want to smell of sex when that happened.

"I am taking a shower," he snapped. "I have a feeling I might want to be prepared for the visit I will have to endure by your family. And you are a troublemaker, Lyra. This will come back and smack you on the ass one of these days."

"Really?" Interest lit her laughter-filled gaze. "I bet it makes me wet."

He snorted. "I have no doubt, you little hellion."

And before his body could overrule his mind, he forced himself into the bathroom, closing the door behind him before he joined her in the bed again instead.

As he stepped beneath the steaming water, he made a note to

contact Braden and warn him to be expecting trouble. He had a bad feeling that plenty of it was now heading his way.

◆   ◆   ◆

Lyra laughed as the bathroom door closed behind Tarek and let the warmth that teasing him brought her fill her heart. She loved the look on his face. For once, the shadows that normally lingered there were gone. In their place may have been irritation or incredulity, but she had seen the happiness there as well.

She made him happy.

She sighed at the thought, an odd satisfaction filling her. Making him happy shouldn't make her feel as though she were glowing from the inside out, but it did.

And it made her want to cook. Something really incredible. Something that would make that bit of confused happiness fill his eyes once again.

She had food. Finally. It had taken her hours last night to convince him to have someone deliver the basic kitchen products as well as some real meat, rather than that stuff he nuked every day.

Yuck. That was nasty stuff.

She shook her head, rising from the bed and pulling on her gown and robe as she ignored the tenderness between her thighs. That and the pulse of desire. She had a feeling that Mating Heat or not, she could forget her response to him ever dimming. He had made her wet the first time she laid eyes on him, and she had a feeling she would be wet for him on her deathbed.

She left the bedroom, padding quickly down the stairs to the wide foyer and turning into the kitchen.

She stopped abruptly. Her eyes widened, terror rushing through her system as her knees weakened.

"Well, it looks like Tarek took a little mate," the intruder sneered, his weapon aimed at her heart. "I bet the Council will have a lot of fun with this one. After we take her Lion out, of course. The only good Feline is a dead one."

Lyra turned to run, only to slam into the hard body blocking her way. The contact sent pain streaking across her nerve endings, causing her to gasp in shock as she jerked away from the other intruder.

What now? Breathing roughly, she fought to hold back her fear, her eyes wide, as hard hands pushed her into a kitchen chair.

"He'll kill you." She clenched her fingers at her side, trying to think, to find a way to escape, to warn Tarek.

"He might try. He'll fail. We were very careful this time. He won't even be able to smell us." Evil, malicious. The taller of the two men stared down at her curiously as he held the weapon on her. "So tell me, what's it like to fuck an animal?"

Lyra swallowed tightly. "Ask your wife."

He grunted at that, smiling mockingly. "Doesn't matter." He shrugged. "The scientists will get the answer."

She had to warn Tarek.

Her gaze flicked to the entrance of the kitchen. He would be finished soon, coming down the stairs, unaware of the danger awaiting him. Unable to smell the threat.

She swallowed tightly.

The Council had tortured him for most of his life, treated him like an animal, refused him even the most basic human considerations.

He had never eaten homemade bread. Had never drunk real coffee. He didn't know how to cook, but from what her brothers had said, many of the Breed labs had been dens of filth and neglect. Yet he kept his home sparkling, free of dust, and took off his shoes at the door. He was a man desperate to live, to be free. A man who knew how to love despite the horrors he had known.

And now these two thought they were going to use her to kill him? She couldn't, she wouldn't allow it.

He belonged to her now. He was her heart, her soul, and she couldn't imagine life without him. She would die without him.

Think Lyra. Her eyes darted around her as the two watched her closely. *Warn him. How could you warn him . . .*

Smell. He could smell arousal. He could smell fear.

Rather than tamping back the horror racing through her, the terror clogging her mind, she gave it free rein instead. She had to warn him . . .

◆   ◆   ◆

Tarek stepped out of the shower, drying quickly before jerking clean sweatpants on and moving to the door to let Lyra know the shower was now free.

He stepped into the bedroom, frowning at the empty bed for a long second before his head raised slowly, a new, intrusive scent reaching his nostrils.

Fear.

He could smell it, sharp, warning, riding the soft trail of Lyra's unique scent. But there was nothing else. No other smell drifting through the bedroom door to give him an idea of what awaited him downstairs.

She was his mate, and he could feel the danger surrounding her pulsing in the air.

He jerked the cell phone from beside the bed and keyed in the alert for trouble before tossing the device to the mattress and striding to the chest of drawers.

He pulled one of the smaller weapons from the drawer before stripping the adhesive backing from the light, skin-adhering holster. Smacking it to the side of the gun, he anchored the weapon in the small of his back before pulling on his shirt.

He grabbed the spare gun from the top of the chest and checked the ammo before moving for the doorway.

Pausing, he listened carefully. There were no lights on, but he didn't need any. And he didn't know who or what was downstairs, but it wasn't a Breed. There wasn't a chance in hell a Breed could disguise his scent so effectively. But sometimes, rarely, certain humans could.

Trainers knew how. It was hard, at times nearly impossible, but it could be done.

As he moved to the stairs he inhaled carefully. He smelled no Breed or human scent other than Lyra's and her fear. It was overwhelming, imperative. But alongside it was a curiously hollow sterile scent. As though something had been cleaned. And another, not quite as crisp, as though something were bleeding away whatever had been used to disguise the evil that filled it.

A cold snarl shaped his lips.

There were two, and one of them was nervous, wary. Perhaps not quite as certain as the other. That one was weak. He would make a mistake.

As Tarek started down the stairs, he laid the extra weapon on a step, close enough to jump and retrieve if he needed it. If he went in armed, they would know he had been aware of them, and they would search him, using Lyra to keep him in place while they took the hidden weapon.

"Lyra, you left the lights out," he called out as he stepped into the foyer. "No more of your games now. Where are you?"

He kept his voice teasing, taunting as he moved to the kitchen where her scent was strongest. He stopped at the entrance, placing his hands on his hips as he surveyed the scene.

Everything inside him clenched with fear as he fought to present a casual attitude. He could feel the growl growing in his chest, his jaw clenching with the need to taste blood.

The two men stood on each side of her, one with his weapon lying threateningly against her temple. She didn't make a sound, but he could see the tears shimmering on her face, her lips moving.

I'm so sorry . . .

"Well, I admit, Tarek, I hadn't thought it really possible." Anton Creighton shook his head as he made a clucking sound. "And to find you so careless. Your Trainers were sloppier than I had thought them to be during your stay at the labs."

Cold, steel-gray eyes stared out of a pale face. A black cap covered his blond hair, but Tarek remembered the color well. His broad, heavily muscled body appeared relaxed, but Tarek could see the tension in it. The other man wasn't nearly as confident as he appeared to be.

And his partner was terrified.

"The stink of your man is starting to bleed through whatever you used to cover him," he informed Creighton coolly. "He's scared."

Creighton's eyes narrowed as Tarek refused to rise to his prodding. His gaze flickered to the other man.

"Good help is so hard to come by." He smiled coldly. "But he did well enough to keep you from detecting us until the time was right."

Tarek nodded with all signs of absent attention as he glanced at Lyra.

"So what do you boys want tonight?" he asked, keeping his voice measured, nonthreatening.

He knew Creighton better than the other man thought he did. He was easy to play with, maneuverable to a small degree, and living on a prayer as he fought to escape both Breeds and Council soldiers.

Creighton was basically a coward. When the labs were attacked by government and independent forces to rescue the Breeds held there, he had deserted the fight rather than risking capture. He was considered a criminal to both sides now.

"Just the girl." Creighton shrugged dismissively. "As soon as I dispose of you, I can use her for a little trade. You should have stayed off my ass, Tarek. But because you're so persistent, I'll take care of you now and ensure my return to the Council ranks with your pretty little mate."

"The Council is disbanded, Creighton." Tarek watched him pityingly. "There's no one to trade with."

A rich chuckle filled the air.

"You really believe that, Tarek?" he asked, shaking his head. "No need to worry, Lion-boy. They're still there. Tucked away nice and safe, but there all the same."

"Shut up, Creighton," his partner hissed. "Kill him and be done with it."

Lyra flinched, her gaze turning wild at the demand.

Damn. She was the wild card, not these two bastards. And there wasn't a damn thing he could do but pray her common sense won out.

"Your boy is a little impatient, Creighton." Tarek mocked as he leaned against the doorframe, crossing his arms over his chest as he watched them. "A little bossy, too, isn't he?"

Creighton's ego was legendary.

"Shut up, Tim," he snapped. "I have him under control."

"You sure he's not a Coyote?" Tarek nodded to good old Tim, with his washed-out hazel eyes filled with fear and lanky dark brown hair. "He shakes like one."

Creighton's chuckle was mocking, grating on Tarek's nerves as the barrel of his gun slid against Lyra's temple in a cold caress.

"He'll do," Creighton assured him as he stared back coldly. "Unfortunately, there's no bounty on your head. But I guess I'm going to have to kill you anyway. If you had just let me be, boy, I would have done the same." He shook his head in mock regret. "Some Breeds never learn though."

Just a little more. Just a few more seconds.

He could smell Braden and another Breed at the back door. But he could also smell the overwhelming scent of fury at the front door. Human fury. A father's fury.

Shit.

"This was really a bad time to come calling, Creighton." Tarek shook his head, almost feeling sorry for the other man now. "It's bread night, you know."

He glanced at Lyra, praying she would get the message. She blinked, amazement and a surge of renewed fear glittering in her eyes.

"Bread night?" Creighton stared at him in confusion. "What does bread have to do with anything? Has freedom rotted your brain?"

"Sadly, for you, I believe it may have."

The back door splintered as the house alarm began blaring. Lyra, bless her sweet heart, was no one's fool. Before Creighton could stop her, she threw herself to the floor, rolling beneath the table as her feet kicked out at Tim's knees as Tarek dropped, whipped the gun from his back, and fired back at the Trainer.

The front door exploded as Creighton went down and Tarek threw himself beneath the kitchen table, his body covering Lyra's as he left the other man for Braden and whoever the hell was screaming bloody-assed murder to take care of.

"I told you it wasn't going to work. You can't play with men who know you so well, Lyra," he growled, reminding her of his warning as she spoke to her father earlier. He pulled her deeper beneath the table, forcing her behind him, sheltering her between his body and the wall as she struggled to push him away.

Braden and Jonas were on the floor, weapons raised ready, as three well-trained Navy SEALs burst into the room, weapons drawn, murder glowing in their eyes.

"Dammit, Tarek, let me go before they destroy the house," Lyra yelled at his ear. "They'll tear it apart."

"Better the house than me," he grunted, holding her in place as the black-clad figures halted at the table, followed by a set of legs clad in jeans.

The father.

Hell.

"Look, I like this house better than mine." She smacked his shoulder before putting her knees into his back and pushing. "And they're going to ruin it."

"Dammit, stay in place, woman," he snarled. "I can rebuild the house, and as I can't kill the bastards because of you, I'd really prefer to stay out of harm's way. If it's all the same to you," he snarled mockingly.

"Moron."

"Brat."

"Well, at least she's alive," a mocking voice drawled as three Navy SEALs hunkered down to stare beneath the table.

Eyes amazingly similar to Lyra's stared back at him. They quickly took in the fact that he wasn't about to let her move just yet, and she was fairly content to be where she was, insults notwithstanding.

"You can't shoot my future husband." She finally managed to wiggle past him.

Heaving a sigh, Tarek glanced across the floor as Braden came slowly to his feet.

"Are those assholes bleeding on my kitchen floor?" Lyra was out from under the table just ahead of him, facing her brothers, hands on her hips. "Why are they bleeding on my floor?"

"Blame your boyfriend under there." The broadest of the four men faced her squarely, his black head lowered to snarl back at her, anger lighting his eyes. "He shot them. We didn't. And since when the hell is this your house?"

"Since *I* said it was." Tarek pulled her back, his instincts flaring at the other man's fury toward his mate. This was not acceptable.

"And who the hell are you?" Violence raged in the brother's expression. A violence he could damned well direct somewhere other than toward Lyra.

"Her mate . . ." His cold smile didn't go over any better than his announcement.

Pandemonium ensued.

· CHAPTER 10 ·

"I can't believe you actually got into a fistfight with my brother." Lyra's expression was none too pleased later that night as she stood before him, inspecting the black eye and split lip he had gained from the effort.

"Neither can I," he grunted, wincing as she pressed the alcohol pad she held to the abrasion on his cheek. "It was wasted effort. You, Lyra, are a troublemaker. I've seen this tonight."

"Me?" She drew back, her eyes innocently wide as she stared back at him in surprise. "What did I do?"

"You antagonize your brothers." He caught her hips as she attempted to move from the bed where he sat. "You deliberately challenge their authority and continually keep them in a state of combat-readiness. That fight was your fault. Had you been a bit more forthcoming, as I encouraged you to be on the phone, they would not have charged in, determined to protect your honor."

Her lips twitched. The little hellion.

"If you had stayed out of it, there wouldn't have been a fight." She braced her hands on his shoulders to hold him back from licking once again at the scratch she had somehow gained from the night's adventures.

The red mark extended from her shoulder, past her collarbone, and although the sting was irritating, it was nothing compared to the fires burning in the rest of her body.

"No man gives you orders but me," he grunted at being denied access to her sweet flesh. He deserved something in reward for the aches and pains echoing beneath his flesh.

"You don't give me orders, either," she informed him imperiously. "What is it with you guys that you think you can?"

He sighed wearily, seeing his life stretching out ahead of him, constantly amazed or exasperated at one small woman. Not that he wasn't looking forward to it. But Lyra had a habit of antagonizing her brothers where perhaps she should be less confrontational.

He was definitely going to have to talk to them alone in regards to this. She seemed to enjoy keeping them upset.

"The fact that you can so easily get into trouble?" He arched his brow mockingly. "Lyra, sweetheart, after discussing this with your brothers, I'm certain you are a trouble magnet."

The fight had been a damned good one. Clean, brutal, fists flying, and curses raging as he and Grant, her oldest brother, proceeded to destroy the kitchen.

When they finished, Lyra had stomped to the bedroom to pout while they agreed to a beer and a heated argument on whether or not Lyra would stay with him.

Not that there was a question of it as far as he was concerned, but in the eyes of her family, he had seen their love for her, and their fears. He wasn't exactly the boy next door. He was a Breed, and he had just nearly gotten her killed. It would be enough to terrify a brother who had accepted responsibility for his headstrong sibling.

And they seemed to accept him and his ability to protect her. Most men would have been hesitant. Thankfully, the prejudices against the Breeds were absent in the Mason family, due to the fact that her three brothers had been instrumental in the rescues of many of the Breed captives.

He pulled her to him then, his chest tightening at the memory of Creighton's gun caressing her temple, the bullet much too close to extinguishing the fire that warmed everyone she touched. How could he endure life without her now?

"You didn't have to fight them." She leaned against him, her slender body flowing easily against him as he lifted her to straddle his lap, his arms wrapping tight around her back as his lips lowered to the mark he had left on her shoulder. "I had them under control."

"You had them in cardiac arrest," he sighed. "Your poor father will never be the same."

Lyle Mason, the father in question, had been most determined to take his daughter home, to wrap her in the protection he felt only he could provide. He had been a man tormented with thoughts of losing the daughter he so obviously adored.

Not that Tarek understood the family dynamics, but he understood the need to protect, the need to love the tiny woman he held in his arms. She was his light. His world. She could be nothing less to anyone who loved her.

He pressed her tighter against him, feeling her rock against the erection straining beneath his soft pants, dampening the material with the damp heat of her pussy.

She wasn't wearing panties beneath her gown. His hands smoothed down the material until he caught the hem and lifted it, his hands gripping her smooth, bare ass.

A moan locked in his throat at the feel of her sliding against him, her breathing deepening, the scent of her heat filling the room.

"Don't leave me, Lyra." He couldn't stop the words from slipping past his lips as he held on to her, lifting her, laying her back to the bed as he rose above her.

"I have no intention of leaving you, Tarek." Her eyes were glowing with emotion, with hunger. "I told you, I love you. And I don't say that lightly. Not to anyone."

He touched her cheek, his throat tightening as he fought past the confusion, the disbelief that this woman could love him. That God, in all His bountiful mercy, had finally adopted him and given him this gift he never thought he could have. Something, someone, to always call his own.

"The next time you start a fight with your brothers, I will spank you, though," he growled as her head raised, her lips finding the hardened nub of his nipple as she nipped at it playfully.

"Sounds like fun. How many fights are we talking about before I get my just desserts?"

He moaned as her fingernails raked down his abdomen before her fingers hooked in the waistband of his sweatpants and began to lower them slowly.

"You are a hellion," he breathed out roughly as he moved from the bed and stripped quickly.

Her gown went flying past him as he shucked his pants. When he straightened, there she was, on her hands and knees, her tongue reaching out to lick the bulging head of his cock.

Her black hair fanned around her face, her blue eyes glowing with emotion and hunger. They were as brilliant as the brightest, purest sapphire, and more precious than gold to him.

Her pink little tongue flickered over the crest of his erection again, leaving a trail of fire around the sensitive hood as he tensed at the pleasure shooting from his cock to every other nerve ending in his body. He didn't think pleasure could get any better—until her lips parted, her heated mouth opening to accept the head of his cock into the damp depths.

Tarek watched as the flushed, straining crest of his erection disappeared between her lips, her tongue stroking the underside with such incredible pleasure he wondered if he could bear it.

His hands tangled in her hair, clenching tight as a strangled growl filled his chest, escaping his lips as she began to suck him with hungry abandon.

Her movements were hesitant, innocent.

She was killing him.

She stared up at him, laughter and arousal gleaming in her gaze as her tongue stroked, her mouth drawing on him, her wicked hand moving slowly up his thigh until she cupped his balls with silken fingers and destructive pleasure.

"Brat," he groaned, fighting for breath. For control.

His tongue was throbbing like a toothache, the need to spill the excess hormone into her mouth making him wild. He could taste the spice, feel its effect on him, feel his cock tightening further, the need to release becoming a near-agonizing pleasure.

And still her mouth moved on him. Slow, delicate licks, deep, drawing caresses until a purely animalistic growl erupted from him.

Tarek tightened his hands in her hair, pulling her back as he felt the pulse of the barb just beneath the hood of his cock.

"Enough."

"Hmm. I'm hungry." She licked her lips sensually, full, swollen lips. "Maybe I want more."

She laughed, a low, sweet sound, as he pushed her back to the bed, spreading her thighs as he lowered his shoulders between them.

There was no time for preliminaries. He had to taste her. Sample the delicate liquid silk of her pussy before he went insane. Or kissed her.

If he kissed her, there would be no waiting. He was riding too close to the edge, her own hunger rising so quickly the scent of it was going to his head.

"I'm going to eat you up," he groaned a second before licking through the bare, syrup-laden silk of her intimate folds. "Every inch of you, Lyra. Until the taste of you permeates every fiber of my senses."

She breathed in roughly, the flesh of her tummy convulsing as he watched it with narrowed eyes. He could see so much there. Each ripple of creamy flesh corresponding with the level of her arousal.

His tongue circled her clit before he drew it between his lips, watching as her stomach seemed to convulse. As he suckled at her, he moved his fingers to the drenched folds of her pussy, opening her farther until he could work a finger inside the hot depths.

She jerked against him, her hips writhing, pressing closer to the penetration as her creamy juices began to flow.

"Oh God, Tarek, you're making me crazy," she cried out desperately, her vagina rippling around his finger. "Stop torturing me like this."

He hummed his pleasure of her taste. Sweet. Addictive. He pushed her closer to the edge of her release, his finger thrusting deeply inside her, caressing the responsive depths as she lifted to him.

"Tease." Her rough accusation was thick with her pleasure. "Fuck me, Tarek. Don't make me have to kill you."

He would have smiled if he weren't so consumed by the hunger for her.

"Tarek . . ." Her half-scream was followed by the tightening of her pussy around his finger, her tummy tightening. "You'll pay for this." Her knees bent, her feet pressing into the mattress as she lifted closer. "I swear I'll make you pay . . ."

He gave her what she needed. Adding another finger to the snug depths of her cunt, he began to pump them inside her using his lips, his tongue, the suction of his mouth to drive her higher, to send her into fragmented explosions of ecstasy.

She arched to him, crying out his name as he quickly rose above her, lifting her, pressing his cock into the convulsing tissue of her pussy as he gritted his teeth against the pleasure.

She was so tight. So hot.

Liquid silk. Lava-hot cream.

He gripped her hip with one hand, lowering his weight to the elbow of his opposite arm as he felt her legs wrap around him.

Her pussy flexed around him, tiny flutters of sensation, tight, rippling caresses washing over his erection as he worked it into her, first short, desperate thrusts and then hard lunges as he began to fuck her with all the strength and desperation of the hunger surging inside him.

His lips lowered to hers, his tongue spearing into her mouth as she moved beneath him, opening for him, taking him with strangled screams and ever-tightening ripples of her responsive pussy.

She was ecstasy. She was life.

The tempo of his thrusts increased as the hormone surged from his tongue to her system, heating them both further, sending them rushing headlong into orgasm.

As he felt his release tightening his balls, the extension beneath the hood of his cock began to engorge, becoming firmly, heatedly erect and locking him tight inside.

Violent shudders shook her as her arms tightened around his neck, her head turning as his lips unerringly found the mark that branded her as his mate as he began to flood her with his semen.

Shocking, violent pleasure. A bonding unlike anything he could have known. And Lyra. Always Lyra. The center of his life.

"Oh God. Tell me that barb thing does not go away with the heat," she gasped when they found the sanity to breathe. "I wouldn't be pleased."

"I guess you'd have to hurt me?" He chuckled weakly as he rolled to his side, pulling her against his chest as he sighed in contentment.

"I'd have to hurt you bad." She sighed.

"But you'd still love me." She'd better.

"I'll always love you." She nipped at his chest before leaning her head back to smile up at him mistily. "Always, Tarek. You might not be the boy next door, but the Breed works much better."

Their laughter was soft, content. His soul was fulfilled.

He wasn't completely human. But neither was he an animal. He was a Breed, a Breed who had found his mate, and his life.

In a
Wolf's Embrace

◆ ◆ ◆

They were created, they weren't born. They were trained, they weren't raised.

They were taught to kill, and now they'll use their training to ensure their freedom.

They are Breeds. Genetically altered with the DNA of the predators of the earth. The wolf, the lion, the cougar, the Bengal; the killers of the world. They were to be the army of a fanatical society intent on building their own personal army.

Until the world learned of their existence. Until the council lost control of their creations, and their creations began to change the world.

Now, they're loose. Banding together, creating their own communities, their own society, and their own safety, and fighting to hide the one secret that could see them destroyed.

The secret of mating heat. The chemical, biological, the emotional reaction of one Breed to the man or woman meant to be his or hers forever. A reaction that binds physically. A reaction that alters more than just the physical responses or heightens the sensuality. Nature has turned mating heat into the Breeds' Achilles' Heel. It's their strength, and yet their weakness. And Mother Nature isn't finished playing yet.

Man has attempted to mess with her creations. Now, she's going to show man exactly how she can refine them.

Killers will become lovers, lawyers, statesmen, and heroes. And through it all, they will cleave to one mate, one heart, and create a dynasty.

I dreamed of a man, lost, broken, and alone.
I dreamed of a woman, disillusioned, weeping,
and forced to roam.
I dreamed of a child, cold, hungry, and without a home.
A wolf cried out.
A lion roared.
And the lonely eagle screamed upon the winds,
where he soared.
And in a dream, a story was born.
Thank God for the dreams.

◆ C H A P T E R   I ◆

NEW YORK CITY
DUBBREE SUITES HOTEL
2023

Two assassinations in one month, each tied to known or suspected Genetics Council members. It was going to be a public relations nightmare for the Feline Breed contingent of the species.

First General Cyrus Tallant. Of course, his assassination had been laid at the feet of the Genetics Council upper-level members. As would this one be. After all, Dr. Benedikt Adolf Albrecht was under just as much, if not more, suspicion of being aligned with the shadowy twelve-member directorate of the council.

Matthias Slaughter knew Albrecht was more than just aligned. Albrecht was an actual member of the council directorate. He was also the director of training. It was his, his father's, and his father's before him, legacy to the hellish existence the Breeds had endured in the labs.

The Breed species hadn't been lucky enough to be born. No, nature hadn't, in all her insight and mercy, thrown a genetic kink in the works of an everyday human. Quite the contrary. In one of her rare fits of humor, she had decided instead to work with what man had created. What monsters such as Albrecht had pieced together. With their genius in genetic engineering and the past atrocities of their forefathers, the council had managed to create the human and animal species they had envisioned as their own personal army. An army that would be the muscle behind their quest for power.

How nature must have chuckled over that one.

Matthias imagined over the years that he had heard a giggle or two from her as well.

Physically, mentally, genetically, the Breeds were everything the council had hoped for, paid for, killed for. Psychologically, they fell far short of the mark. Like their natural cousins, the predators of the earth, the Breeds worshipped freedom, and they worshipped their own honor.

Many had died remaining true to that inner code, an ideal rather than a set of rules. An instinctive hunger and drive to attain the freedom their wild cousins knew.

They were animals in men's bodies. Primal, savage, predatory. And intelligent.

That intelligence had been the downfall of the council's plans. And it found him here now, more than a century after the first Breed had drawn his first breath.

The technical wizardry of another Breed enforcer was ensuring that the security cameras didn't record Matthias's entrance or later his exit. It was ensuring that the council itself was blamed for this death, as well as the generals before him.

The council must be cleaning house.

Matthias grinned at the headlines he imagined. The grin was quickly gone, as the sound of the penthouse's double doors opening had him waiting expectantly.

He didn't tense. Not so much as breath disturbed the air, as he inhaled carefully. Albrecht was known to travel with several bodyguards, though tonight, as they had every night during this short stay in New York, Albrecht's bodyguards were heard entering their separate room farther down the hall.

Excellent. Albrecht was known to depend on the Dubbree Hotel's security. Arrogant bastard. He thought his position protected him. That his genius in genetics and his fortune in pharmaceuticals could possibly shield him from retribution. But he had always flaunted security. Just for the hell of it. After all, who would dare attempt to harm him?

"Cretins." The heavy German accent had Matthias's lip curling to reveal the wicked canines at the side of his mouth.

Benedikt Adolf Albrecht wasn't well known for his respect toward his bodyguards.

Lights flared in the entryway, the doors closed, Matthias waited.

His prey was a creature of organized habits. Albrecht believed an organized mind was a stable mind. That could explain the accusations Matthias regularly received in regards to his own sanity. Or lack thereof.

He waited patiently in the darkened living room. The bar sat across from him. Albrecht would go there first.

And just like clockwork, the low lamps flared to life, all but the two that sat near Matthias, and Albrecht moved slowly toward the bar.

Albrecht looked like a cadaver. Tall, skinny, thin gray hair lying close to his scalp, and pale, almost bleached flesh. He stalked to the bar, as Matthias lifted his weapon from his lap.

Ice clinked in the glass, liquor splashed into it. Matthias aimed, pulled the trigger, and watched the back of Albrecht's head crack from the bullet. A second later the council member fell over the bar. Crystal carafes rolled, broke, scattering glass and the scent of liquor. But even that couldn't drown out the sound of horror from the entrance.

A woman's shocked gasp, the scent of fear—and of recognition. For the first time in his thirty years of life, Matthias felt regret, and a tinge of sadness. Because he knew his own fate had just been decided.

Matthias turned to his side, a snarl on his face, a growl in his voice. "Goddamnit, Grace."

Static crackled in the communications link at Matthias's ear.

"Get her out of there, Matthias. I can control the security monitors for five minutes, tops. Use the stairs, proceed to the ground floor. Lawe will be waiting with the van at the exit."

Matthias was moving, even as Jonas barked the orders into the receiver at his ear. He was across the room before the slender, doe-like figure of Dubbree's assistant manager, Grace Anderson, could run.

Her lips were opening, her lungs filling. Before the scream could leave her throat, his hand was over her lips and nose, his other arm jerking her against his chest, compressing her lungs and causing instant unconsciousness.

He slung her over his shoulder and strode quickly from the suite, pausing a precious second to make certain her prints didn't show anywhere on the doors, and securing the locks before moving down the hall.

He picked up the sounds of the bodyguards in the next room, the television they were watching, someone was showering. He strode by the door, slipped down the stairwell, and began taking the steps at a quick run.

Grace's weight was slight, her scent wrapping around him like silken regret. She shouldn't have been here. He had watched her get into her car and move into the traffic that congested Manhattan that afternoon. She was supposed to be on her way out of town, on vacation, leaving the city for the peace and relaxation of the mountains.

She wasn't supposed to be here. And she wasn't supposed to be anywhere near Albrecht.

The assistant manager of the exclusive hotel had earned herself a well-deserved break from the city. She had laughed with him about it and invited him to join her when his business in town was completed. Sun and fun, clear streams and lots of trees, she had teased.

And he had promised her, first thing in the morning, he would follow her.

Dammit to hell, why had she come back?

"Lawe's in position, you have three minutes," Jonas spoke in his ear. "You have to clear that exit and be in the van before the cameras go to normal operation again."

The scheduling of the security upgrades was top secret, even the floor security personnel had no idea when it happened. Jonas, miracle worker that he was, had managed to find out not only when it would happen, but how to ensure how long it would take.

"I'll have ten seconds to spare," he muttered, racing down the stairs, his steps silent, his movements sure despite his burden. "Have the doors open."

"Open and ready," Law reported. "Get a move on big boy, this area won't stay secure the full time."

Get a move on. He grunted at the order. As though he wasn't going fast enough.

"Break the girl's damned neck and dump her." Another voice came across the line. "She's a liability."

A growl rumbled from Matthias's throat, though his pace never faltered.

"Shut up, Simon," Jonas ordered. "Two minutes, Matthias."

He would make it in plenty of time if Sleeping Beauty didn't decide to wake up and pitch a fit. And she could pitch a fit. He'd met her during the mugging Jonas had staged for Matthias to save her from. If he hadn't moved in when he had, Simon might have been charging the Breeds extra for hazardous-duty pay.

Thankfully, she stayed quiet. He hit the exit, ducked, and disappeared into the interior of the van, with two seconds to spare. The door slammed shut, barely missing Grace's head. The van was accelerating away from the exit less than a second later.

"Security system active. All monitors showing normal operational status. The Monarch Suite is locked and secured. Good going, Matthias," Jonas congratulated him.

Matthias placed his hand protectively against Grace's head, shifted her from his shoulder, and laid her on the tarp-covered floor of the van.

Simon watched him, smirking. The blond-haired mercenary with the smooth southern drawl was a pain in the ass under normal circumstances. A blue-eyed ladies man and self-professed rogue, the mercenary was also a tactical genius.

Beside him, Jonas, the director of the Bureau of Breed Affairs, sat in the secured chair in front of a bank of monitors and finessed a keyboard like it was a lover. The military cut of his black hair revealed an imposing profile, though his eerie silver eyes were damned odd for a Lion Breed.

Breed Enforcement agent, Lawe Justice, drove, and Rule Breaker (hell of a set of names for cats) watched him expectantly from the front passenger seat.

"He didn't kill her," Simon stared down at Grace almost mournfully, as he tipped his cowboy hat back and flicked a glance at Matthias. "What the fuck are you going to do with her, wolf?"

"My problem." Matthias moved to peer over Jonas's shoulder at the monitors that recorded the hotel's security, tracked personnel, and alarms.

"No alarms." Jonas moved between the monitors using keyboard commands. "Your entrance or exit wasn't recorded or seen. We're in the clear."

Jonas turned in his chair, and Matthias retreated to rest his back against the wall of the van, as Jonas stared down at Grace's unconscious form.

"Why didn't you kill her?" Jonas repeated Simon's question dispassionately. "If she was in Albrecht's suite this late, then she was a part of him."

Matthias stared back at him coldly. "I won't reward her help by snapping her neck."

"Then I will," Jonas decided, moving as though to do just that.

Matthias lifted his lip in a growl, causing Jonas to pause.

"Matthias, she's a risk. She can identify you and place the weapon in your hand. What other choice do you have?" Slashing quicksilver eyes clashed with Matthias's gaze.

"I'll take care of the situation."

"And when she's reported missing? I managed to have her vehicle picked up by one of my enforcers, but she only had a week's vacation. What then?"

Matthias shifted his gaze from Jonas's to Grace's face. Her features were relaxed, her dove gray eyes closed. Rosebud lips were softened, and her creamy flesh was pale.

He had terrified her, but there hadn't been time for gentleness.

"I'll take responsibility for her," he stated firmly.

"And when she reports what she saw?" Jonas asked, his voice hard. "When she reports that a Breed, a known associate of the Bureau of Breed Affairs, killed Dr. Albrecht. What then, Matthias? You're risking the whole community, not just yourself."

"Touch her, and I'll kill you next," Matthias growled, a hard rumble of violence that had the tension in the van spiking to heated levels. "Think about harming her, and I'll kill you."

"Then hide her." Jonas shrugged. "And hide her well, wolf, because if she even breathes the truth of tonight's events, I'll make sure she never takes another breath."

◆　　◆　　◆

Jonas watched, several hours later, as Matthias loaded his conscious, bound and gagged little burden into the folded-back front seat, secured her into place, and drove away.

He leaned against the outside of the van and grinned, hell if he could help it. Sometimes, his people just amazed him, especially those who hadn't yet heard the truth of the mating heat, or the first signs of it.

Common sense was the first casualty to the heat, and he almost regretted letting the Wolf Breed drive away to parts unknown. It would have been fun as hell to watch.

"He's gonna mate her," Simon drawled from inside the van. "That look in his eye was impossible to mistake. I thought he was going to rip my throat out when I suggested breaking her neck."

"He came close." Jonas smirked.

"You should have warned him," Lawe sighed.

"You should have had him dragged back to Sanctuary for those stupid tests," Rule snarled. "If they don't find a cure for that shit, I'm never going to fuck again. It's starting to give me the jeebies."

Jonas chuckled. "We need to understand it, you can forget about curing it. Besides, Ely and the Wolf Breed scientists have enough victims. No sense in adding a new pair to the mix."

"And if he can't convince her to keep her mouth shut?" Simon voiced the question rolling around in Jonas's head. He grimaced at the thought of the answer to it.

"Track him," he ordered the other man. "If he can't convince her not to talk, then we'll have to."

Permanently if necessary. He'd hate it. It would sicken his soul, but he had done worse to see to the Breeds' survival, and he was certain he would do so again. Shedding innocent blood would add to the nightmares, though, and that he wasn't anticipating. As far as Jonas was concerned, he had enough nightmares to fight.

◆ C H A P T E R 2 ◆

She should have changed out of the short black skirt and white blouse she wore to work. She should have worn jeans. Pants, anything but the leg-flattering little skirt she was so fond of. Because it was now around her thighs. So indecently around her thighs that Grace felt herself flushing.

And while she was considering her recent mistakes, she should have let someone know she had returned. Checked in. Put off dealing with Albrecht's complaints. Anything but what she had ended up doing.

But she just had to come back for that stupid little bathing suit she had stuffed in the pocket of her jacket. And when she had, Mr. Albrecht's message had been flashing on her machine. Irate. Demanding action over some slight by the staff.

She had listened to the message, erased it, because she was anal about stuff like that, and then had gone to Albrecht's suite. That had been her biggest mistake.

The door had been slightly open, but Albrecht was known for that kind of absentmindedness. He was so arrogantly certain no one would dare attack him under the eagle eye of the security cameras that he ignored every precaution. Security had warned him repeatedly that they could not ensure his safety if he didn't stop leaving the suite door open. Normally, one of the security personnel contacted his bodyguards in the other room and had them do it. Tonight, security hadn't taken care of it. Which meant they were updating the security system. Which meant the damned system, as well as the backup, was off-line. *Which meant no one knew what the fuck had happened to her!*

Ten minutes. The system had been off-line for ten freaking stupid minutes, and one of their most influential residents was dead.

It didn't matter that he was an asshole. He was still dead. And Matthias had killed him.

Her breath hitched as she battled the tears filling her eyes. The man she had fallen in love with was a killer.

She glanced over at him.

His expression was imposing in the low lights from the dash. The wicked scar that slashed over his forehead, across his eye, then to the center of his cheek was hidden from her view. His profile revealed only the dark curve and slash of arrogant bones, the arch of black brows. Thick, coarse black hair, as dark as night, flowed down his neck and was caught at the nape of his neck with some sort of elastic band.

Broad shoulders and a body so tight and hard it gave a girl damp panties. He was dressed in his customary black leather pants, shit-kicker boots, a T-shirt, and black leather jacket.

The gloves he had worn on his hands had been black as well. They were gone now.

And to top it all off, he was a Wolf Breed. Powerful, charismatic, scarred, and dangerous. All the things that made a girl's heart go thump in the night.

And he was a killer.

She flinched as his hand moved, then drew in a shaky breath as the gag was removed from her mouth. He didn't stop to untie her, or to release the restraints holding her to the lowered seat. But at least she could speak now.

"Just how damned stupid are you?" The words broke past her lips before she could think. "You should have killed me back at the hotel, because I swear to God I'm going to watch you fry."

She tried to tear herself loose, jerking and writhing against the bonds furiously.

"Keep it up, and I'm going to see more than just those pretty thighs, Grace." His husky voice had her stilling, her gaze jerking to where he was glancing at her thighs before looking down her body.

"Oh yeah, as if you haven't already made certain you could see more," she yelled, flushing at the knowledge that her skirt had ridden to the crotch of her panties. Her damp panties. "What are you going to do now, rape me before you kill me?"

He stared down at her with whiskey-colored eyes. Those eyes almost mesmerized her.

"If I intended to kill you, I wouldn't rape you first," he promised her mockingly. "Somehow, that just reeks of foul play."

"And murder doesn't?" She gasped in outrage.

"Albrecht was a member of the Genetics Council." The sound of his voice, low, husky, nearing another of those dangerous growls she had heard just before he grabbed her, had her flinching. "That wasn't a murder, Grace, it was an act of mercy."

She stared back at him in shock.

"He was a mean old man," she admitted in disbelief. "But he couldn't have been part of the Genetics Council any longer. He was so absentminded he forgot to close his stupid doors. If he *had* been a member, he had likely forgotten it by now. Which makes it murder."

She hated liars.

"You were using me all along." Fury filled her at the thought. "Was the mugging a setup, too? A way to get on the stupid manager's good side? Is that what it was? And here I didn't even get a mercy fuck for my trouble."

He hadn't wanted to be seen with her, she had thought it was because of her plain looks. He said it was because he was a Breed, he didn't want to see her hurt. It hadn't been. It had been because right there in her living room, shoved into her little bookcase, was all the information he would have needed to get to Albrecht.

But how had they known when the security would be off-line? And was it just Matthias, or were there others?

"I have your luggage in the back," he told her, obviously gritting his teeth. "Your car has been taken care of."

"Should I thank you?"

He ignored her again.

"I liked the thought of joining you at the cabin. I checked the place out last week. It's a nice little place. I thought I'd escort you up there, maybe stay a while. Discuss some things with you."

Her breath stilled in her lungs. The cabin was by a lake. He could drown her there, and no one would ever know what had happened to her.

He was going to kill her. She had been falling in love with the man who was going to murder her. Now this was just a hellacious ending to a perfectly fucked up love life.

Her father had been right all along. Grace had finally jumped into something that was going to get her killed. He had been predicting it since she was four and she climbed her first tree. Now, it seemed it was going to happen.

"I'm not going to hurt you, Grace."

"Oh yeah, that's why I'm trussed up like a Christmas turkey and heading to a conveniently out-of-the-way cabin." She had to fight back her tears. "Does that mean you're going to just kill me fast?"

Oh man, she had really stepped into it this time. Wasn't she the one wishing for adventure, just a few months ago? Surely she wasn't the one that had taken one look at Matthias after he rescued her from a mugging and thought he was some kind of dark, sexy knight. He wasn't a knight, he was a monster.

Yeah. He wasn't going to hurt her. He was just going to let her waltz right into the police department and identify him as Albrecht's assassin and wish her good luck with the future. Uh huh. She could see that happening.

"Damn, you're melodramatic, do you know that?" He slanted her a look from the corner of those sexy, exotic eyes of his, and her stomach clutched at the look.

He looked at her like that a lot. Like a man with sex on his mind, but he had yet to touch her, to kiss her. That look was as much a lie as everything else about him had ever been.

"I tend to get that way when I see harmless old men assassinated and I get kidnapped. It has a decidedly melodramatic effect on my life, Matthias."

He glanced at her again. But not at her face. Once more, his gaze slid to her thighs.

"Yeah, I can see where that would be upsetting." His gaze finally slid to her face. "But I said I wouldn't hurt you."

"Like you said my mugger was gutter trash," she retorted. "Tell me, Matthias, was that a setup?"

He jerked his head to face forward, his expression tightening, as she stomped her feet into the floor of the vehicle.

"Damn you. Damn you. Damn you." The curses were throttled screams, as she then slammed her head back against her seat. "Let me go! Just let me go, so I can kill you myself."

She had been terrified. Terrified and so damned grateful to the man who had saved her that she had overlooked every sign that he was trouble. And the signs were there. The diamond glittering in his left ear. The scar on his face. The tattoo she had glimpsed on his bicep, the nipple ring, the faint outline of which she had seen beneath his T-shirt.

He looked like a thug, but he carried himself with such supreme confidence, such arrogance, that every stupid feminine instinct she had possessed had been drawn to him.

"Your mugger *is* gutter trash," he finally muttered.

"So you didn't set that up?"

"I didn't set it up."

Her gaze narrowed. "Was it set up for you?"

"I had to find a way to make you trust me, quickly," he admitted. "That was the only way."

Anger vied with fear. Damn him, there wasn't a chance he could let her live. She might as well go down letting him know exactly what she thought of him. She'd already watched him blow another man's head off. It wasn't like it could get much worse.

"You lied to me." She gritted her teeth in fury, surprised at how much it hurt.

"I didn't lie to you, Grace," he finally sighed. "I stretched a few truths and didn't tell you exactly why I was there."

"You used me to kill a man."

"I rid the world of a monster, and I'll prove it to you," he said. "What you do after that, is up to you."

"And if I go straight to the police?" Of course she would go straight to the police. Was there any question of it?

"Then I'll do everything in my power to protect you." The regret that shimmered in his voice had her chest tightening. "But once I'm behind bars, others will kill you. I won't be able to save you then."

He was lying to her again, of course.

"Grace. Give me a chance." His hand lowered from the steering wheel to her knee. The shock of his calloused, scarred hand against her bare flesh for the first time sent a riot of sensation cascading through her.

It was his *hand*, for God's sake. On her *knee*. It wasn't like it was tucked between her thighs.

"I gave you a chance." She tried to jerk away from him, but his hand only tightened, holding her bound legs in place. "And look where it got me. More lies. And more threats. No thank you, Matthias, I think I've trusted you too much already."

Matthias felt his fingers tighten on the fragile width of her knee and forced himself to relax. He wouldn't hurt her, and he didn't want to frighten her further.

Already the scent of her fear was nearly overpowering the soft, subtle scent of the arousal that filled her each time he was near her.

It was one of the reasons he had rarely touched her over the past weeks. He had kept his distance as much as possible, knowing that until he had dealt with Albrecht, he didn't have the time to deal with what he knew was coming with Grace.

Jonas thought it was such a closely guarded secret that Wolfe Gunnar, the leader of the Wolf Packs, adhered to the strict order of silence on the subject of mating heat. But Wolfe wasn't a fool. He knew his enforcers were a danger to themselves if they weren't aware of what could happen at the most unlikely moment.

Matthias knew what mating heat was, just as he knew that Grace was his mate.

The glands beneath his tongue had been sensitive for weeks, and he could feel them becoming swollen tonight. Those glands were filling with a mating aphrodisiac, a hormone that would push sensuality, sexuality, into the bounds of extremity.

It would affect Grace worse than it would affect him. She would be unable to deny her natural response to him, unable to hide from it. She would be as helpless within it as he would be once he began touching her.

The fine, almost imperceptible little hairs along his body were prickling with another hormone, one more subtle, but no less intense. His cock was rock hard. His balls were drawn tight. And he had learned in the past week that jacking off only made it worse. There would be no satisfaction until he found his release within the snug depths of Grace's body.

And there the problems would truly begin. If what Wolfe, Jacob, and Aiden had explained to their enforcers months ago were true, then during his mating with Grace, he would become more of an animal than he could have ever imagined.

Even now, as his fingers lingered on the flesh of her knee, he found a pleasure in that small touch that he had never known before. Even in the midst of the most sexual acts he had performed during his sexual training in the labs, he hadn't felt such pleasure as he did now in simply touching.

He was one of the younger Breeds. Barely thirty, but he hadn't escaped that phase of training. Not that the scientists had included sexual training for any pleasurable benefits. As in everything else, even that phase of training had held more sinister purposes.

When entranced by their lover, a man or a woman could be convinced to trade their soul for the love of the one capable of giving them such extreme pleasure. Powerful figures could be blackmailed, the sons and daughters of such figures could be used for information. Wives could be seduced, husbands could be tempted. It was all the same to the council. Every weakness could be exploited.

In the years since his release, Matthias had never used the talent he had found to please a woman, to betray one. Until Grace, he had refused to involve any woman in the dangerous, bloody life he led.

He was an assassin. The council had taught him how to be an

assassin. He carried the scars from his failed attempts during training, and he carried the marks of his successes since his escape.

He didn't kill for money, and he didn't kill from hatred or greed.
He killed for mercy. He killed to make the world a safer place, not
just for his own species, but for the humans as well.

Council members, scientists, trainers, and soldiers—many had
been released once they were revealed. If they were smart, they lived
the rest of their lives without picking up their old ties. If they weren't,
then Matthias or one of his kind made house calls. And there were
many who eagerly, if more secretly, renewed those old ties.

He had gotten lucky with Albrecht, though. He was impossible to
forget. And Matthias just happened to have been at the right place at
the right time, before the Breed rescues ten years before. He had seen
Albrecht with several scientists, heard the scientists refer to him as
"director." Only council members were given that distinction.

Matthias had remembered, and he had given the bastard a
chance. A chance Albrecht had deliberately ignored. The proof of
that was in the bloody, broken bodies of the mated Breed pairs he
had managed to capture over the past years. Young Breeds, independent. Rather than seeking the Wolf or Lion Breed compounds when
mating heat overtook them, they had tried to figure it out on their
own. And they had died in the effort.

The horrifying evidence that Albrecht was once again experi-
menting with Breeds was too much to ignore, and Matthias had been
called in.

He had used Grace to make his house call, and gaining her for-
giveness wouldn't be easy.

"Where are we?" she finally asked wearily, staring up at the
ceiling of the SUV, trying to hide her response to his touch.

"We're about two hours from your cabin," he told her softly,
enjoying the feel of her satiny knee and the flesh in the curve of her
leg against his fingertips.

"You researched me well then," she said, fighting to control her breathing.

The scent of her arousal was growing. The glands in his tongue were thickening. He should stop touching her, he should place both hands on the steering wheel and concentrate on driving the vehicle rather than driving them both crazy with lust.

"I researched you for months," he admitted. "I followed you at night when you jogged and tracked your movements otherwise. You were under surveillance for nearly six months."

He hurt her. He could smell the scent of her inner pain, and he hated it.

"Why did you choose me? Why not the head of security? Or the head manager? Why a lowly assistant manager with limited power?"

He snorted at that. "You mean the lazy manager who has shifted all the work, responsibility, and information to your shoulders, while claiming the fruits of your labor?" He asked. "I didn't have to smell the laziness on that woman to know the truth of her. All I had to do was read the file that had been prepared on her."

"How did you know Albrecht would be here during the security upgrade?"

"I have my sources." He shrugged.

"How many of you are working together?"

Matthias flashed her a grin. "How many of us did you see?"

"You had help," she bit out. "How else did you manage to get my luggage or have my car moved? You couldn't have done this alone."

"I kill alone and this is all that matters." He wouldn't tell her different. There was always a chance she wasn't the person he thought she was, and he didn't dare betray the others. "Stop asking me questions, Grace. We'll talk when we get to the cabin."

"Stop touching me then. And I swear to God, if your fingers go any higher, the first chance I get I'm cutting them off your hand."

His hand had slid higher, inches above her knee, and despite the vehemence of her order, she was enjoying it. The smell of her arousal was now covering that of her fear. The air around him was indolent with the scent of a wicked storm. He could feel the wild pulse of her blood beneath her flesh, and he knew it matched his own.

"I've been dying to touch you, Grace," he finally admitted. "Holding back these past weeks has been hell on my control."

"Well isn't that just too damned bad," she snapped, though he could hear the breathlessness, the hunger inside her. "Because you don't have a chance in hell now. Unless it's rape you're after, big boy, you fucked up when you pulled that trigger. I wouldn't sleep with you now if all that mating heat crap the tabloids printed were true."

He almost winced. Those tabloids had no clue. And neither did she. Because he would have her, and by the time the mating heat was finished with them, they would both be begging for it.

✦　✦　✦

She couldn't believe this mess. She couldn't believe Matthias had actually killed, in cold blood. He hadn't even given Dr. Albrecht a warning.

She shuddered at the memory of it. The memory of his face, so dispassionate. There had been no anger, no fury, it hadn't even been emotionless really. Just unconcerned. What he had done had caused not so much as a flinch of remorse.

How many others had he killed? Would he kill her the same way?

Grace turned her face away from him and stared at the door of the SUV. The seat was reclined fully: that, in combination with the dark night and the rural area they were driving through, left her completely out of sight.

She was stretched out, bound, helpless. Most women would have been begging for their lives, screaming, crying. She was trying to think instead. To wait. To steal a chance to escape. If one came.

She had a feeling one wouldn't come. And begging would do her no good. It wouldn't have done Albrecht any good, either.

She had been falling in love with Matthias, and perhaps that was the part that hurt the most. They had spent most of her breaks sharing coffee in her small office, and the evenings enjoying quiet dinners together, or long walks in the park.

He fascinated her. Drew her. Knowing what he was, the horrors he had experienced had pricked at her heart, and her woman's heart had wanted to erase those horrors with softness.

She had even told her family about him. About the Wolf Breed whose eyes were so filled with loneliness. Who smiled as though he hadn't known he could do so. Who watched her in a way no other man ever had. Her father had wanted to meet him. Her mother wanted to cook for him. Her brothers offered to teach him to play football.

She blinked back her tears at the loss. At both their losses. He had no idea what he was missing out on when he lost *her* family.

She liked to say she was fully a part of reality, and reality demanded that she accept that Matthias wasn't just going to let her go. He couldn't afford to. The whole Breed community would suffer for what he had done tonight, if the authorities ever learned of it. And Grace was well aware of his loyalty to not just the pack he claimed as his own, but to the Breeds in general.

She closed her eyes as she felt his fingertips stroking her leg again. His palms were horribly scarred, the faint ridges from those past wounds rasped over her flesh, and her soul. They brought pleasure and pain. Pleasure from his touch, pain at the knowledge of all he had endured.

She thought she had gotten to know him. She knew he *could* kill. He'd told her of some of the assignments he had been sent on during his time in the labs. She'd known he had killed since then in the confines of the investigative work he did. She hadn't imagined he could kill in cold blood, though. Shooting a man from behind, without warning, somehow seemed worse than killing one face-to-face.

She knew there were rumors that Albrecht had been part of the Genetics Council. Rumors that he had ordered deaths, worked on the genetic alterations, and perhaps even been a part of what the press called the twelve-member directorate. He had been the head of the Genetics Council—the shadowy figures that financed, directed, and oversaw each stage of the Breed development.

All Grace had ever seen was a mean, disillusioned old man, though. One who didn't even have the common sense to close the door to his suite and was constantly searching for his appointment journal.

If the rumors were true, he should have been arrested rather than released after the inquest into the Breed atrocities. He shouldn't have been killed the way he was.

"Grace, the smell of your fear is killing me." His voice was soft, gentle. "I promise, I'm not going to hurt you."

"And I'm supposed to believe that?" She turned her head to stare back at him, seeing the flash of somber regret in his gaze before he turned back to look at the road.

"You will believe it," he said, his voice as heavy with regret now as his gaze had been. "But you won't die. Not by my hand, or by any others, as long as I can protect you."

"What? You think you can make me forget what I saw?" She hated the tears in her voice, but even more, she hated the damned disillusionment. She hated looking at him and fighting herself to believe what she had seen with her own eyes.

"Not forget it," he admitted. "I'm hoping, though, that you'll understand it enough to keep the knowledge of it to yourself."

He was crazy. That was all there was to it.

"Oh, well, if that's all you want, then I'm all for it." Living was worth lying for. "Let me go now, and mum's the word. I promise."

He flashed her a chiding smile.

"I can smell your lie as easily as I can smell your arousal, Grace. Have you forgotten that?"

Her eyes widened. Cream flooded her pussy and wept to her labial folds, rushing to surround her clit. That little bundle of nerves was pulsing now, engorged and swollen. The sound of his voice was rasping, filled with male lust and determined aggression.

"You never mentioned the arousal part," she gasped.

"I didn't, did I?" His fingers slid higher on her thigh, and, traitorously weak, her legs trembled, her breathing became rougher, and her juices thicker.

His fingers grazed the damp crotch of her panties, and Grace heard the low, weak moan that betrayed her slip past her lips.

"The scent of your arousal has made me crazy." His voice deepened, as a growl rumbled in his chest. The sound should have frightened her; it turned her on instead.

Sensation was humming through her body, tingling in her clit and her nipples, making her gaze heavy as his fingers continued to brush lightly against the damp cotton of her panties. That slow, deliberate caress held her spellbound.

He was using the hand that had held the gun that killed Albrecht. But it wasn't death she felt. And it wasn't disgust. It was pleasure. A hot, insidious pleasure that held her mesmerized.

"Matthias, this is wrong." She wanted to tell him to stop, but the words wouldn't push past her lips. "Don't do this to me. Please."

"You do it to me, Grace," he accused her darkly. "Each touch you've given me, no matter how innocent, made me weak. Made me hard. I've been so damned distracted by you, my head so filled with the memory of your scent that I didn't know when you entered that suite. I should have known. I should have sensed you and been able to pull back. To hide until you were gone. But you were already so much a part of me, that I carry you with me, whether you're actually there or not."

The SUV slowed. It didn't stop, but it was definitely slowing as he glanced at her. A second later he jerked his gaze back to the road, but his hand didn't leave her, his fingers didn't pause in their caresses.

The implications of his declaration seared her mind. There were rumors, tabloid tales and obscure reports of Breed mates. Mates that were rarely photographed, rarely seen by journalists. It was said that in the ten years since the Breeds had been revealed, that the mates to those Breeds hadn't aged. Tabloids ran stories almost weekly of a sexual frenzy during what they called "mating heat." And then there were the wild tales of orgies and animalistic behavior.

There were also stories of other animalistic occurrences. Reports that the Breeds' sexuality was closer to that of their animal cousins than that of humans. Feline Breed males were said to lock inside their females during ejaculation, with a penile extension just beneath the head of the cock, referred to as a barb. And as for the Wolves . . .

Grace stared at Matthias's taut profile. Wolves were supposed to lock within a female with a heavy swelling known as the knot.

It couldn't be true. She'd scoffed at the stories then, and she refused to believe them now.

But she couldn't refuse to believe the heavy, lethargic arousal overcoming her. He was barely stroking her, his fingers were but a slight pressure against the covering of her panties, and still, it made her too weak to protest. And the cotton covering was becoming damper by the second with her juices.

"You need to stop," she whispered, her lashes fluttering with sharply rising need. "Please, Matthias . . ."

· CHAPTER 4 ·

Grace's family cabin sat in the Catskill Mountains northwest of New York City. The heavily forested area called to the wildness of Matthias's spirit. The sounds of the night wrapped around him, but the scent of Grace filled his mind.

The two-story cabin sat next to a small, unpolluted lake. The crisp scent of the water was refreshing, the sound of a waterfall played somewhere in the distance. It should have been relaxing. It would have been, if the fever to take his mate weren't filling his insides with a burning hunger.

He sat his restrained captive in a wide, padded porch chair and dug the keys from her purse. She glared at him, her tapered, dark blonde hair falling over her brow and shadowing her eyes.

The door opened easily. Matthias inhaled deeply, searching for any scent other than that of an empty cabin. Satisfied that they were alone, he picked her up, carried her to the heavily cushioned couch, and left the cabin again.

He carried her luggage and his bag to the large downstairs bedroom then checked the well-stocked cabinets and refrigerator. Once he had assured himself of the security of the cabin, he disconnected the phone lines, locked the front door, and turned back to her.

Grace remained silent. And she was still aroused. He could smell the arousal, and it was killing him. But he could also smell her fear and her anger. She had judged him the moment she saw him pull that trigger, and if she had her way, he'd be locked up forever.

It was a heavy burden, to understand the event from her viewpoint. Her innocence couldn't understand the conditions under which the Breeds had been trained, the forces that had shaped their lives from conception to escape. The nightmares were nearly as brutal as the reality of it had been. Even now, ten years later, Matthias could feel the agony of those years.

"Why did you do it, Matthias?" When she spoke, her voice was agonized, filled with tears and disillusionment. She had already tried him and found him guilty.

Matthias knelt in front of the couch, his hands moving to the restraints that bound her hands and feet, his fingers massaging the slight welts on her flesh as he frowned down at them.

The beatings, the hours of mental torture, and the deaths. Imprisoned behind bars and forced to watch as friends and littermates were murdered with such brutal means, that even now, Matthias had trouble sleeping for the horrific memories.

All in the name of training. Of numbing the Breeds to the sight of pain, cruelty, and death. Turning them into emotionless machines that responded at the council members' beckoning.

"I was created in Albrecht's lab," he finally answered her, lifting his head to stare back at her. "I know his cruelties. I know the monster he was." He lifted his hands from her flesh and stared at the palms. The scars that crisscrossed them had been put there by Albrecht's knife. A punishment for a failed mission.

"He was released after the hearings about Breed atrocities. You had no right to kill him after that."

His gaze jerked back to hers. "He was released on his oath that he was not a part of the council directorate, which I know was a lie. He was released on his oath that he would never again attempt to create or imprison Breeds. Ten years ago, he was released. And he never stopped. We found the bodies, his scent covered them as well as the marks of his abuse. He never stopped."

To know they hadn't found all the Breeds, even in the ten years of searching, was like a poison in Matthias's soul. The council scientists and soldiers who had escaped had taken the young with them and turned them over to the council, to be hidden in other, even more secret labs. And now those children, ten years older, were turning up dead, horribly tortured. The experimentation that had been done on them was brutal. But even worse were the mated pairs, those that had known freedom for but a short time, recaptured, and tortured to death.

"We were the test models. The first generation of Breeds to actually survive the first few years of life are barely older than forty. They had their first success nearly a century ago—Lion Breed who managed to escape with one of their scientists. But it took them another several decades to get it right again, because the first Leo destroyed everything in that hellhole of a lab as he escaped. We were the disposable models." Fury twisted his expression. "Imagine watching your friends, your brothers and sisters being dissected, live. Being beaten until they died, broken and still trying to fight. Or so drugged they were no more than the animals whose genes they carried. I watched Albrecht do this. For years. For so many years." He pushed his fingers through his hair and moved away from her.

The blood. He could still smell the blood and death.

"Had he finished, I would have walked away from him, as I was ordered to do." He turned back to her, his eyes narrowing on the tense set of her expression. "I would not have killed him, Grace, had he not continued those atrocities."

"You should have gone to the authorities."

"The authorities had their chance. I took care of it. He will never rape another young Breed. He will never dissect another while they scream in agony, and he will never, ever attempt to prolong his own misbegotten life because he lucked out and found a mated Breed pair."

That had been the final nail in his coffin. They had found the bodies. The two young mates, so horribly mutilated, the signs of experimentation so monstrous, that even he and Jonas had thrown up.

"That doesn't make sense. What would two lovers have to do with prolonging his life? You're lying to me, Matthias. Don't do that."

Matthias shook his head. It would do no good to argue it with her—until she experienced the mating, she would never believe it.

"One of these days, you'll know the truth," he said heavily. "Are you hungry? I could fix us something to eat."

Grace stared back at him in disbelief. One moment he was talking of death, the next he was willing to cook? She shook her head as she moved, tugging her skirt farther over her thighs, before shrugging her restrictive jacket off.

"What are you going to do with me?" she asked. "You promised not to hurt me."

He nodded. "I won't hurt you."

"Even knowing I have every intention of telling the police what I saw?" She couldn't lie to him. He would smell it.

The hurt that flashed in his eyes shouldn't have bothered her, but it did.

"Even knowing that," he answered. "I'm going to spend this week with you. Let you come to know me better. Try to make you understand . . ."

"Why?" She crossed her arms over her chest and glared at him. "What does it matter if I understand or not? You murdered a man, Matthias."

"And if you report it, and I'm arrested, then I can't protect you. Other Breeds will come for you, and they will kill you before you ever have the chance to testify. Is that what you want? Do you want to die?"

"The authorities will protect me."

"Don't be so fucking naive, Grace," he snarled, causing her to flinch. "Don't be stupid. You know better than that."

Yes, she did know better. She knew she didn't have a chance at living if she ever breathed a word of what she had seen. Perhaps, in some small way, she could even understand why he had done it. Now that the shock had worn off and her mind had accepted the fact that he had done it, it was her own anger driving her instead.

"Just leave then." She rose to her feet and breathed out roughly. "I'm smart enough to know the rules, Matthias. That doesn't mean I ever want to see you again. Just get out."

"It doesn't work that way." He shook his head, his whiskey gaze remote.

"Why not? You can smell a lie, then fine, you know I'm not lying. Albrecht may have deserved every agony you could have possibly given him, but I can't accept it. We have laws in this country for a reason."

His bark of laughter shocked her. "Do you, now?" He crossed his powerful arms over his chest and watched her, mocking. "Let me tell you about your laws, little girl. Laws that allowed all your fine politicians to stick their dirty little fingers into the Breed pie before the world learned of us. How they sent their Special Forces teams after the small pride that was hiding in Kentucky. How they turned a blind eye to the tortures that were inflicted on us. Until the world learned of us and drew a horrified breath. Those same fucking bastards faked their outrage and had no choice but to back us. Back us or be revealed as the lying sons of bitches they were."

Throttled rage filled his voice and glowed in his eyes. Grace had never seen such fury, such banked violence in any one, in her life.

There were reports of this. News articles and documentaries, but until now, Grace hadn't been certain what was the truth and what were lies told to enhance the popularity of the Breeds' right-to-life laws.

She licked her lips, knowing he wasn't lying. Her chest ached for him, ached about the pain he had endured. But he had killed an unarmed man. Without remorse.

She nodded, swallowing tightly as she let his furious gaze capture hers.

"I won't report it," she whispered. "But I won't condone it. Whatever was growing between us, Matthias, if anything other than your need to use me was there, is over. Please, just leave."

"It's not going to happen."

Grace watched his expression harden, his eyes darken in determination.

"What do you mean, 'it's not going to happen'?" She watched him warily.

Had he been lying to her? Did he mean to kill her after all?

A tight smile curled his lips. "I already smell your distrust," he growled. "I don't lie, Grace. I'm not going to kill you. And I won't torture you."

"Then why stay?"

"Because you own me now. You're my mate."

· CHAPTER 5 ·

Grace stared back at the wild man standing in the middle of the cabin's living room. Dressed in black leather and facing her with an arrogant determination that had once appeared sexy. Now it was downright scary.

"What do you mean, I'm your mate?" The tabloid stories were rocking through her head, and she really didn't have time right now for the perversions they had reported.

She should have known better than to read that trash. But, like most Americans, she had been fascinated with the discovery of the Breeds. Fascinated and outraged by their creation and the horrifying abuses they had endured.

But, did he answer her? Hell no. He shook his head slowly, his lips curling at one corner, as he continued to watch her with those dark golden eyes. And he kept inhaling slowly, reminding her that she was still wet. So wet from his earlier play that her panties were literally clinging to her pussy.

"Matthias, right now is really not a good time to pull the silent Breed act on me," she snapped. "I'm about two minutes from a nervous breakdown. This has not been a good night for me."

Instantly his expression altered. From arrogance to sensual delight. His facial features softened as he moved toward her, his arms dropping from his chest, his shoulders flexing as he drew the black leather jacket from them. He tossed it to the couch as he neared her.

Grace took a step back. The sensuality in his gaze made her even more wary than the earlier anger had.

"Don't touch me," she ordered him roughly.

"Poor Grace," he crooned, a hint of a rumble in his voice sending a shiver racing down her spine as he moved behind her. "Yes love, it's been a very hard night for you. Seeing your mate for what he is, for who he is, hasn't been easy." She felt his breath on her hair, then his hand as he smoothed it over her shoulder. "I had hoped to ease you into it."

"Ease me into what?" She tried to jerk away, but the hand that suddenly gripped her hip wasn't allowing that to happen. "Into murder? Not going to happen."

"Into this."

Her knees nearly buckled as his lips brushed across the nape of her neck, a hint of the damp warmth of his tongue stroking along it.

"Stop it, Matthias. You can't seduce me into approving what you've done."

"I don't care if you approve of me, Grace. I only care that you accept me."

Oh my God. His teeth raked over her neck.

Grace blinked, fought to clear her vision and to remain on her feet. Because that little scrape of his extended canines did nothing to return her common sense. On the contrary, it only dampened her panties further.

"Get away from me." She tore from his clasp, turning to face him furiously, fighting her arousal and the drugging pleasure his touch brought. "I don't want you to touch me."

"Your body is begging for my touch." He grinned as he sat down on the couch and began removing his boots.

"What are you doing? Put those back on." Shock dumbfounded her. He had murdered a man in front of her, and now he was undressing? As though it were normal?

"Come on, Grace." He flashed her a seductive smile. "I'm tired, and you're snarling. Let's take tonight to rest, and tomorrow we'll revisit this little disagreement."

"Little disagreement? You *killed* a man."

"He wasn't a man." Matthias shrugged as he set his boots to the side. "He was a monster."

"That doesn't make it right."

"And it doesn't make it wrong, either," he sighed, his expression flickering with regret. "It doesn't make the need for it any less. I don't have to like what I do to realize the fact that it has to be done. Now, let's go find the bed and try to rest."

He gripped her wrist and began drawing her through the house.

"I'm not sleeping with you."

"Fine, I'll sleep with you."

He tugged her behind him like a recalcitrant child, tugging at her arm and drawing her into the bedroom before locking the door behind them.

"Matthias, stop this." Frustration, fear, and arousal converged inside her as he finally released her. "You can't believe there's any way to fix this. Surely you can't."

She couldn't let him believe it could be fixed. The past weeks were over. They were gone. She would never forget the look on his face as he killed, and she couldn't forget how easily he had done it.

He pulled her suitcase from the bed and laid it on the nearby chair. Her frilly, girly bedroom had never held a man as intensely sexual and powerful as this one. He filled it with testosterone and stubbornness to the point that she was nearly choking on it.

"I'll find a way to fix it." He opened the suitcase and drew out the plain white, long summer gown and robe she had packed.

"Matthias." She stared back at him in confusion. "You're more logical than this." How could any one man be so stubborn? "You know you can't fix this."

"I know I don't have a choice." The gown and robe were flung at her, causing her to catch them in surprise as he stared back at her with furious intent. "What I found with you is too important, Grace. I won't let this destroy it."

She shook her head slowly. "It was destroyed the minute you pulled that trigger."

"The minute I made certain another Breed never died. The minute I ended the agony for untold mates in the future that he would have captured. The minute I fucking destroyed a nightmare," he snarled. "I should do as you ask and fucking walk away from you now, because by God, you have to be the most judgmental, self-righteous creature I have ever known."

Grace's lips parted in shock. "That's not true."

"Isn't it?" He flicked her a hard, heated look, his lips curling in a little half sneer. "What did you do when you learned of the lives the Breeds led? When you read your little news report on your PDA and went about your life? Did you think, *Oh, poor creatures*? Did you even download the pictures of those labs they found? Did you even take the time to see what those sons of bitches did?"

She hadn't. The reports alone had given her nightmares. She couldn't bear to see the pictures. And now, she felt ashamed of that.

"Live through it, then tell me how wrong I was," he snapped. "Watch your baby sister die beneath the rutting of soldiers. See your friends, those you call family, die screaming in agony, and then tell me you wouldn't have done the same."

She could see it in his face, in his eyes, and it broke her heart. She had to blink back her tears, force her lips not to tremble as she thought of the horror he had faced in ways she never had.

The scars he carried, the shadowed horror that sometimes reflected in his eyes, the bleak, hollow sound of his voice.

"I'm so sorry, Matthias," she whispered huskily, clutching the gown to her chest. "What you endured was hell. But you are not a judge and jury."

"No, I'm the executioner." He stood before her without remorse. "He had already been judged and his sentence was passed. I merely carried it out. Now get that fucking gown on and get your ass into bed before I lose what little control I have tonight."

With that, he stalked from the bedroom. Even in bare feet he seemed to stomp, his steps heavy, fury pulsing in every line of his body before the door slammed behind him.

Grace sat on the bed slowly, staring at the closed panel, knowing, somehow, she had managed to do more than merely hurt him.

She stared at the gown, pushed her fingers through her hair wearily, then rose to her feet and did as he had ordered. She was exhausted. So tired she could barely think straight. Maybe tomorrow she could find a way to make sense of it. Maybe she would realize it had all been a horrible nightmare that would just go away.

The thought of escaping Matthias flitted through her mind. She should at least try. After all, she had seen him kill, he could still kill her.

As she drew the blankets over her shoulders and stared at the bedroom window, she knew she had at least a chance of escape. And yet here she lay, and she didn't know why.

All she knew was that as she stared into the darkness, all she could think about was the horror his life must have been. Never having anyone. Never being able to care for anyone. How alone he must have felt.

She had seen that loneliness in his eyes the night she thought he had saved her, during that stupid staged mugging. She had dragged him into the hotel with her and made him drink coffee with her. He had watched her as others might watch a snake, expecting her to strike at any time.

He had touched her heart that night, with the scar slashing across his forehead, over his eyelid, and onto his cheek. With his sexy, sensual lips and whiskey-brown eyes, his obvious discomfort with a smile.

But she had made him smile that night. Not a whole, unbridled smile. A tentative smile, as though he were trying it out first, waiting to see if it was going to hurt.

Three weeks. He had come into her life just three weeks before, and he had become such a part of it that now she wondered how she was going to do without him.

She looked at the window again. She really should run from him.

A tear slid down her cheek instead, because she couldn't run from him. But she could never have him, either.

.

It wasn't a nightmare. The next morning Grace awoke to the knowledge that she couldn't just escape the events from the night before any more than she could escape Matthias, and she couldn't run from them.

She brushed her hair and teeth, stared at her pale reflection, then grimaced and headed to the kitchen. She could smell coffee, and she was dying for it. The need for caffeine was crawling through her system, with the same craving that desire for Matthias was clenching between her thighs.

Dreams had tormented her through the night. Dreams, nothing, she had been tormented with visions of sexual delights that had her blushing at the thought of them. She should have had nightmares of blood and death, not dreams about what that bulge beneath those black leather pants could do to her.

"Good morning." He came to his feet from the kitchen table, another pair of leather pants covering his muscular legs. His feet and chest were bare.

Grace stared at the broad, hairless chest, as she came to a sudden stop. She'd been wanting to see that nipple ring she had glimpsed under his T-shirt. Now that she was seeing it, her mouth watered, her lips tingled with the need to capture it, to tug on it. But as sexy as the sight of it was, nothing could detract from the thin white scars that crisscrossed his chest and abdomen.

He pulled a shirt from the back of the chair and shrugged it on, covering the horrific scars. They weren't thick and ridged, but they crisscrossed his flesh like a road map.

"Sorry about that." He turned away from her, walking across the cheerful, bright kitchen, buttoning the black shirt. "I made coffee."

She couldn't help it. Grace moved quickly across the room, facing him as he turned back to her.

"I have to see it," she whispered, her fingers going to the buttons of his shirt. "All of it, Matthias. You don't have the right to hide it from me now."

His hard, sharply defined features tightened, as her fingers undid the buttons of his shirt. She pushed the cotton shirt from his wide shoulders, and tossed it over a chair.

"Did *he* do this?" she whispered, her fingertips touching the evidence of the cruelty he had experienced.

Some of the scars were older, almost invisible. Tough, darkly tinted flesh rippled under her touch, as he glared down at her.

"He enjoyed using the whip. The scientists needed to know under what conditions we couldn't fight or complete our objectives. We were put through a variety of simulations. Torture being the favorite of them all. If we didn't succeed in the objective given us, we died."

Her breath hitched in her throat, as tears flooded her eyes. She followed the scars on his chest, his side, then moved around him to stare at his back.

"Oh God, Matthias." The scarring was worse on his back.

She leaned her forehead against his back, clenching her eyes tight at the incredible pain he must have endured.

"It doesn't hurt any longer, Grace," he assured her.

Grace lifted her head, her gaze going to his shoulders. On his left shoulder was the Breed marker. A genetic shadow of a paw print. Within that print, four bloodred teardrops had been tattooed into his flesh. Around the paw, a precise tattoo of what appeared to be dark smoke had been drawn, a single feather, tipped with blood, caught within it.

"Why this one?" She touched the bloodstained feather wrapped in wire.

"The price of submission," he growled.

"And this one?" A line of carefully disguised bones, wrapped in the same barbed wire, the wire twisting from the base of his spine to the middle of it.

"Friends who died for their freedom," he answered.

"And this?" She touched the bloodred teardrops encased by smoke.

"The tattoo was made by a tribal medicine man. It's a protection symbol, to hold the evil within it from marking my soul." His voice was heavy, filled with pain.

"The teardrops are the evil?" She asked. "Why?"

"They mark each council member I've killed."

Grace froze, her fingers trembling over the four markers.

"The larger one denotes a directorate member. The two medium-sized ones are scientists, the smallest are trainers. I don't bother to list the coyote soldiers, they aren't worth the need for protection." Disgust for those Breeds colored his voice.

"And Albrecht will add to it," she whispered. "What happens when you run out of room?"

"Then I return for another protected circle and begin again." His back tightened, as rage thrummed in his voice.

"And does it help the nightmares?" she asked, "or make them worse?"

Matthias stared over the room, his soul bleak at the sound of her voice. He could hear the pain and compassion in her voice, the need to understand. And despite the blood that stained his hands, all he could think about was touching her.

"Sometimes, it stills the nightmares," he answered, as he turned to her. "And sometimes, they only grow worse."

His hands gripped her shoulders, the softness of the cotton hiding the warmth of her flesh from him.

"Would you stop?" she asked.

Matthias could see the hope in her eyes, the innocence. That innocence alternately lightened his soul and weighed it down. He had never meant for her to know what he was, he had thought he could keep that part of what he did hidden after he claimed her.

Because he couldn't stop.

"We have other things to discuss," he said, rather than answering her. "We need to discuss *us*."

"There's no *us*, Matthias." The regret in her voice tore at him. "I won't report what I saw, but whatever we had is over."

She tried to move away from his touch. Despite the arousal he knew she felt, the tender feelings he knew hadn't died, still, she moved away from him.

Once she had come to him with a smile, her pretty eyes lighting up in pleasure. Now, her dove-gray eyes were dark and shadowed, knowing the truth of what he was.

"It doesn't work that way." He had to tell her the truth. He couldn't force her into the mating, as much as he wanted to. He couldn't pull her into it without her knowledge.

"Of course it works that way." Her lips turned down in a sad smile. "I decide who I sleep with."

"The mating changes that." He kept his voice low, gentle. "You can never just walk away now."

"Watch me." She tried to pull away again.

"How many nights can you handle the arousal without me in your bed?" He asked as his grip tightened on her shoulders. "Without my touch? It's been building since the night we met, the need to touch, to kiss, to lie beneath me. Admit it."

"Once you're gone, I'll get over it." The confidence in her eyes was overshadowed by her arousal.

Matthias continued to touch her, his hands moving over her arms, sliding the robe past her shoulders, touching her bare skin, his fingertips lingering to relish the feel of warm silk.

"It won't go away, it will be there. It will become worse some nights, easier others, because we've never kissed. Because my lips haven't touched your flesh. But you'll never be free of it."

He watched the suspicion grow in her eyes.

"You're trying to frighten me," she chided, her lips trembling now.

"No, I'm trying to be honest," he said. "You laughed about the tabloid stories, the Breed community sneers at them, but there's truth to some of them, Grace. There's a bond, a hormonal, biological bond once a Breed comes in contact with his mate. It doesn't go away. It doesn't lessen . . ."

"No." She shook her head desperately. "That's not possible."

"There are small glands at the side of my tongue. They fill with a very powerful hormone once the mating begins. It takes no more than a lick on your flesh to make you burn. A kiss will turn you inside out with the need to be fucked. Eventually, the fires burn so hot and so desperate, that nothing matters but easing the hunger twisting inside you. How long it lasts depends on each couple. But it never completely goes away. In each case, though, there is love. There is emotion to make the bonds created endurable. It only occurs between a couple that would have loved, despite the heat."

He watched her pale. Her small hands flattened on his sweat-dampened chest. He was already burning for her. The glands in his tongue had become fully engorged the night before, and already the hormone was spilling into his system.

"Let me go, Matthias."

"Listen to me, Grace. You were loving me, I know you were, before last night."

"Last night changes everything," she cried out, her expression fraught with fear. "Let me go."

He released her, feeling the damning sorrow that weighed at his soul, as she put the length of the room between them.

She stared at the palms of her hands before wiping them on her gown, staring back at him in disbelief. Her gaze flickered from his face to his thighs, then back again.

"How long have you known about this reaction? That it could happen between us?" she asked.

"Since the beginning," he answered her honestly. "The night of the mugging, when I touched you, when I wiped the tears from beneath your eyes, I could feel something inside me shifting, changing. Within a week, I could feel the itch in my tongue, the arousal that wouldn't abate. I knew then."

He had known even before then that she would hold his heart. Months he had spent watching her, investigating her, learning things about her that softened him toward her. She was a good woman. Loyal. Honest. She worked hard, she had friends, and she often went out of her way to do good things for them. Taking them soup when they were ill, visiting them in the hospital. Late nights on the phone, when one of them lost a lover.

"God, you infected me with something." She was staring back at him in horror.

Hell, he should have just kissed her and let nature take care of it.

"Not fully." He finally shrugged. "But I will, before this week is out." His muscles tightened in determination. "You are my mate, Grace. I won't let you just walk away from me. No other woman will ever be as important to my soul. No other woman will ever bring me the pleasure you do, with just your smile. And you know you will never forget how I make you feel. You know it."

She was shaking her head desperately. "You can't do this to me! I won't let you."

"I can't control it," he said. "Tell your body it can't happen. Tell your heart you don't care. By God, Grace, fix it and then tell me how you've done it, and I'll let you go. Until then, I can't walk away, because it would rip my soul from my body to do so."

"You don't love me," she cried.

"I cherish you," he growled. "But even more than that, for once in my misbegotten life, I have a chance at real freedom, and you're it. The chance to be more than the animal I was created to be. With my mate, I can be a husband, a father . . ."

Grace flinched at the sound of his voice when he said the words *husband* and *father*. He softened, a sense of wonder flashing in his eyes. He stared at her as though she meant something, as though she were important, as though she held his soul.

That look overrode her horror at what he was telling her. It diluted her anger. And nothing should have been able to dilute her anger.

"You knew all along. That's why you made me fall in love with you," she accused him, trying to hang on to the fury. "You deliberately made me care for you."

He pulled his shirt back on, though he didn't button it.

"Only because I cared as well," he stated, his voice rough. "All my life I've had to hold back. I've had to force myself to care for no one, because I knew they would suffer for my emotions. Once I escaped the labs, that restraint was so much a part of me that even forming friendships has been difficult. Until you." He shook his head, his dark gold eyes locked on her. "You gave me a chance to know what I've been missing all my life, Grace. You still the fury inside me, and you made me hope there was more to my life than the constant battle for freedom. You made me love you. Why shouldn't I respond in kind?"

She had hoped he would love her. She had teased him, she had tempted him, she had done everything to draw him into a touch, a kiss. She had laughed with him, and knowing he was a Breed, tried to show him a softer, gentler side of life. She had set out to bind him to her, believing this scarred, shadowed wolf she was coming to love needed her.

And maybe he did, in more ways than she knew. But he was a killer, wasn't he? He had taken Albrecht's life without remorse, hadn't he? Or had he?

The bloodred teardrops on his shoulder told another story. Teardrops, a sign of pain and regret. They told a story she knew he would never admit to. Teardrops denoted sorrow, bloodred teardrops, grief. She wondered if he even realized the grief that lurked in his gaze, and in his soul?

God, he was killing her. He stared at her with such longing, with such hunger, that it broke her heart.

"I would give my life to touch you and not have you pull away from me now," he whispered, moving slowly toward her. "If I swear not to kiss you, would you let me touch you?"

Wild, unquenched hunger rose inside her.

"Matthias, that's not fair to you." She shook her head desperately as she backed against the door of the refrigerator.

"Not fair to me?" His lips quirked mockingly. "It's far more than I deserve. I need it, Grace. Just this once, let me touch you."

CHAPTER 7

She wasn't a virgin. Grace liked to consider herself a well-rounded, experienced woman, but even for her, the way Matthias touched her made her feel almost innocent. She felt unable to deny him, unable to reassert her common sense and run like hell.

It was one thing to know the ways of the world, and in some cases, the ways of men. But with Matthias she was finding out that everything she had learned over the years was just wrong.

Matthias didn't act like other men. He didn't react as other men, and he sure as hell didn't go after what he wanted as other men did. If he had argued, gone dominant, arrogant, and stubborn, she could have walked away, she told herself.

But he stared at her with such hunger. A hunger he didn't attempt to hide or push away. She wasn't a threat to his independence. The way he watched her, she was imperative to his survival.

"You're so pretty," he whispered, as he stopped before her, causing her to ache as she stared up at the wonderment of his expression. "I look at you, and sometimes, I'm afraid of touching you. Of giving you the power to destroy me. Most people have a little healthy fear of Breeds, but you stand before me, knowing in your soul, I'd never harm you."

The backs of his fingers smoothed over her cheek, sending curious tingles racing through her body.

"I'd die before I ever harmed you, before I'd ever see you harmed. Do you know that, Grace?"

She could feel it, see it in his expression and in his eyes. This wasn't stalker material, nor was it an edge of desperation. This was a man, a strong, powerful man, stating his intent, nothing more. It wasn't tinted with fanaticism or with a threat. It was a clear statement.

"Matthias, you need someone—"

"No." His fingers covered her lips, stopping the words. "I need whatever you'll give me, right here and right now. Nothing more. Just my hands on you, Grace. Let me touch you."

His thumb smoothed over her lips as she leaned her head against the refrigerator and stared back at him, torn, uncertain.

"I touched silk three months after our rescue from the labs," he whispered, as his fingertips moved over her jaw. "I swore there was nothing softer in all the world, until I touched your hand."

His hand smoothed down her arm, lifted her wrist and brought her palm to his stubbled jaw. "Your hands were warm and so soft. As soft as innocence itself."

His eyes closed, and he held her hand against him as he worked his cheek over it. She let her fingers touch his cheeks, smooth over them, and his expression shifted to one of bliss.

"I'm not innocent," she told him, but she meant the reminder for herself. Because he made her feel innocent. He made her feel nervous, excited, uncertain, but without the fears of virginity. He made her feel so much a woman that it was frightening.

"But you are innocent." He laid his cheek against hers, his lips at her ear, as he pushed her robe over her shoulders. "Innocent of deceit and corruption. When I smell your scent, I smell summer. I feel warmth. All the things I wondered if I would ever know."

Grace shivered with excitement at the guttural sound of his voice, the latent growl that bordered it. He was breathing hard and deep, his chest rasping over her gown-covered nipples and sending shafts of pleasure to tighten around them.

"Matthias, what are you doing to me?" Her head fell to the side, as his chin stroked over her neck.

"Just touching sunshine," he said softly. "Heat and magic. Warm me, Grace. Just for a minute."

At this rate, she was going to forget all that pertinent information he had just given her on what sex with him would be. Hormonal aphrodisiacs, mating heat, and biological bindings be damned. Her clit was screaming a silent demand for touch, and her sex was clenching in need.

And he hadn't even kissed her. His rough cheek and jaw were doing no more than smoothing over her neck, her shoulders, as his hands slowly did away with her gown.

Her gown.

Grace gasped as the material pooled at her feet, leaving her naked but for the high-cut cotton and lace thong she wore.

"Shh. Easy, Grace," he whispered. "I'm just touching you. That's all. No kisses. No demands. Ah God, just a little touch."

His hands cupped her breasts.

"Matthias. It's more . . ." she sucked in a hard breath as his thumbs raked over her nipples. "More than little touches."

"It warms me, Grace." He pressed his forehead into her shoulder, his black hair falling to the side, covering the swollen mounds of her breasts. It was cool and heavy, another sensual stroke against her flesh.

Suddenly, nothing mattered but warming Matthias. She knew the hell he had lived through, had triumphed against. She knew the pain and blood his life had been filled with.

So he had killed the bastard who had caused it, her dazed mind pondered. Would she have done any less? Her life had been filled with laughter and love, with acceptance. Things Matthias still fought for. Things she had dreamed of giving him.

✦ ✦ ✦

Matthias fought to control the shaking of his body, the need to lick and taste her flesh as he stroked her. He could smell the sweet heat of her pussy, drawing him, making his mouth water for the rich syrup he knew flowed from her.

His hands were filled with her swollen breasts, her pebble-hard nipples poking against his thumbs. But he had promised. He had promised not to let the aphrodisiac filling his mouth touch her.

It was killing him. The glands were pumping the hormonal fluid into his mouth, filling his system, burning him alive with the need to fuck her. His cock was so hard, throbbing so viciously he had to fight to hold back his growls.

He let his cheek touch her, his forehead, praying the sweat gathering on his skin didn't have the aphrodisiac effect. He moved along her neck, her shoulders, bending to her to allow his cheek to caress her upper chest, then the hard mound of a breast.

His hand slid to her waist as he panted, his lips a breath from her hard nipple, her little whimpers of pleasures causing him to clench his teeth to hold back.

"Matthias, you're killing us both like this." She trembled in his arms. "Don't do this."

"Are you asking me to stop, Grace?" Please, God, no! He couldn't bear it. He had to touch her, if he didn't touch her, he was going to die.

"Matthias," the soft protest dragged an unwilling growl from his lips.

"I dream of holding you." He rushed his cheek over her nipple and moved lower.

He went slowly to his knees, his hands and face alone touching her, stroking skin so soft he knew it couldn't be real. This had to be a dream. God had been merciful. Somehow he had died, and God had given him an angel to love. It had to be. Because she was so warm and soft, all the things he had dreamed of with none of the scent of death surrounding her.

When he reached the elastic and lace band of her panties, he felt a hard spurt of pre-cum erupt from his cock. He jerked at the pleasure of the small ejaculation, his fingers tightening on the band, as he forced himself to go slowly.

"I can smell you," he sighed against her hip. "Like hot cream and sweet syrup. Have I mentioned, I have a weakness for cream and syrup?"

Her hands were on his shoulders, her fingers kneading them beneath the shirt he wore, as wicked little cries left her throat.

He pulled at the band of her panties, sliding them slowly from her hips, then along her rounded thighs. The little swell of her belly drew him. He wanted to lick it, longed to taste it, but contented himself with pressing his cheek against it instead.

"Matthias, I don't think I can stand this," she gasped.

"Sweet heaven, just a few more minutes, Grace." His eyes had opened, and he was treated to the prettiest sight of his life.

Sweet honey gold curls beaded with her female cream. Luscious little drops of it clung to the soft curls that shielded her pussy, glistening with arousal and heat.

"Oh God, Grace." His hand was shaking, as he touched a single droplet with one finger, easing it from the curl before rubbing it against his lips.

His eyes closed, his nostrils flared, and the growl that tore from his chest was animalistic, hungry, almost violent.

He licked the taste of her from his lip, drowning in the need for more and relishing even that smallest hint of passion.

"I've dreamed of going down on you." He clenched his teeth desperately, as he fought for control. Maintaining it was iffy. "Licking your flesh, seeing these pretty curls wet with your need for me. Breeds don't have body hair, you know?"

"I know." Her voice was thin, her breath panting as he parted her legs further.

"I've never taken a woman like this," he told her softly. "With just my hands, just this touch." His hand slid up her thighs, his fingers parting the curl-shrouded folds with a reverent touch.

God help him. She was hot. So liquid hot his dick was burning for it. Another hard ejaculation of pre-cum jerked the engorged flesh, warning him, that for him, the mating heat was progressing too quickly. That wasn't just pre-cum. It was a slick hormone-filled lubrication that eased the tender flesh of the vagina, preparing it for his penetration.

Wolf Breeds were thickly endowed. Most women, even female Wolf Breeds struggled to accept the girth. But during mating heat, a Wolf Breed's hormonal responses prepared the female. The preseminal fluid aided that, but only during the mating heat. It helped relax the tender muscles, built the arousal, ensured that the sexual act progressed without undue pain, and prepared the feminine sheath for what would come later.

Mother nature was a bitch. Breed mating was wickedly sexual and sometimes, for the females, it could be terrifying.

"Matthias, you're making me weak," Grace moaned, dragging him back from the sight of his index finger piercing the swollen lips and gathering her moisture to it.

He had to taste her again. He couldn't put his lips to her, but maybe, like this.

He looked up at her, brought the sweet juice to his lower lip and smeared it there. When his finger had eased back, he licked.

He moaned at that rich taste. She cried out, her nails piercing his shoulder, as her hips jerked forward, almost slamming her pussy into his lips.

"Stop. Grace. Easy, sweetheart."

"Damn you!" She cried out. "This is killing me."

It was the expression on his face that was killing her. Absorbed, intent, so filled with pleasure it humbled her. His face was flushed, his eyes glittering with rich, golden browns, almost a fire inside the dark orbs.

He was staring at her pussy as though it contained all the secrets of his pleasure. His fingers slid through the slick folds again, parting them, easing inside her.

Easing inside her, when she needed more. Her hips jerked, her pussy convulsing around the single finger as it rubbed against the sensitive tissue.

"Matthias, please. Please. I need more." She was shaking, sweating. God, she had never before perspired like this in the height of sex, let alone foreplay.

Her muscles were tightening, pleasure was streaming through her bloodstream, her clit was on fire, engorged and needy.

"Easy, baby. I have you." Two fingers slid inside her as his thumb slid against her clit, circled it, rasped along the bundle of nerves and sent her exploding into a cascade of pleasure.

Violent, white hot, blistering in its intensity, the orgasm that tore through her had her crying out his name. Her nails dug into his shoulders as she lifted on her tiptoes, tightened on his fingers, and felt her juices rushing around them.

She felt one arm surround her hips, his head digging into her belly, and she wasn't certain, but she could have sworn she heard an animalistic snarl.

Nothing had ever been so good. No pleasure she had experienced, or had imagined, could prepare her for something so perfect, so intense, or mind shattering.

Nothing could have prepared her for Matthias.

Matthias needed to give Grace time to accept him on her own, without the mating heat clouding the issue or making her feel that she had been forced into something she didn't want. But the next day, he was beginning to wonder if that would happen.

After he had driven her to climax, she had escaped to the shower, and for the rest of the day, and now into the next morning, she watched him with a wariness that tore at his soul.

He had never been forced to see himself from another's eyes, especially one who had never known the horrors of those labs, or the price of Breed freedom. He had accepted his part in the scheme of preserving Breed independence and establishing their position on earth. It wasn't as though there was another planet they could escape to.

He had been trained by his creators to kill. He now used that training to make certain that those who created them could never repeat the horrors of the past. At least, not for long.

Until Grace, he had never considered how the non-Breed population of the world would view this, how they would view him.

He stood beside the lake outside the cabin, as the sun rose high in the sky, resting on his heels, as he looked out over the water and frowned at the thought.

The blood of monsters shouldn't stain a man's soul. He had saved countless lives, both Breed and non-Breed alike, by the actions he had taken, and he had never given it much thought, until now.

He marked the kills within the smoke circle and gave their souls up to a higher being to judge. He didn't consider himself judge and jury. He was merely the means to stop the atrocities they committed.

Or was he just making excuses for himself?

Bending his head, he picked up a smooth rock from the sandy ground and rubbed his thumb over it, frowning as his thoughts held him captive.

He considered himself neither a good man, nor a bad man, but he was questioning his own actions now, because of one small woman. She saw blood on his hands, whereas he saw peace from the fact that one less monster existed. She saw an injustice, where he saw justice. And he now found himself in conflict with his very beliefs and his perceived place in the world.

He was a Breed. There was no changing that, and he had just as much right to exist in this world as any other creature did. He had the right to laughter, the right to dream, and the right to love. But did he have the right to kill?

A part of him howled *yes*. A part of him questioned that belief. Could he ever do his job again, now that he had seen the look of horror and betrayal in Grace's eyes?

And he knew he wouldn't. Whether she accepted the mating between them or left at the end of the week to resume her life alone, Matthias knew that this part of his life was over.

The smoke assassin would exist no more. He would drift out of men's minds with the same ease that he had slipped into their most secured areas and destroyed the monsters. All because of a woman.

His lips quirked at the thought of that woman.

She was the softest creature on the face of the earth, as far as he was concerned. Gently rounded and tender of flesh as well as emotions.

Stubborn. He could see the stubbornness in the sharply rounded chin, but he saw her compassion in her pert little nose and rosebud lips.

Her gray eyes were always soft, even when she was angry, and when she was aroused, they were like a storm. Dark, shifting with color, and firing with hunger.

She moved him. She made him wish for things he had never believed he would want. Made him dream of things he had never believed he would dream of. Things like a home, perhaps children, but at the very least, her soft smile filling his heart before he slept each night, the warmth of her body curled against his.

He wanted to protect her, he wanted to laugh with her, as he had done before she had seen him take a life. She had kept a smile on his face with her gentle teasing and her determination to make certain he knew what the finer things in life were.

Such as a pillow fight. She had whacked him over the head with a couch pillow one evening in her apartment and informed him that even Breeds needed to learn the rules of a pillow fight.

He had nearly kissed her that night. She had dusted him in the pillow fight, but he had retaliated by wrestling her to the floor and stealing her pillow.

He smiled at the memory. Her need for the kiss had filled the air, and only the thought of what would come had kept him in control.

She needed the choice. He wouldn't surprise her with it, he wasn't going to force it on her.

She had cooked him dinner many nights then made him help her wash the dishes rather than using the dishwasher. Another evening she had made him help her cook. He doubted she would repeat that exercise very soon. They had ended up eating from room service, but they had laughed.

They had taken long walks through Central Park, holding hands. He had gone shoe shopping with her. She had helped him pick out a new pair of boots. He'd talked her into a leather miniskirt, she'd made him buy a pair of jeans, and then they wore their new clothes in the privacy of her apartment, as they ate popcorn and watched a comedy movie she'd been wanting to see.

She could bust his ass playing poker, but he had her on Monopoly. They had fit. Despite the sexual tension that had steadily grown between them, there had been something about being with her that fit him, all the way to his soul.

And he couldn't help but think that finally he belonged to someone.

Breeds weren't born, they were created. They belonged to the labs. They were no more than expensive tools and experiments, until their escapes. After that, they belonged to no one. They were without family, in many cases they were without friends. They were part of the pack they had trained in, but true belonging went deeper. It went to the soul. And his soul belonged to Grace.

But he was beginning to realize that perhaps Grace really didn't want to belong to him. He stared at the rock in his hand, then, feeling the bite of that knowledge as it tore at his heart.

Walking away from her would destroy him. It would mean that there truly was no place in the world that he would fit, and he didn't want that to be true.

He had fought for ten years to make the world safe for Breed mates. With each year, the knowledge of the mating might not be publicized, but the knowledge of the danger to them was. The world was standing behind them, and in several cases where Breed mates would have been kidnapped, regular citizens had raised the alarm.

The Council Directorate was finding it harder with each successive year to strike against known, registered Breeds. They were too well known in the communities they had come into. They were well liked and considered members of the community. Even the pure blood societies were reportedly finding it harder to gain members outside the fanatical few.

There was still a long road to travel in making peace with society at large. And there were still too many Breeds dying needlessly. But inroads were being made.

Now, if only Matthias could make his own inroads.

Straightening, he turned his head to the cabin, eyes narrowing, as Grace stepped out onto the porch. She hadn't tried to run yet, and he had given her every chance to do just that.

She stood just outside the door, staring at him across the clearing. She wore a stretchy, snug top with thin straps and a pair of cutoff jeans. Her silky hair fell around her face to her shoulders in several natural shades of blonde. Even from here he could see the somber reflection in her soft eyes.

Breakfast and lunch had been so silent between them that it weighed in the air like a heavy fog. He had left the cabin to escape it, to escape the pain he knew he was causing her.

Matthias felt his body tighten as she stepped from the porch and moved down the steps before coming toward him. Her steps were slow, the air of reluctance that hovered around her had his teeth clenching.

He dropped the rock he held back to the ground, shoved his hands in his pockets, and waited for her. He felt as though he had waited for her all his life, only to watch her slip from his life once he found her.

"You're not a very conscientious kidnapper," she informed him, as she stepped up to him and brushed the hair back from her face. "You don't even watch me properly."

His lips twitched, as amusement flooded him for a brief second.

"I'm new at this," he bantered back. "You'll have to forgive me my mistakes."

She sniffed in apparent disdain. "I think I'd drop it, if I were you. It's one of those things you either have a talent for, or you don't."

"Perhaps you're right. I'll give it some thought."

Silence descended between them once again. Matthias was forced to curl his fingers into fists to keep them in his pockets, to keep from touching her. She had no idea about the forces that were beating inside him. The hormonal changes in his body were ripping him apart, the taste of the aphrodisiac filling his mouth reminding him by the second that she was his mate.

It would take so little to ensure she never left him, he thought. So little. A lick to her neck as she slept, perhaps. The scrape of his canines against her skin. A kiss. Just the softest kiss, and he would have her forever.

Her body anyway. But it wasn't just her body he wanted, it was her heart, her woman's spirit, and her capacity to love. He didn't want more of her condemnation, or her hatred. And she would hate him, if he stole the choice from her—she would never forgive him. And he would never forgive himself. Prison would be preferable to that. Or death.

"Why did you target me to get to Albrecht?" she finally asked, though now her voice was devoid of anger.

"It gave me an excuse to get close to you," he admitted. "I had been watching several of the hotel's employees. You were just one of them. But you were the one that fascinated me."

Being honest with this woman about such things would never be easy.

She looked out toward the lake for long seconds, following his stance and shoving her hands into the pockets of her cutoffs.

How forlorn she looked. He would give anything, everything to go back and change that moment that she had seen him kill.

"I was falling in love with you, Matthias," she finally whispered.

"I know." He nodded. "I already love you, Grace."

And he did. He loved her so much it was ripping his guts to pieces.

"I've never loved before," he told her quietly. "It wasn't hard to realize what you meant to me. You made me laugh, you lightened my soul."

"And you set out to destroy it." Anger flashed in her gaze.

Matthias sighed bleakly. Perhaps he should just leave, give her a chance to think, to consider being without him. But God help him, he was terrified to do that.

"I won't explain my actions again." He shook his head before staring up at the deep blue of the sky. When he looked back at her, she was watching him somberly once again.

"Go back into the cabin, Grace," he finally told her. "Or work in your flowers or whatever it is you do on vacation. You're straining my control."

A frown snapped between her brow, and her eyes darkened in anger. "I can't relax. I can't do that while you're kidnapping me. Maybe someone will return the favor on your next vacation."

"I would first have to experience such a thing," he growled.

He had never had a vacation. There was still too much to do. There were ten council directors still free, funding the pure-blood societies and training them to kill Breeds. There were trainers still at large and coyote soldiers still lurking. Who had time for a vacation?

"You've never had a vacation?" Disbelief colored her voice. As though it were yet another crime that she marked against him.

"I wasn't taught vacations in the lab," he snarled. "Remember?"

"As though that's an excuse." She sniffed with such ladylike disdain that she fascinated him.

"Grace, I'm going to warn you one last time," he ground out between clenched teeth. "Remove yourself from me, or you are going to regret it."

"It's my property. You remove yourself from *me*." Her hands went to her hips, as her little chin tilted stubbornly. "I did not kidnap you, Matthias. It was the other way around."

"*Fine!*" He knew he flashed the sharp canines at the side of his mouth as he snarled the word out, because her gaze narrowed, and her lips tightened. "Then you can accept the consequences if you stand there so defiantly, much longer."

"What consequences? Are you going to tie me up again and restrain me to my seat? Oh wait, why don't you just re-kidnap me, that was scary enough."

"Why don't I kiss you?" he suggested ferally. "Why don't I cover your lips with mine, shove my tongue in your mouth, and force this be-damned hormone into your system, to torture you as well? Why don't I make your pussy so wet, so hot, that you would use your own fingers to tempt me to fuck you? That you would beg me to be inside you? Why don't I do that, Grace?"

He could feel the blood pumping harder, faster inside him now. Adrenaline was mixing with the hormone, and that wasn't a good thing, pumping the effects through his body, straight to his cock. He was so ready to fuck, his cock was about to rupture.

His hands had torn from his pockets and gripped her shoulders now, as he glared down at her.

"My dick is so hard it's agony. I think of nothing but being inside you. Of feeling you, hot and melting around my cock, as you did my fingers. Perhaps you should remember exactly what will happen if I do that."

Grace pressed her hands into Matthias's chest, feeling the thundering of his heart beneath her hands, the tension in his body. She stared into his eyes, feeling as though she were drowning in them as he snarled down at her. What was she supposed to remember? Oh yeah, uncontrolled nympho-sex. Needing him so badly it hurt.

Hell, it hurt now.

"What, Matthias, all that incredible control you've had over the last three weeks is finally fraying? Poor baby. So much for all that Breed training to control your baser impulses."

Had she really said that? Obviously she had, because he was staring at her as though she were crazy.

"Have you lost your mind?" He asked her slowly. "Do you think that now in any way resembles the last three weeks? Sorry, baby, I hadn't tasted that hot little pussy then. I have now, and trust me, the need for more is wearing my control thin."

"It was a decision *you* made, not me." Her finger poked into his chest. "How many low-cut blouses did I wear? Would you like to know how many times I didn't wear panties under my skirt or took my bra off after we came to my apartment? It didn't bother you then, why should it bother you now?"

And he was right, she was crazy. She was aroused, and she was mad. This was her damned vacation, and he was messing it up. What was worse, he had been messing her life up for three weeks, and now she found out that she couldn't even have a hot one-night stand with him without committing for life.

She would be damned if that was fair. Because she knew he was right. Sex with another man would never satisfy her, because he held her heart. She was in love with a killer, and she wanted to kill him for it.

"Do you think I didn't know what you were doing?" His head lowered, his lips only inches from hers as he scowled down at her. "Do you think it was easy to try to be one of the good guys? To not take advantage of you and force you into this heat?"

"One of the *good guys*?" Her eyes widened, as her voice rose. "Where in the hell do you see yourself as a good guy? You are so fucking *bad*, you give the word a new meaning."

· CHAPTER 9 ·

Grace stared at Matthias in shock, as the words slipped past her lips. Amazingly, he didn't become angry. He didn't take her accusation in the worst light, and that wasn't how she had meant it.

Though, she wasn't certain how she had meant it. She just hadn't meant it in the sense of the killing she had witnessed. The thought of that had her sobering further.

His eyes crinkled at the corners. "You like bad boys," he accused her. "You told me you did."

"That's beside the point," she huffed. "And stop making me crazy. You *are* making me crazy, you know."

"Because you love me." There was so much confidence in his voice that she grit her teeth in agitation.

"Don't tell me how I feel, Matthias. I don't like it." She glared back at him. "You have to be the lousiest kidnapper in history."

"Should I tie you to your bed?" he mused, his expression strained, despite the amusement in his eyes.

"You'd enjoy that too much," she finally sighed before turning away and moving a few paces along the finely ground dirt that bordered the lake. "Would you give it up?" she finally asked, turning back to him.

"Give what up?" he asked, but she saw in his eyes that he knew what she was talking about.

"What you do." The killing. The bloodshed. The danger.

He pushed his fingers through his long black hair. The moment he released it, an errant wind blew it back around his face, giving him a savage, warrior appearance.

He breathed in deeply, stared out over the lake, then turned back to her. "For you. As long as no danger threatens you."

She felt herself trembling, hope surging through her, burning through her mind, as he stared back at her, his expression stoic.

"You wouldn't hate me for it?"

"Grace, dammit, I love you," he snarled. "Do you think I'm unaware that things have to change if you accept me? That what is acceptable as an unmated male would be unacceptable as a mated one? For God's sake!" He glowered down at her. "Do you think I was born stupid?"

She shook her head slowly, a smile trembling on her lips. "No. You weren't born stupid, Matthias."

"What about you?" he growled. "Could you forget Albrecht? Could you forgive what you saw for a life with me?"

She licked her lips slowly. "I understand why you did it. Why you feel you had to do it. Because of what he did to you and to those you knew, you would have had no choice."

But she couldn't face a life with him, never knowing who he would kill next, or why, or living with the fear that the day would come when he would make a mistake. That he would take an innocent life. No man was perfect, and eventually she feared, he would shed innocent blood. That she found too hard to accept.

"So I make this promise to give it up. It doesn't mean I won't continue to fight for Breed rights. I won't sit back and watch my people die without working to help them."

"I understand that."

"The least I can do is be an enforcer, an agent for the Bureau of Breed Affairs."

"I can handle that." She knew about the bureau and their work.

He nodded slowly. "Then come here, mate, take me."

Instantly, Matthias's expression transformed from pure self-assurance, to wicked, carnal arrogance. His lips became fuller, his gaze darker, his thick black lashes lowering as a hard flush stained his cheekbones.

The sensuality he had kept locked inside was finally free. It glittered in his eyes, turned them to dark, whiskey fire, as he watched, waited for her to come to him, for her to accept him.

Grace cleared her throat. "An aphrodisiac in your tongue, huh?"

His lips quirked with a decidedly anticipatory grin.

"Hot, uncontrolled sex?"

A growl rumbled in his throat.

"Well, in for a penny, in for a pound." She stepped to him, her hands sliding from his chest to his shoulders, as his head bent and her lips touched his.

There was no drugging sensation, only sweet, hot pleasure. His lips moved slowly over hers. They both learned the shape and texture of each other, held back, and relished this first touch.

Grace lifted one hand from his shoulder, her lashes lifting, so she could stare into his face with dazed fascination, as she touched his whiskered cheek.

He looked disreputable. Wild and bold. And he was all those things. But his gaze, though burning with arousal, was tender, his hands gentle as one threaded through her hair and the other gripped her hip.

"Like sunshine," he whispered against her lips. "That's how you taste, Grace."

Her lips parted, accepting his again, her tongue reaching out to lick at the harder curves of his. He jerked, his hands tightening on her, as he pulled back.

"Come on." He gripped her wrist and began striding quickly to the cabin.

"Wait." She stumbled along behind him. "What happened? What are you doing?"

"I refuse to take you outside," he snarled, moving up the steps to the porch. "We're going to the bedroom."

"Well, you could have kissed me properly, just once," she argued a bit peevishly. She had been waiting for that kiss.

"Once I get my tongue in your mouth we're both goners." He slammed the door behind them, set the security alarm on the doors and windows, and continued toward the bedroom.

As the bedroom door slammed behind him, he turned, wrapped his arm around her hips, and jerked her to him.

"Now," he groaned. "Sweet God in heaven. Now!"

His lips descended on hers, parting them, making way for the stroke of his tongue and the spicy, heated taste of lust.

Grace had never imagined that lust had a taste, but it did. It was spicy hot, a hint of jalapeño and the taste of a tropical breeze. It was fine whiskey with an undertone of honey, and it was addictive. Once she had the first taste of him, she knew why he had hesitated to kiss her. Because she could never get enough. She wanted his kiss inside her forever.

Her lips surrounded his tongue, hers battled with his and suckled at it with delirious demand, arching in his arms. She moaned into his lips, felt his groan and his hands. Hands that pulled her clothes from her body. Hands that moved her fingers to the band of his pants.

She tore at the metal closures, releasing the band quickly, before sliding her hands inside to test the muscular contours of his sexy male ass.

"You taste good," she moaned, as his lips lifted from hers to lower her to the bed. "I need more."

"More is what you'll get."

He sat on the bed, jerked his boots off, then straightened and removed his leather pants. Of course, he went commando. No underwear. She wished he had worn underwear, she might have been better prepared for exactly how well endowed he was.

It wasn't so much the length, which was impressive, but he was thick, thicker than she had expected. Thicker than any other man she had ever taken.

Fascinated, she sat up on the bed, reaching out with a single fingertip to touch the throbbing head of his cock. Of course, it was pierced. A silver bar pierced the ridge of its head, the locking balls at each end glittering in the sunlight that slanted through the window. It matched the piercings in his left nipple and ear.

"Any reason for this?" She touched the curved silver lightly. Then her gaze was caught by the two rune tattoos inside his thighs. She knew those. Strength and wisdom. He was both.

"Later," he growled. "I'll explain it later."

Shadows flashed in his eyes, and she didn't want them there. She wanted the flaming arousal back in full force. She wanted all his attention on her.

Grace lowered her head, parted her lips, and let her tongue swipe over the damp crest, pausing to pay particular attention to the silver piercing. She rolled her tongue over it, gripped the small locking ball with her teeth, and tugged at it gently.

Matthias froze. But the shadows were gone. His expression was watchful now, dark with sensuality. Grace parted her lips further and slowly lowered her mouth onto the straining, engorged crest of his cock.

"Ah, fuck!" His groan was followed by a hard, powerful clench of his abdomen. A second later, it was Grace's turn to freeze.

That wasn't just pre-cum that spurted into her mouth, and it wasn't the consistency of semen. The taste was like that of his kiss, honey and spice, pure lust.

She stared up at him, her tongue licking over the thick head and the piercing, as she tried to analyze it. Tabloid rumors, fanatical accusations of perversions and animalistic characteristics flitted through her mind.

Maybe they weren't all lies. Maybe the past ten years of accusations against the Breeds' sexuality was more than just supposition. If it were, it gave a whole new meaning to the idea of wild sex acts.

She eased back, her lashes drooping over her eyes, as he watched her carefully.

"What's next?" She breathed over the head of his cock, watching his cheekbones flush from arousal, as carnal knowledge lit his gaze.

"It's a surprise," he growled, the fingers of one hand curling around his thick shaft. "If I tell you, it would spoil it."

Oh, he was bad.

"Could I convince you to tell me?" She lowered her mouth over the straining crest again and sucked it deep. She watched his face, as she worked his flesh with her tongue, with the suckling heat surrounding him. She gripped the silver that pierced his flesh with her lips, tongued it, then sank her mouth over his cock head once again.

His lashes drifted closed, as his body tightened further. A ragged growl rumbled in his chest. She loved that sound. The hotter he became, the more aroused, the deeper it became.

She knew what was coming, she could sense it. She could feel it. Her hand brushed his away, stroking the thick flesh slowly. She could feel the tension in the middle of the heavy length, a harder pulse of blood, the flesh more heated.

Another spurt of the pre-cum filled her mouth, as a groan ripped from his throat. His cock throbbed, the blood beating furiously through the heavy veins.

"Enough." He drew back, ignoring her frantic attempt to hold him in her mouth.

She could feel the back of her throat tingling, a deeper hunger rushing through her.

"You'll wait," he snarled, pushing her back. "You'll not destroy my control this time."

"You have control left?" Her arms curled around his shoulders, as his lips moved down her neck. "I don't think that's fair. Mine's gone."

She could feel the burn now. It was racing through her, licking over her nipples, her clit. She arched to Matthias, rubbing the hot tips of her breasts against his chest, feeling the fine, silken body hair that was almost invisible to the naked eye. Damn, it felt good, though. Like rough silk rasping over her nipples.

"Do you feel it, Grace?" He whispered as his lips moved lower, his canines rasping over her collarbone. "Do you feel the need building? Burning inside you like its been burning inside me?"

She felt it. Her eyes closed in delirious pleasure with it. The sensations were nearly painful, the arousal building inside her until her womb was rippling with it.

"I'm going to make it burn hotter." His voice was guttural now, hoarse with his own arousal just before his tongue licked over a nipple.

"Oh God, yes. Suck it." She arched, driving the tight peak against his lips. "Suck my nipples, Matthias."

Another growl. But his lips parted, and he sucked the tender tip inside.

Wet liquid fire wrapped around her nipple. He sucked her deep, his mouth hungry, his tongue stroking and licking, as her nails bit into his shoulders.

"Oh, that's so good," she moaned, her hips arching to grind her pussy against one hard, lean thigh, as he held himself above her. "It's so good, Matthias. I love your mouth. I love your tongue."

He caught the peak between his teeth, his tongue lashing it as she writhed beneath him. Tingles of electric sensation tore from the tip to her womb then struck with brilliant heat to the heart of her pussy.

She jerked in his arms, arched, cried his name.

"Sweet, Grace," he whispered, kissing the swollen slope of her breast reverently, before pressing more kisses between the two mounds and easing slowly down her body. "I can smell your pussy. Sunlight and syrup and sweet cream. I'm going to eat my fill now. I'm going to lick that pretty pussy so slow and easy."

"Oh yes," she moaned, writhing beneath him, her legs falling farther apart as he neared the agonized flesh there.

Her hips lifted, as his lips grazed her hipbone. Her hand tangled into his hair, holding him to her as he whispered over the curls at the top of her pussy.

"Matthias, please." Her heels dug into the bed as she lifted to him. "Now. Touch me now."

His hands slid beneath the cheeks of her rear to hold her in place. Locking his gaze with hers, his tongue distended, sliding through the saturated slit with a long, slow lick.

Spikes of sensation shot through her. Tingles and flares and fingers of electricity arcing from nerve ending to nerve ending as the breath caught in Grace's throat.

Sheer pleasure.

Her eyes closed, and her head tipped back as a keening cry spilled from her lips.

◆ C H A P T E R 1 0 ◆

Matthias licked at delicate, creamy flesh, humming his pleasure in a long, low rumble. She tasted better than honey, better than sweet cream. The luscious juices spilling from her pussy were tinged with spice and spiked with pure sweet fire.

His hands kneaded her ass. Sweet delicate curves that clenched beneath his fingers as she lifted to him without reservation. And he accepted. He ate her with a greed he didn't believe was possible, terrified he couldn't get enough of the sweet, addictive juices spilling to his lips and tongue.

Stretching out along the bed between her thighs, he lifted her closer, staring up at her absorbed expression as slowly, so slowly he pushed his tongue into the gripping, spasming channel he had dreamed of.

Her pussy was like silk. It flexed around his tongue as she cried out again, her hands clenching in his hair, pulling him closer.

Matthias could feel the hormone spilling from his tongue into the sweet depths of her cunt. The potency of the taste was diluted by the sweet juices he sipped from her. He rimmed the opening, lapped at it like the favored treat it would now become. He could eat her for hours and never get enough. Lick her forever and die with the hunger beating at his soul.

"Oh yes," her trembling voice speared through his senses. "Oh,

Matthias, it's so good." She stretched beneath him, arching closer, as her hips worked her pussy onto his tongue.

His cock throbbed, the pre-cum spurting from it to the blankets beneath him. He wasn't ready to fuck her yet, he thought desperately. Not yet. He had waited his entire life for this moment. For that one perfect moment, when touch, taste, moans, and whispered passions came into sync.

Everything melded together with Grace. Her taste was perfect. There was no scent of promiscuity, no taste of another who had gone before him. The Breed sense of smell and taste was often too good. But with Grace, there was only the sweet, heated taste of her woman's passion.

Slick, silken, her juices clung to his lips, to his tongue, as he slowly drew back from her.

Swollen glistening folds of flesh drew his gaze. Silken damp curls, ruby red, passion flushed, her pussy lured him. He licked again, hearing her cry, then drew back to gaze at the slickness again.

Had any woman ever been so wet for him? He knew there hadn't been. Only Grace. Farther up, her clit was swollen, fully exposed and flushed with need. He reached out with his tongue, curling around it and groaning at the taste of it.

Grace jerked, and more of her juices spilled from her.

He needed more. A rumbled growl fell from his lips, as his tongue pierced her core again, and he allowed the tip of his nose to caress the hard nub of her clit.

"Oh God, Matthias." She never called him Matt. He liked that. He wasn't a Matt. He was Matthias. It was the name he had chosen for himself, the name he preferred, and she never used anything else.

"Yes." She stretched beneath him again, her hips rolling, pressing his tongue deeper inside the clenching muscles of her cunt. "Lick me there. Right there."

She was vocal. He liked the sounds of her passion, the feel of it. And he liked knowing she enjoyed his tongue. He licked as she pleaded, caressing into tender tissue as she gasped then cried out for more.

"Your taste," he groaned as he pulled back, licked the outer folds once again, and then caught the spill of sweet liquid from the opening of her pussy. "So sweet, Grace. Your pussy is like nectar. Soft and sweet and addictive."

He lifted his head again, his tongue curling around her clit, as he pressed two fingers inside the grasping depths of her pussy.

She was shaking in his arms, shuddering. Each muscle of her body was drawn tight, and her pussy was so snug he was suddenly thankful for the unique hormones that would prepare her for him. He couldn't hurt her, the thought of hurting her destroyed him.

"Matthias. Oh God, Matthias, what you do to me," she cried out hoarsely, as he drew her clit into his mouth.

She was close to orgasm. He could feel it pounding in her clit, in the tender muscles of her pussy and knew within seconds she would explode beneath him. He wanted it. He needed it. Sex had never been like this. This hot, this desperate. The need for *her* pleasure overriding the need even for his own.

When it came, growls tore from his own chest. Her clitoris, that delicate little nub of flesh expanded, swelled further, and the sweetest taste fell from it, as he felt her vagina tighten and pulse forth more of her slick juices.

The taste of her clitoral response was incredible. Slight. Fresh. New. As though no other man had drawn it forth before.

She was screaming his name. He could hear it, distantly, feel it vibrating through his soul, as this unique taste tempted his tongue. And Matthias knew he would never be satisfied, never be tempted to taste another woman again. Because nothing could ever be this good again.

◆   ◆   ◆

Grace couldn't breathe, she couldn't draw enough oxygen into her lungs, couldn't seem to find the instinct to force it in, as everything, conscious and subconscious, centered on the orgasm imploding inside her.

She shook her head desperately, fighting for air, but she couldn't get enough. Her eyes opened wide, her chest straining as the resulting panic caused the breath to still in her chest. She had warned him. Overexcitement. It happened every time.

"Easy, Grace." Matthias came over her, holding himself above her, one hand easing from her stomach to between her breasts with a gentle, caressing movement. "It's okay, my love. Slow and easy."

"Matthias," she gasped, feeling his fingers lower to massage her diaphragm.

"It's okay, Grace," he soothed her tenderly, his lips lowering to her neck and pressing against the flesh there in a soft, heated kiss. "Relax, love. It will ease."

Her hands were clenched in his hair, tight. It had to be hurting, but there was no strain in his voice, no attempt to loosen them.

"You're so sweet, so responsive," he whispered deeply. "I won't let you come to harm. I swear it."

His palm eased the horrible tightness, relaxing her, making breathing easier. As she drew sweet, clear air into her lungs, her breath caught again.

Oh God. His cock was poised at the entrance to her vagina, parting her folds, thick and hard. The shudders that raced through his body coincided with each deep spurt of heated fluid that erupted from it.

She could feel it heating her inner flesh, doing something so odd, relaxing it, yet sensitizing it further.

"What . . . ?" She stared back at him in shock.

"It's preseminal fluid," he groaned in her ear. "Hormonal. It eases the tender flesh inside, makes penetration easier. Sweet God, Grace." He shuddered. "I need you now. *Now.*"

His lips lowered to her shoulder, as he began to ease inside her.

The pressure, the heat, was incredible. White hot tingles filled her pussy, causing her to lift to him, desperate to still the little fingers of sensation that dug into her muscles.

He stretched her. Then stretched her more. She could feel her flesh parting, burning with a pleasure so intense it bordered on pain. Or was it pain so intense it merged with pleasure?

"Matthias," she gasped his name as he worked his engorged crest slowly inside her.

"It's okay, Grace." The hand that had been stroking below her chest now moved to enclose a swollen breast. "Slow and easy. I promise. I'll take you slow and easy."

She heard the desperation in his voice, the need to ease into her rather than ravish her. But she heard the hunger as well. He was burning as hot as she, his body shuddering with the same force that was trembling through hers.

He was thick, hard, and heavy, and she needed more. Grace lifted to him, working her hips closer, rolling them, taking the shaft deeper, as a groan ripped from his throat and his hand clamped on her hip.

"Easy," he snarled.

"You go easy," she panted, lowering her head to nip his neck demandingly. "I don't want easy."

His hips jerked, burying another hard inch inside her and stretching her with burning intensity.

"God yes." Her neck arched, her hips rolling again. "Fuck me, Matthias. Like I dream."

"Can't hurt you." He was the one fighting to breathe now. "Easy, Grace."

She twisted, digging her heels into the bed and lifted closer again. Her eyes went wide, and the blood thundering through her system went wild. Another hard blast of the pre-cum, and the sensations burning inside her increased. Her pussy rippled around his cock, flexed, spasmed.

"Hell's fire, woman," he bit out. "Don't do that."

It happened again. His hips jerked, and with a snarl he buried inside her, full length, the thick shaft overfilling her, the engorged head pressing demandingly against her cervix.

And it wasn't enough. She needed strokes. She needed taking. She needed . . .

"Fuck me." She nipped at his neck. "Now, Matthias. Fuck me now."

She felt it coming before he moved. The muscles of his back flexed beneath her hands. His thighs tightened, then with another hard growl, he began to move.

It wasn't easy. It wasn't a slow, peaceful loving. It was as wild as Matthias, as hot as her most wicked fantasies, and Grace knew she would never be the same.

"Like this." His hands lifted her legs around his hips, and he sank in farther.

She could feel his balls slapping against her rear, hear the hot, wet slap of flesh against flesh, and feel the hot burn of a possession so intensely carnal it would be branded into her very being forever.

His lips were everywhere. Kisses on her neck, her shoulder. He bent and suckled her nipples with deep hard draws of his mouth, lashed them with his tongue. His hips drove his erection inside her with furious thrusts, and she accepted him with hoarse cries for more.

"So hot and sweet." He nipped at her ear. "So giving. God yes, Grace, give to me. Take me."

The tension was gathering in her womb again. It flexed and

spasmed with the power of the pleasure racing through her now. Sensations that tore through her, stripped her control, and left her racing toward an edge of ecstasy that should have been terrifying.

Matthias groaned against her breast, his body bowed over her, his cock moving hard and heavy inside her. The fierce strokes stretched and burned and sent fiery fingers of absolute pleasure tearing through her. He fucked her with wild hunger, his cock shafting into her with desperate strokes, as her legs tightened around his hips.

He pumped inside her demandingly, stroking and igniting flames of devouring lust. It rippled and burned through her body, left her gasping, begging for release.

Her nails dug into his back, as his lips returned to her shoulder. Sweat coated them, their moans blended, mingled until Grace's turned to screams.

This orgasm didn't just implode inside her. It exploded through her, tore past her body and lit her soul with fireworks. Her pussy tightened on his shuttling cock to the point of pain, as she felt the release of her juices wetting her further. Then something else happened.

She should have been prepared. He hadn't hidden it from her. He had warned her.

She felt his release build, heard his throttled male groan at her shoulder a second before she felt his canines bite into her flesh.

There should have been pain. There should have been a rending of flesh. There wasn't.

There was a sharp, fiery blast of sensation, as she felt the first spurt of semen, then the sudden thickening of his cock.

It thickened. And thickened. And thickened. Just in one place. Burning through the thick, heavy muscles that gripped him so tightly, exposing nerve endings she couldn't have known existed, stretching her, secured inside her, as he shot his seed straight to the opening of her cervix.

He was locked inside her. Pulsing violently, stroking her pussy, even though he was still inside her. It throbbed with his release, the feel of the blood pounding through it, throwing her into another orgasm so violent that she didn't have to worry about breathing, because she knew she must have died.

Nothing could be so incredible and still allow life afterward. This was the pinnacle. This was ecstasy, and she would never survive.

◆ CHAPTER 11 ◆

Matthias found himself gently massaging Grace's diaphragm after the explosion that tore through her body. She was trying to laugh and gasp for breath at the same time, her face flushing with an edge of embarrassment.

He was still locked inside her, his muscles tight and rippling with the final spurts of his own release. His long black hair fell over his face and hid her expression, like a dark cocoon, insulating them from the world.

Tenderness filled him, as her soft gray eyes watched him with a pleasure reflected in her gaze. Her hands stroked his shoulders so gently, as his palm pressed beneath her rib cage, easing the tightness.

"That's so embarrassing," she finally whispered, stroking his hair back from his face, as he kept his gaze locked on her.

God he loved her. Loved her until he could think of nothing but her.

"Overexcitement," he whispered, kissing her cheek tenderly, as he felt his cock finally, blessedly, ease in its stiffness. "And a bit of fear, perhaps?"

Her lips tilted teasingly. "You have a few aspects that are a little overwhelming," she admitted. "But it's not totally your fault. Sometimes, I panic a little."

A little? Her diaphragm was relaxed now, and her breathing, though a little quick, was coming easier.

"Has it happened often since you were a child?" he questioned, easing from her, shuddering at the snug grip of her pussy as he slid out.

"Oh." She breathed out hard at his movement. "That still feels good."

Her hands slid over his shoulders and stroked down his chest, as he moved to lay beside her. She was a gentle weight against his chest now, one slender leg tucked between his, as she pushed his hair back from his face once again.

"It doesn't happen a lot," she finally answered him. "It used to happen all the time when I was little. New situations or if I got scared or excited. My dad was in the army. Every time we heard of a new battle near his area, or if he was late coming home on leave, it would happen."

Stress, perhaps, Matthias thought as he tucked her closer to him.

"It hasn't happened since I hit my twenties. But then again, I've never been so excited in my life," she laughed, pulling her head back to stare up at him.

"Or perhaps so frightened?" he asked.

She shrugged, a wry smile on her face. "But it didn't happen when I saw you in Albrecht's suite. Or when you kidnapped me."

"Because you trusted me." He cupped her face in his hand, feeling his chest tighten at the knowledge of how much she had trusted him without even knowing it. "You knew I wouldn't kill without reason, Grace. Just, I think, as you knew that Albrecht was all he was accused of being."

She didn't turn away from him now, nor did she avoid his look. "I knew," she finally whispered. "Inside. But you still scared the life out of me."

"Not enough to steal your breath," he reminded her.

A soft smile from remembered pleasure shaped her well-kissed lips, this time as she shifted against him, her hand stroking down his arm. "No, it's your touch that steals my breath, Matthias. Maybe, if we practice a whole lot, I'll learn how to control it."

"Hmmm, perhaps that's the answer." He leaned down, allowing his lips to rub against hers, to feel the passion and desire in her acceptance of him.

He hadn't expected this. The price of keeping her wasn't so very bad, though. No more assassinations. He could live with that. Jonas could use him at the Bureau of Breed Affairs. He had requested his help there on a full-time basis many times, and Matthias had refused. Maybe he could talk to the director about that now, see what was needed.

There were very few Wolf Breeds in the bureau. The pack leader, Wolf Gunnar, was now on the Breed Ruling Cabinet and met often with the human and Feline sections of the Breed community. The separate Breed races were slowly coming together, adapting and learning how to ensure their place in the world. Matthias could help with that. Grace could help with that. He had seen her at the hotel managing the staff. She was like a little general directing the running of the establishment.

"I think I'm hungry," she finally sighed, as his head lifted. "Starving, actually."

Matthias touched her cheek with the backs of his fingers. "Then I better get you fed," he said. "Because the heat will build again, Grace. And soon."

Grace stared back at him in surprise, as he moved from the bed, then helped her rise as well. The surprise quickly changed to admiration. He was hard from head to toe. His body was lean, his muscles flexed with power without being ungainly.

She could understand now why her childhood panic had returned. Her difficulty breathing was due to stress, to emotional overloads, as the doctors had coined it. That was Grace, too damned emotional sometimes. She could handle watching her lover kill a suspected monster, but she couldn't handle the knowledge that he was imperative to her happiness.

Just as her father had been. Just as the knowledge of the danger he had faced had brought on the emotional attacks.

She had thought she was over them. Her father had just retired from the army a few years before, but she hadn't had an attack in more than six years. Until Matthias.

Because she loved him.

She shook her head as she followed him to the shower. They washed quickly, hunger of a different sort driving them now.

Showering with Matthias was a unique experience, though. He loved the water, and he hogged it. She had to push him back several times to get her share, and a wrestling match ensued for possession of the stream of water. She lost, of course, but he did hold her close enough to make certain she was both washed and rinsed from head to toe.

Then he made certain she was dry as well. By the time he finished, Grace was ready to head back to the bed rather than to the kitchen.

"Food first. I need my energy." He inhaled slowly, his lashes lowering, as sensuality filled his expression. "Then we'll go to bed. Perhaps we'll even sleep sometime tonight."

He backed her against the bathroom wall, the heavy length of his cock burning against her lower stomach, as her hard nipples raked his chest.

Grace ran her palms over his biceps, then his shoulders, as his head lowered, and he licked the small spot where he had bitten her earlier. Sensation sang through the small wound, a clenching pleasure so deep and hot she rose to her tiptoes to prolong it.

He was definitely a bad boy. Tattooed, pierced, and arrogant as hell. She had seen that arrogance more than once over the past weeks. But he was gentle with her. He touched her like a dream, and he kissed her like fire.

"Food," he whispered regretfully against her lips, drawing back and staring down at her somberly. "Are you sure you're okay?"

"I'm fine." She was so damned horny now she thought she might melt in a puddle at his feet.

They dressed in the bedroom and headed through the cabin to the kitchen.

The refrigerator was filled with cold cuts, vegetables, and cold water that the caretaker had stocked before her arrival. The freezer held a variety of packaged steaks and other frozen goodies.

She grabbed the meat from the refrigerator and some lettuce and tomatoes. Thick, fresh bread was wrapped and stored in the cabinet. She removed it and set it on the counter.

Matthias was unusually quiet as he moved through the kitchen, the living room, then back to the kitchen. His expression was somber, the way he watched her finally grating on her nerves.

"Is there a problem?" She laid the bread knife down and watched him closely. "If you're still considering killing me, I should point out that has to be against the rules, or something."

His lips quirked as he shook his head. "That would be worse than suicide."

"Then what's bothering you?" She set the bread on plates and began heaping them with meat, cheese, and veggies.

"I just thought of something." He slid his hand into the pockets of his leather pants as he faced her. "What were you doing in Albrecht's suite?"

"He left a message on my machine, demanding my presence. I thought I would see what his problem was before I left."

"Why did you come back?" He was frowning curiously.

Grace waggled her brows. "My bikini. I forgot it. It was new, and

I wanted to wear it while I was on vacation. I love swimming in the lake."

The frown eased away, as his whiskey eyes lit with arousal.

Grace snickered at the look, as she picked up the plates and moved them to the kitchen table, before grabbing two bottles of water from the fridge.

"A bikini, huh?" he asked, taking his seat across from her. "What kind of bikini?"

"A little black bikini." She clenched her thighs, the burning in her clit was becoming a bit irksome. Surely to God she could get through a meal without attacking him?

"I'd like to see it," he murmured, picking up his sandwich and biting into it with strong, white teeth.

Teeth that had bitten her. She could feel the mark at her shoulder throbbing and irrationally wished he would lick it again.

She ate her sandwich with more determination than actual hunger now. After they finished, she quickly cleaned the dishes. And Matthias was still quiet.

He had moved from the kitchen to the living room, where he stood in front of the wide picture window, staring out at the lake.

He looked almost regretful.

Maybe Breeds didn't like women with a weakness, she thought morosely, remembering how her breathing had seized up. It was a stress reaction, it wasn't like she was terminally ill or anything. To be honest, her climaxes had terrified her. She had never come so hard, never felt such pleasure ripping through her. It was no wonder she had panicked a little, especially when his cock had thickened, spreading her further and sending her into another, sharper series of orgasms.

"The panic attacks aren't a big deal," she finally said as she stepped into the living room. "They go away eventually."

He turned to stare at her, his eyes narrowing, flicking to her breasts. Her nipples were poking against the soft material of her dark blue shirt, and her pussy was clenching in need.

Violent need.

It didn't make sense. Before, she hadn't ached like this, not to the point that it was physically painful.

"I'm not worried about the panic attacks. If you were ill, I'd detect the scent of it."

Okay. That told her.

She pushed her fingers through her hair and glared at him.

"Then why are you moping around like it's the end of the world? Did I do something wrong?"

Maybe she hadn't pleased him sexually. A man could get a little out of sorts when a woman failed to pick up on something he was wanting but was too stupid to ask for it.

His jaw clenched as he inhaled roughly. "You didn't do anything wrong."

She nodded sharply. "You know, I understand that being a Breed could make you more testosterone-impaired than most men tend to be. But I can't read your thoughts any more than I can read other men's. If something is wrong, I'd prefer you just get it out in the open rather than making me miserable by pulling the silent treatment. Trust me, I have several brothers, I can handle your delicate sensibilities."

His brow lifted, as amusement glittered briefly in his eyes. Amusement, arousal, and something undefined. Anger, perhaps.

"My male sensibilities are functioning fine," he assured her, the corner of his lips tilting wryly.

Grace crossed her arms over her breasts, almost gasping at the feel of the material of her shirt raking over her hard nipples.

"Then what's your problem?"

"You're in pain," he said softly. "Aren't you?"

Grace shifted uncomfortably. "Not really."

"I wanted to hide from you exactly what the mating would do to you," he finally sighed. "There's still so much we don't know about it, or its effects. I should have waited."

"Now, you're starting to frighten me, Matthias."

"Do you know that only two of our wolf mates have produced children? In one of those, the wolf's genetics were so recessed that the scientists theorize that it made conception easier for his mate. The other was so brutally experimented on that she still has nightmares."

Grace flinched at the thought of such pain. "The Felines seem to have no problem."

"More than you know," he sighed. "It's true, the original pride initially had success in conception, but after that, the heat continued during the females' ovulation periods, and no other babies were conceived. It's been ten years. Scheme Tallant, the mate to the Felines' head of public relations, is now carrying twins. One child has been born to Merinus and Callan, one to Veronica Andrews, and one to Kane Tyler's mate, Sherra. There is one child born to Dash Sinclair and his mate, and to Aiden's mate, Charity. For the Wolves, conception has proved extremely difficult, and the heat extremely severe."

His voice was heavy, his expression dark, remorseful.

"I tried to be honest with you, Grace." He shook his head, his lips tightening with what she now knew was self-anger. "But I hungered for you." A frown creased his brow, as he stared back at her as though that hunger still confused him. "Even now, my control is less than it should be." His frown deepened. "I tried to tell myself it would be different between us, but I knew better."

Her sex clenched as slick juices spilled between her thighs.

"Do you think explaining it any further to me would have made a difference?" she asked "I'm not a child, and I'm not completely ignorant. Once you told me what you had, I remembered the tabloid stories, I knew I could be looking at more than you were telling me. Evidently, I didn't care."

His head tilted as he watched her with confusion. "How could you not care, Grace? It will change your life forever. Place you in danger. It will restrict your life and will turn you into a target for the scientists out there, who are determined to destroy us."

"And that's what bothers you the most," she said softly. "That danger. Admit it, Matthias. You're frightened."

His lips tightened. "I will protect you."

"No matter the cost," she guessed. "You're afraid that your attempts to protect me will cause me to hate you."

He growled. That sound sent rapid little bursts of near-ecstasy to explode through her vagina, as it tightened her clit further.

"That isn't all," he admitted. "They want our mates." He stared back at her, tortured, desperate. "The mating causes a decrease in aging. The couples who have mated are aging only one year per every five to ten years. You will live far longer than you ever imagined, and it's because of this that the rogue scientists are so desperate to get their hands on mated pairs."

Okay, now that was shocking. Grace stared back at him, her lips parting in disbelief.

"How much longer?" she asked.

He swallowed tightly. "We aren't certain, but there's rumors that the first Lion Breed created more than a century ago still lives, and that he and his mate are still in their prime."

"Whoa!" She breathed out, moving to the chair beside her and sitting down heavily. "That's definitely a decrease in aging." Her hand pressed against her lower stomach. "Does it stop after conception?"

He shook his head sharply. "Not that we've seen. Conception is so difficult that our doctors and scientists believe this is nature's way of ensuring the species. Until the babes have grown and we see how this aging affects them, we can't be certain of anything."

"Well, this definitely throws a little kink into things," she breathed out roughly. "You said Merinus and Callan have only one child? The reports state three. I remember that."

He shook his head. "There are three pride children. The press mistakenly reported the children as all belonging to the pride leader and his mate, and they didn't bother to correct it. They keep their mates closely guarded while they're pregnant, and out of the public eye. It's the only way to ensure their safety."

"And the wolf mates?"

His jaw flexed, a muscle ticking violently just under the flesh.

"No one knows where Dash Sinclair hides his family. Aiden and Charity stay on the Wolf Breed compound in Colorado and never leave it. Their child will be born under as much restriction as we were created in."

"And if I conceive?" she whispered.

"We'll have no choice but to return to Colorado. If it happens."

• CHAPTER 12 •

Grace rubbed at her bare arms as she stared back at Matthias, the irritating pinpoints of sensation racing over her flesh were driving her insane. She needed him to touch her, not stand there trying to explain things neither of them could change at this point.

"So, you're regretting not telling me all this before?" She leaned back in the chair and licked her lips, watching as his eyes darkened, his dark cheeks flushing a brick red, as his lips became fuller, his expression darker with lust.

"I should have told you." His nostrils flared as she lifted her hand and stroked it over her collarbone. Every inch of her body was tingling now, begging for him.

"Consider me told," she stated.

"What?" He was staring at her, almost dazed now, his hands slowly pulling from the pockets of his black leather pants. Pants that did nothing to hide the straining length of his arousal beneath them. He was thick and hard. She was wet and wild, and she needed him now.

"Look, this is all very interesting, and I'm sure I'm going to have questions eventually. You know, once the ramifications of the whole mating thing hits me? Sometime after you get your wolfie ass over here and fuck me."

His eyes narrowed, as his hands went to the black shirt he wore, his fingers sliding buttons from their holes, and his gaze gleaming now with pure lust.

"My wolfie ass?" he asked her softly, his voice dark, rough.

Grace slid her shorts from her body, leaving only the silk panties she wore, as his shirt was tossed to the floor. Her own shirt came off easily, as he sat down and pulled his boots and socks off.

She rose to her feet, and before he could rise from the wide, padded stool he had been sitting on, she was in front of him.

"You're slow." She knelt before him, pushing him back against the chair behind the stool, her fingers moving for the metal closures on his pants.

"So I am," he growled, his tight abs flexing as she parted the edges of the pants and revealed the straining length of his cock.

The piercing gleamed against the dark flesh.

"Why the piercing?" she asked, lowering her head to let her tongue worry the little ball at one end of the bar.

His hands slid into her hair, a tight groan leaving his throat.

"A reminder," he panted.

"What does it remind you of?" She held the hard shaft, turned her head, and sucked the upper side of the crest between her lips to allow her tongue to stroke around the jewelry with flickering movements.

"Freedom," he bit out. "It reminds me of freedom."

"Why?"

He tightened further as her teeth gripped the bar.

"We weren't allowed piercings or tattoos in the labs. Nothing that would identify us. Nothing that would make us individuals. It reminds me. I'm free."

Her heart clenched, and her soul bled for the pain that resonated in his voice. His freedom came down to his choice to be pierced and marked. His ability to be an individual.

She sank her mouth over the engorged head of his erection and sucked him in deep. She wanted the memory of that place wiped from his mind. She wanted it replaced with need, with hunger. For her.

He belonged to her.

He growled her name as he leaned back against the chair, sprawling across the stool and the chair cushion behind him. Her fingers stroked the thick shaft as his hands clenched in her hair, guiding her movements, showing her how to please him best.

He liked to feel her teeth raking gently along the crest. The way her tongue played with the bar piercing his flesh.

As she sucked his cock head, her hands pushed at his pants, sliding them over his thighs, and pushing them down his legs.

There, now she could explore flesh she had been dying to touch. His scrotum was silky and smooth, only the faintest hint of silky hairs covering it. It tightened as she cupped it in her palm then slid her nails over it.

"Grace," the growl in his voice was warning. "Leave me control, sweetheart. Don't push this."

Oh, a dare.

She opened her eyes, lifting them to meet his as her lips lifted from the throbbing crest and began to slide down the straining shaft.

He was breathing hard now, his hands gripping the arms of the chair rather than her hair.

"What control?" she whispered. "I don't have any, why should you?"

She wanted that loss of control. She wanted the wild man she glimpsed in his eyes, the bad boy she knew he was. Her lips moved lower, her tongue licking until she came to the tight, silky flesh of the sac below.

"Dammit. Grace," he cursed, but he arched to her, allowing her the freedom to lick over the tight flesh, to feel the straining tension there.

As she watched, a small spurt of pre-cum spilled from the slit on his cock head. He growled again, a thick rumbling sound of hunger that had her heart racing in excitement.

She used the slick fluid to ease the stroking of her hand along the shaft, feeling it flex beneath her fingers as her lips investigated his balls and her tongue flickered over the silken, tight flesh.

"You don't know what you're doing," Matthias snarled. "What you'll cause."

The fingers of her other hand moved lower, beneath the tense flesh of his scrotum and found the ultrasensitive flesh beneath. She couldn't have anticipated his reaction.

She was only stroking the flesh between his balls and his anus, but he jerked, his hands gripping her shoulders and pulling her back as he jackknifed from the chair.

"I warned you," he bit out, his voice tight and hard, wicked with a sensual threat. "You want to play games, mate. Let me show you what happens when you do."

She had somehow released more than she had bargained for. Within seconds she found herself bent over the stool, Matthias behind her, and before she could stop him, his lips and tongue were moving along the cleft of her rear.

She should have been frightened, terrified. She had never been touched there, refusing to allow any previous lovers that freedom.

But Matthias wasn't asking for anything. His tongue was ravenous, licking and stroking, as his hands parted the full curves and he delved lower.

"Matthias!" She cried out his name, trying to lift herself from the wickedness of the caress, the stroke of his tongue over the entrance to her rear. Another stroke, then an entrance so shocking she began to shudder.

"I've been dying for this," he groaned behind her, his hands caressing over her ass as he rose, his cock tucking against the entrance.

"It's not going to fit," she gasped.

At the same time, she felt the first blast of the preseminal fluid explode from the tip of his cock and his cock sinking into the tight orifice.

Grace tried to writhe beneath him, but his hands held her in place, his cock parting her flesh marginally as the forbidden channel began to burn.

Sweet God, what was he doing to her? What was in the silky fluid that both lubricated and eased the passage she knew he was preparing to take?

With each spurt, he was able to sink deeper inside her, stretching the unbreached entrance, burning it with a pleasure/pain that had her screaming beneath him.

"I love your ass." His hands kneaded the curves. "I would watch you when you walk, my cock so damned hard I thought I would die, imagining this. Imagining taking you here, feeling you accept me. Submit to me."

Submit.

That was it. Grace could feel it in him. The dominance and power he had kept hidden from her. He had let her make nearly every decision in their relationship until now. He was ensuring his dominance now. Reinforcing the fact that he might give up a few things for her, but he still controlled this. He controlled her response. He controlled her sexuality.

She arched before him now, feeling another heated spurt of the fluid that relaxed and eased, even as it intensified sensation. She could feel the burn inside her anus, demanding more, demanding the hard stretching, the submission required to take him in.

"You're mine!" The declaration was made with a rough demand. "Say it, Grace. Mine."

"Yours," she panted. She wasn't about to argue. Not now. Not when he could stop and take the incredible sensations away from her.

He was thick and hard, hot and demanding, and with the aid of the slick, forceful jets of heated fluid, he was taking her, stretching her, forging inside her until his scrotum was pressed into the wet heat of her pussy, and his cock was fully embedded in her rear.

Then he was moving. He didn't pause. He didn't wait for her to make sense of the pleasure that mixed with the pain or the burning need and heated resistance.

His hands gripped her hips, and he began fucking her with slow, forceful thrusts. Each time he slid back another spurt of heated fluid sensitized her inner flesh further. Each forceful thrust was taken with slick ease and with a desperate cry.

He moved one hand from her hip, sliding between her thighs, his fingers surrounding her clit, stroking and milking it as his thrusts increased.

She could feel the drag of the bar that pierced his cock, an added sensation that dragged a desperate breath from her lungs. His thighs braced hers, his balls slapped against sensitive flesh, and within seconds Grace felt her release racing through her.

She bucked beneath him at the hard explosions that began to shudder through her. Pleasure became an agony of ecstasy. Sensation became waves of desperate, clenching release that she was certain she would never survive. As one would recede, another would build. As the thickening of his cock filled her ass and his spurts of release began to burn inside her, another took her, shook her, and had her fighting to scream.

She was writhing, jerking beneath him, held still by his body as he came over her, his lips covering the mark he had made on her shoulder earlier, his tongue stroking it as his sharp teeth held her in position.

She was lost. Lost in the orgasms pouring over her, and the mental and physical submission racing through her. She belonged to Matthias, just as he belonged to her. And the knowledge wasn't scary. It was right. For the first time in her life, belonging to someone was just right.

· CHAPTER 13 ·

The horrible craving for Matthias's touch had finally eased as the day gave way to night. He forced her into the shower again, chuckling as she leaned against his chest and tried to doze while he bathed her. It was a good thing he still had some strength in his legs, because hers was shot.

She was limp, physically and mentally sated, and sleepier than she could ever remember being in her life. When he finally carried her to the bed and tucked her in close to his chest, a satisfied little sigh left her lips.

Her lips smoothed over the curved bar, secured at both ends by small silver balls that pierced his nipple. The metal was warm from the warmth of his flesh and reminded her of what he had said about his reasons for getting the piercings. To remind him of his freedom, his individuality. He was pierced and tattooed, scarred inside and out, and he was the most beautiful creation on the face of the earth, as far as she was concerned.

The thin scar that ran from his brow, across his eyelid, and half-way down his cheek was barely noticeable to her, though she ached often at the thought of the pain he must have felt when he was wounded.

He was a bad boy. There was no doubt about that. Wicked, carnal, intense, and arrogant. But when he held her, his arms were gentle, his hands tender as he soothed her closer to sleep.

"My dad would like you." She yawned as she snuggled closer to him. "My brothers would, too."

She felt his hand still on her back where he had been stroking her spine.

"Do you think they would?" His voice might sound unconcerned, but Grace knew him now, and she knew that strained edge to his tone was one of hope.

"I know they would." She was confident of it.

"Why would they like me?" he asked her. "I don't look like any man's vision of a son-in-law, Grace." Stark, almost bleak, his regret washed over her, forcing her to blink tears from her eyes.

"You're strong, honest. You stare people in the eye when you speak to them, and I love you. Trust me, Dad won't be able to resist you. And of course, Mom is just going to be in heaven. She'll think you need to be fattened up. She'll bake you homemade pies and bread and spoil you every chance she gets with her best dishes."

"Why would she do that?" Confusion lingered in his tone.

Grace moved her head back, staring up at him in the dark. "Because she'll love you, Matthias. That's what mothers do. My brothers will teach you how to play touch football, and their wives will ogle your ass when they aren't looking. My sisters-in-law are exceptionally intelligent. They know a fine male form when they see one."

Matthias stared down at her, frowning. She was talking as though his acceptance within her family was a done deal, without him having to make concessions or scrape for it. That couldn't be true. Nothing had ever come so easily to him. He had to fight for everything. It was accepted.

"Your father and your brothers will see me for what I am, Grace," he warned her, hating that fact. "They'll want you to choose another man. Accept that now."

He felt her surprise, then her amusement at the soft laugh that wrapped around him. "Oh, Matthias, you just don't understand families," she whispered into the darkness. "Daddy will take one look at you, and he'll take you out to his shed where he tried to fool us into believing he's building something. He'll give you a beer and interrogate you for hours as he puts you to work sanding this or that, or using a hammer. That's his form of acceptance. Trust me. He's going to love you."

"I don't know how to sand or hammer." For the first time in his life Matthias wondered if he was feeling an edge of fear.

"My brothers will follow along, of course," she informed him, as he felt a curl of trepidation. "They'll grin and smirk, as Daddy questions you, throw out a few questions of their own, then grab the football and rescue you."

"I don't know how to play football." He cleared his throat nervously.

"That's okay, they don't either," she assured him drowsily, confusing him further. "And while the neighborhood guys gather around in the back lot to teach you how not to play football, Mom will be cooking up a storm, and me and the sisters-in-law will be admiring your manly butt and broad shoulders. But don't wear leather to play football in. You need jeans."

"I always wear leather." It was slicker, harder to grip. It didn't make as much sound when one moved, and he had grown accustomed to it.

"You wear jeans to meet Mom and Dad, so you can play ball with the boys." She yawned again, as though compliance with her little demands were a foregone conclusion. "And remember, Mom makes the best cherry pie in the world. And she still makes homemade vanilla ice cream. You'll love it."

He was certain he would, but that wasn't the point.

"Grace, don't get your hopes up," he whispered, pressing his cheek to the top of her head, as his eyes closed in despair.

She wasn't like him, she had a family, interaction, a life outside of him. He only had her.

"You'll see." She sighed, her body relaxing against him. "You'll see, my family is going to love you."

Her father and brothers would likely warn him away from her with a weapon. When that didn't work, they would complain to the Bureau of Breed Affairs. When that didn't work, they would attempt to turn Grace against him.

He hadn't considered this, the reaction of her family. Hell, he hadn't considered her family at all, and that had been a mistake. He could hear her love for them in her voice. They were important to her. She would hate losing them. She would hate him, if she lost them because she was bound to him by the mating heat.

Matthias could feel sweat beading on his brow. What the hell would he do when that happened? Grace didn't know, she had no concept of how important she was to him. She was his life. She was every dream he had ever dreamed in the hell of the labs. And after his release, the thought of the woman who would eventually fill his life had been his every hope for the future. The first time he had seen her, he had known she would carry his soul through eternity. Life or death, it wouldn't matter, he belonged to Grace Anderson.

And she belonged to her family.

There had to be a way to ensure her family's compliance, he thought. He had money. He could make certain they had no legal difficulties. He could kill their enemies.

No, no killing. Grace wouldn't like that. Okay, he could make their enemies wish they were dead. He had a few resources he could draw on. Men understood such matters. At least, the non-Breed men he knew understood such matters. Were fathers and brothers somehow different?

Surely they couldn't be. They were still men. He might not be good enough for Grace, but he could find a way to ensure that they didn't hurt her by turning their backs on her when she refused to toss him free of her life, like she should the mutt he was certain they would believe he was.

He resumed stroking her back, using just his fingertips, relishing the feel of her satiny flesh. He knew she longed to live closer to her parents. He could buy her a home near them, that would surely earn him a few good points.

Damn. He would have to make plans to deal with this one. Research her family before he went to meet them. He would have to research them extensively. Perhaps he'd get lucky, and if worse came to worse, he could find something to hold over their heads to ensure that Grace wasn't hurt.

Because there wasn't a doubt in his mind that they would want him out of her life. He was a Breed. Part animal. He wasn't a man, he was a creation. A freak of science. No man who loved his daughter would want such a mate for her. Hell, he wouldn't want it for his own daughter, why would her father want such a thing?

And he was a killer. Or, he had been a killer.

A smile quirked at the corners of his lips. He had a feeling that before it was over with, many of his habits would be changing. But, that was okay. He was looking forward to it. She was soft and gentle, and as long as he could forestall the problems he knew would come with her family, then he could ensure she stayed soft and gentle with him.

Losing her would kill him, he knew that. Even without the mating heat, his soul was already bound to her in a way that he knew he would never be free of.

He kissed her head, loving the feel of her against his chest, a delicate weight that warmed him to his core.

He would figure out this family thing, for her. He wasn't so certain about the football, though. He had never touched a football in his life, though he had watched other Breeds attempting to learn during his stay on Wolf Mountain in Colorado.

Dealing with her family's hatred of him would be a small price to pay to have her in his life. He would pretend not to notice it, make himself as unobtrusive as possible, and should they need any help in anything, he would take care of the matter.

He nodded with a barely discernible movement. That should work. And if worse came to worse . . . He sighed. If worse came to worst, he would deal with it. She was worth it to him.

"I love you, Grace," he whispered against her hair.

He loved her laughter, her smile. The way her nose wrinkled when he teased her, the way her ears twitched when he kissed them.

She shifted against him as though trying to burrow deeper into his chest, and he let a smile tilt his lips and gathered her closer to him. His arms surrounded her, his head bent over hers, and he let her legs tangle with his.

His body was now as bound by her as his soul was. Silken limbs encased him, and soft breaths fell against his chest.

For the first time in his life, Matthias closed his eyes and slept while a woman lay tangled with his own body. He had never before been able to relax with a lover. But damn if he could help it. She had worn him out. She was as enthusiastic in their sex play as she was at everything else she did. Maybe a bit more so, he thought, as he remembered her nails raking his back and her demands for *harder, faster, now*, echoing in his head.

Yeah, definitely more enthusiastic in their love play was his last, distant thought as he breathed out in exhaustion and let sleep throw its final web across his senses.

Dawn wasn't far from making its first appearance over the horizon when Matthias came awake with a start. The scent of diseased perversions and hatred filled his senses, as he pressed his hand over Grace's lips and brought her quickly awake.

"Danger," he growled softly at her ear, while he pressed the panic button at the side of his watch. Jonas was their only hope. "Dress quickly."

He moved out of the bed, pulling her with him and tossing her the clothes he had insisted she keep by the bed, just in case. Jeans, a T-shirt, and light jacket. Thick socks and hiking boots.

He jerked his leather pants on, a black shirt, socks, and boots. Within seconds he was dressed and pulling his duffel bag away from the wall.

His weapons were there. The tools of his trade. He strapped the pistol to his thigh, knives against the underside of his arms. He tucked a backup pistol in one boot, a dagger in the other. He grabbed the shorter model automatic rifle he used for warfare.

"Matthias?" Grace whispered in fear, as he grabbed her wrist and moved her quickly from the bedroom.

They didn't have much time. He could feel the coyote soldiers moving in, could smell their blood-drenched souls, but they hadn't surrounded the house yet.

"It's okay. Just do as I say, and we'll be fine."

He prayed. Oh God, he prayed, as he quickly unlocked the window on the far side of the living room and lifted it soundlessly.

He dropped to the ground, then lifted Grace from the ledge, as she attempted to follow him. She was shaking, but stayed silent. Silent was good. It could have been their ticket out of there, if it weren't for the smell of her heat.

The soft scent of mating arousal was unmistakable. There was no way to hide it. That meant their asses were in a sling, if Jonas didn't get here fast.

Matthias made certain they were downwind of the coyote soldiers, who had attempted to come in downwind themselves. But the winds in the mountains were capricious. At some point they had shifted, betraying the coyotes' advance while hiding his escape with Grace, for the time being.

He didn't dare use the vehicle they had driven up in. The sound of a motor would betray them instantly. That left their feet. He only prayed he could get her far enough away to ensure a fighting chance at saving his mate's life.

What the hell had made him think he could have this time with her? That he could possibly steal just a few days of peace?

Somehow, he must have missed the signs that he was being watched. Only a coyote could have scented the mating heat building between him and Grace before he kidnapped her. But how had he missed a coyote trailing him?

Matthias kept Grace close to his side as he moved from the house to the sheltering trees that ran along the rough track leading into the cabin. He kept to the far side, knowing the coyotes were moving up along the upper side.

The breeze drifted around him, bringing the smell of them to him and causing his lip to lift in a snarl of hatred. If he were alone, he would have gone hunting. He would have killed every fucking mongrel that thought he could blindside Matthias this way.

But he wasn't alone. At his side, his mate was struggling to keep up with him, trying not to breathe too hard, to stay as quiet as possible.

As a twig crunched under her feet, he throttled a curse and wrapped his arm around her waist, lifting her off the ground. Her arms wrapped around his neck, and he felt her tears against his shoulder. Tears he wished he could shed.

There was no time for tears now. He had to get her as far away from danger as possible. There were a few other cabins farther down the mountain; there had been vehicles there as they drove in. If he could steal one and get a head start . . .

That wasn't going to happen.

He caught the scent of the coyotes' change of direction and knew he was fucked. Somehow, they had figured out that he and Grace had left the cabin, and now they were on his ass.

"Leave me," she whispered in his ear, as he found a faint animal path and began to move faster along it. "You can get away on your own."

"It's you they want, Grace."

She shuddered at his words and pressed her face tighter into his shoulder.

"It doesn't matter." Her voice trembled at the words. "I know how to hide. You can get away and go for help."

He would have howled then, if he could have. She honestly thought he would allow her to sacrifice herself? For him?

"You're wasting your time," he growled. "I won't leave you."

Even in death, he would follow by her side. But he didn't intend to die. If ever there had been a time when he intended to live, then it was now.

"Four. I have you."

Matthias slid to a stop at the sound of the number he had been known by in the labs. Not a name, by all means they shouldn't believe they had the rights that even pets had. No, they were known by numbers. He had been the fourth Breed created in the Albrecht lab in the German mountains.

Matthias stared at the six coyote soldiers that stepped from the surrounding trees. Behind them stood Vidal Velasco, the Spanish directorate of genetic protocols.

It was this bastard who had chosen the women who were kidnapped for the European labs and used for their ovum and life-giving wombs. It was he who had decided which woman would be released and which woman would be bred to death. It was this bastard who had slit the throat of the surrogate that had birthed Matthias.

Matthias had been five when Vidal had gathered three of the Breed children in that lab together, called this woman their mother, then slid his blade over the weakened female's throat. Even then Matthias had recognized the thankfulness in the woman's eyes at her realization that the horrors she had been suffering were over.

"I hear you have chosen a name for yourself, Four," Vidal's mocking, aquiline features were illuminated by the glow of the full moon, as it peeked from the clouds above.

Vidal was much older now, nearing his seventies, Matthias knew, but he moved like a much younger man, his black eyes glowing in the night, his short gray hair gleaming.

Even now, he wore a dark gray suit. His black shirt was dull against his swarthy flesh, his gray tie cinched snug at his neck. Matthias bet he was wearing the overly expensive leather shoes he was partial to, as well.

Vidal was nothing if not precise and neat in appearance and action. Even when he was killing.

Matthias lowered Grace to her feet, keeping his arm wrapped snugly around her, as he checked the position of each coyote. He held his rifle in one arm, his finger on the responsive trigger, as the coyotes began to spread out behind him.

"You picked the wrong night, Vidal," Matthias growled. "I'm not in the mood for you."

Inside, he was praying. He needed the coyotes closer together, not farther apart. He needed just one chance to catch them in a spray of bullets and to keep them from shooting Grace.

If he died, he would die knowing he left his mate to these monsters. He couldn't allow that to happen. Grace must survive.

"Is she breeding yet, Four?" Vidal asked him in his precise, flawless English. "I hear wolves are having a difficult time transitioning from animal to man when they take their mates. Have you managed that yet?"

Matthias watched Vidal carefully. He stood just behind two of the protective coyotes whose weapons were aimed, not at Matthias, but at Grace.

"When the shooting starts, I'm taking you out first, Vidal," Matthias said. "My bullets will tear right through your coyote pets and enter your chest. I won't miss."

Vidal frowned. "Now, Four, we don't have to be antisocial about this," he chastised Matthias. "Just give us your pretty girlfriend, and we'll let you run for a while longer."

Matthias lifted his lip in a mocking snarl. "I think you know that's not going to happen. I'm well aware of the experiments the council scientists are running. I'd kill her before I'd let you get your hands on her."

Vidal crossed his arms over his chest, as Matthias tracked each soldier with his eyes and with his senses. He would have one chance to get Grace out of this alive. If the coyotes continued to surround him, he would have just enough room to drop and roll Grace to the small, rocky crevice next to them. It would provide the barest cover, but perhaps enough for him to cover her body with his own, as he tried to take the coyotes out.

"I can't believe you allowed yourself to be caught so easily."

Vidal's teeth flashed in the darkness. "You had a coyote on your ass the whole time you were courting Miss Anderson and never realized it. Have you grown soft, Four?"

Matthias shook his head. He had wondered about that.

"There was no coyote tracking me. You got lucky, nothing more. Seems fate shines on the diseased and soulless at odd times after all."

The scent of Vidal's anger began to pour around him. It made the coyotes nervous, as well it should. Vidal never could handle a Breed who dared talk back. It was one of his failings.

"Why did the directorate decide to send you on this little mission anyway?" Matthias shifted closer to the shadowed natural indention in the earth, as he watched Vidal. "Did they decide they didn't like you after all?"

"I am part of the directorate, you ignorant mutt," Vidal snapped.

"But not the head of it," Matthias pointed out, knowing well the ego that filled the bastard. "Are you certain they didn't send you on a suicide mission, Vidal? Every assassin you've sent after me has failed. What makes you think you could succeed?"

"I tracked you. I trapped you. With your mate," the other man gloated.

"Everyone gets lucky sometimes." He turned to glance around him, shifting ever closer to the rocky ledge that dropped into a four-foot ditch that water and erosion had created. "I think you just got lucky this time." He turned back to Vidal once more, giving him a cool smile. "Will your luck hold out?"

"Give me the woman, or the coyotes will fill her with holes, Four. My patience is wearing quite thin with your taunting."

Grace was shaking in his arms, but for each move he made, she slid into place with him. Her hands gripped the arm wrapped around her waist, and her body was tense, prepared. He could smell her fear, but he could also smell her determination to live.

Unfortunately, for them to live, their enemies had to die. The thought of shedding more blood in front of her was abhorrent to him. He had promised her the killing would stop. He had promised himself that for her, he would no longer kill. And yet, the cycle the council had began couldn't be stopped. Not for Matthias, not for any of them.

"I'll just have a bullet put in your head," Vidal sneered. "And I'll take your woman from your lifeless body. I hear it's quite painful for a woman after having been mated by you creatures, to be touched by another. Perhaps I'll get lucky, and my coyote was right when he sensed the possibility of her fertility. Is she carrying your pup?"

"Perhaps." He felt Grace's start of surprise. She wasn't carrying his child, he would know it if she were. But the thought of that could keep the coyotes from directing their bullets at her. "But you'll never know one way or the other," Matthias assured him. "Because you'll be dead."

"I will listen to her screams, just as Benedikt and I listened to the last bitch we dissected to get the brat she carried," Vidal sneered. "Her mate begged for her life, Matthias. Will you beg for your mate's life?"

And what of the child? Sweet God, what were those monsters doing now? Matthias remembered the sight of the female mate. She had been cut in so many places, sliced to ribbons. There had been no way to tell exactly what the scientists were looking for. If they had successfully removed a fetus from her body, though . . . His stomach twisted at the thought.

He lowered his head just enough to whisper, "I love you."

Her fingers tightened on his arm.

"Whispering your good-byes?" Vidal sneered.

Matthias moved.

His fingers tightened on the trigger, fire erupting into the night, as he threw Grace into the shallow ditch, then twisted and jumped in behind her, his gunfire still lighting the night, as he pushed her to move.

He could smell the blood behind him, but he could also hear Vidal's enraged screams. Matthias pulled Grace up the small gorge rather than running down it. Just ahead was a stand of boulders. If he could reach it, he might be able to hold them off long enough for Jonas to make it.

He had felt the answering vibration at the back of his watch against his wrist moments before. Jonas was on his way, and he wouldn't be too far off. The locator on the watch only sent out a short-range signal. He wouldn't have been able to detect Jonas's reply unless he was within range of the watch's tracker.

He pushed Grace behind the boulders, cursing as bullets rained around them. He pushed her to the rocky ground, moving to a crack between the boulders, and began shooting back.

A slender hand jerked the Glock remake from the holster at his thigh. Sensing her intent, Matthias quickly shrugged the ammo pack from his back and prayed she knew how to use the weapon.

"Grace, if anything happens to me . . . ," he growled back at her.

"Shut up and keep shooting. Nothing's going to happen to you." Her voice was shaking, terrified.

Matthias sighted a coyote soldier moving in closer, using the trees for cover. He gave the bastard one last chance to stay in place, and when he moved, Matthias fired.

One down, but there were more. And they were smarter about keeping cover.

"Jonas is on his way," he told her. "We just have to stay in place and stay alive. We'll be fine."

"Of course we will." Her voice was weak, thready.

The smell of gunfire filled the air, as Matthias continued to fire into the darkness, praying he would get lucky.

"Four, you're making me angry," Vidal called out. "You know I'll punish the woman for this."

Amazingly enough, Grace was the one that fired. She was kneeling at his feet, aiming low. A scream of coyote rage echoed in the night. She had obviously hit what she had aimed at.

"Stay put, and stay down," he ordered her, as he glimpsed a flash of gray moving through the underbrush. Vidal was trying to move into sight of the only weak point of their cover.

"I've got your back." Fear seemed to be making her voice tremble.

Matthias moved to the opening behind them, slipped past it, and waited. Behind him, Grace was firing. Occasionally a grunt or curse could be heard from the darkness. The smell of blood was thick in the air, but the smell of Vidal's treachery was thicker.

He moved closer. Closer.

Matthias lifted the rifle and watched, waited. Just a little to the right, he thought. He almost had him.

Vidal's graying head peeked from the tree that had been sheltering him, and Matthias fired. The bullet zipped through the night, struck Vidal's forehead, and the bastard went down.

Enforcers filled the area at the same time. Dozens of them were falling from the sky, sliding down black nylon ropes suspended from the night-black, silent heli-jet that had moved in overhead.

Matthias shook his head at Jonas's timing and slid back into the shelter to collect his mate.

Grace had never given much thought to death. Her thoughts since meeting Matthias had been filled with dreams for the future and plans to show him all the little intricacies of being part of a family. But when she felt the bullet tear into her chest, death was uppermost in her mind.

Strangely, it wasn't pain she felt. It was cold, not hot. It seemed to fill her body with ice rather than the burning pain she would have imagined. She was numb, yet able to move.

She had to move. She had to help Matthias. Just this one last time, she had to do something for him.

She managed to get his gun out of his holster and help hold the coyote soldiers back, determined to at least take a few with her if she did die. Matthias couldn't help her until this was dealt with, so she fought to hold back the ragged cries that tore at her chest.

Not from pain. She was numb to the pain, just aware of it. She wanted to cry because of what she was losing. As she felt herself growing weaker, felt the haze of blood loss engulfing her mind, she thought of leaving Matthias forever. She thought of the pain he would feel when she was gone.

It had taken her weeks to get a smile out of him, and she remembered the thrill the sound of his first laugh had brought her. She had a feeling Matthias hadn't often had occasion to laugh.

As Grace lay on the ground staring into the crack between the boulders, the gun dropped from her hand, and a whimper of agony left her lips.

She didn't want to leave him. She wanted to watch him play football with her brothers. She wanted to see her mother fuss over him and realize her father's approval of him.

"Matthias," she whispered, finally feeling him beside her again.

The gunfire had abated. Were the coyotes all dead? She hoped they were. She wanted them all dead.

"Grace. *Grace!*" She heard the panic in his voice, felt his hands as he turned her over, and knew he saw the blood.

She blinked up at him.

Shock, rage, agony creased his face, filled his dark eyes, and sent pain raging through her. She hated seeing the pain in his face.

Dawn was moving in, lighting the shelter they hid in, shadowing his scarred face, his incredible whiskey eyes.

He was screaming. She could hear him screaming, though what he said didn't make sense.

She lifted her hand to touch him. Just one last touch. Oh God, she didn't want to leave him. She wanted to lie with him one more time, she wanted his kiss again, to feel his touch.

"Matthias," she whispered. She loved his name, loved his face, and his heart.

"Don't you leave me, Grace." He was pressing something to her chest. "Do you hear me? Don't you leave me."

He was so arrogant. He was glaring at her, as though his refusal to let her go was all that was needed.

"Grace I swear to God, if you die, I'll never wear jeans. I'll never eat pie. I'll shoot fucking football players. Don't you die on me!"

She smiled. She was so glad it didn't hurt. That was so strange, the pain should have been agonizing.

"I love you, Matthias," she told him softly. "Like the earth loves the rain, like the flowers love the sun."

She was so tired. So tired and so frightened. She didn't want to leave him.

Her breathing hitched as the tears she couldn't hold back any longer began to fall from her eyes.

"Grace!" He was screaming at her, as her lashes fluttered. "Ah God, Grace, stay with me! Stay with me!"

She was so tired. She touched his face, feeling his hand clasp her fingers to his rough cheeks, and she fought to smile back at him.

Like a flower loves the sun . . . that thought drifted through her mind again. He warmed her like that. The sun warmed the flowers. "I love you."

She couldn't stay with him any longer. She tried. She tried until a silent scream was echoing in her head, because she could feel herself drifting away from him, and she couldn't stop it.

As her eyes drifted closed and rich darkness engulfed her, she could have sworn she heard a wolf cry.

Matthias . . .

◆   ◆   ◆

"Let the medic work on her, Matthias!" Jonas was screaming in his face, as Matthias fought the hands pulling him away from Grace.

She was so weak. The smell of her blood was in his brain, and agony beat at him with blows harsher than any he had received in the labs.

Matthias fought like the beast he was to tear away from the Breeds restraining him. To get to Grace. To hold her to him.

"You mangy fucking wolf, listen to me." Jonas's forearm slammed into Matthias's throat, driving his head back against the boulder.

Matthias let out another bloodcurdling howl of agony.

"She's alive, Matthias, but if you don't fucking calm down, we won't be able to help her. Do you understand me? We won't be able to help her."

Silver eyes flashed in the dawn light, the savage expression of the Lion Breed who was helping to restrain him finally took shape.

"Jonas! Grace . . ."

"Help us, Matthias, don't go wild on me," Jonas snarled, his canines flashing dangerously. "She's alive. If we're going to keep her alive, we have to move fast, and you have to keep your head."

The forearm across his throat flexed powerfully, as Matthias struggled against him again.

"Can you keep your fucking head, Matthias?" Jonas yelled in his face.

"As long as she breathes," he screamed back.

"Good! Let's get going." Jonas released him, and only then did Matthias see the basket that Grace had been strapped into and the medic working furiously to keep her alive.

"Jump in." Jonas pushed him to the wide metal basket used to transport the wounded from the ground to the hovering heli-jet above. "You and the medic. The hospital has been notified, and doctors Armani and Morrey are en route."

Matthias clutched the side of the basket, as he knelt on one side of Grace, the medic on the other. An IV was strapped to her arm, a compress on her chest.

Sweet God, they had shot her in the chest. He felt the grief raging inside him now, the knowledge he could lose her, and he knew he would never bear the pain of it.

She had to live. Without her, he would never be warm again.

As the Breeds waiting in the transport heli-jet secured the basket, the hum of the craft grew louder.

He heard the report the medic was transmitting to the hospital in New York City. Her vitals, the site of her wound and its depth. She was on oxygen and had an IV. Surgeons were waiting, and the Breed doctors were on their way.

Within minutes the heli-jet was landing, and they were taking

Grace away from him. She was loaded onto a stretcher and rushed across the roof as a second heli-jet landed and deposited the two doctors, who had been redirected from a flight to Virginia just minutes behind Jonas.

Doctors Armani and Morrey rushed across the landing area and followed the gurney. Within seconds, the heli-jets lifted off and left Matthias alone.

He stood on the hospital roof, staring around at the blinking lights, the buildings that rose like sentinels around them, and felt a striking loneliness fill his soul.

They had taken Grace away from him. Because of him, she was hurt, possibly dying. Alone.

Matthias stared down at his scarred hands and saw her blood, heard the ragged growl that tore from his throat. He was lost.

He stared around the rooftop again and realized that clear to his soul, without Grace, he was simply lost.

CHAPTER 16

Joe Anderson entered the surgery waiting room, his wife, sons, and their families closing in behind him. He knew him the moment he saw the young man Jonas Wyatt had told him to look for.

Wearing black leather, streaked with blood, his face resting in his broad hands, as long, night-black hair flowed around them.

He sat alone. The other families awaiting word on their loved ones were gathered at the other side of the room, casting wary looks his way.

Matthias Slaughter.

Grace had told him about Matthias, of course. Not what he looked like, or about the air of danger that surrounded him. She told him things only a woman would think of. Things like his sadness, his wariness, and how he made her feel.

Joe sighed heavily. This man made his daughter feel alive. Grace had said, "As though there's adventure around every corner, Daddy." And she had laughed. But he had heard the love in that laughter.

This was his daughter's man. That made him family. No matter what.

Matthias's head lifted, and the scarred face looked around, as he swiped the overly long black hair back from his face. He was an imposing figure. Standing to his feet, Matthias paced over to the windows, looked out, paced back to the small table, sat down, and tried to blend into the shadows of the room.

Joe could see the man's attempts to become invisible, and it both-ered him. Jonas hadn't said much about this Wolf Breed enforcer, but Joe had learned years ago how to read between the lines. And what he had sensed rather than heard, made him ache for the young man.

Joe fought back his own fear, his own anger at the thought of his daughter lying in surgery, a bullet in her chest, her life hanging on the line.

Daddy, I love you like the flowers love the sunshine. And you know they love it, 'cause they open right up and spread their petals like arms. Have you noticed that, Daddy? They hug the sun, because it keeps them safe and warm. That's why I love hugging you, Daddy. You keep me safe and warm.

He had to blink back his tears at the memory of her, barely ten, trying to wheedle her way out of some trouble she had gotten into at school. Grace had been his wild child. She had fought and scrapped, climbed trees, and jumped into water that was invariably over her head. Just as she had this time.

And just as he had always known she would, she had picked a man strong enough to follow her into adventure. Grace loved adven-ture. She restrained it now, worked hard, and never got into trouble. But she still liked to climb trees, and she still liked the deeper waters.

"There he is. Joe, why are you just standing here?" His wife, Janet, moved around him, her still-shapely figure drawn tight with fear for her daughter and worry for this Breed that their daughter spoke so highly of.

Matthias Slaughter was streaked with dirt and their daughter's blood, and his expression was haggard, bordering on savage. The sight of him broke Joe's heart.

As Joe stood there, Janet and his three daughters-in-law left him alone with his silent sons. Grace's older brothers were a lot like Joe. They watched and assessed.

Joe looked back and saw their eyes, and knew the boys saw the same thing he did. A man almost broken. The Breeds had lived horrifying lives. If that Jonas Wyatt's expression was anything to go by, then this Breed had known hell as few others had.

If he loved Grace as Wyatt said this man did, then the fear he would be feeling right now would be staggering.

He watched as Janet, with her mussed, shoulder-length gray hair and petite figure, fearlessly walked right up to that Breed.

The man's head lifted, and his eyes were alive with rage and agony, as he stared up at Janet. Joe knew the moment Matthias realized who she was. His expression clenched, his reddened eyes turned moist, and he whispered in a rough, growling voice, "She's my sunshine . . ."

Joe knew in that moment, Matthias Slaughter was family.

◆   ◆   ◆

Matthias wasn't ready for Grace's family. They would be angry, enraged at the danger he had brought to their daughter. There would be no buying or threatening their acceptance now. If she lived, they would demand his immediate removal from her life, and by God, he couldn't blame them.

He stared at his hands. He couldn't wash Grace's blood from them, it was all he had left to hold on to, her blood covering his flesh, reminding him that her love hadn't been a dream. It had been real. As real as the fight she was waging for her life right now.

When he looked up at the figure that moved to stand beside the table, he had immediately been snared by Grace's eyes. Soft, gray, tear-filled eyes in a lined face.

"Matthias, I'm Grace's mother." Her voice was soft, like a whisper of acceptance, and his heart clenched at the pain of it.

"I love her like the sun," he whispered, needing them to know before they accused him, before they raged at him. "She's my sunlight," he repeated.

And he could have never expected what happened next. Tears fell from those soft gray eyes, as she wrapped her arms around him and laid her head on his shoulder.

His arms gripped her, as she began to cry. His eyes lifted to the other women surrounding him, and to the men who watched him silently.

There was no condemnation. They all looked at him with compassion, especially the older man, the father, whose eyes reddened from the tears he held inside.

"I'm sorry." He was, to the bottom of his soul, so bleakly sorry that she had taken that bullet instead of him. He would give his life to trade places with her. He had offered his life to God to take him instead. He had prayed, bargained, raged, and begged the Almighty not to take his sunlight.

The father nodded once. He moved forward then, drew his wife from Matthias's embrace, pulled chairs back from the table for both of them, and introduced Grace's family to him. As though he weren't the enemy. As though it was important he know who they were.

"Not the first time she's been in surgery." Joe cleared his throat, as he sat beside his wife and wrapped his arm around her. "Remember when she was six, Janet?" He cleared his throat as Matthias stared back at him in confusion. "She fell out of that tree and started bleeding internally. I thought we were going to lose her then."

The three sons nodded, the women smiled watery smiles.

Matthias stared at them. "I have money." He clenched his hands on the table. "I have some small connections." They stared back at him questioningly. "I know I didn't protect her well this time." He stared at the blood on his hands. "I'll do better." He lifted his gaze to the father. "I'll make certain I do better in the future." His teeth clenched. He had sworn he would beg if he had to. "Don't take her from me."

Joe blinked, lowered his head, and shook it.

"I won't let it happen again."

Joe lifted his eyes once again. "Matthias . . ."

"I can't live without her." He meant to beg, but it came out as a growl of fury. "She would be torn between us. I don't want this . . ."

"Matthias." It was Janet that reached out to him. She placed her hand on his, over Grace's blood, and caught his eyes with hers. "We all love Grace. And if she loves you, then you're family. You don't buy acceptance, son. You don't bargain for it. It's there or it's not. You love her, and we accept you because of that. But, she loves you. Because of that, you're family."

"You don't know me." He shook his head, terrified and confused, certain they had to hate him. They had to be hiding it, for Grace's sake.

"We'll get to know you." Joe's voice was a warning.

Matthias latched onto that. A warning. He knew how to handle that.

He stared back at the father, whose lips suddenly quirked with hidden knowledge. "Trust me, we'll all get to know each other. Grace will make certain of it."

He could handle that. Matthias nodded sharply before sliding his hand back from Grace's mother's touch. He breathed out roughly, stared around the room, then froze as Dr. Armani, the head Wolf Breed doctor and scientist, entered the room with her Feline counterpart, Elyiana Morrey.

He jerked to his feet. Their expressions were pale, their lab coats wrinkled, and exhaustion marred their features.

"Nikki." He took a step toward her, then froze again.

They were watching him quietly, their gazes flickering over the family, who finally also came to their feet.

He had prayed over the past hours. He had bargained with God.

He had begged for just one more chance and offered his life for hers. He had pleaded with a being that hadn't created him, but one Matthias prayed would bless him.

"It was close," Nikki finally said, a smile creasing her dark, exotic features. "But she's alive, Matthias . . ."

TWO MONTHS LATER

"I told you to wear jeans." Grace was laughing at him, her gray eyes shining with happiness, as tears of mirth rolled down her cheeks. "Didn't I warn you to wear jeans?"

"Shut up, Grace," he growled, attempting to peel the wet leather from his legs as he stood in the middle of their bedroom, dripping from sweat and the pain. "Those brothers of yours are fucking insane," he snarled violently. "Have I ever mentioned they are fucking crazy?" His voice rose at the accusation.

She was laughing. She was standing in the middle of the floor, her arms across her stomach, and she bent over, struggling to breathe as she laughed at him.

She was barely healed from the wound she had taken the night the coyotes attacked them. It had been slow progress, until Dr. Armani had given her a transfusion of Matthias's blood. After that, her recovery had moved quickly. Although the blood they had given her in surgery saved her life, her body had attempted to reject it. The unique qualities of the hormones in her body had fought it, and fought her recovery, until Matthias's blood had been added to it.

It shouldn't have worked. Their blood types didn't match, and his Breed blood should have been an instant poison to her system. Instead, from the moment it was introduced, she had begun to heal.

Now, two months later, she was standing here laughing her ass off at him because he was coated with mud and grime and struggling to get his damned pants off.

"I told you, jeans," she reminded him, finally straightening. "Geeze, Matthias, you need a shower." Another peal of laughter left her, as a mud-sodden hunk of hair fell over his face.

He swiped it back and glared at her.

"Poor little wolfie," she crooned, as he kicked his pants free and stood before her, naked. And aroused. Horribly aroused. He had felt the mating heat returning in the past week, tormenting him with the need to possess her. To taste and touch her.

In the weeks since her surgery, as though her body recognized its need to heal, the heat had only been a slow simmer inside them both. Now it was blazing inside him, and the scent of her heat filled his head.

His lashes lowered, as he flicked a look over the shorts and T-shirt she wore.

"Shower with me." He moved toward her, his body tightening with hunger. He had been like this for days, and it was killing him. If he didn't touch her, take her, he would go insane.

Her tongue swiped over her lips, as she pushed her hair back from her face, sensuality marking her features.

Grace hadn't forgotten for a second what she had almost been taken from. Over the past two months she had made certain Matthias became an integral part of her family, so that, should the worst ever happen, he wouldn't be alone.

He fought her, of course. He knew what she was doing. But when she awoke in that hospital room, saw his pale, haggard features and his agonized whiskey eyes, she had known. Had she died, Matthias wouldn't have been long behind her. His soul was a part of hers. She wondered, even now, if either of them could survive without the other.

God she loved him.

She leaned against his damp, muddy chest, her eyes closing, as she felt the warmth of him surrounding her. She loved him like flowers loved the sunshine. They embraced it, drew in its heat, and basked in its approval. That's what she did with Matthias.

Her hands slid over his powerful forearms, as they enclosed her, his hands gripping the hem of her shirt and drawing it away from her body.

Tossing the material aside, his lips went instantly to the mark throbbing on her shoulder.

"Like the flowers love the sun," he whispered at her ear, echoing her thoughts. "That's how I love you, too, Grace. I can't survive without your warmth. Without your love."

She turned to him, her head tilting back, her lips accepting his, as his tongue swept into her mouth. Honey and spice. That was his taste, and she gloried in it. Her tongue wrapped around his, drew the hormone from the swollen glands beneath it, and she let the fire have her.

Kissing her, touching her, Matthias lifted her into his arms and carried her to the shower. He didn't take his lips from hers as he adjusted the water. He sipped at them, licked at them, shared his taste with her, then lifted her beneath the spray of the dual showerheads.

The glass doors closed behind them, wrapping them in steamy intimacy, as his hands coasted over her body. His lips moved down her neck, to her chest. Just beneath her collarbone, he licked the scars the bullet and subsequent surgery had left. They were still a little tender, but the stroke of his tongue was like the sunlight.

Grace lifted herself against him, her head tipping back, as water ran over her head, soaking her hair, running in rivulets over her face, down her neck, to his lips. Lips that were moving from the scar to her nipples.

He sucked the hard points inside his mouth, drew on them deeply, growled in pleasure as she rubbed her leg along his thigh. The tiny, nearly invisible hairs that grew there, soft as a whisper of silk, caressed her.

Her hands weren't still, and neither were his lips. As he sucked at her nipple, scraped it with his teeth, her head lifted to allow her lips to touch his brow. Her hands smoothed over his shoulders, over the bulge of his arms.

Warmth and pleasure filled her. Wicked, sharp pleasure that clenched her womb and had her breath catching with an overload of sensations.

She had missed this. She had missed his touch, his kiss, the heat of him flowing over her and through her, until she didn't know where he ended and she began. He was her dreams, her adventures. Her sunlight.

"Poor Grace," he whispered against her breast. "I can smell how hot you are, how sweet."

"So fix it," she demanded breathlessly, leaning back against the shower wall, as his tongue swiped between her breasts, followed by a hungry growl.

She loved that growl. A bit of a rumble, a latent vibration of pleasure. She could distinguish between the sounds. Matthias growled a lot. Especially when he reached the saturated, slick folds of her pussy.

"Oh God." He shuddered beneath her hands. He did that a lot, too. "I could eat you for hours. For days." His tongue licked through the narrow slit, circled her clit, and had her shuddering.

She was supposed to stand when he did this? When his tongue licked and stroked, and sent fingers of electric heat whipping through her?

"I don't think I can hold out that long," she panted, feeling the excess juices that gathered and built between her thighs.

She ached for him. Ached with a need that went beyond the heat that seared their hungers, one that went to her soul. She wanted him inside her again. She wanted that affirmation, that proof that they were alive.

"You don't have to hold out long, Grace," he groaned, his fingers parting the tender flesh as he tongued her clitoris.

Sensation raced from the bundle of nerves, struck her womb, clenched it, and sent her arching, tilting her hips closer, as the need for orgasm began to thunder through her. She was desperate. Didn't he know she was crazy for this now?

"It's been too long," she cried out, as she felt his fingers fill her rather than the thick length of his cock.

It was good. It was wickedly good, the feel of his fingers caressing her inside, parting her pussy and rubbing against sensitive nerve endings. But it wasn't enough. It wasn't what she hungered for.

Even as his fingers slid deep inside her sex, flexed and stroked the tender tissue, she was begging for more. His tongue licked around her clit, tightening it with agonizing need, as the nerve endings pounded with the need for release.

He nuzzled his lips against it, drew it inside his mouth, and suckled her with firm heat and disastrous results. Grace exploded in pleasure, the clitoral orgasm whipping through her, jerking her muscles tighter, and causing her nails to bite into his shoulders, as he rose before her.

The violent contractions of release were still thundering through her body, when he gripped the backs of her thighs and lifted her.

Grace curled her legs around his hips on instinct, forcing her eyes open to watch him in drowsy pleasure, as he tucked the head of his cock against the mouth of her vagina.

"I love you," he groaned raggedly, as he began to press inside her, the silky preseminal fluid filling her, sensitizing her further. "Like the flower loves the sun, the earth loves the rain. You're my life, Grace Anderson Slaughter."

She felt her heart melt for him all over again. That happened at least a dozen times a day, and it was always fresh, always new.

"I love you," she gasped, as he continued to slide inside her, stretching her, parting her, burning her. "You're my soul, Matthias. My sun and my rain." Her back arched, as he seated his erection fully inside her.

Grace felt her muscles flexing, tightening around the width of his cock, and sending brilliant shards of exquisite pleasure racing through her. They raked her nerve endings, embedded her soul, and whipped through every cell of her body.

Words weren't needed now, only gasping cries of pleasure and the hard thrusts and acceptance of the heat burning through them. His cock shuttled inside her hard and deep in luscious strokes. Grace twisted in his grip, taking him, stroking him, tightening on the hard, heavy length of his cock, as she began to tremble in his arms.

She could feel her orgasm coming now. It was tightening in her womb, through her muscles. Her clit was distended, her nipples hard and aching, as they raked against his chest. She was on fire. Burning. Sweating, despite the water rolling over them, and exploding in his arms as she screamed out his name.

His release followed. The thickening in the center of his cock spread across her sensitive pelvic floor muscle, causing it to spasm and contract, to milk tighter at his flesh, as a snarl of pleasure left his lips. The additional swelling didn't affect the entire length of his cock, just that one portion, the section that aligned just above the delicate vaginal muscle, effectively locking him inside her.

The blast of his semen inside her triggered another orgasm, not as fierce or as hard. This one was gentler, easing through her rather than exploding over her nerve endings.

As it ended, Grace found herself still pressed against the shower wall, as Matthias trembled against her. Cool water sprayed over their overheated bodies, washing away the perspiration that would have coated them, but doing little to still the heat that had raged through their bodies.

Her hands stroked his shoulders, her lips pressed against his neck. Grace held him to her, absorbing the hard spasms that gripped his muscles with each spurt of his release.

With each eruption, the hard swelling inside her throbbed, pulsed, and sent tremors of response racing through her. Like mini-orgasms clenching her womb. With each spasm, she tightened on that thick swelling, causing another pulse of his release to blast inside her. Causing him to shudder and groan in her arms.

"This . . . this is ecstasy," he whispered at her ear. "This, Grace, is home."

She felt tears fill her eyes. *Home.* Matthias finally had a home, and it was her. She buried her head against his broad shoulder and thanked God for the Breed that had found her.

"That was worth waiting for," she panted minutes later, as the swelling of his cock receded and he slid out of her, groaning.

"I couldn't handle having to wait like that again," he informed her, his breathing hard and heavy, as he lifted his hand and touched the scar on her chest. "Never again, Grace."

Her hand covered his. "I'll always be a part of you, Matthias. No matter what. Just as you'll always be a part of me."

He shook his head. "I took a job at the hotel. I'm head of security. You're assistant manager, and I have every assurance you'll be promoted to manager before much longer. We're going to live nice, sedate lives from now on. Do you understand me?"

He looked so arrogant. So dominant.

Grace grinned. "I still get to climb trees."

A
Jaguar's Kiss

◆ ◆ ◆

For Natalie.

For your friendship, your willingness to listen,
and your patience in the face of so many
different versions of one story.

But most of all, just for being you.

They were created, they weren't born. They were trained, they weren't raised.

They were taught to kill, and now they'll use their training to ensure their freedom.

They are Breeds. Genetically altered with the DNA of the predators of the earth. The wolf, the lion, the cougar, the Bengal: the killers of the world. They were to be the army of a fanatical society intent on building their own personal army.

Until the world learned of their existence. Until the Council lost control of their creations, and their creations began to change the world.

Now, they're loose. Banding together, creating their own communities, their own society, and their own safety, and fighting to hide the one secret that could see them destroyed.

The secret of mating heat. The chemical, the biological, the emotional reaction of one Breed to the man or woman meant to be his or hers forever. A reaction that binds physically. A reaction that alters more than just the physical responses or heightens the sensuality. Nature has turned mating heat into the Breeds' Achilles' heel. It's their strength, and yet their weakness. And Mother Nature isn't finished playing yet.

Man has attempted to mess with her creations. Now, she's going to show man exactly how she can refine them.

Killers will become lovers, lawyers, statesmen, and heroes. And through it all, they will cleave to one mate, one heart, and create a dynasty.

· PROLOGUE ·

Natalie Ricci stared at the tall, imposing figure standing on her doorstep and reminded herself to breathe. A woman who fainted over a dark, arrogant, exceptionally handsome man deserved whatever happened to her while she was out cold. And anything this man did, she would want to be awake for.

"Can I help you?" She brushed back the dark bangs that grew over her forehead and tried to restrain the nervous jitter playing patty-cake in her stomach. Tall, dark, and handsome was good, real good, but that gleam of powerful male assurance in his eyes warned her this man would be impossible for any woman to ever comfortably control.

"Natalie Ricci?" Even his voice was worth shivering for.

There was no discernible accent, and she was fairly good at identifying accents. His voice was well modulated, perfectly pitched, and stroked over her senses like black velvet.

Black hair, thick and lustrous, was pulled back from his face and bound at the back of his neck. His fallen angel features were composed, almost emotionless, but those eyes, eyes like emeralds, gleamed with intelligence, sensuality, and a spark of primal intensity from within his sun-bronzed face.

There were shadows in those eyes as well. A latent, hidden pain that a part of her, the feminine, caring side of her that she wished she could ignore, longed to ease.

Dark jeans cinched low on leanly muscled hips while a dark blue chambray shirt stretched across his powerful chest. And he wore boots. Well-worn, scarred, and totally masculine boots.

"I'm Natalie Ricci." She had to clear her throat to answer him, had to tighten her stomach to stop the little flutters of longing that attacked her womb.

Whew, if ever there was a man to tempt her hard-won self-control, she was betting it would be this one. What he was doing on her doorstep she had no idea, but whatever he was selling, she was certain she was ready to buy. Empty bank account notwithstanding.

It was really too bad, too. She had sworn off men. Until she could figure out how to play the game, how to protect her heart and her independence, then men were out.

As luscious and sexual as this man looked, she had a feeling he would be just as controlling, domineering, and arrogant as any man born. Probably worse than most. Definitely more than her ex-husband, whose control tendencies had managed to destroy their marriage.

"Can I help you?" she asked again, wishing she had worn something other than old faded jeans and her brother's too-big, paint-spattered T-shirt.

He inhaled slowly, as though he had caught the scent of something that intrigued him.

"Ms. Ricci, I'm Saban Broussard, liaison to the Breed Ruling Cabinet. I'm here to discuss your application to teach in Buffalo Gap." He pulled the slender identification wallet from the back of his jeans and flipped it open. The Breed law enforcement badge, his photo, and pertinent information were all displayed.

She froze in shock. Well, shock and the sound of his name, or the way he said his name, Saban, a soft little sigh of the *S*, the subtle *a*, and the *bahn* at the end. But what caught her, what had her senses standing to complete attention, was the vaguest hint of a Cajun accent in his voice after her certainty that there had been no accent.

If he was Cajun, she was just lost. If there was any sexier accent created, then she couldn't think of it at the moment.

It took several breathless seconds for her senses to stop reeling, to focus on who he was and where he was from. When she did, her eyes widened in shock.

"Did I get the position?"

She wanted that position with a desperation that had left her shaking when she filled out the application more than a year ago. She had known, had been warned that there were thousands upon thousands of applicants on the waiting list for a teaching position in the small town just outside the Breed headquarters of Sanctuary.

She had taken the chance, filled out the application, and sent it in, praying. She had prayed for months, and when nothing came of it, she settled back into her own routine and tried to make other plans.

"May we speak inside, Miss Ricci?" Saban Broussard turned his head, stared along the tree-lined street, and lifted his brow at the residents that had managed to find one reason or another to come to their porches or to work on their lawns. She should just charge admission and have done with it.

She bit her lip, knowing the questions that would be coming before the hour was out.

"Come in." She stood back, holding the door open and allowing him to step inside the house.

He brought the scent of the mountains with him, wild and untamed, dark and dangerous.

"Thank you." He nodded as she led the way into the small kitchen off her living room.

The living room was almost empty, filled with taped boxes rather than furniture as Natalie packed her belongings.

"Have you already taken another position?" He stopped in the center of her kitchen and stared at the boxes there.

She shook her head. "I haven't. Simply moving to an apartment closer to the school where I currently work. My ex-husband gets the house and all its glorious payments. I get an apartment." And hopefully a little peace.

He stared around the kitchen again, his jaw bunching before turning back to her.

"I was sent to inform you of the opening of the position and to escort you to a meeting with our pride leader, Callan Lyons," he said then. "I'll then stay to help you get things in order before escorting you to Buffalo Gap."

She really needed to sit down, but she had given the table and chairs to a distant cousin that had recently made the monumental mistake of getting married.

"How did I get the position?" She shook her head in confusion. "I was told there were thousands of applicants just waiting for one to open."

His lips quirked. "I believe the pride leader, Callan Lyons, stated it was close to forty thousand applicants. You hit the short list on the first stage of the selection process and managed to gain the position by what I'm told was a very long, tedious, and exacting investigation into the backgrounds of those on that list. Congratulations, Miss Ricci. You'll be the first teacher hired in the county in close to seven years."

Natalie blinked back at him. He stood confidently, his arms held loosely at his sides, his eyes seeming to take in everything as she stared back at him, certain she must look like a complete lunatic.

"How soon can you be ready to leave?" He stared around the house once again. "Callan Lyons of the Breed Ruling Cabinet will be flying into the capital, Columbia, tomorrow evening, if this is convenient for you, to outline the position and discuss the specifics of the job, though we do need to arrive ahead of him to complete other matters and sign the endless forms, contracts, and so forth that will go with the job."

Natalie shook her head in confusion. "I thought the Breeds didn't interfere in Buffalo Gap? I heard that somewhere. Wouldn't I be meeting with someone from the Board of Education instead?"

"Not if you're being hired to teach Breed children. Those children are very well protected, and any hiring done in that regard comes under the sanction of the Breed Ruling Cabinet. Until that decision was made, the Board of Education has allowed the Breed Ruling Cabinet to select any additional staff required." He tilted his head and watched as she gripped the small bar she stood beside to keep herself from falling. "You are still interested in the job, are you not?"

She nodded slowly. "Oh yeah," she assured him. "I would say that's an understatement."

"Very well. I was hoping we could make arrangements to leave for Columbia this afternoon, if possible?" He stared around the kitchen, his gaze touching on the boxes. "Sanctuary's heli-jet is waiting on the private airfield outside of town to escort us there. Is that agreeable—"

His words broke off at the sound of the front door slamming open, hitting the wall in the small foyer she had led Saban Broussard through and echoing through the near-empty house.

Before she could do more than gasp, she was pushed behind the bar and within a blink Saban was across the room, weapon drawn from somewhere as he slammed her ex-husband's body against the wall and jammed the muzzle of his weapon beneath Mike Claxton's jaw.

Mike's pale blue eyes widened as his face blanched in terror. Saban's lips were drawn back in a snarl, lethal canines flashing as a growl rumbled in his throat.

"Call him off," Mike gasped, his gaze latching on Natalie in desperation as he wheezed out the plea.

"For God's sake, let him go!" Natalie stalked across the room, glaring at the Breed. Obviously a Breed. Only they had the unique, terrifying, wickedly powerful canines such as this one had. "He's not dangerous, he's just stupid. Dammit, do I have to be plagued with stupid males?"

Saban drew his weapon back, but only reluctantly. He wanted to pull the trigger. He wanted to rip the bastard's neck out and watch him bleed, taste his blood, feel the terror that filled him as he knew death was coming.

Because his scent was in this house and to a small extent, lingered around the woman. The reaction was an anomaly. It wasn't a part of who or what he was. He cared for no woman, and he certainly didn't care which male touched them. Until this one, this Natalie Ricci, whose brother called her Gnat. Whose mother laughed at her childhood antics with loving amusement.

Until this woman, Saban had never known a time when he would have killed a man over his possession of a female. But this one, he knew he would kill man or beast over her.

The possessiveness had grown over the past weeks, during his surveillance of her. He had seen her on her back porch shedding tears after this bastard had stalked from her home. He had heard the screaming, stood outside her back door and prayed for the control to restrain the violence that rose inside him.

Brown-haired, weak, full of his own self-importance, Mike Claxton had no business near Saban's Natalie, no reason to breathe her air, to be here in this house, as she attempted to leave the home he had stolen from her in the divorce.

"Let him go before I kick you both out of the house and end up costing myself a job I wanted. You won't like me much if I have to do that."

Saban glanced at her from the corner of his eye, aware of the weak-minded fool gasping for air, his hands clawing at Saban's wrists as he was held securely to the wall.

The feminine ire, frustration, and promise of retribution filled her gaze and did something Council soldiers, scientists, or rabid Coyote assassins couldn't do. It caused a small core of wariness inside him to awaken.

If he was going to charm her, tempt her, and steal her heart, then starting out with her upset with him, possibly frightened of him, may not be the wisest course of action.

She looked furious and fierce, eyes the color of molasses, dark and gold swirling together as she glared up at him, demanding the release of a man whose scent of dishonor was cloying and offensive.

He released Claxton slowly, uncertain why he did so when he wanted nothing more than to crush him, and reluctantly holstered his weapon.

"Consider it your lucky day," he told the other man as he collapsed against the wall, fighting for breath. "I'd leave if I were you. I'm not known for mercy or for my patience where fools are concerned. The next time you enter her home, I would suggest knocking."

"You know," Natalie commented, her tone stern and perhaps just the slightest bit concerned, "I have a feeling you and I are not going to get along if this is your normal attitude."

Saban smiled. A flash of canines, the expression of innocence he had seen other males adopt around their mates when they had managed to test their women's patience.

"We'll get along fine, *cher*," he assured her before turning, locking his gaze with Claxton's, and praying the other man read the silent warning there. "This one, though, he may have cause to worry."

"Natalie, what is this?" Claxton massaged his throat as he glared at Saban.

There was fear in his eyes though, and Saban let himself be

content with that for now. Maybe later, he told himself, perhaps once he'd secured his place in Natalie's heart, then he would take care of this bastard.

"This is Saban Broussard," she bit out as she moved away from both of them and went to the counter across the room to pour herself a cup of coffee.

He could feel the anger pouring from her now, the uncertainty, and he flashed Claxton another hard look before letting a hard growl rumble in his throat. Because of this son of a bitch, she was mad at him, and if Claxton weren't very careful, Saban would take it out of his hide.

He was satisfied to see Claxton pale further, but when his gaze slid to Natalie, he nearly paled himself.

What an interesting reaction. Saban felt the clench of his chest, the awakening knowledge that he cared if this woman were upset with him. And she was very upset with him.

"He's a Breed enforcer, if you haven't guessed," she snorted, a cute little feminine sound that he found he liked. "He's here to escort me to meet with members of the Breed Ruling Cabinet. I've accepted a job with them."

Ah. Saban's gaze slashed to Claxton as fury, rich and satisfying, poured from the man. Perhaps this fool would give him the reason he needed to slash his throat after all.

Evidently he was doomed to disappointment. Claxton narrowed his eyes, his lips thinned, and his weak hands tugged at the polo shirt he wore, but he made no move toward Natalie.

She moved to the end of the bar with her coffee, leaned her hip against it, and regarded both of them rather curiously as she sipped from her cup.

Was she weighing the differences between them or seeing similarities? There were no similarities, Saban decided. Better she see that now rather than later.

"We need to be going," he told her. "I arrived in time for you to contact Sanctuary or your local law enforcement for confirmation of my assignment and the arrangements that were made to transport you to Columbia. We're running out of time."

She sipped at the coffee again, her gaze going between the two of them.

"I can't just run out of the house with you, Mr. Broussard. Even Callan Lyons should know that. I do intend to contact Sanctuary as well as the police department, my parents, and the principal of the school that I've been teaching in. I'll then shower, dress, pack, and get ready to go. That won't be accomplished in a matter of minutes."

His body tightened; lust slammed through every bone and muscle that comprised it as he stared at the defiance in her eyes. When was the last time anyone had dared to defy him, to make him wait?

"I'm not leaving you here alone with him," Claxton snapped, but there was very little heat in his voice.

Saban slid his gaze to the other man. "Bet me," he murmured, letting his gaze meet the pale blue orbs and allowing the lust that fired his body to gleam in them.

Better this bastard knew up front that Saban intended to claim what the other man had so carelessly thrown away. Some men were just smarter than others, it appeared.

"Bet me." Natalie's cup struck the counter, jerking Saban's gaze back to her.

She didn't bother to shoot Claxton that gleam of anger burning in her eyes, but Saban felt it clear to the soles of his feet. It made him horny. Made him want to show her exactly who she would belong to, who would control all that fire and passion inside her.

But that wasn't going to happen if he let her remain angry with him.

What had those dating books said? The ones little Cassie Sinclair had heaped on him the year before? Charm, soft words, praise, and the ability to compromise would show a woman his innate ability to please her on both the emotional as well as the mental level.

He could do this.

"Cher." He let the soft breath of his accent free and tried to keep from strutting as her eyes widened, her face flushed, and a hint of aroused heat flowed from her body. "I apologize for this. He came in threatening." Explaining himself nearly had him clenching his teeth in irritation. "I thought he had come to harm you or perhaps even myself. I am a Breed." He shrugged, knowing it was self-explanatory; Breeds were attacked on a daily basis. "My only thought was to protect you and myself as well." He smiled at Claxton. All teeth, sharp canines and the male promise of future payment. "Pardon my reaction to your entrance, but perhaps you should have knocked first."

Silence filled the kitchen for long moments.

"And here I thought my day couldn't get worse," he heard Natalie mutter then. "I was so wrong."

Years before, Natalie could have sworn there was no one harder to get along with than her brother. Ill-tempered, overbearing, and certain of his place in their mother's affection, he had tortured her. Tormented her. Pulled her hair, hid her dolls, flushed her goldfish, and generally kept her in a state of distress.

She was of a mind to forgive him now, because she had found someone more overbearing, more ill-tempered, and much, much harder to get along with.

So would someone tell her, please, why she could feel herself being charmed rather than irritated? Why it was becoming so damned hard to maintain her distance and not smirk at his antics?

She was pissed, she told herself. It was all a game—she could feel it, sense it—but his efforts to get her attention were beginning to draw much more than her interest. She was beginning to like him. No, not just like him, and that was the scary part.

She'd been in Buffalo Gap less than two months, and she had tried, she knew she had tried not to be charmed with the arrogant, conceited, smirking Jaguar Breed that Jonas Wyatt had saddled her with, but God help her, it was getting harder by the day.

She should be angry with him, because to tell the truth, there were times she just didn't know what to do with him.

Such as the time he had followed her to the doctor. Had he stayed in the waiting room? Of course not; he had tried to breach the examination rooms. Had become so threatening that Natalie had been forced to ask the nurse to allow him to stand in the hallway.

Not so much because of his protective determination to be there, but because of his eyes. She almost sighed at the thought of that. The shadows in his eyes had been bleak, and Natalie knew if she had forced him outside the doctor's office entirely, then the animal DNA that had somehow decided she needed protecting would have pushed them both over a line they were delicately balancing on, even then.

It was distracting though, even a little embarassing. Even her ex-husband hadn't attempted anything so forward as to try to horn in on her examinations.

That had just been the first week. The first week. It had been one frustrating episode after another.

She understood that they were still acclimating themselves to the world. She really did. It had to be hard, even now, ten years after the Breeds were first discovered and adopted by America and all its enemies and allies. They were the unknown element in the world now, a different species, kind of like aliens. There was speculation, rumor, prejudice, and pure human spite. It couldn't be easy functioning normally. But this . . . this was impossible.

She needed groceries, but after less than ten minutes in the store, she was ready to leave her cart sitting, the Breed standing, and forget about eating. He had her hormones racing in arousal and her frustration level rising as she fought to ignore his surprisingly endearing antics.

"I believe you need more meat," he whispered from behind her, his voice suggestive as he leaned toward the cooler and picked up the thick, rolled roast from inside. "This one looks promising." He held the meat up for display, and she felt her face flame as the butcher smirked at her from behind the cold display case.

Natalie jerked the roast out of his hand, thumped it in her cart, and kept going.

"*Boo*, surely you aren't gonna continue in this silent campaign," he sighed behind her. She could hear the amusement, wicked and insidious, vibrating in his voice as thick as his accent. His Cajun accent.

She really wished he wouldn't call her *boo* or *cher* or *chay* or *petite bébé*. He could call her by her name, just once, couldn't he? So her heart wouldn't thump so hard in excitement.

Except, the few times he had, the syllables had rolled off his tongue like a caress and sent a shiver spiking through her body. And she liked that too damned much.

She continued through the aisle, picked up milk and eggs, a package of processed cheese, then watched as he picked up a package of Monterey Jack. She managed to glare over her shoulder at him.

"I've never tried it," he said softly, suggestively. "But I've heard it's quite good."

Saban Broussard was wickedly handsome. Too damned handsome for his own good with his long, black hair, gleaming emerald green eyes, and patrician features. He looked wild and wicked, and he was irritating, frustrating, and driving her insane.

He refused to give her a moment's peace, and Jonas Wyatt, the director of Breed Affairs, flat-out refused to give her a different bodyguard.

Not that she had really tried too hard for that one. She restrained her sigh of self-disgust. She kept putting off forcing the issue, afraid she would miss him if he was gone. Even if he was driving her crazy, there was something about him that drew her. And she hated that part the worst. She could have handled the rest if she could be assured that she could handle the forceful personality she knew he was holding back.

As the first teacher for Breeds in a public school, Jonas said he considered her a resource and a liability, so he gave her the best to protect her.

A Jaguar Breed. A Cajun who had been buried in the swamps for most of his life, a Jaguar that he had promised was as antisocial as any Breed living. She wouldn't even know he was around.

Fat chance.

"You shouldn't eat that." He took the TV dinner that she had picked up out of her hand and replaced it in the freezer. "Fresh meat is much better for you."

Her teeth clenched tighter as a young mother giggled across the aisle, and her dimple-cheeked baby waved shyly at Saban. Evidently, he was social. The young mother blushed prettily, and the little girl's smile widened as Natalie jerked the dinner back from the shelf and plopped it in her cart before moving on.

This wasn't going to work. She was going to end up jumping his bones, and if she did that, she might as well shoot herself. Why wait for those sneaky Council soldiers she was told still lurked in the shadows? She'd take care of it herself.

"That boxed food will give you a heart attack before you're forty," he murmured as he followed her. "Are you always so stubborn?"

She clamped her lips tight and moved on.

All she wanted to do was buy some groceries, go about her business in relaxed comfort, and get ready for the coming school year. She didn't want to deal with a Breed who didn't have an antisocial bone in his tall, hard, handsome, too-damned-arrogant body and made her heart race, her lips tingle for a kiss, and her thighs weaken in need.

"You are going to hurt my feelings, *boo*, if you keep refusing to talk to me." He sighed as she moved into the checkout lane and began lifting her purchases to the counter.

He moved to her side and began taking items out of her hand and placing them himself with an amused quirk to his lips and laughter gleaming in his dark green eyes.

That laughter was almost impossible to ignore. Bodyguards were to be seen, not heard, she told herself.

Who could have known that the normally taciturn, sober, somber, *quiet* Breeds could have a complete anomaly in their midst? This Breed was a maniac. He drove a twenty-year-old four-by-four black pickup that sounded like a monster growling. She couldn't even step in it by herself for God's sake.

He flirted. He cooked food so spicy hot the fire department should be put on call, and he watched cartoons. He didn't watch action movies or the news, hated the world events channel, and flat-out refused to watch any of the documentaries concerning the Breed creation.

If he wasn't watching cartoons, he was watching history or baseball. He watched baseball with such complete absorption that she wondered if he would notice a Council soldier walking in front of him.

He was taking up more room than her ex-husband had and invading her life more fully. It was going to have to stop before she lost her heart.

As her cart emptied, she moved forward, paid for her purchases, and smiled at the young man bagging and loading them back into the cart. That smile froze on her face as she heard a growl behind her. The lanky young man loading the bags paled, fumbled the bag that held her eggs, and swallowed tightly, his Adam's apple bobbing in his throat.

Yeah, that was something else he did. He growled. He growled at the delivery guy, he growled at the mailman, and he actually snarled when one of the other Breed males had stopped to talk to her while she was in a department store in town.

Natalie wiped her hand over her face and took her cart after paying for her purchases. She stalked outside to her car, fury pumping through her system.

This was supposed to have been an independent move. Away

from friends and family and her ex-husband. Away from precon-
ceived notions of who or what she should be so she could just be
herself for a change. Instead, she was babysitting a snarly Breed male
who made zero sense to her and threatened to invade her heart as
well as her life.

"Here, *boo*, let me." He took the keys from her hand as she pulled
them from her purse and moved to open the back of the compact
SUV the Breed Ruling Cabinet had given her to drive while employed
to teach their children.

She was the first teacher to be allowed to teach Breed children
who wasn't a Breed. This was also the first year a Breed child had
been allowed in a public school. And she was going to have a nervous
breakdown before the news of it ever hit the world.

"I'll follow you back to the house. I have one of those barbecue
grills that I saw on television the other day. I could fix steaks tonight."
He gave her a mocking yet hopeful look.

"You didn't buy steaks." She broke her silence, it was just too
much. A Breed who was going to grill steaks, and he hadn't even
bought any.

He smiled, satisfaction curving lips that were too damned eatable for her peace of mind. She wanted to take a bite out of them.
Taste them. Devour them. And there wasn't a chance in hell she was
going to allow that to happen.

"They're in the cooler in the truck." He nodded to the black behe-
moth parked beside her little dove gray front-wheel-drive SUV. It
gleamed, black and sinister. She almost smiled, almost softened.

Natalie shook her head, jerked her keys from his hand, and
stalked to the driver's door of her own vehicle. She hit the lock release
on the key and pulled the door open before stepping into the swelter-
ing confines of the interior.

She didn't check to see where he was; checking meant she cared,
and she wasn't giving in to it. She drove back to the little two-story

house just outside town, pulled into the driveway, and stormed to the house. She didn't bother with the groceries; he was just going to beat her to them anyway.

Instead, she left the door open and entered the house, aware of the disapproval that followed her inside. She wasn't supposed to enter the house without him; she wasn't supposed to breathe without him testing the air first; and by God, she was not supposed to melt inside because he did it with such subtle moves that she felt cuddled rather than smothered.

"*Chay*, you and I are gonna have a talk." Just as she suspected, he stomped into the house, six feet four inches of irritated male, decked out in denim and boots as he plopped the groceries on the table.

Natalie stared at the bags and wondered if her eggs had a hope in hell of having survived intact. Anger surged inside her, but it was at herself more than at him. Anger that she was letting another man close, risking her heart and her independence on a man she knew would be impossible to get out of her system.

"You know," she finally said carefully, "I do have a name."

She lifted her gaze to him, adopting her most severe expression. The one she reserved for the most difficult of children. And it didn't even seem to faze him.

He glowered down at her, his head bent, his shoulder-length, straight black hair falling around the face of a fallen angel. Green eyes glittered with sparks of irritation, and his expression was too damned sensual to be scary in anything but the most primal of ways.

Oh yeah, Saban Broussard terrified her. She was scared to death she was going to lose control and jump his bones one night when he was parading half-naked around her house. Wouldn't that look good on her résumé?

"I know your name, *boo*," he growled. "As well I know who your bodyguard is. Me. You do not run from me like a scared little rabbit scurrying from sight. I won't have it."

"You won't have it?" She widened her eyes in amazement. "Excuse me, Mr. Broussard, but you do not have a leash around my neck or ownership papers with my name on them. I do as I please."

"You do not." His head lowered, his nose nearly touching her, as anger sparked inside her like wildfire flaring out of control.

Her hands pushed out, flattening against his chest and trying to push him back. Trying, because he wasn't budging an inch.

"You're fired," she snapped.

"You can't fire me; you can only quit." He smirked. "Until that time you will obey the precautions made for your safety, or you will deal with me."

"I'm just real scared of you!" Her hands went to her hips, her lips flattened. "What are you going to do, growl me to death? Make me watch baseball until my eyes fall out of my head? Oh no, wait, you're going to take all my TV dinners." Mock fear rounded her eyes. "Oh, Saban, I'm so scared. Please don't."

He growled. It wasn't a hard vibration of sound, rather a subtle rumble that had the more cautious part of her brain urging wariness. And she might have paid attention if she weren't so damned mad.

"You are in my way." She lifted herself until her nose touched his. "Get out of it."

His expression changed then, shifted. His eyes narrowed, and the savage, remorseless determination she'd heard all Breeds possessed flashed in his eyes.

She should have run then and there. She should have turned tail and run as fast as those rabbits he'd mentioned earlier.

The minute his hands latched on her upper arms, the second she realized his intention and his head lowered, she should have slammed her knee into his groin and had done with it.

If she'd had time.

Between one second and the next his lips covered hers, his tongue pushed between her lips as they parted in surprise, and oh hell in a handbasket, she was lost.

Those eatable, kissable lips were devouring hers. His tongue stroked inside her mouth as the taste of heated spice filled her senses.

His kiss had a taste. Not the normal tastes a kiss had, but the taste of a wild promise, a desert afternoon, heated and filled with mystery and hunger.

Natalie found herself melting against him. She shivered. That hard, luscious body braced her weight as his hands cupped her rear and lifted her closer. His head slanted, the kiss grew deeper, a hard growl rasping his throat as she let her lips surround his probing tongue, and she sought more of his taste.

It was there, each time she caressed the tongue twining with hers, subtle, urging her to consume more, to hold him closer, to devour this kiss.

And it terrified her. She felt her independence, hard-won and imperative, fighting beneath the claiming she could feel coming, screaming out in warning until she jerked back, struggled, stumbled from his grip as she stared back at him, panting from the need suddenly tearing through her.

She lifted her hand, touched his lips. Lips that mesmerized her, left her aching, a miracle of pleasure, just as she had known they would be.

"You're mine." There was no sexy teasing in his voice, no flirty seductiveness. His dark eyes glittered with predatory awareness and with triumph.

Her hand dropped away from him.

"You're insane," she gasped.

"Mine."

· C H A P T E R 2 ·

Saban watched as Natalie's eyes grew wider, a hint of fear flashing in the molasses depths, mixing with the anger and the arousal.

He knew what he had done. Knew he had spilled the potent mating hormone to her system in that kiss, and he knew he should feel guilty. He should feel remorse pounding through his head rather than satisfaction.

"You feel it now, don't you, Natalie." He drew her name out, tasted it on his tongue and relished the sound of it.

He had kept himself from using it, held it back, knowing he couldn't say it without the breath of ownership in his tone, as it was now.

And she heard it, as he had always known she would.

"I feel your insanity." She moved quickly away from him, wariness tightening her body.

Saban watched her, letting his gaze track each movement as he inhaled the scent of her, tasted her against his tongue. He could still taste her; beneath the taste of the mating hormone was the taste of her passion, of the needs she kept tightly bottled inside her and the battle she waged to hold it all in.

His Natalie, as intelligent as she was, as softly rounded and sensual as the feminine core of her was, was disillusioned, hurt, all because of one weak-minded, inept man that hadn't the good sense to see the gift God had given him.

And now he faced that woman, knowing he had committed the ultimate crime in her eyes once she learned what that kiss actually meant. He had taken her choice from her. He had begun something which tied her irrevocably to him and thereby took away the control she so highly revered.

"I'm not insane," he finally sighed. "At least no longer." He swiped his hands through his loose hair and stared around the kitchen.

Damn, he should have known better than to listen to Cassie and her lectures on women who did not possess Breed DNA. He had taken advice from an eighteen-year-old, had seriously considered every word she had said, and now he'd pay for it.

"What do you mean? No longer?" Her eyes were narrowed, and her body was burning.

The sweet, spicy scent of her desire wrapped around his senses and had him clenching his teeth at the need to taste it, to taste her.

"What I mean doesn't matter now." Saban rubbed at the back of his neck before lowering his hand and staring back at her.

She had the width of the kitchen between them, the scent of her coffee mixed with the soft fragrance of the apple pie she had baked yesterday morning and the scent of the woman herself. It was as powerful an aphrodisiac as the mating hormone.

She watched him closely, perhaps too closely. He could see her mind working, see her sorting out the odd heat that came from his kiss, the taste of the hormone in her mouth and her need for more. And he watched as she began to suspect the truth.

His chest actually ached, and regret shimmered in his soul as his Natalie swallowed tightly, and her eyes darkened.

"The tabloids aren't all bullshit, are they?" she whispered. "There is some kind of virus that you spread with a kiss."

Saban snorted at the simplicity of the statement.

"The tabloids are the ones who are insane." He shifted his shoulders, uncharacteristically nervous in the face of this explanation.

"It's called mating heat," he finally said softly, wishing he was holding her, that he had just taken her, that he had bound her to him more fully before he had to explain this. "There's no explanation for it, and so far, it seems it happens only once. Only one woman was meant to be my mate, and that woman is you."

She crossed her arms over her breasts, her lips pouting with instant denial, though she only said, simply, "Go on."

Go on. Hell, he was no good at this.

"Simply put, you are my mate. The mating hormone ensures that you won't deny me or my claim instantly. It's rather like an aphrodisiac. Like an addictive aphrodisiac."

Her lips flattened. "It's not a sickness? A virus?"

"You will not become ill," he snapped, more to distract her from this line of questioning than for any other reason. "Merely aroused. Very aroused." *Damn.* He growled that last word, his anticipation thickening in his voice as he felt the need inside him burning hotter than before, flaming across his nerve endings.

She was his. She may as well resign herself to this now. He would give her as much explanation as he had been cleared to give, but no more.

"And if it's not what I want?" Slow and precise, the words dripped from her lips like a death knell. He was very certain this was not what she wanted. And in ways, he couldn't blame her, but unlike those who did not carry the Breed DNA, Saban had a very healthy respect for Nature and all her choices.

"Once the heat begins, it can't be reversed." It could be eased, but he didn't have to tell her that yet. There were many things he couldn't tell her yet.

"So anyone you kiss—"

"No! Only my mate. Only one woman, Natalie, only you."

"I knew this was a bad idea!"

Saban almost jumped back at the sharp, furious words and the sparks that lit her molasses eyes.

"What was a bad idea?" he asked carefully.

His senses were already prime to claim her, his teeth ached to mark her, and she stood, her angry, defiant, slender hands propping on her hips as her expression became outraged.

"Letting you stay here. Listening to that insufferable, arrogant Jonas Wyatt, and allowing, for even one second, for your impossible, frustrating, completely insane ass to stay here." Her voice rose, but it was the flush on her face, the scent of heat, both anger and arousal that whipped through the room that held him mesmerized.

She was like a flame burning with incandescent beauty; even her dark, nearly black hair became brighter, shinier.

Damn, there went his chest, clenching again, those emotions he hadn't yet figured out rioting through his system.

"So it would appear you were right." He inclined his head in agreement. "But I wouldn't have left, and Jonas knew it. Now, we can deal with this."

"Deal with this?" Her brows arched in angry mockery. "Oh Saban, we're going to deal with this all right. Right now."

She stomped to the phone, jerked it off its base, and her finger stabbed at the button programmed to ring in Callan Lyons's main office.

Saban frowned. "Callan has nothing to do with this."

The look she flashed him would have silenced a lesser man. Hell, it almost silenced him.

"Mr. Lyons." Her voice was sugary sweet and lifted every hair on the back of Saban's neck. He could only imagine Lyons's expression and the frustration that would be twisting his savagely hewed features.

"Oh yes, we do have a problem," she said politely, her smile tight. "You're going to have a dead Breed in, oh, I'd give him twenty minutes, if someone from Sanctuary doesn't pick him up. I do believe he's rabid. Someone needs to save him, or I'm going to put him out of his misery."

As she listened, the sides of her nose began to twitch, and Saban had to restrain his grimace.

"I don't care if Coyotes are swarming Sanctuary with grenade launchers. Get some of those badass Breeds you prize so highly out here to collect him, or I'm going to kill him. And after I kill him, I'll hang his mangy, worthless hide in my front yard to show everyone else exactly how it's done. Twenty minutes." She slammed the phone down.

"One of your handlers will be here to pick you up soon. Don't let the door hit you in the ass, and don't find yourself anywhere near me after that."

She stalked across the kitchen, her pert little nose in the air, her face set in lines of rejection, denial, and fury.

His mate was denying him. Not that he had expected anything less, but with a spirit as strong as his Natalie's was, there was only one way to combat it.

He caught her as she attempted to brush past him, swung her around, surrounded her with his arms, and before more than a gasp could pass her lips, he had them in a kiss.

His arms tightened around her, lifted her, bore her through the doorway until he was able to find the couch and fall into it, one hand cupping the back of her head and holding her lips to his.

She wasn't fighting it.

She was furious, enraged, but she wasn't fighting his kiss. Her greedy lips were suckling at his tongue, and it was heaven. Her hands were in his hair, twining in it, tangling in it, and pulling him closer as a ragged female sound of hunger tore through his senses.

She was like a flame burning in his arms, blistering with her kisses, with the ragged sound of her pleasure, tightening his cock, his balls, hell, every muscle in his body with the need to possess her, to claim her so deeply that she could never deny him again.

"I hate this!" Snarling and filled with outrage, her voice stroked over him in shades of arousal and need as his lips lifted from hers.

Saban framed her face, his hands relishing the feel of her flesh as he stared into her eyes, read her inability to deny the pulsing desperation of his touch.

"I thank God for this . . . and for you," he whispered, allowing his thumb to brush over her swollen lips, his tongue to taste her on his lips. "Hate me as you please, Natalie. Curse me, revile me until hell freezes over, but it changes nothing. It can change nothing. You're mine."

Natalie struggled beneath the statement, fighting to refute it, to find some way to counter it. But how was she supposed to fight anything when desire clawed through her system with talons of fiery lust and pulsing heat?

She had wanted him before; God knew she had. Fighting that need night after night had made her insane, snappy, frustrated. But now—now it was like some demon of lust clawed at her womb, tore at her clit, and tightened bands of wicked, agonizing heat around each.

She arched, totally involuntarily, against his hips as they pressed between her thighs, the ridge of his erection digging into the tender flesh of her pussy as the subtle flexing of his powerful thighs stroked the denim-covered ridge against her.

She could feel her juices spilling from her sex, moistening her panties and preparing her for him. Preparing her for something she knew would tie her to him forever.

That was the warning her brain had been screaming for weeks. To get away, to escape while she could still run, and to put as much distance between her and the luscious Jaguar as possible.

"You can't do this," she gasped as one of his hands smoothed down her neck and gripped the slender strap of her camisole top.

"I was born to do this," he growled.

The feel of the small strap sliding over her shoulder had her lungs pumping for oxygen, her lips parting to draw more in. How was she supposed to breathe? He surrounded her, sucked all the air out of the room, and he was touching her. Undressing her.

"I have dreamed of nothing but this since the moment I laid eyes on you." He traced the rising flesh of her breasts as they spilled over the top of her lacy bra. Her nipples hardened violently, becoming so sensitive she wondered if she could orgasm from the rasp of the lace against them.

"Saban." She licked her lips, tasting him, needing more of him.

The hormone, as he called it, was worse than addicting. Already she could feel the need for it overtaking her senses, battling with her common sense, and topping it with little struggling.

"Ah, here, how pretty is this." He smoothed the strap of her bra over her shoulder, then eased one cup away from a straining breast.

Her nipple was cherry red, swollen and needy. She was almost embarrassed at the state of it. A testament to how long it had been since she had been touched? Or a testament to the power of that freaky hormone he was talking about?

She needed his lips there, needed his mouth suckling her, stroking her past the point of sanity.

"Look how sweet, *cher*." He touched his fingertip, strong, calloused, to the hard tip.

Natalie felt the breath rasp from her throat. Her back arched, driving her nipple into his touch as her head fell back and she let her eyes close. She just wanted this touch. Just this once. Right now.

"Please, Saban." Was that her? Her voice? Her begging for something she knew would destroy the independence she had fought so hard for? Was she insane?

"*Cher*, sweet petite *bébé*," he groaned. "Anything. Anything you need."

She felt his lips first, brushing against the violently sensitive puckered flesh. Then his tongue, swiping over it, hot and wet and wringing a cry from her lips a second before she lost the ability to breathe.

His mouth surrounded the tip as the fingers of one hand caught its mate. He covered the heated flesh, burned it, licked it, sucked it into his mouth, and fed from the hunger that began to pour from inside her.

Natalie was unaware of time, place, or reality. Nothing mattered but the hunger. Nothing mattered but his touch. One hand on her other breast, the other pushing the elastic waist of her cotton pants down her hips, delving beneath them.

She knew what was coming. Natalie was no virgin to be seduced, so she knew where he was headed, and she knew the worst thing she could do was let him actually get his hand in her pants. She would be lost. Any more pleasure, and she would never tear free of him. He would try to own her, control her.

She whimpered at the thought and fought for the strength to pull free, to drag his lips from her breast, to pull free of the hand moving closer, closer to the saturated flesh beneath her panties.

It was hard to tear him away though when her hands were tangled in his hair and trying to pull him into her flesh. When her thighs were sprawled open, her hips arching, her desperate mewls urging him on.

She sounded like a cat in heat, which might be fitting, considering what he had told her, and when his fingers met the humid, blistering need spilling from her pussy, she knew she was lost.

Natalie's hips arched, a cry tore from her throat, and rich, sweet, overwhelming lust spilled from his kiss as he took her lips once again.

"I thought she said she was going to kill him. Are you sure you didn't get that message mixed up, Callan?"

· C H A P T E R 3 ·

It was a science fiction nightmare, and Natalie was caught in the middle of it. The director of the Bureau of Breed Affairs, Jonas Wyatt, and the pride leader of the Breed Ruling Cabinet hadn't come to whisk their irritating Breed back to Sanctuary. To the contrary. They had brought the heli-jet and whisked Saban as well as her back to the estate and far belowground, where the Breed laboratories were now set up.

It was definitely a nightmare. Hours of tests, drawing blood, examinations that shouldn't have been so uncomfortable, and questions so damned personal Natalie kept blushing.

The explanations were even worse than the examinations and the questions, though. The explanations were nearly more than her mind could comprehend.

Natalie liked to think she was a fairly intelligent person. She was always open to the paranormal; she questioned everything that confused her and tried to understand. She even believed in psychics and reincarnation for pity's sake. But this?

A pheromonal, biological, chemically based reaction that resulted in the swelling of tiny, normally hidden glands beneath the Breed's tongue. Those glands then filled with a hormonal aphrodisiac, addictive and potent, ensuring that those affected actually had sex.

When Natalie asked if there was a cure, Elyiana's only answer was that they were working on it. Does it go away? They were working on it.

They were working on it. The day was over and edging into night when the doctor was finally finished with her, and she knew no more then than she did when she arrived, but she was fairly certain there was a truckload of information they weren't giving her.

By the time the heli-jet landed in the wide side yard beside her house and she and Saban were reentering her house, she was angrier than she had been when she first called Callan Lyons.

Fat lot of help he had been. He and Wyatt both refused emphatically to change her bodyguard, and they refused to keep Saban away from her long enough for her to understand what the hell was going wrong with her own body.

And it was wrong. It had perspiration beading on her forehead, her womb clenching, and the aches at her clit and in the hidden depths of her vagina were nearly too much to bear. She felt off center, uncertain, and scared.

In her life there had been few times she had actually been frightened, but she admitted that she was definitely scared now. She was tied, bound to a man that she was certain she might not even like.

Well, she didn't actually dislike him, she thought as she stood back voluntarily and let him open the house, let him smell the air then step inside to be certain it was safe while checking the security system wired into it.

"It's safe, *cher.*" His voice was gentle, patient, as he returned to the door.

"Someone could have shot me from the road while you were checking the place out," she informed him, her voice so brittle she nearly winced as he closed the door behind her and locked it.

"The chances were slimmer. My senses are degraded a bit tonight; I wanted to be certain you weren't walking into an ambush before you came in. The sensors on the heli-jet would have detected weapons in the area or hidden assassins."

She shook her head. She didn't want to talk about the heli-jet.

"I'm going to take a shower and go to bed." She turned away from him and headed for the stairs.

"Cold water won't help the heat. You won't be able to sleep through it; you won't be able to make sense of it or to apply logic to it. But we could discuss it."

She turned back to him, her jaw clenching as she fought the emotions rising inside her.

Damn him, as frustrating as he was, she did like him despite her reluctance to admit it. She had liked him playful, she had liked him teasing, but this part of him, the part she had sensed he was hiding, this she doubted she would like.

He stared back at her, calm, self-possessed, determined. That determination was like a silhouette over his entire body, a shadow he could never escape.

Fortunately, he wasn't ordering her to discuss it. It was the only thing saving his life at the moment.

Natalie met Saban's eyes. Just for a second, she had been scared to do that, afraid of the satisfaction, the triumph she would have glimpsed there. There was none. Those dark eyes were somber, brooding. And she thought, for a second, she might have glimpsed regret.

"And what would we discuss that I haven't already learned?" She kept her voice low, though she knew the fear inside her was throbbing through it.

Breeds were amazingly perceptive. Hiding emotions from them just didn't work.

He breathed out deeply before raking his fingers through his hair and stepping one step closer toward her.

"I endured the tests today as well," he said.

Natalie flinched, those tests had been more than uncomfortable; they had bordered on too painful.

"The heat has advanced further inside me, the hormone building in it." He came closer. One step. "Weeks, from the moment I first saw you, I knew what you would be to me. Each day that the heat builds inside, the harder it is to endure another's touch, no matter male or female, until the effects of the heat begin to ease. My flesh is sensitive, my distaste at another woman's touch nearly violent."

Natalie jerked her gaze from his and stared over his shoulder, fighting the tightening of her throat, the tears that wanted to rise.

"Natalie," he drew the sound of her name out, as though he were relishing each syllable. "I can cook. The steaks are in the freezer. Let me care for you this evening and answer your questions."

One step closer, his hand reached out, touched her cheek. "Let me care for my mate, if only briefly, if only in this small way."

"I hate what you're doing to me. What this is doing to me," she muttered, feeling the defenses she had been building through the day crumble. He wasn't demanding anything, he was asking, and it wasn't a ruse. He wasn't pretending.

Saban grimaced, his nostrils flaring. "In this moment, I don't blame you for hating me, *boo*. Perhaps, at this moment, I hate myself as well. Let me take care of you." He held his hand out to her. "Just a little bit."

Natalie stared at his hand, fighting herself now as much as she was fighting him. This was a side of him she hadn't seen. There was no teasing, no flirting, no deliberate male innocence, which hadn't gone over well with her at all.

She wondered for a moment who this man was, this Breed whose eyes were so somber, whose expression wasn't dominating but rather filled with quiet pride and confidence.

She lifted her hand and placed it against his, feeling the roughness of his palm, the strength of his fingers as he clasped it and led her to the kitchen.

"A young Breed teenager, the daughter of a mated pair, she knew you were coming into my life," he said as he led her to the kitchen table and held her chair out for her.

Natalie sat, uncertain now what to say.

"She's psychic or something." He shrugged. "Cassie Sinclair has gifts none of us have really been able to determine, but sometimes she knows things. She told me more than a year ago that you were coming into my life." He turned from the freezer and cast her an amused, baffled smile. "I didn't believe her. But she pushed dozens of books off on me: *How to Charm Today's Woman*, *Sex and the New Generation*." He shrugged before pulling the steaks from the freezer and moving to the counter. "Asinine."

"But you read them?" Natalie pushed her hair back from her head and tried to breathe through the flash of heat that suddenly tore from her.

And he knew. His head jerked around, a frown pulling at his brows as his eyes suddenly flashed with primal awareness.

"I read them." His voice was harder, thicker. "If you were going to arrive in my life, then I wanted to be ready."

The heat tore through her vagina then, causing her to tighten her thighs and hold her breath against it.

Saban's fists clenched on the counter as his body tightened.

"Saban, I need to go upstairs."

She moved to rise from the table.

"You need me." He kept his back to her, but he snarled the words, a declaration, an agonized certainty.

"Not like this." She breathed out roughly, then tried to draw enough breath into her lungs to breathe through the building contraction of heat tightening in her abdomen. "I trusted you enough to allow you to stay in my home. I trusted Lyons and Wyatt enough to make certain nothing happened to me. You've forced me into this."

He shook his head slowly.

"You know you did," she whispered, tears finally thickening her voice. "You knew when you kissed me what you were doing."

"You belong to me." He turned then, his eyes glowing in his face, hunger and need tightening his features into savagely hewn lines. "You've had one day to feel what has grown inside me for weeks. One fucking day, Natalie. I've burned for you through the days and the nights. I've ached for your touch, and even that you would not give me. I flirted, I teased. I did everything those fucking books said a man should do, and nothing worked."

Natalie stared back at him, confused, uncertain. "And you thought throwing me into this would?" she finally asked bitterly. "That forcing my compliance was the only step left? You forced this on me, Saban. How is it any different from rape?"

How was it different? His lips opened, fury pounded in his head that she would think such a thing, that she could ever believe he would force such a choice from—

Saban felt it then, the knowledge, the certainty, from her point of view, that it was exactly what he had done. He had given in to his own frustration, his anger at her defiance, his hunger, and he had unleashed it on her in a way she could never fight, one she could never escape.

He had never raped a woman in his life. The Cajun swamp rat who had raised him would have been horrified that the young man he had such pride in at his death, had done something so vile.

The sickness of it clogged his throat, tore at his conscience.

"Ely gave you the hormonal treatment, didn't she?" he finally asked.

"That injection? Yeah, she shoved something up my veins and

slapped a bottle of pills in my hand before we left. Wyatt didn't give her much of a chance to explain them though."

He nodded quickly. That sounded like Jonas. Jonas would do that for him, but he had done Saban no favors, no matter what he thought.

"They ease the heat." His throat was so tight he could barely speak now. "They adjust the hormones during this phase, allow you some ease." He grabbed the steaks and stalked to the door. "I'll fix your dinner. Take them. Bath, shower, whatever you need."

He slammed the door behind him and took a hard breath of fresh air, fighting to push the scent of her need and her anger from his head.

God help him, it was the same as rape.

He slapped the steaks in their protective containers on the narrow table beside the new grill before bracing his hands on the wood and staring along the forests that bordered the house.

He needed to run. He needed the mountains and the silence, he needed the peace that came with it to clear his mind, to think.

God in heaven, he hadn't meant to do this to her. To make her feel this way. She was everything he had dreamed of for so long. Gentleness, sweetness, intelligence, and determination—and his. Something meant just for him. A gift, an affirmation that he wasn't a freak of science but instead a product of nature and God's mercy.

He had waited for her for so long.

Deep into the darkness of night his arms ached for her, even when another woman had lain within them. His heart had beat for her, his soul had burned for her. He hadn't known who she was, where to find her, but he had known she was there. Known that she belonged to him.

And what had he done to this gift he had so wanted to cherish?

He had taken her will, her control, with a kiss that he still remembered with the greatest of pleasure. A kiss she had met with equal force. One she had been waiting for; he knew she had been waiting for that kiss. But it didn't excuse it. He had known what he was doing, what would happen; she hadn't.

"I'm sorry." The back door opened, and the scent of her wrapped around him then.

"For what?" Rather than looking at her, he lifted the lid to the grill and ignited the flames that curled over the ceramic briquettes inside.

"It's not the same as rape."

Saban clenched his teeth and fought the need to fist his hands.

"You decided this for what reason?" He lowered the grill lid and watched it, as though in watching it he could make it heat and burn away the shame inside him.

"Because I already suspected the truth of it," she finally said. "I knew it existed, and I pushed anyway because you were frustrating the hell out of me. It wasn't rape, Saban, but neither was it right. And now we'll both have to deal with this. But I won't deal with it with lies between us. Not from either side."

How could she have said something so vile to him?

Natalie felt everything inside her cringing, searing from the knowledge that she had struck out in the most unacceptable way and accused him of something so vicious.

This man, who had set aside his pride to read those stupid dating books, who had tried to charm her, tried to ease her into his arms rather than taking what he wanted.

And it had almost worked. Hell, it was working, and she had known it; it was the reason she had been confrontational. It was the reason she had fought each overture he made so fiercely. Because he was making her feel, making her want things she told herself didn't exist.

She had suspected, in some ways she had known after she met Callan Lyons and his mate/wife, Merinus, that the rumors of a strange mating hormone/bond, and the deceleration of aging that the tabloids ran such stories around, were true.

Neither Callan nor Merinus had aged so much as a year in the past ten years; the same went for the others who had played prominent roles in the Breed freedoms and had married. Or mated, as the Breeds referred to it.

He stood stiff, still, in front of that grill, struggling, she knew, with his own emotions. She had seen the struggle in his expression before and saw it now in the tense set of his shoulders.

She wanted to touch him, ease him, and yet the fear of pushing her own arousal to that point terrified her. But she couldn't leave him hurting, believing she felt that. She moved to him, laid her head against his back, and felt his hard indrawn breath, the minute easing of the tension.

"I'm sorry," she whispered again.

His nod, a hard jerk of his head, was enough.

Moving back, Natalie sat down in the padded chair that was next to the patio table. Saban's back was to her, his arms spread until his hands rested on the wooden table sides of the large grill. The muscles of his back were tense, his head lifted as he stared into the forest. She could almost feel his need to run.

Just as she had felt it before over the past month. A unique tension that gripped him despite his usual teasing manner. She wondered how much of it was an act and how much was truly a part of Saban Broussard.

"Most of what you know of me is a lie then." He shrugged, his back still to her. "I'm snarly, I'm arrogant, I hate jokes, and baseball fascinates me." He glanced down then. "I do like to cook."

"The teasing and flirting?" Parts of it she had liked; others she realized she had somehow known were all an act.

"I'm not much of a lady's man, *cher*," he grunted. "I'm a killer. I was created a killer, raised as one, and once I escaped, I killed to stay free."

Natalie watched as he turned to her, his expression still and composed; only his eyes raged with emotion.

"I know what the Breeds are, Saban," she murmured. "And now I know why you tried to be something you weren't." She shook her head stiffly.

God, this arousal stuff was killing her. It was bad enough before that kiss, but now it was tearing through her system, nearly making her ill.

And he knew it, he could smell it, he could feel it.

"Natalie, take the hormones," he said, his voice gravelly as she watched his fingers form fists against the wood. "Go inside. I'll fix the steaks, and I'll be in in a bit."

"Has it been like this for you since the beginning?" She needed to know what she was dealing with, who she was dealing with.

"A week before I came to your door and introduced myself, I watched you." She jerked in surprise, watching as his head lifted to the soft breeze that fell from the mountains around them. "You were alone in the house, your bedroom window was open, and the scent of your arousal drifted down to me. You were masturbating."

Natalie felt her face flame and had no chance to hide her embarrassment as he swung around and crouched in front of her chair.

"I could taste your sweet scent on the air," he growled, his face only inches from hers. "Needy, aching, your pussy throbbed for satisfaction, and you found none." His lips pulled back from his teeth in hunger, his eyes burned with it as his voice lowered. "And I knew I could ease you. I knew I longed to ease you with a strength that overcame even my need to kill the bastards who hunted us for so many years. And I knew, tasting the scent of your juices in the air, that you were my mate."

"How?" Desperation filled her, longing, fear, so many emotions, so many needs she couldn't make sense of. "How could you have known, Saban?"

He took her hand before she could draw back and flatted her palm over his heart. "That night was the first time in my life that I realized my heart beat. In my life I have never known fear, nor excitement, or nerves. I was always calm. Always steady. But that night, Natalie. That night, I felt all those things, *cher*. I felt them rip inside me, tear through my soul, and fill me. Without control. Without volition. I had no choice, because you're the other part of me. My soul, *boo*. My mate."

He should have looked ridiculous, kneeling there in front of her, her hand pressed into his chest, unfortunately, he looked anything but ridiculous. He looked arrogant; he looked like a man determined to claim his woman.

Sexy, savage, hungry. He wasn't pleading, he wasn't asking permission for her heart. He was claiming it, and as far as he was concerned, it was that simple.

"It doesn't work that way." She could feel his heart beneath her hand, strong and steady. "Just because you want it—"

"Doesn't make it so." His lips twisted with an edge of bitterness. "But the mating heat does make it so, Natalie. What you said, about the choice being taken from you, may be true from your perspective, at this moment. But it isn't true of mine. If you weren't meant to be my heart, and I yours, then it would not have happened."

"Saban, there are no guarantees in life," she snapped, frustrated, feeling the pressure his certainty brought her. "I just walked out of a marriage that nearly destroyed me with one controlling man. I don't need to jump out of the frying pan into the fire."

As the last word left her lips, heat bloomed in her womb, between her thighs. Her teeth clenched on the agonizing pleasure. It wasn't pain. It was a need for pleasure, and it was sharp, intense, destructive to her self-control.

"I took the damned pills," she groaned, wrapping her arms around her stomach, pressing, fighting against the clenching, spasming need that tore through it.

"The hormone in the kiss raises the arousal level," he said softly. "The hormone in the male semen eases it somewhat."

He pushed her hair back from her face, his hard hands stroking pure pleasure along the sides of her face.

"I suspected." She shook her head. "The tabloid stories, all those silly articles. When I came to Sanctuary and met Callan and Merinus, I suspected parts of them were true."

And she had been intrigued, curious about the Breed who watched her with hungry eyes and pretended to be something, someone he wasn't.

"Parts of them are true," he agreed. "Let me ease you, Natalie. Let me take away the pain."

His lips touched hers, a butterfly kiss that had her own lips parting and a breath of need escaping her lips.

"I'm going to regret this." She knew she was.

Natalie opened her eyes and stared back at him, desperation, need, and fear roiling together inside her. "I can't handle shackles, Saban. I can't be controlled." The fear of it was ripping through her mind, destroying the balance she had found after her divorce.

Because she was being controlled. By the mating hormone he had spilled into her system, by her own body, by needs she couldn't deny because everything inside her was demanding his touch.

"I'll call Ely," he growled. "She can strengthen the pills."

Natalie shook her head, her hands jerking up to cover his as he moved to straighten away from her.

"Touch me. Just touch me." She could feel the perspiration pouring from her face now, the weakness invading her body. "Saban, this is worse than she predicted. Oh God, this is bad."

Dr. Ely Morrey had explained what she could expect in the first stage of the mating heat. But she'd said it only got worse after mates had sex that first time. Before that, the arousal would stay steady, a little uncomfortable, until she and Saban actually had sex.

If it was worse than this later, then she didn't know if she would survive it.

She stared back at Saban, seeing the agony in his eyes, the knowledge that he hadn't expected this either.

"*Cher*, Natalie." His thumbs smoothed over her cheeks. "Go inside, away from me. I'll finish this meal for you. You can eat."

She shook her head.

"If we stay out here, *bébé*, we'll end up fucking out here." He was breathing hard, his chest moving fast and hard as his hands tightened around her face. "The scent of your arousal is making me insane. My control is thin enough as it is."

She licked her lips nervously. "Come in with me."

The fact that she had made the decision, that she was actually considering having sex with him at this point shouldn't have surprised her, but it did. This arousal wasn't painful, not in the sense of levels or degrees of pain. Instead, it was imperative, desperate; her skin was crawling with the need to be touched, her mouth watering for the taste of him.

"Go in," he said tightly. "I'll bring the food back in and come to you."

She shook her head.

"Get away from me, Natalie," he snarled, jerking to his feet, surprising her with his vehemence. "Go inside. Five minutes. Give yourself five minutes away from me, make certain without me that your wisest choice isn't to call Ely first."

"You started this." She jumped from the chair and faced him, anger rising inside her, pounding through her blood and spearing through her senses as it strengthened along with the lust. "You shot this freaky hormone into my system; now you can take care of it."

If she could just get past the need, just for a few minutes, just long enough to think again, then she could figure it out. But she knew, until he touched her, until he took her, there wasn't going to be a clear thought in her head.

A growl rumbled in his throat. "It's too strong right now," he grated. "I won't take you easy."

"If you tried to take me easy, I might have to kill you," she raged back, her hands fisting in his shirt as she felt the flames of need licking over her flesh. "Saban, please, just touch me. Do something, anything so I can think."

"So you can figure a way out of this?" Bitterness filled his voice, but he was touching her, easing her backward into the house, the steaks forgotten.

"So I can figure out how to handle this." Maybe she was accepting there was no way out of it, but she didn't accept what she knew was coming from it.

She liked Saban. She hadn't realized how much she liked him until she had to think about it, had to categorize the relationship that had developed. She cared for him. She would miss him, God, miss him so bad if he wasn't here, but she didn't love him. She didn't want to love him. And she didn't want to be controlled by him or some damned hormonal aphrodisiac.

The door locked behind him, and Natalie found herself lifted against him, his arms like steel bands around her as his kiss became a tease. He licked and nibbled at her lips, giving her just a taste of the spicy, storm-laden essence of his kiss. He made her crave more. Made her moan, her arms tighten around his neck, her tongue dip past his lips to taste more of him.

"We won't make it to the bedroom if you keep this up," he warned her, his voice dark, rough, a growling rasp that sent a shiver racing through her as one hand pushed beneath the elastic band of her pants to cup the curve of her cheek.

"So?" She didn't care.

As he held her against him, her hands slid from around his neck to the buttons of his shirt. She wanted to feel him, wanted to touch him. The weeks he had followed her through the house that image had played out in her mind. Turning, ripping the buttons free and jerking the material from his body before rubbing against him like a cat. Like he had a habit of rubbing against her every chance he had.

She wanted him. She didn't have to fight that want now; something had forced her into it, taken the choice out of her hands, and she suddenly wondered if that wasn't a good thing. Would she have ever gone after the powerful, sexual beast this man was on her own?

Natalie tore her lips back from him, the teasing little tastes driving her insane. Her hands locked in the front of his shirt, and she ripped. Buttons scattered as a snarl left his lips, savage, animalistic, but his chest was finally bare. Sun-bronzed, hard, and tough, and free of hair except the nearly invisible, incredibly fine pelt that covered him.

"Oh God." This was better than chest hair. Perspiration gleamed on it now, making the soft hairs easier to see, and Natalie realized nothing could be more sensual. The thought of it rubbing against her sensitive nipples made her pussy clench, her juices spilling between the swollen folds between her thighs.

She had to taste him. As he carried her through the kitchen to the short hallway and the stairs, she licked his chest. His muscles jumped beneath the caress, his arms tightening as he stumbled against the wall.

The taste was there, and she lapped at it, kissing and licking her way to the flat, hard disc of his male nipple. Her teeth raked it, nipped at it. Natalie wondered vaguely if she had needed the hormone to become addicted to him, to hunger, to ache for his touch until she thought she'd die without it. Saban could be addictive on his own, she decided.

"Yes. Sweet mercy, *cher*." He pressed her against the wall, his head falling back as she tongued the hard disc, licking at the stormy taste of perspiration, the heat and hardness of tough male flesh.

"You taste like your kiss," she whimpered, licking over his chest again, little small laps that tasted his flesh and fired her blood. "Kiss me, Saban. I need your taste."

The growl that came from his lips should have been frightening; it should have caused at least an edge of wariness to cool the lust burning inside her. Instead, it tightened her stomach, caused wet heat to spill from her vagina again. And when his lips covered hers, his tongue pushing inside, there was no room for wariness or for thought, only for hunger, only the desperate need inside her to replace the shadows in his eyes with light.

That thought pierced her as she felt him stumble up the stairs. She had seen those shadows when she first met him, wondered at them, ached for them.

She stroked her hands over his bare shoulders as her head bent, her lips suckling at the storm-ridden taste of his kiss. She loved storms. The smack of thunder, the flare of lightning, and it was all there in his kiss, in the desperate hunger she knew no other man had felt for her.

"Not gonna make it to the bed," he groaned, tearing his lips from hers to pull at her shirt. "Take it off."

She took it off and flung it behind them as he shed the scraps of his shirt and went to his knee on one step.

Natalie's eyes widened as she straddled his thigh, the heated muscle pressing into her pussy, the force of her weight against him applying a teasing pressure against her clit. And when he moved her—oh Lord, his hands rocked her on his thigh, stroking her clit as his lips covered an inflamed nipple.

"Yes!" She hissed the word, her head falling back as she rode him in slow, undulating movements.

The rasp against her clit was exquisite, if she could just get the right pressure, the right position.

It was shockingly ecstatic, poised on the pinnacle of orgasm, certain when it came, it would take the top of her head off.

"Not like this." Hard hands gripped her hips. "Inside you. I'll be inside you when you come for me, *cher*. I'll be damned if you'll go without me."

He had to make it to the bed. God, he couldn't take her here on the stairs. He had promised himself, the first time, when he completed his claim on her he would do so in the bed he had made for her. The one he'd made certain was in place before she came to this house.

The king-size bed made of heavy cypress posts, carved and detailed, made especially for the woman who would one day hold his soul.

He dreamed of claiming her there. Not here, not on stairs where she couldn't possibly know the comfort of soft sheets and the finest mattress he could provide.

Growling, his lips still holding the tight, sweetly succulent flesh of her nipple captive, he forced himself to his feet then nearly lost all strength he possessed as her legs wrapped around his hips and the heat of her pussy seeped through his jeans to his cock.

He locked his hands on her ass, and he forced himself down the short hall to her bedroom. He pushed his way through the doorway, slammed the door closed, and barely remembered to lock it before he stumbled across the room to the bed.

He felt the power of it the minute he collapsed to the mattress with her. The comfort, the peace. Entwined with the prayers of the swamp rat that had saved him, carved into lightning-struck cypress were ancient symbols of protection and peace. It was a work of art by an artist the world had never known as he taught the craft to the strange boy he had rescued from the hurricane-ravaged bayou.

It was the bed Saban had dreamed of building at an age when most boys were still tied to their mother's apron strings. The bed where he knew he would one day create his family.

"Here," he sighed, lifting from her, giving her nipple one last lick before levering himself from the curvy sweetness of her supple body.

He pulled her legs from around his waist, gripped the band of her capris, and pulled them quickly down her legs. Disposing of her strappy little sandals was easy, as was removing the silk of her damp panties.

And then he paused, held himself still, and stared down at the perfection of the woman who was his mate.

Her breasts that filled his hands perfectly, the flare of her hips, the gentle weight of her thighs, the smooth, curl-less folds of her sex. Her pussy was bare, silken, and beautiful. But how much more beautiful, he thought, if he could convince her to allow those soft curls to return?

All the sweetness in the world was held there, and he was a man who thrived on his sweets.

His head lowered, his tongue distending, and he swiped through the soft cream, a rough growl leaving his throat as he found the swollen little nub of her clit and her soft, needy cry filled the air.

Sugar and cream, that was her taste, and he could become drunk on her. He licked through the slick juices, nectar, the wine of the gods, it had to be. His lips opened, and he kissed the delicate folds of flesh, licked at the taste of her, devouring the passion that flowed from her.

And she loved it. He could feel the pleasure twisting, climbing through her body as she writhed beneath him. He had to clamp his hands on her hips to hold her still, but she lifted herself to him.

Her knees bent, her feet pressed into the mattress as he knelt beside the bed. Her hips angled, and his tongue found paradise. Rich, heady, living passion flowed to him as he heard her cries sinking into his head.

He had never known lust this hot, this wild. He fucked his tongue into the gripping, heated depths of her pussy and growled. An involuntary sound, wild and primitive, as he fought to slake his hunger for her taste.

The scent of her arousal had filled his head for weeks. Heated and mesmerizing, it had built a hunger for her that he feared he would never sate.

Mating heat be damned. This woman had consumed him long before the mating heat had begun affecting him. And now he would consume her, become so much a part of her that she could no longer run, that she realized they were bound: bound in ways she didn't want to escape.

"I want you!" Natalie clawed at his shoulders as his tongue pumped into her pussy, driving her to the point of madness with the wicked, incredible pleasure tearing through her.

She wanted to touch him, wanted to give him the same pleasure he was giving her, but she couldn't think. She couldn't push herself away, and she couldn't help but beg, to plead for more of his wicked tongue and evil fingers.

Fingers that were pressing inside her, filling her as his lips moved to the hard knot of her clit and surrounded it.

Her eyes jerked open, stared down her body, met the dark green fire in his as he licked and suckled at the violently sensitive flesh.

She was going to explode. She could feel it. She was right there. So close.

"You taste like a dream." He kissed her clit, once, twice, then licked around it slowly, his slumberous eyes locked with hers. "I could eat you forever."

She could barely breathe.

"But I want to be inside you when you come for me the first time."
He pulled back, despite her attempt to tighten her legs and hold him
in place.

"I've dreamed of this, *cher.*" Anticipation filled his voice, his
slumberous gaze as he jerked at the laces of his boots and quickly
pulled them free.

Licking her lips, Natalie moved as his hands went to his belt. She
rose, sat on the side of the bed, and brushed his fingers away.

"I want you now." She slid the buckle free then went to work on
the metal buttons, pulling them free, the hard, thick ridge of his cock
making the task difficult at first.

As the material parted, Natalie drew it down to his thighs, left it
there, and cupped her palm over the thick flesh hidden only by the
cotton briefs he wore.

She heard his breath hiss from between his teeth as she gripped
the band of the underwear and drew it slowly over the swollen length
of his erection.

Weakness flooded her. Her juices pooled on the ultrasensitive
folds of her flesh, and she swore her womb was clenching in trepidation. Because he wasn't a small man in any way.

"*Cher,* leave me a little control, eh?" His voice was strained, but
his hands were gentle as he brushed the hair back from her face.

"No." She gripped the hard flesh with both hands and brought it
to her parted lips.

He said something. Something foreign, thickly accented, but she
didn't catch it. The blood was thundering in her ears, rushing
through her body, and her mouth was surrounding the wide, hot
crest of his cock hungrily.

She had dreamed, too. Dreamed of him taking her in this big
bed, dreamed of taking him, just like this.

She stared up at him, tasted the heat and male lust, the hunger and the need on his flesh. Sweat gleamed on his chest, ran in small rivulets along it, and added a subtle male fragrance to the air.

It was his eyes that held her though. A green so dark now she wondered if they weren't closer to black. They glowed in his face, as startling as the wicked white canines that gleamed at the side of his mouth as his lips pulled back in a desperate snarl.

Hard hands were in her hair, twisting in it, tangling in it as she sucked his cock head inside and swirled her tongue over it slowly, tasting him.

He wasn't watching her in detachment, he wasn't analyzing her performance, he was enjoying it. Enjoying it to the point that she moaned at the additional pleasure that the expression on his face brought her.

Savage pleasure tightened his expression, pulled his lips back and had growls leaving his throat. It was the most exciting, erotic sight she had known in her life.

"Ah, *cher*," his voice whispered over her. "Sweet *bébé*."

She sucked him deep, tasting the subtle essence of pre-cum and wild, desperate lust.

She tasted and teased, tempted and tormented until she felt the control she had always sensed inside him break.

Between one second and the next she was pushed to her back, his jeans and briefs discarded, and he was moving purposely between her thighs. The length of his erection was iron-hard, throbbing, the prominent veins ridging the flesh, the engorged head darkened and pulsing in lust.

"Saban, please—" She bit her lip, holding back her words. She wanted to ask him to go easy, to take her slowly at first, but she could see the hunger raging in him, brewing into a storm of lust that darkened his emerald eyes.

"Do you think I would hurt you?" His jaw clenched, his chest heaved as he fought for breath, and the thick head of his cock tucked against the folds of her pussy.

His voice lowered to a primal growl. "Do you think I don't know, Natalie? That I didn't feel more than your sweet, slick heat?"

His hips bunched, tightened, pressed forward as his lips lowered, and he lifted her hands to his shoulders. "Hold on to me *cher*. I'll take care of you, I promise."

Small, stretching thrusts did just that. Eased inside her, parting the snug tissue gently, working his cock into her with fiery, delicious strokes that were both pleasure and pain.

Ecstasy whipped through her system, fiery trails of lashing pleasure tore across sensitive nerve endings, and as Natalie stared up at Saban, she saw something she had never seen in her marriage to Mike: shared pleasure. The need to please her as well as to be pleasured.

Saban wasn't rushing. He wasn't intent on pushing boundaries as much as he was intent on sharing the burning need, which was more erotic than any boundary she'd ever had pushed.

"What are you doing to me?" It was more than pleasure. With her gaze locked with his, the patience in each thrust, the taut hunger on his face, sweat gleaming and running in slow rivulets down the side of his neck, he was the picture of a sex god at work. But his eyes. Emotions glowed in his eyes, emotions she didn't want to face, didn't want to battle, within him or within herself.

"I'm loving you, *cher*. Whether you want the love or not." He leaned forward, nipped her lips. "Just loving you, *bébé*."

One last thrust, slow and measured, buried him inside her as his lips took hers in a kiss that fired her soul. Her body she could have understood. The heated hormone spilling from his tongue hit her system like a fireball and began speeding through her bloodstream. But her soul? It should have been protected, closed away from any and all male influence.

But she felt her chest tightening, her heart racing from more than excitement, and the almost hidden acknowledgment that this was more than she had ever dreamed loving could be.

The growl in his chest deepened as his thrusts began to increase. His cock stroked once-hidden nerve endings, buried to the depths of her, and stroked there before beginning again. Natalie became a creature of sensuality, of pleasure. Thought, caution, and fear receded beneath the agonizing pleasure burning through her body.

Her hands gripped and caressed sweat-dampened muscles. She writhed beneath him, thrusting back, needing the fierce, hard thrusts now that she had grown used to the width and length of the erection buried inside her. She twisted beneath him, gasping, crying his name as she felt the heat burn hotter, the pleasure flame higher. Each stroke of his flesh, no matter which part of her body it touched, drove her higher. She was flying. Oh God, she had never flown.

"Saban!" She screamed his name, fear suddenly coalescing inside her, the sensations building, burning, rising to a crescendo that threatened to terrify her.

"I have you, Natalie." His lips moved over her jaw, her cheek. "Give to me, baby. Give to me. I'll hold you here. I swear it."

Husky, rough. His lips skimmed over her neck, her shoulder, those wicked canines scraped against the tender flesh between neck and shoulder, and his thrusts became stronger, hard, driving into her, fucking her with such complete abandon that the waves of ecstasy building inside her began to crash over her.

Her orgasm exploded, ruptured, imploded. It tore through her with a force that she was certain destroyed her mind as she felt those canines rake her flesh again, then a hungry growl left Saban's throat.

She couldn't have anticipated it. She should have. His teeth pierced her shoulder, his mouth clamping over the wound, his tongue stroking, laving, as his body jerked in its own release.

She felt the head of his cock swell, throb, then she felt *it*. The extension swelling from beneath the head of his cock, moving inside her, stroking her, locking his cock in place as his semen began to spurt inside her.

The second orgasm that shook her stole her breath and her sight. Her nails locked into his shoulders, her muscles trembled, shook, and she swore she saw the flames racing over both their bodies as her wail filled the air.

She had never known, never believed so much pleasure could exist. That she could orgasm, from her vagina and her clit at once, that the orgasm could race through her body and explode through every cell, every molecule of flesh. Or that in that orgasm she could feel herself, a part of herself she never knew existed, finally awakening.

There were times in a woman's life when she didn't have a choice but
to admit that she was in over her head, and Natalie admitted the next
morning that this was one of those times. She didn't like it, didn't
like having to reprioritize her life, or acknowledge that she had no
choice but to deal with a relationship that she had been certain was
highly ill-advised.

Saban, despite his easygoing manner, was no pussycat, and she
knew it. She sensed it clear to the core of her being and had no idea
how to handle waiting for the other shoe to drop where he was
concerned.

And she didn't like the fact that the mating heat had forced this,
rather than human nature alone. Of course, how she could expect a
Breed to be ruled by human nature, she couldn't imagine.

He had proved beyond a shadow of a doubt in the bed the night
before, throughout the night, and into the morning that he was
much more than a man or an animal.

He had been tireless, but then, so had she. The hunger that had
driven them had kept them going at each other well after midnight
before throwing them into an exhausted slumber, only to bring them
awake hours later, hungrier, more desperate than ever before.

She wanted to blame it only on the hormonal reaction. Unfortunately, she clearly remembered awakening, that abnormal heat finally

sated, only to have her curiosity and her needs aroused once again without that stupid hormone coming into play.

She had wanted to stroke him. Stroke him, kiss him, hear those primal growls that rumbled in his chest, and feel the strength of him when he finally had enough and tumbled her beneath him.

Now, as morning began to edge into afternoon, she found herself trying to find sense in something she knew she didn't have a hope in hell of making sense of.

What the hell had she managed to get herself involved in? But even more to the point, why wasn't she angry over it? She should be furious. She should be screaming at Lyons, threatening Wyatt and the Bureau of Breed Affairs with all manner of legal actions for not informing her of the hazards of consorting with Breeds. Instead, she was standing in her kitchen as she watched a shirtless Saban frown down at the grill he was currently attempting to figure out.

It had worked perfectly last night. This morning, it seemed to be intent on driving one Jaguar Breed insane. That, or he was trying to buy time the same way she was, by focusing on something other than the situation at hand.

She had finally given up on that herself an hour ago.

She glanced at the steaks lying on the counter, the potatoes ready to go into the microwave, and pushed her fingers through her hair before forcing herself to turn away from the sight of it. All that luscious, bronzed flesh displayed was too much for any woman's senses to deal with for extended periods of time.

She was on edge, uncertain, and trying to deal with something totally out of her realm of understanding.

The ringing of the doorbell had her jumping, swinging around, and staring through the house as the back door opened, and Saban strode in, jerking his shirt over his shoulders as he glanced at her.

His eyes were cold, hard, causing something inside her to chill as she followed him through the house. He hadn't pulled a weapon, so she assumed he knew who was at the door.

She moved quickly behind him, pulling at the hem of the long shirt she wore, drying her palms on the sides of the denim shorts.

Saban paused at the door and stared back at her as the bell rang again.

"Remember one thing," he suddenly growled, causing her to tilt her head and stare at him in surprise. "You're mine now, Natalie. I won't tolerate another man in your life. Or in your heart."

Her teeth snapped together a second before her lips parted to sling a searing retort his way. He chose that moment to jerk the door open and face the sheriff and her ex-husband, Mike Claxton.

Mike looked frustrated, furious, his blue eyes snapping in anger as the sheriff of Buffalo Gap shot Natalie a resigned look before turning to Saban with an edge of wariness.

Sheriff Randolph had the broad, heavy build of a linebacker, dwarfing Mike's smaller, leaner frame. His dark hair was cut military short, his dark eyes sharp and intelligent.

"Sorry to bother you, ma'am, Saban." He nodded to Saban. "But it seems we have a complaint."

"Mike, what are you doing here?" Natalie stepped forward, only to pause as Saban sliced a hard, warning look her way.

She almost rolled her eyes, but something about the set of his expression, the ready tension in his body, warned her that he wasn't quite ready to shelve the whole protective, possessive male thing.

She hated the thought. Hated the thought that the trust and the independence she needed could be wiped away so easily in his mind.

"Look at her, Sheriff," Mike suddenly snapped. "I told you something was wrong with her. Are you ready to listen to me now?"

Shock had Natalie backing up a step as Mike turned his enraged gaze on her. This was one of the reasons their marriage had been doomed from the first month. Jealous rages, an almost fanatical certainty that Natalie was always looking at other men, lusting for them.

She shouldn't have been shocked, much less surprised.

Natalie shifted her gaze from Mike to the sheriff. "Sheriff Randolph, it's good to see you again." She gave him an uncomfortable smile. "You haven't caught me at my best this morning."

"I apologize for that, ma'am." He shifted on his feet uncomfortably. "Mr. Claxton here seems unwilling to accept the fact that you're hale and hearty though."

"Look at her, she's pale. She looks drugged," Mike accused as he started to step into the house.

"You have not been invited inside." Saban stepped forward, his low voice dangerous.

"Get out of my way, Breed." Mike was shaking now, his voice holding a nervous tremor as Natalie watched him fight stepping back. "I want to talk to my wife."

"Ex-wife." Natalie didn't wait for Saban to answer to that one. She turned back to the sheriff instead. "I'm sorry you were bothered."

"Dammit, Natalie. Pack your things, you're coming home. This foolishness has to stop somewhere," Mike bit out virulently, his fists clenching at his sides as he was forced to stare around Saban rather than walking through him. "I'll take you home."

"Your new friend has a death wish, Ted," Saban told the sheriff. "Get him out of here."

"Now, Saban, let's be reasonable about this." The sheriff pulled his hat from his head and swiped his hand over the short cut of his hair. "Mr. Claxton just wants to talk to her. Let him see her, see she's not under any undue influence, and then he'll leave."

Saban's body jerked tighter as a ready, dangerous tension filled him.

"What sort of undue influence would I be under?" Natalie turned back to watch Mike suspiciously. He could be paranoid, he could be a bastard, but he wasn't normally insane.

Normally. She was starting to revise her opinion of that. He had that bulldog look on his face that assured her he was about to go off the deep end on her with one of his paranoid accusations.

"I want to talk to her away from him," Mike snapped at the sheriff then.

Sheriff Randolph grimaced as he glanced at Saban almost hesitantly. "Mr. Claxton, I can't make her talk to you alone." He glanced at Natalie then, his dark brown eyes intent, somber as he studied her. "It's up to you, ma'am."

"What the hell are you pulling here, Ted?" Saban snarled then. "Take your friend and get the hell out of here."

Sheriff Randolph wasn't buying something here. Natalie could see the suspicion in his eyes as he glanced from her to Saban, and she could see Mike's anger growing.

"Saban, that's enough." The tension in the air was thick enough to choke on. "Why don't you and the sheriff go get coffee—"

"You think I'll be relegated to the kitchen like a recalcitrant child and leave you alone with this madman?" He turned his head, his fierce green eyes pinning her with cold fire. "I don't think so."

She breathed in deeply and prayed for patience.

"I think you're going to take the sheriff to the kitchen for coffee, and you're going to do it without growling like a temperamental five-year-old." She smiled back at him, a thin, furious curve of her lips. "Don't make me think of an 'or else.' That's just so tacky, and I do hate appearing tacky."

Sheriff Randolph cleared his throat, obviously fighting a chuckle as Saban glowered back at her, one side of his lips curling back to display those wicked canines.

Canines that had pierced her shoulder, holding her in place more than once through the night as his tongue laved, and the hormone burned the wound.

He was a part of her. In a way no man could ever be a part of her. He was in her head, her blood, and she very much feared he might be a part of her heart. A part that would be destroyed if he continued to try to smother her.

"I don't like this," he growled. "He's not stable."

"I'm not stable?" Mike burst out, his eyes glittering with rage as he pinned her with his gaze. "For God's sake, Natalie, look at what you're shacked up with and tell me anything about that is logical. He's an animal."

"Enough!" Natalie swung to him, instinctive, heated anger filling her at the accusation. "If you want to discuss anything, Mike, then keep a civil tongue in your head."

His lips flattened as the sheriff watched both of them with flat, hard eyes. He had his own agenda, Natalie thought. Questions he couldn't ask, so instead he watched.

"And I'm to leave you in the same room alone with this man?" Saban questioned her with an edge of disgust.

"Listen to me, you rabid bastard!" Mike tried to push into the house, rage burning in his face now, splotching his cheeks as the sheriff grabbed his arm and Saban blocked the doorway. "Let me in there. You've done something to her, and I know it. Look at her. She's pale and scared. Look at her, Sheriff. He's done something to her. He's a fucking animal. He shouldn't be here with her. He shouldn't be around her."

Natalie stepped back from the doorway as Saban's hard body blocked Mike's furious attempts to get past the door. She had never seen him like this, so enraged that his own personal safety wasn't uppermost. Surely he knew Saban could break him like a matchstick if that was what he wanted.

"Mike, that's enough!" She snapped out the order, firming her voice, hardening it. "For God's sake, have you lost your mind?"

Saban was struggling not to hurt him, Natalie could see that. He was blocking the doorway with his own body, holding Mike back as the sheriff gripped his arm and dragged him forcibly away from the door.

"Get him out of here, Ted. Jonas will be in your office within the hour to file a complaint. I want him kept away from her."

"Fucking animal! You don't make that decision." Mike struggled against the sheriff. "That's my wife in there. You don't touch my damned wife."

Mike fell back as Saban snarled, a primal, dangerous, feline sound unlike anything Natalie had heard as he rasped. "Ex-wife, bastard."

"My God, this is insane." Natalie pushed past Saban, slapping at his hard stomach as he tried to hold her back. "Take your hands off me and stop this crap. Are all of you insane?"

"Natalie, listen to me." Mike reached for her, his hands closing around her arm, his fingers biting into her flesh.

The sensation of his touch caused an immediate reaction, one she didn't understand, couldn't make sense of. Her skin felt as though it were shrinking, physically trying to draw away from his touch as shards of brittle, sharp distaste filled her brain.

A shocked, hoarse cry came from her lips as she tried to jerk away from him, staring at where his fingers wrapped around her flesh just below the elbow.

A vicious snarl sounded behind her, and before Natalie could process the lightning-fast events, Mike's neck was gripped in Saban's powerful hand, his fingers loosened from her arm, and he was tossed, physically, through the air into the yard beyond the porch.

She stared down at her arm, then back to Mike before she rubbed at her skin slowly, trying to wipe away the feel of his touch. It was still there, the sensation of his skin on her, causing a sickness to roil in her stomach as nausea rose in her throat. She felt invaded, molested, as though Mike had touched an intimate part of her flesh rather than merely gripping her arm. The sensations had bordered on agony, unlike the mere feeling of distasteful discomfort when the Breed doctor had examined her.

Shock slowed reality, had her head lifting, watching as Saban jumped to the ground, lifted Mike from the lawn, and nose to nose snarled furiously, flashing the sharp canines in his mouth as his fist struck with lightning quickness into the soft padding of Mike's belly.

The sheriff tried to tear them apart, tried to force himself between the two men, but Saban was too enraged.

She heard her own voice screaming his name as she jumped to the ground, rushing to the fray and gripping Saban's arm as it came back for another round.

Mike's eyes had rolled back in his head, his body slumped as Saban stilled, his head whipping around to Natalie, his eyes slicing to where she touched him.

"Let him go." Thin and reedy, she had to force her voice to work, force herself to think. "Let him go now."

She stared back at him, shaking, shuddering with the force of the knowledge tearing through her now. Whatever he had done to her had more far-reaching effects than an arousal gone haywire.

"Let him go." She lifted her other hand, wrapped it around the wrist where his fingers were still clenching Mike's neck. "Please."

Mike was gasping for air as Saban opened his fingers slowly and allowed him to collapse to the ground where the sheriff jerked him back up and hustled him back to the cruiser.

Natalie stood beneath the hot summer sun, distantly aware of the neighbors that had come from their houses to watch in horrified curiosity.

"What's happening?" she whispered. She could still feel Mike's touch echoing painfully through her arm. She couldn't wipe it away, couldn't stop the churning in her stomach.

Saban grimaced, turned to her, then wrapped one hand around the nape of her neck and lowered his lips to hers. His tongue speared past her lips, tangled with hers, and in a second she was devouring the taste of him, suddenly, horrifyingly craving the dark taste of lust that spilled from his tongue.

It was a brief moment in time, no more than a touch, a taste, but when his head lifted, Natalie felt as though the energy had been sapped from her body, but so had the pain. She laid her forehead against his chest, her breath hitching in fear.

"What have you done to me?" she whispered. "Oh God, Saban, what have you done to me?"

◆   ◆   ◆

Mike watched the scene in the front yard. That animal touching her, kissing her, his arms going around her as he pulled back and Natalie rested her head against his chest.

She leaned into the Breed, let him support her, let him hold her through whatever pain she was feeling, and he hated it. He wanted to rip the bastard apart, cell by cell. The son of a bitch had what should have belonged to Mike. He was stealing it, had been stealing her away from him for God only knew how long.

This was the reason she had been so all-fired determined to divorce him, to walk away from him. This was the reason she never depended on him, never leaned on him and let him guide her, because of this Breed, this animal.

He wiped his hand over his face, feeling the sweat building there, running down his temples. The soldier that had come to his apartment just after she left town was right. Mike hadn't believed it, couldn't believe that those bastard animals could have the control over a woman that he was told they had.

But he was seeing it with his own eyes. He had seen her, unable to bear his touch, her face going white, the shock of it darkening her eyes a second before the Breed had torn him away from her.

And now the animal was holding her rather than the husband she should have never divorced.

God. What was he going to do? He had to get her away from that bastard. He had to get her to the doctor the soldier had waiting so they could fix this.

This was why she divorced him. He shook his head in amazement. He hadn't understood it at the time. He was her husband, he had the right to have her home when he wanted her home, the right to protect her and look over her. To keep her safe from bastards like that animal Broussard.

He let his eyes lock with the glowing green of the Breed's and swallowed tightly at the promise of retribution there. Broussard would kill him if he had the chance. Mike would have to make certain he didn't get the chance. There would be a way; he would find a way to draw Natalie away from this, to save her, to get her to that doctor so he could cure her. So he could wipe the effects of whatever had been done to her out of her mind.

He knew her. The Breed didn't. He could do it.

"Man, you have a fucking death wish." The sheriff got into the driver's seat and glanced back at him pityingly.

Pityingly, as though Mike didn't have a chance. He did have a chance. He just had to get Natalie where they could help her, that was all.

"She's my wife," he snapped.

"Ex-wife," the sheriff reminded him with a sneer.

Mike glared back at him.

Shaking his head, the other man turned and started the vehicle before pulling out of the drive.

Mike continued to watch Natalie. She was arguing with the Breed now. He knew that look on her face, had become intimately acquainted with it in the year before their divorce.

He had wondered what had happened to his wife. The woman who loved him, who obeyed him. This was what had happened to her. This Breed. And Mike was going to have to fix it.

He should feel guilty, he should have a conscience, shouldn't he? He should feel pain: the same pain she felt that she was bound so irrevocably to him that even the touch of another male brought her distress.

But he wasn't. And the true problem lay in the fact that he couldn't hide that he wasn't. That was why he had to rush to keep up with her as she stormed into the house, nearly slamming the door in his face before he could get past it.

"You know, *cher*, I'm a man," he stated as she whirled to confront him in the living room. "I am a Breed male. Possessive, confrontational, and territorial. You can't ask me to be any different."

"I could ask you not to drag me into it. I could ask you not to show your ass on the front lawn simply to stake your pitiful claim, and I could ask you not to commit murder while the sheriff is watching. For God's sake, some things should just be private." Her voice rose as she spoke, anger spiking each word, clipping them until they rolled off her lips like a curse on the head of the unwary.

"He touched you." That was enough for Saban. "He caused you pain."

"Oh yeah, and he knew that gripping my arm was going to cause that freaky hormone you infected me with to send knives slashing into my flesh." Disgust colored her words.

Her molasses eyes were hot, boiling with temper, her face flushed with her fury, and he swore even her hair seemed to have picked up fiery highlights. She was like a dark flame burning before him, searing him with the wonder of her. That and pure male ownership.

She was his woman. His. The one thing nature had created solely for him. If she thought for even one second he would allow another to touch her, to claim her, then she had best think again.

"I should have warned you of that perhaps," he grunted, though he was certain that warning her of it would have done no good. "I would have thought Ely had taken care of that."

"Expect discomfort." She pushed the words past her lips like some filthy curse. "Expect a few side effects. Tell me, Saban, what the hell else should I expect now that you've actually fucked me?"

He felt his teeth clench at the derogatory tone of voice.

"Don't push me, Natalie," he warned her softly. "My own temper hasn't yet cooled from watching that bastard attempt to claim you."

"No one claims me." Her fists balled at her sides, and he could have sworn she nearly stamped her foot.

How interesting. It was definitely a sight to be wary of, because he could smell the pure violence simmering inside her. Her patience with him, with Breeds, with males in general was rapidly reaching its limit. He wondered, though, and couldn't help but be fascinated with the idea of her losing that patience and temper.

There was a warrior inside her; he could feel it. A woman ready to take on the world when it counted and to flay a Breed at twenty paces should he deserve it. And he definitely deserved it; hell, he was almost looking forward to it. From what he had seen of his pride leader, Callan, and Callan's mate, makeup sex could be damned satisfying.

The books Cassie had pawned off on him had assured him that it was satisfying. Often the best sex of any relationship. Though, to be honest, if it got better than last night and this morning, he may not survive it.

"Did you hear me, Saban Broussard?" Her voice roughened, rasped with her anger. "No one claims me."

"That mark on your neck proves otherwise." He shrugged as he stared back at her calmly. "I've claimed you, *cher*, for better or worse. There is no divorce, there is no separation, and there will be no ex-husband believing he can rescind that claim."

Saban kept his voice calm though firm. He had a feeling that if he lost control of his hot Cajun temper, then he would have lost this battle from the beginning. Because with the temper came a resurgence of the heat, hotter and brighter than before, as he knew Natalie was now learning.

Nature did not allow the Breed mates to confront each other without a safeguard in place. They may fight, they may rage, but they would not deny each other.

In the face of her anger, he could feel no guilt. He wasn't a man to do anything by half measures; he had been trained to know what to do, how to do it, and not question himself over every decision made.

But as he stared back at Natalie now and saw the flash of hurt and fear beneath the anger, he wondered at the ache in his chest. Guilt? Perhaps. He'd never known that emotion either until Natalie, so it was hard to be certain.

Her independence had been hard-won, and now she felt it threatened. He didn't blame her for her anger, but he would not allow her to deny him or the mark she now carried.

"You should leave." Her voice was thick with unshed tears and unresolved fury. "Now!"

"Well, *cher*, I'll just make certain I do that," he growled. "With your ex-husband prowling around like a demented coyote and that fool sheriff sticking his nose in where it don't belong. Oh yeah, I'm jus' gonna pack up and head on out, eh?"

He was growing tired of being told to leave her.

"I have to get out of here." She shook her head. "I have to get away from you before you drive me completely crazy."

"Until your ex-husband showed up, you had no problems with me." He felt like snarling, like roaring in his own frustration as the thought hit his mind. "Does he mean so much to you that now you have to run from me?"

The look she cast him was so filled with disdain that had he been a lesser man, he may have flinched.

"Don't pretend to be stupid, Saban; you just don't pull it off well," she informed him caustically. "I don't know what your Breed rule book says, but common decency should keep you from acting like a complete moron just because it suits your purposes to do so. You threatened Mike. You nearly killed him. And you shouldn't be standing in front of me as though this mating heat bullshit makes it all right."

"I will protect you." He stepped closer, glowering down at her as the animal part of his brain demanded that he show her, again, just how much she was his woman. "Claxton wasn't being reasonable, Natalie, you know that."

"And you were?" She crossed her arms over her breasts and glared at him. "You were choking him to death. One-handed."

"Would you have preferred I used two hands? I thought it sporting to give him a handicap at least, but next time I'll make certain I do the job right." The next time he would just kill the bastard and have done with it.

The look she flashed him spoke volumes of her fury and her opinion of that statement.

He watched, fascinated, as she restrained her rage. Her arms unfolded, her body tightened, until he wondered if her spine would snap.

"I have things to do today," she informed him then. "Things that do not include you. Excuse me."

She headed for the stairs, dismissing him as though the argument were over, simply because she deemed it over?

"Not so fast, mate," he bit out, moving quickly to slide between her and her destination. "This argument has not yet finished."

"Why? Because you haven't gotten fucked yet?" She flicked a glance at the evidence of his erection beneath his jeans. "I'm not in the mood."

He growled at that. "You damned sure are ready to fuck, but that wasn't on the agenda quite yet. Your anger at the moment is, because it's completely illogical. Claxton was gearing himself up for violence, Natalie, and you know it. Better he found that outlet with me than with you. It ensured his survival."

"Mike wouldn't hurt me." A frown flashed between her brows. "I was married to him for years, Saban, he never touched me in violence."

It was the way she said it, the telltale flicker of her lashes, the scent of deceit. She wasn't lying to him, but she wasn't telling him the entire truth either.

"What did he do then?" he asked her carefully.

The sudden evasion in her eyes was proof that he had done something.

"He never hit me, and do you know what else he never did, Saban? He never started fights with men over something so asinine either."

"No, he likely started them with you." Saban could feel the renewed need to rip the man to shreds, one limb at a time. "Is that why you divorced him, Natalie? Why you fight the mating with me so hard? Did he attempt to control all that wild, beautiful fire inside you? Or did he attempt to douse it?"

"Conversation is over." She said it calmly, but he could sense, smell the hurt and the anger raging inside her.

Like those flames Claxton had wanted to control, she pushed it back, buried it, hid it beneath that mask of calm self-control. She could teach a Breed about self-possession.

She could definitely give him lessons in it, because he wasn't handling this nearly as well as she was, but also, he knew, he had already accepted what she was to him. She still had that journey to make.

"This conversation is not over." He bared his teeth in frustration; he could feel that frustration rising inside him now, threatening the boundaries of his control. "Hear me well, Natalie. It doesn't matter who it is, man or woman; any threat to you will be dealt with. Any strike against you will be retaliated against. So much as a thought, a flicker of threat, and I will be there. Whether you like it or not, whether you want it or not."

"Whether I want it or not." Her voice was bitter, cutting like acid into his soul. "Because you decree it. Stand wherever the hell you want to stand, Saban. As long as it's well away from me."

It hurt. Natalie couldn't stem the hurt rising inside her, the fear, the certainty that the loss of control where Saban was concerned would be her undoing.

"I don't need you to fight my battles." She needed to fight her own battles, dammit. "Especially where Mike is concerned."

She turned to move away from him, only to be confronted by his broad chest once again.

"Get out of my way, Saban."

"So you can run and hide?" he bit out. "Rather than facing this problem and fixing it, you're going to run away."

"There's no fixing it," she pushed between gritted teeth as her fingers clenched at her side. "You think you're right. You always think you're right. Big, bad Breed knows it all."

Silence met her accusation. Natalie lifted her gaze then, met his, and had to fight the thickening in her throat as she saw not anger as she thought she would find, though there was a little of that there. Instead, he watched her broodingly, as though searching for an answer or trying to find the question that eluded him.

"You didn't smell what I smelled," he finally said gently. "The rage, the need for violence that was filling him. You divorced him, Natalie, for a reason, and you know this. Just as you knew that violence was brewing within him before you forced him out of the home."

She wasn't going to let him be right about this. She couldn't. If she did, how could she ever stand up to him later? Mike had done this at first, used logic, used a shield of understanding and patience to tear down her self-confidence.

"How my marriage ended in a divorce is my business. How I deal with Mike now is my business. Not yours."

"You don't truly believe that, Natalie." He shook his head as he shoved his hands in his back pockets, obviously restraining the need to touch her.

Unlike Mike.

Not that Mike had ever hit her, but it came close too many times. His temper could be ugly, hands bruising, his tongue sharp and cutting.

"I said it, didn't I?" She forced past clenched teeth as the irritation and the arousal combined into some funky kind of tingles that radiated from her womb outward to the rest of her body.

She was certain that in another place and time, in any other situation, this could have been amusing. If it was happening to someone else maybe.

"Why can't you do just one thing like a normal, everyday person?" she snapped, wanting to pull at her own hair as frustration began to build in her.

The anger was bad enough. But being angry and dying to fuck that hard body? No woman should have to deal with this.

His expression eased slightly from the predatory determination, and sensual amusement darkened his eyes, lowered his lashes as he bent his head closer to her.

"*Cher*, if you haven't noticed yet, normal is not a part of my genetics. Should I give you another example of this?"

She backed up as his hands came out of his pockets and rested comfortably at his sides instead.

"Sex is not going to get you out of this," she hissed. "There's not enough sex to make up for deliberately attacking someone who hadn't attacked you."

"He touched you. He caused you pain." Saban shrugged, though his expression tightened. "That is all the reason I need."

Then he turned away. He turned away as though it didn't matter, as though his decisions were all that mattered and were all that was important.

"Don't you do that." Natalie could feel herself shaking inside and out.

"Do what? Drop this little spat we're having?" He turned back to her, a smooth, powerful flex of muscle as he faced her once again. "We won't agree on this, Natalie. Whether you want to believe it or not, Mike Claxton means you harm, and I won't allow it to happen. You disagree, and that's fine. That doesn't mean that I'll not put a stop to it. Now, if you're not willing to cool off that heat building inside you with a little therapeutic sex, then I could use a snack. Are you hungry?"

Was she hungry?

Her lips parted in shock. He didn't want to argue? He wasn't going to fight over it?

"Since when?" She followed him rapidly. "Since when do you not want to fight? You're male, right?"

He flashed her a wicked grin over his shoulder. "You should know by now."

Oh God yes, she knew. She knew his hard, calloused hands holding her to him, the feel of his mouth devouring her, his cock destroying her. And she knew the cold, icy fury in his face when he had held Mike's neck in his grip, slowly choking him to death.

"You can't just attack people who piss you off, Saban. Especially men. I have to deal with men daily at work, I can't afford this."

"Then they'd best have the good sense to keep their hands off you." He opened the door of the fridge, bent, and looked inside before pulling free a gallon of milk.

Natalie stood and stared at him, anger shuddering through her body.

"It doesn't work that way, dammit," she cursed.

He set a glass on the counter, poured it full of milk, then, lifting the glass, turned and faced her.

"Bet me." His eyes gleamed in amusement as he lifted the glass and drank.

A man drinking whiskey was sexy. A man with a bottle of beer could be sexy. But a man drinking a glass of milk should not have been sexy. Unfortunately, Saban could make it erotic, especially when he lowered the glass and licked over his lower lip with sensual male awareness.

Natalie felt her stomach tighten, felt her pussy cream furiously as she remembered the enjoyment on his face as he licked her just like that.

"You're being unreasonable." She forced her fingers to uncurl from the fists they were making, to stretch as she strove to make sense of this attitude. He'd been ready to kill Mike. Now he was watching her with amused playfulness.

"You do not attack anyone for something so insane as touching me when they aren't aware of this stupid mating heat," she retorted, feeling off center, uncertain of her own anger now. It was damned hard for a woman to fight with a man when he was watching her like a piece of candy that he was dying to taste.

"We'll see." He crossed his arms over his chest.

"We'll see?" she pushed through her teeth, that anger rising again, along with the need, the hunger. She hated this. It was insane. The madder she got at him, the hornier she got, and that wasn't a good combination. "The next time you attack someone, I'll have you arrested myself," she threw out rashly. "I won't allow it."

His expression changed then. Predatory, arrogant. This was the Jaguar Breed, the frightening, sensual animal she always felt lurking beneath the surface.

"You won't allow it?" His voice rumbled with a growl, slurring the words with just enough primal power that it sent a chill racing down her spine.

"I won't allow it." She felt the shudder that tore through her body as the amusement fled his gaze, and savage arousal filled it instead.

He moved toward her.

Natalie wasn't retreating. She wasn't backing down on this, and she was not going to allow him to railroad her into agreeing that he could attack whenever and wherever he chose. If she didn't put her foot down now, if she didn't stop it now, then there would be no end to it. He would believe he could run over her anytime he wanted, however he wanted.

Start as you mean to go on, her mother had always warned her. She had tried doing that with Mike, tried to stay firm, and he had run over her. He had frightened her, her love for him had excused him, and she had spent three miserable years trying to make a marriage work that was doomed from the start.

"I pulled back for you," he rumbled as he came closer. "I let the bastard go, because you said 'please,' because the pain in your voice for that piece of shit was more than I could bear. Did you see the look on his face when he gripped your arm, when he saw the pain it caused you?"

Natalie shook her head, denying the question.

"Oh, you saw all right, *boo*." His lip curled in anger. "You saw the satisfaction, the glee in his eyes, and I smelled it. I smelled it, and I swore I would kill him for it."

"You can't just go killing people over something like that." She smacked her hands against his chest, tried to push him back.

His hands lifted then, smoothed down her arms, and a shiver raced across her flesh.

"He still breathes," Saban snarled.

"Barely!" she bit out. "Do you think that makes what you did okay?"

"I think it made it very dissatisfying," he said softly, dangerously. "Killing him would have been preferable at that time, but losing you over it wouldn't have been worth it. That doesn't mean I'll allow him to get away with it. He'll be more careful in the future, and so, mate, will you be more careful. The next man that comes at you in anger, get the hell out of my way. Because the more harm he causes you, the greater his chances of meeting his eternal maker." Each word shortened, roughened, until he finished with a harsh, furious growl.

Natalie opened her lips to blast him, to argue further, though the words tumbling in her head refused to find coherency. Before she could speak, his head lowered, his hands jerked her to his body, and he nipped at her lips.

It wasn't even a kiss. He nipped at them, then licked them, watching her through narrowed eyes as her tongue jumped to the lower curve of her lips to taste him. To savor the spicy, stormy essence that lingered there from the hormone that infused it.

A broken little groan came from her throat.

"You taste me." He licked her again. "You feel me, Natalie. Tell me, tell me you know I'd do nothing to harm you. Including killing that miserable little bastard unless he actually endangered your life."

"You'd hurt him." She tried to shake her head, tried to fight the need beginning to burn in her blood.

"Oh, *boo*, for sure I would. I'd hurt him bad." The Cajun slipped free, lazy, guttural, spiked with hunger and dangerous intent. "I'd make him run crying to his momma for daring to harm, to believe he could ever take what is mine alone. And you know, *cher*, you are mine alone."

His.

Her lips parted, and his covered them, a weak, whimpering little moan leaving her lips as she tasted him fully. As he sucked her tongue into his mouth and then gave her leave to play. To lick at him, to tease until his tongue came to her, until she could suckle it, sweeping her tongue over it, drawing the taste of him into her mouth.

"No!"

Natalie jumped around him, ignoring the little growl that sounded behind her.

"Don't tell me no, mate," he retorted heatedly. "I smell your need, and even more, I smell the fact that you know I'm right. You'll not run from this or from me."

"I'll run whenever or however I want to." She pushed her fingers through her hair and backed out of the kitchen. "Leave me alone, Saban. Just leave me the hell alone."

She turned and stalked to the steps. She had to make sense of this; she had to find a way to balance the things she was learning about him.

He couldn't just attack people. This mating heat stuff was bad enough. How would either of them survive it without some control? Without one of them thinking sensibly, and it was real damned clear that the one thinking clearly wasn't going to be him.

All she had to do was get away from him, just for a little while. Away from the sight of him, the remembered taste of him, the aching need for him.

She hit the stairs almost at a run, aware, so very aware that he was behind her, moving with lazy speed, gaining on her, his expression taut, hunger burning in his eyes.

Her breath hitched in her throat; a ragged moan left her lips as she felt his hands grip her hips halfway up the steps, stopping her as his hands moved quickly to the front of her jeans and began working the snap and zipper loose.

"What are you doing?" she screeched, scrambling to capture his wrists, his hands, to stop the quick release of her clothes even as he jerked the material over her hips. "Dammit Saban . . ."

She went to her knees as a large hand pressed into her back, pushed her forward, and he came over her, dominant, forceful, his lips covering the wound he had left on her shoulder the night before.

Natalie froze as pleasure streaked, exploded, tore through her from that single caress. The area was so sensitive, so violently receptive to his lips, to his stroking tongue, that it stole her breath.

"This won't solve anything," she gasped as the head of his cock pressed between her thighs, slid through the slick moisture there, and found the entrance it sought.

He didn't move his lips; instead, he growled against the wound as his hips pressed forward, burying his erection inside her as Natalie felt needle points of ecstatic pleasure begin to attack every nerve ending he stroked.

"This doesn't change it," she panted, fighting the pleasure, fighting her inability to refuse it. "It doesn't make it right."

Her back arched as a mewling cry left her lips, and his cock pressed to the hilt inside her, filling her, overtaking her.

"Tell me you're mine." He nipped at the wound, causing her head to jerk back against his shoulder, one hand to reach back for him, clamping on his hip as he held her to him.

"I won't let you control me."

"Tell me," he snarled, licked the bite mark, sucked at it with a hungry growl.

"I won't let you do this." Her cry was weak, a pitiful, pathetic attempt to defy what she knew, even now, was the truth. A certainty as nothing else in her life had ever been.

His hips flexed, causing his cock to stroke her internally, to rasp against her inner flesh, the swollen, flared head caressing, enflaming tender, sensitive flesh with small thrusts. His lips grazed the wound at her neck once more, then his teeth raked over it, sending violent shudders to race down her back as her senses became overwhelmed, her common sense lost beneath the rush of pleasure.

"Tell me." Insidious, flavored with dark sensuality, rough and primal, his voice stole through her mind, as his touch stole her reason.

"Yours." Her cry was rewarded, her submission accepted, and the animal within him broke free.

It was burning, pleasure-pain; each thrust was hard and heavy as control was lost for both of them. As though her admission of his conquest was all he needed to allow his own pleasure free rein.

It was more pleasure than she could process; it was heated and liquid; it burned through flesh and bone and filled her soul where she hadn't known she had been cold. Cold and lonely and searching for that something more, that reason to give her inner self to another.

She didn't have a reason, but that didn't matter. She felt it melting, felt it flowing through her body, pouring from her cells, wrapping around him and drawing his essence into her. And breaking her heart.

In the moment between agonizing pleasure and climax, Natalie admitted it to herself. It wasn't Saban she was fighting; it was herself. Because she was losing herself in him, giving him parts of her soul that even Mike hadn't known existed. Giving him parts of her that she hadn't believed she could share.

And when the climax exploded through her, when it sang through her senses and quaked through her body, she knew she was lost.

Behind her, Saban jerked, snarled. The head of his cock throbbed, the barb, that thumb-sized extension, became erect, pushing past the underside of his cock head and stroking areas too sensitive for touch, already primed, already enflamed as his semen spurted inside her.

He had marked her. Taken her. He possessed her. And unlike Mike, Natalie had a feeling Saban truly could destroy her.

There was a wariness between them, days later, that Natalie couldn't figure out how to overcome. She didn't know if she even wanted to overcome it at this point.

The mating heat had her off balance; her emotions, her independence, and the fear Mike had instilled in her through their marriage of being controlled again all battled within her head and within her heart.

A part of her wanted to reach out and take everything Saban seemed to be offering her, yet the other part held back, watched and waited. Nothing could be as easy as this. The mating heat, the sense of everything coming together when his body moved within hers.

The new school season was coming closer by the day. Classes were on a year-round basis, but the six-week break between the final semester and the beginning of new classes gave students and teachers a much-needed vacation before classes began. And it was during that time that the Breed Cabinet had given Natalie a chance to get used to the town and to review the files she had been given on the students assigned to her.

The classroom she had been given was one of the finest she had seen. The computers were state-of-the-art, the room was bright and airy, the tinted windows that lined one wall looked out on the green, well-manicured grounds that surrounded the school.

She knew the glass to those windows was specially made to

ensure an assassin's bullet couldn't find its way through. Just as she knew that the Board of Education had approved a variety of security measures that would place Breeds in close proximity in and around the school to ensure the protection of the Breed children who would be attending classes.

It was a chance of a lifetime. She would always be known as the first non-Breed teacher to be a part of the education of the exceptional children rumored to have been born of the unions between Breeds and non-Breeds.

That had been part of the excitement of having been chosen for the job, until she met Saban.

Natalie paused in inputting the class schedules she was making up into her personal PC at that thought. Yeah, Saban had changed things. From the day he had arrived at her home, she had known he would change things within her, and because of it, she admitted, she had fought the attraction rising between them.

She had fought him, snapped at him, acted like a shrew and a spoiled brat, searching for ways to irritate him past the wickedly sexy looks he had given her.

A part of her had wanted nothing but to run from him, while another part of her had held on to every look, every word, every second of attraction sizzling between them.

Until she found herself here, staring sightlessly at the half-finished class schedules and the room prepared for incoming students as Saban rechecked the security control room that the Breed children's bodyguards would use during class.

She looked to the open door, aware of the murmur of his voice, too low to make out what he was saying, but comforting nonetheless. Comforting just because she knew he was there, close, protective.

God she was totally losing her perspective here. The same protectiveness that terrified her when he was defending her against Mike was now comforting.

She shook her head at the thought, just as she mentally kicked herself for not having anticipated what Mike would do. He had been fine with the divorce and the mistress he'd had on the side the last year of their marriage until he thought she might have someone else in her life.

Then it was all over but the screaming, the fighting, and the accusations. She was well acquainted with all of them.

The surprising part had been that he had actually stayed away from her since the confrontation at the house. She had been terrified he would try to get in again, that he would bring his insanity back to where Saban could choke it out of him.

As she dragged a hand wearily through her hair, her gaze still on the doorway, Saban stepped through it. Tall and rugged, dressed in jeans, a T-shirt, and boots, a black Breed Enforcer badge clipped to his belt on one side, his weapon worn comfortably in a shoulder holster.

He looked like what he was, a badass Breed ready to fight if the situation warranted it. Ready to love if she would give him half a chance.

He strode across the room, powerful legs eating up the short distance, his brilliant green eyes eating her alive despite the forbidding line of his mouth.

The flat, severe expression was a warning, and one she knew she wasn't going to like.

"What's happened?" She rose slowly from her chair, all manner of nightmare visions flashing through her head. Heading it was the fear that Callan Lyons, pride leader of the Ruling Cabinet, had changed his mind about allowing the children to attend the public classes.

He moved to the front of her desk, his brooding gaze flickering over her face before he propped his hands on his hips and scowled. The irritated, aggravated look took her aback.

"I've just been informed that your ex has attempted to order Callan Lyons to have me removed from your home based on his suspicions that you have been unduly influenced by me and therefore not in possession of your full mental faculties. He's threatening to sue me, the Ruling Cabinet, and the Board of Education for being conspirators in my evil designs upon your very luscious body and demanding that you be released from your contract and escorted immediately to his location where he will then return you to your home and get you medical care."

As he spoke, Natalie felt her lips parting in shocked amazement.

"He wouldn't dare," she breathed.

"Oh, he's dared," Saban snapped. "Now, tell me again why I shouldn't kill the son of bitch and put us all out of our misery."

She only wished he was joking.

"Because it would piss me off?" She flattened her hands against the desk and glared back at him. "Do you think I want bloodshed over someone's insane jealousy? For God's sake Saban, why the hell do you think I divorced him?"

"I'm wondering what possessed you to marry him to begin with," he snorted irritably before running a hand along the back of his neck. "He's out of control, Natalie. I'm warning you now, the Breed Ruling Cabinet is considering a measure to have him arrested and barred from the area. If he ignores the injunction, he'll be jailed."

"Saban—"

"Don't Saban me," he growled. "Do you have any idea the threat he poses to the very tenuous agreement the Ruling Cabinet and the Board of Education came to here? Or the threat he poses to you, personally? I've warned you, he's not sane, and this merely proves it."

"Mike is a little intense sometimes." She grimaced. "He'll get tired of this and go away." She hoped.

He leaned forward. This time he was the one that flattened his hands on the desk as his nose came within inches of hers. "You are fooling yourself."

Perhaps she was. Shaking her head, Natalie moved away from the desk and walked to the windows. She stared out onto the lush grounds, the tall, thick trees that bordered it, and wondered what she would do if Mike managed to destroy this chance for all of them.

"You should let me talk to him." She turned to Saban, knowing, even before she did, what she would see.

His eyes narrowed on her, denial reflecting on the hard, savage lines of his face.

"Not gonna happen," he informed her with a menacing purr. "Do you remember the last encounter? Did he look as though he would listen to you then?"

No, he hadn't. She breathed out roughly.

"He's not a bad man," she finally said softly. "He just wasn't a good husband."

"He's insane. Stop trying to defend him. He'd cart you out of here physically no matter your wishes, if you gave him only half a chance. I don't intend to give him that chance."

No, she didn't either. But Mike had never been dangerous, not really. He was suspicious, paranoid, and sometimes a little over the top, but she couldn't believe he would hurt anyone.

"When are you going to stop defending him, Natalie?" He crossed his arms over his chest and glowered back at her.

"I'm not defending him." She hunched her shoulders against the accusation. "I just don't want you killing him."

"And if I promise not to kill him?" he rasped coldly. "What then? Will you accept that he's fucking crazy and at least allow me the satisfaction of throwing him over the county line?"

Her lips almost twitched. He might be a Breed, but at the moment he was pure arrogant, irritated male.

"You should let me talk to him," she said again, shaking her head. "You have to know how to reason with him, that's all."

"Well evidently you don't know how to do it either, or you wouldn't have ended up divorced, now would you?"

"Yes, I would have." She met his gaze without flinching. "Reason or not, Mike couldn't accept my need to be myself, and I couldn't accept his need to control me. It was that simple, Saban. Everything else aside, that was what destroyed our marriage."

"You loved him." And he hated it. She could see it for the barest second, flashing in his eyes, the knowledge that she had felt something for another man.

Natalie nodded slowly. "When I married him, I loved the illusion he gave me. I loved the man I thought he was."

His nostrils flared; if it was in anger or in an attempt to scent the truth of her statement, she wasn't certain.

His arms dropped from his chest as he shook his head then, turning from her and running his hand along the back of his neck as though to rub away the tension there.

"I had a life before you, Saban. Just as you had one before me," she reminded him.

"I never loved until you." He turned back to her, that arrogance stronger, tightening his features, brightening his eyes. "But I don't blame you for the emotions you had for him. Sucks, but there it is. My problem with this is your refusal to admit how dangerous he is."

"A danger to himself." That was the sad part, and what Natalie had admitted to herself before taking that final step to divorce him. "He's not a danger to me, Saban. If he hurt me, he couldn't continue to be the martyr he sees himself as. The world is against him." She spread her hands helplessly. "That's how he sees it. Use force or violence against him, and it's only going to make him worse."

She moved then, not certain why the memory of that had her moving to him, walking into the arms that opened for her. Why did she even need to be held? Mike was out of her life, at least for the most part. She didn't need comforting, and she knew Saban sure as hell didn't need it. He was arrogant enough for a dozen men.

But there she was, folded against his chest, his hands rubbing against her back, his warmth enfolding her.

The arousal that had remained a low throb inside her all day wasn't building; the hormonal adjustments the doctor had made the day before had made it safe for her and Saban to actually leave the house for longer than five minutes. So it wasn't overwhelming hunger driving her.

She felt his lips press to the top of her head, though, and couldn't stop the smile that tugged at her lips.

For two days they had avoided the subject of Mike, as though he were a grenade in danger of exploding between them.

"Something will have to be done about him, Natalie," he said softly, one hand curling beneath her chin to lift her face to allow his eyes to meet hers. "This won't continue."

She nodded slowly, regretfully. Yes, something would have to be done, and she knew she would have to do it. She couldn't allow Mike to be hurt. He wasn't a bad man, as she had told Saban. He was just a very needy man, a man who refused to accept that things couldn't always go his way. Once he accepted he had lost, though, he would give up, lick his wounds, and torture some other poor woman who didn't have the sense to see through the sad stories he wove.

She had seen through them a long time ago, and now, as she stood in Saban's arms, she was willing to admit that she didn't want Mike's accusations and his paranoia to damage what she was finally admitting to being between them.

She had a chance here for the love she had dreamed of, for the life she wanted. She couldn't let Mike destroy that. She couldn't let herself destroy it, because she was learning that Saban just might be a man she could depend on. A man she could be free with.

✦ CHAPTER 10 ✦

She was up to something. As the day went by, Saban could watch the gears working in her mind. It was fascinating, watching her, sensing her turning the problem of her ex-husband over in her mind until he wanted to snarl in jealous fury at the knowledge that she was thinking about him.

He didn't want her thinking about another man. He wanted to wipe Mike Claxton with his smarmy smile and avaricious gaze completely out of her memory.

Knowing he couldn't grated at his temper. Knowing she was trying to figure out how to do his job and get rid of the bastard only made things worse.

He watched the process, though, and cataloged each shift of expression, each changing scent of emotion as she worked in the schoolroom, and later as they ate dinner at one of Buffalo Gap's better restaurants.

The hormonal adjustment Ely had given her the day before, as well as the adjusted capsule she took that morning had eased the heat enough to allow Natalie to think rather than to fuck with instinctive abandon. He would have preferred the abandon, he had to admit, because there was no hormonal treatment for the males.

The effects were different, the agonizing heat not nearly as uncomfortable. Or perhaps it wasn't as noticeable as pain. Saban had known pain. Pain so agonizing, so brutal that the need to fuck, no matter how vicious, was more pleasure than agony.

But it was bordering on intensely irritating as he checked out the house. He went over the security diagnostics and then ran the secondary sensors for electronic listening devices, explosives, and a variety of threats.

His dick was spike hard and threatening to rip his zipper from his jeans, but if he was going to fuck in peace, then he had to make damned sure the house was safe first.

Moving back to the living room, his gaze moved instinctively to his mate. She was curled in the corner of the couch, watching him, molasses eyes dark and hot, her body vibrating with arousal.

She was perfection to him. It didn't matter that another had taken her, that she had loved another, he told himself. But did she still love him? Were there emotions that had carried over from her marriage that now hampered her ability to see her ex-husband as he was?

"You're watching me with that predatory look in your eyes again," she announced, her voice husky, edging into passion.

God, he loved the sound of her voice when she desired him. When the heat was building and her pussy was creaming.

"Perhaps I'm considering dessert." He moved closer to her, his teeth clenching at the needs suddenly rocking through him.

The heat building in her wrapped around his senses, intoxicated him, made his blood boil. It had been like that the moment he had laid eyes on her, watching her from afar. She had been an assignment when he landed in Nashville, where she had worked in a small public school as a teacher. Within hours she had become the most important thing in his life. In the weeks since, she had become even more. She had become his soul.

That knowledge made his need for her harder, sharper. It made him all too aware that his position in her life was precarious, despite the mating heat. As much as he hated it—and he did hate it—there had been another male in her life at one time, and that male was encroaching on his territory.

Saban had been created and trained to deal with such irritations with maximum force. He had been raised by an old man he called Broussard to know compassion and to follow something far greater than death.

As he stood there, staring at his mate, he wondered which would win. The training or the upbringing, because at this moment he wanted nothing more than to shed blood and to protect his mate. Because something inside him—that primal, primitive part of him— warned him that his mate needed protecting against Mike Claxton.

"You don't look like a man considering dessert." She unfolded herself from the couch, a sinuous, sexy move that had his nostrils flaring to both draw the scent of her into his head and to maintain control. The scent tested the control, but he resisted for the moment.

"I'm a man considering many things." Foremost, he was considering the best way to maneuver his very intelligent, very confrontational little mate.

Her low laugh was knowing, sexy. The scent of her was like sunrise, like spring and innocence, and like a woman moving slowly, confidently into her place in her mate's life.

He liked that scent. He liked all the feels and the textures of watching her claim what was hers alone.

Perhaps Claxton wouldn't be such an issue. Not that he would ever let her confront the man herself, but perhaps he could not shed blood. And maybe he didn't have to worry about securing her heart. She was coming to him, the scent of her was mixing with his, his scent was mixing with hers.

Her fingers slid under his belt.

Saban's head jerked down. His gaze slashed to those graceful fingers, curled as they were between his jeans and the shirt tucked into them.

The heat of her fingers branded his flesh through the shirt and flashed to his balls, drawing them tight.

It was a first for them. The first time she had come to him. He lifted his head back to her, saw the flash of vulnerability in her eyes, and took a firm hold on the hunger tearing through him.

"I'm yours," he told her. "Do as you will, mate."

"Mate," she whispered the word almost questioningly.

"Much more than a wife." He kept his arms still at his sides rather than touch her as he wanted to. "The most important part of who I am."

Her expression softened, though her gaze gleamed with nervousness and with a twinge of uncertainty. It didn't stop her need, though, and it didn't stop that small step into awareness of her power over him.

And she had a great amount of power over him. He would do more than kill for her—he would die for her. But even more, he would fight to the very limits of his training to live for her.

"I want you." She said it simply, and with that she stole any remaining part of him that he may have held separately from her.

The breath literally stalled in his throat as she worked at the buckle of his belt. Slow, sure movements, her slender fingers easing the belt loose then slipping the metal button free to slide the zipper down, over the heavy ridge of flesh throbbing beneath.

He growled involuntarily, the muscles of his abdomen flexing violently as her fingers gripped the hem of his shirt and pulled it up his torso.

Saban lifted his arms, bent enough to allow her to pull the shirt free, then nearly roared out his pleasure as her head bent and her sharp little teeth raked his chest.

"*Mercy*, my *cher*," he growled, forcing his hands to merely skim along her back.

She was fully dressed. He wanted her naked, and he wanted her naked now.

He gripped the hem of her shirt and drew it off when he wanted to rip it off. He forced back a hungry snarl as he felt her satiny flesh, and then a roar as her hot lips moved down his chest to his abdomen, then to the straining length of his cock.

He stared down at her in amazement as she went to her knees. Her breasts were framed in black lace, pale and swollen and pretty as hell. Nothing could be as pretty as those pale pink, luscious lips surrounding and consuming the head of his cock though.

Damn. Nothing could be as good.

His fingers slid into her hair. The warm strands tangled around his fingers like living silk. She sucked the head of his cock deep inside her mouth. She sent his senses exploding.

Saban felt his head fall back on his shoulders then forced himself steady to stare down at her. He felt the rumbling growls that came from his chest, and he growled her name. He snarled his need for her, and he fought for control. He prayed for control, because he wanted this to last. He wanted this touch, the way her eyes blazed up at him, the sight of his flesh held intimately in her mouth seared into his memory.

A shattered groan ripped from his chest as her tongue swirled around the head, caressing the swollen crest with wicked licks. And there, just beneath the crest, her curious little tongue probed at the flesh that covered the barb. The extension wasn't erect, but it throbbed beneath the flesh, ached with the need for release.

"I'll not stand much more," he groaned as she sucked the head back into her mouth and whispered a moan over the thick crest.

"Natalie, *cher.*" His thighs tightened against the need to come, his balls drew up in agony.

With one last, slow lick, she pulled back slowly.

"I want to take you."

Saban stared down, dazed, sweat forming on his forehead as she rose to her feet, her slender fingers stroking over his erection.

"I want to take you right here." She toed off her shoes as she unsnapped her jeans.

"Here?" He swallowed tightly, watching as she wiggled from the snug denim like a fantasy present, unwrapped one slow inch at a time.

"Here." Her smile was pure sex, pure need. "Do you have a problem with here?" She kicked her jeans free before reaching behind her and unclipping the bra.

The cups fell away from the firm, sweet flesh of her breasts, and control was suddenly the last thing on his mind. Sweet, succulent nipples topped the flushed mounds, and he was lost.

"Here works."

Hell, he didn't care where it was, as long as he was inside her, holding her, her holding him, a part of each other.

Saban sat back on the couch, watched in wonder and pleasure as she straddled his thighs and came to him.

His hands shackled her hips as he reclined into the back of the couch.

She flowed over him like hot honey. Soft, saturated, slick flesh enclosed his cock head, then by slow, agonizing inches took the shaft of his erection. Tiny, whimpering cries left her lips. Her sharp nails bit into his shoulders, and her dark eyes were nearly black in her pleasure.

"I'll not last long. I'll make up for it." He was fighting to breathe.

He could feel the sweat beading on his flesh, feel the wildness invading both of them.

"You can make it up all night." She leaned into his chest, her hips lifting, dragging the tight, clenching flesh of her pussy over his cock, and he lost it.

Who cared about control? This pleasure, the touch of her, the taste of her, the feel of her was all that mattered. Gripping her hips,

Saban shifted and began to move inside her with hard, desperate thrusts. Nothing mattered but fucking her now. Fucking her so hard and deep, with such pleasure that she never forgot what it meant to belong to him.

Natalie was wild above him, meeting him thrust for thrust. Sharp little nails pierced his back as her teeth bit into his shoulder.

The tiny pinpricks of pain were nothing, more pleasure than anything else, but enough to tear away that last strip of control he had kept reined in. He gripped her hips harder, his cock shafting into her with furious strokes as he felt her orgasm rip through her body.

He laid his mouth over the mark he had given her, his teeth scraping it as he gripped her flesh and let go his own release. The barb beneath the head of his cock thickened, hardened, the pleasure-pain of it drawing a snarl from his throat as ecstasy poured through him. Sweet heaven, the pleasure of it. The feel of her pussy against flesh so sensitive the agony was too much for him. He felt it pulse, throb, spilling more of the hormone into her even as he spilled his seed inside her.

The barb locked his cock in place, caressed hidden flesh, and sent them both hurtling into a brilliant, burning sphere of pure pleasure.

He would figure the rest of it out later, he promised himself as he bore her back against the couch cushions and came above her. As his release spilled inside her and the aftershocks of rapture tore through them both, he swore he would hold onto her, no matter the cost. Jealousy be damned, it wasn't worth losing the faith she was finding in him. And it wasn't worth losing the loyalty he could feel growing between them, a loyalty born of emotion and, he prayed, of love.

He didn't want to shackle her to him with sex. He wanted to hold her to him with love. Nothing more.

Natalie had tried desperately not to think about Saban or the emotions twisting inside her where he was concerned. She'd used frustration and aggravation, she'd tried to hide, and she'd tried to deny them. She'd wanted to deny feeling anything for him, because otherwise she would have had to face the fact that within a matter of weeks, less than two months, she had let a man steal a part of her heart that even her ex-husband hadn't possessed.

And here she had been the one to promise herself she would never let another man affect her again.

She almost snorted at the thought the next morning as she put on coffee and began preparing breakfast. Saban sat at the small kitchen table, dressed in his Breed Enforcer uniform.

Strapped to his side in a shoulder holster was his weapon, to his left thigh a sheathed dagger. He would have more weapons hidden on him, she knew. Weapons she couldn't see, weapons he knew how to use with deadly efficiency.

And why that brought her comfort rather than freaking her out, she wasn't certain. She should have been frightened of Saban from the day she learned he'd be living in her home with her, following her, protecting her.

It was one of the reasons she had fought him so far, she realized as she finished the bacon, eggs, and toast. It was why she hadn't wanted him here. Why she hadn't wanted him to be a part of her life. Because she had known he would become a part of her heart.

And he was. Right there in living color, bronze muscle covered by the military-type black uniform with the Jaguar insignia on his shoulder.

She almost shook her head at herself as she poured two mugs of coffee and moved to set his on the table. Turning away from him, she couldn't help it, she just couldn't help but to let her fingers skim over the thick, black silk of his hair.

"Hey." He caught her hand, his head jerking up, his gaze connecting with her in lazy awareness of her. "You don't have to try to sneak and touch me."

He placed her palm against his cheek, turned a kiss into it, then went back to work on the small electronice notepad he had attached to the palm Internet link he carried.

Natalie threaded her fingers through his hair, a smile twitching at her lips as he leaned into the caress, even though his brow was furrowed with concentration.

He didn't mind being touched. And he didn't think a light caress meant running straight to the bed as well. Mike hadn't wanted to be touched unless he was ready for sex.

She let her fingers linger a moment longer then moved back to the stove and breakfast.

Strange, how easily Saban has slipped into her heart. She hadn't wanted it, she had given it the good fight, but he was there.

She paused at the stove, felt the sharp blow to her heart, and realized she loved it. It stole her breath, when she knew it shouldn't have. It shook her to the core, even though she realized she should have known all along what was happening.

She had fallen in love with a man a hundred times more dominant than her ex-husband had been, and he had managed to slip so much deeper inside her soul than Mike ever could have.

She stared sightless down at the bacon and felt the anger that began to build inside her. It wasn't an anger toward herself or toward Saban. But toward Mike.

He had come to Buffalo Gap to destroy not just her independence but what she had found with Saban. He had left his bimbo, his job, and the home he had stolen from her to make certain she lost anything she could have found in this small community.

He would do it, too, she realized. He wouldn't physically hurt her, but he would destroy the respect and the good standing she was building here. He would make it impossible for her to teach the Breed children before he would make himself appear as a threat to her and to them.

And he knew what he was doing. And she knew she was going to have to stop him before he destroyed this chance she had at happiness.

"I need to check a few things in the truck." Saban rose from his chair as she turned to him. "I'll be right back."

He strode quickly from the room as she drew in a slow, hard breath. As she heard the front door close, she jerked the phone from the wall and punched in Mike's cell phone number.

She was going to take care of this between her and Mike. She wouldn't have Saban's hands bloodied because of her ex-husband's stupidity, and she wasn't giving him the chance to nearly destroy her career again.

"Natalie, thank God you called." He answered on the first ring. "Are you okay?"

The pseudo concern in his voice was nearly too much.

"Go home, Mike," she snapped. "I divorced you for a reason. To get you out of my life. Don't make me get another restraining order on you. You know how bad that's going to look if you have to actually get another job."

"You didn't used to be so hard, Natalie." There was a wealth of sorrow in his voice. God, didn't he ever see what he was doing to himself?

"You didn't used to be so stupid," she hissed. "I left Tennessee to get away from you. I'm happy here, Mike. Happier than I ever was in our marriage. Go back to your bimbo and leave me the hell alone."

Silence filled the line for long moments.

"I just want to see you first," he finally said, his voice soft, regretful. "Is that so much to ask?"

"Yes, it is." Way too much to ask, because she couldn't blame Saban for being concerned, and there wasn't a chance in hell he was going to agree to this.

"Five minutes, Natalie. Anywhere. I don't care. Just give me five minutes to say good-bye."

"And you'll leave?"

"I swear, I'll leave."

"Five minutes," she retorted. "I'll be at the mall later today sometime around four. I'll meet you at the outside entrance to Sally J's." Sally J's was one of the women's-only clothing stores in the large mall just outside town. "You'll have five minutes. I'll call you right before I step outside."

"Will your furry friend be with you?" he asked bitterly.

"He'll be around," she finally sighed. "But I'll talk to you alone. Be there at four, Mike. And remember, five minutes. That's it."

"Five minutes. That's all I need, Nat."

She hung the phone up and moved back to the stove as the front door opened once again, and seconds later Saban strode back into the kitchen.

As Saban sat back down at the kitchen table and took a healthy sip of the decaffeinated coffee he'd slipped into the canister days ago, he drew in a slow breath.

Sometimes his sense of smell was a curse rather than a blessing. Times such as moments before, when he had smelled the emotion pouring from Natalie. Rich and saturated with arousal, tempestuous with need, and overlaying it all, the deep, heady scent of love.

Love had a scent, though it varied from person to person and couple to couple. It wasn't easy to detect and often wasn't even apparent except in high-stress, personal moments.

What was she thinking of? he wondered. What had caused that well of emotion to open inside her and break free and then to touch him. To touch him of her own volition, as though testing her ability to do so or his patience in allowing it.

God help them both—he would lie at her feet until hell froze over to feel again what he had felt when she had touched him so timidly. Sensation, like an electrical current had run over his scalp and sizzled down his spine. He'd barely restrained a weakening shiver, and he cursed himself for it. For a second, he'd been like the pitiful cub he remembered himself as, so long ago. Staring at the scientists from his metal pen, hungry for something that went beyond the need for food. And now he knew what that hunger was, not for just a touch, but for one filled with emotion.

That touch had set his nerve endings on fire, and now, long moments later, it had him on edge, off balance, and filled with his own emotions.

"I'd like to postpone the trip to the mall that you planned for today," he told her, keeping his voice level as she set the plate of food in front of him. "There are still some safety issues I'd like to have taken care of first."

His control not withstanding, the report Jonas had sent out via the eLink wasn't happy news.

"I can't postpone it."

Saban's head snapped up. Her voice was carefully bland, nonconfrontational, but he heard the nervousness behind it. The same nervousness he sensed every damned time she disagreed with him. Did she think he was going to beat her for disagreeing with him? That son of a bitch, Claxton, had a lot to answer for; unfortunately, Saban had already come to the conclusion that he would have to allow Jonas and his team to take care of getting the bastard out of town, rather than taking care of it himself.

Natalie might not like his methods.

As he watched her, he noticed that she didn't meet his eyes. She took her seat, salted and peppered her food, sipped her coffee, and said nothing more.

He could see the pulse beating a ragged rhythm in her throat though, and he could smell her trepidation.

"Very well." He lowered his gaze to his own breakfast and dug in. "I'll contact Jonas and have a few extra men assigned around the mall just to be on the safe side. An enforcer caught sight of a suspected Council soldier in town last night. The Council has been attempting to capture Breed mates for years, so we need to be careful."

"Why?" She lifted her head then, suspicion flickering in her gaze.

Did she believe he would lie to her? Saban wanted to growl, he wanted to throw something, wanted to beat her ex-husband until he was nothing but bloody pulp.

"Why are they attempting to capture our mates? Or why do we need to be careful?"

Her lips pursed as mocking patience filled her expression. "What do you think?"

Saban smiled, making certain to add just enough wicked sensuality to the look. "Many things, but I'll concentrate on your question. They want our mates to experiment on the phenomenon, which by the way, they saw as early as the first Breed's creation more than a century ago. Unfortunately for them, that first Leo escaped in his twenty-seventh year of creation. The mating hormone and the genetic viruslike condition it creates is of interest to them."

"What sort of interest?" She was eating, but her attention was caught, he could see.

Natalie was a curious little thing, and that curiosity was rarely a problem. Until now.

He finished his breakfast, pushed back his plate, and stared back at her coolly. "It creates a condition that decreases aging in both the Breed and his or her mate. In ten years, Merinus and Callan have aged perhaps a year. There are rumors the first Leo, who should be nearing the age of one hundred and thirty, is still alive and still in his prime. And that, my dear, is the reason the Council scientists would do anything to capture our mates."

◆ CHAPTER 12 ◆

It was hard to take in. Hours later, as Natalie entered the huge, two-story indoor mall just outside the town's limits, she felt as though she had been sucker punched with the information.

Saban had answered all her questions, he had even offered to take her to Sanctuary to allow her to discuss some of the more advanced effects of the mating heat. Nothing dangerous, he had assured her. There was nothing life threatening in being a mate. Why, hell no, just an advanced life span and only God knew what problems in the future. Not to mention mentally defective, in her opinion, Council scientists and soldiers drooling for a chance to slice into a body verified as a mate, Breed or human.

It amazed her at odd times, the destructiveness that men could force on each other. The horror and cruelties didn't exist in the animal world. It was survival of the strongest there, and in some ways, that was how the Breeds saw living now. Survival of the fittest.

Did nature see it that way as well? Was that the reason for the mating heat? The reason for the advanced life span once mated? She knew that women, Breeds and those who were married or mated to Feline Breeds, conceived quickly without the hormonal treatments Dr. Morrey had worked up. But after the first conception, it then became much harder to conceive. And Saban had told her that the Wolf Breeds had had an even harder time of it until only recently, when their doctors had detected additional hormones, so far unknown, within one of their mates.

The whole mating process was confusing as hell, but according to Saban, the one constant in it all was the emotion the mates shared. So far, in over eleven years since the announcement of their existence, a mating had always resulted in love. And the look he had given her as he related that information had been filled with heat, emotion, and the unvoiced question she wasn't ready to answer yet.

Yes, she loved him, and knowing it terrified the hell out of her.

As they neared Sally J's, Natalie checked the watch on her wrist surreptitiously and glanced around at the crowds mingling from store to store. She had ten minutes to meet Mike on the other side of the store.

The restrooms were on the other side, with two entrances and exits into them. She was hoping she could enter from one side and move quickly to the exit on the other side, beside the doors that led to the outdoor parking.

Five minutes. That was all she was giving Mike, and she intended to do that talking. Enough was enough. They were divorced, they had divorced for a reason, and she wasn't going to turn the new life she wanted for herself into an international incident. Which was what it would become if he became the first recorded non-Breed to die from jealous rage.

She trusted Saban, she did, with her own life. But Mike's, she wasn't so certain of.

"I'm going to the ladies' room." She paused by the entrance. "I'll be out in a few minutes."

She had to force herself to tamp down nervousness, to hold back fear, which she was terrified was damned near impossible. But after one narrow-eyed look, Saban nodded slowly before leaning against the wall with all the resigned patience of any put-upon male.

She almost smiled.

Moving into the ladies' room, she picked up her steps, walked quickly past the stalls, then out of the exit on the opposite side of the curved room. It was only a few steps to the outdoor exit through two sets of double doors and onto the sidewalk that surrounded the mall.

Mike was waiting for her directly across the small road, arms crossed over his chest, his expression causing her chest to clench with a spurt of familiar panic. He was angry. Mike wasn't always rational when he was angry. He didn't care if he caused a public spectacle of himself or her, and he rarely listened to reason. She almost turned and walked back into the mall.

Instead, she glanced at her watch then back at Mike, a silent declaration that she wasn't walking over there. At least this close to the doors, there was a handy escape route if one of those Council soldiers was lurking around the mall.

She looked around just to be certain and saw no one suspicious. The parking lot was busy, the traffic fairly thick.

She watched Mike curse before he moved across the street, his shoulders thrown back, his expression pugnacious.

"We couldn't do this in the shade?" He sneered. "You always have to be difficult, don't you, Natalie? Big-time Breed teacher has to call all the shots."

"I can go back inside, and we can forget this," she retorted. "Saban's waiting just inside the doors, Mike. Make this fast."

"I want you to come home. Dammit, you have no business here. You're my wife."

A sharp, amazed laugh left her throat. "Drop it, Mike. We both know this has nothing to do with you wanting me back and everything with losing control of me. I'm not your wife. I'll never be your wife again, and if you don't get that through your thick skull, then you're going to end up dead."

"Siccing that rabid animal of yours on me, Nat?" Disgust filled his voice. "How can you let that thing touch you?"

Natalie wanted to roll her eyes but knew it would only make this little fight run longer.

"Mike, I agreed to meet you so you'll see this isn't happening with me." She tried to keep her tone soft, gentle. Sometimes it worked. "Our marriage was over the first year; I just didn't want to admit it. Now, let it go, and go back to Tennessee. Don't make this harder than it has to be."

His lips flattened, his face flushing with anger.

"Don't you see what those Breeds have done to you, Natalie?" He pushed his fingers through his hair as fury flashed in his eyes. "They've done something to you. They drugged you." He reached for her, his teeth clenching violently as she jumped back. "Look at you, you can't even stand to be touched by anyone but that bastard fucking you."

"Stop this, Mike. You don't know what you're talking about, and it's not a discussion we're going to have. You need to leave. I didn't want you before I came here, and I don't want you now."

His nostrils flared, a telling sign. Only at his most furious had Natalie ever seen that. Those were the times he had wrapped his hand around her neck and pounded the wall beside her head. When he had smashed furniture and spent hours accusing her of screwing every man they both knew.

"You're my wife." He advanced a step, and in his eyes Natalie saw something she had never seen before. A fury so violent she knew Mike would never keep his control.

Had he truly been working his way up to this over the years? How had she not seen it, not suspected that he would retaliate like this the moment he knew he was no longer a part of her life? Forget the divorce, the bimbo; he had still controlled her. She hadn't dated, she hadn't sought out friends, because she knew Mike, and she knew he wouldn't have tolerated it.

And she hadn't even suspected she knew until now.

She stepped back warily toward the doors now, wishing she

hadn't slipped away from Saban, that she had just fought it out with him, made him at least let her try. She would have been safe. Or safely in her bed screaming in pleasure as Saban argued his side. Either one would have been preferable to this.

"They drugged you, Natalie. The doctors that talked to me after you left told me all about it. This drug their bodies make. It makes you addicted, dependent."

Oh God. Oh God. She looked around frantically, knowing what was going on, certain Mike had set her up.

She turned to push through the entrance doors into the mall, to run, to escape back to Saban.

"You fucking bitch, you're not running back to him."

Natalie almost screamed as his hand locked over her upper arm, pulling her back as she scrambled to grab the handle to the door, to get away from him.

The pain, though not as severe at first, became mind-numbing as he dragged her back. She felt his arm lock around her waist, his chest against her back as she clawed at his flesh, guttural whimpers leaving her lips as she tried to scream for Saban.

She heard screams, but they couldn't be her own. A haze of pain covered her eyes, filled her brain, and with it came terror.

Mike was cursing, raging. She could hear tires squealing and she knew, oh God, she knew he was taking her away. Taking her away from Saban and the dreams she hadn't known she had.

"You bastard!" Fury, rich with terror and mixed with adrenaline, spiked through her mind.

Her hands curled back, her nails clawing back at Mike's face as she tried to tangle her feet with his legs, throwing him off balance.

They hit the street as horns blared and a siren began to scream through the air. As she rolled to her stomach, she felt hands grab her ankles, pulling at them, trying to drag her back as she kicked, screaming, trying to roll, fighting for release.

There were too many voices. Too many hands touching her, and a second later she froze in a terror so thick, so horrible it nearly stopped her heart.

A feline roar of rage split through the chaos of sound as she heard the rapid, staccato bursts of stunners and bullets ripping around her.

One last kick, and she was free of the manacles at her feet. Crawling to her knees, she lifted her head, fighting to see. There were people everywhere. Black uniforms surrounded her. Someone was screaming from behind the barrier of enforcers, and she swore it sounded like Mike's screams.

"Saban! Oh God, Saban!"

"Stay the hell where you are!" The growling roar from her right had her twisting, searching for him, her mind still dazed, the pain of Mike's touch still ripping through her senses.

But he was there. Through the blur of tears and pain, she saw him, then she felt him, one arm curling around her and pulling her into the mall as the gunfire behind them suddenly ceased.

His eyes were blazing into hers, filled with rage, his expression twisted with it. "If you wanted him that fucking bad, I would have readily released you," he snarled. "Now keep your goddamned ass here, and I'll see if I can save the son of a bitch for you." He turned around, stood aside for the two female Breed Enforcers who crowded into the small area. "Watch her and keep her here if it means shackling her to the fucking door."

Shock froze her, parted her lips on a cry, and left her staring at his retreating back as he left her sitting there between the street entrance and the mall entrance.

She curled her arms around her waist, and as she fought the pain and the need for his touch, she laid her head against her knees and let the tears fall.

She knew what she had done. Without meaning to, certainly without desiring to, she had betrayed her mate.

Saban stared at the mess four Council soldiers made as they bled out on the asphalt of the street outside the black panel van they had been attempting to get Natalie into.

The scientist was still alive, a little bit wounded, but he was breathing, and the EMTs seemed certain he would keep living. If it weren't for the information they needed from him, Saban would have finished the job and put a bullet in his head.

Mike Claxton was sitting on the ground, his head in his hands, a bandage wrapped around one arm and another binding his ankle.

The bastard had been damned lucky. The fact that Natalie had managed to trip both of them had saved his life, taking him out of the line of fire when he, Jonas, and the other Breeds swarmed out of the mall into the parking lot.

Saban braced his hands on his hips and stared at the man and wanted to howl in rage. He could smell the weakness, both physically and mentally, that poured from Mike Claxton. He wasn't a fitting mate for Natalie; hell, he hadn't even managed to be a fitting husband to her, and yet she had run to him.

He couldn't even find it in him to excuse her, to find a way to understand it. It simply came down to the fact that Claxton had meant more to her than her own life, than Saban's life, had. And that broke his heart.

Shaking his head, he moved to the man, then hunched in front of him, his elbows resting on his knees, as he stared at Claxton's bent head.

Mike's head lifted. Miserable, damp blue eyes met Saban's.

"You set this up." They knew that. He had arranged with the scientist and the soldiers to take her.

Claxton sniffed back his tears. "They have a cure for her. Whatever you did to her, it made her leave me, divorce me. She loves me, Breed. Not you."

The pain of that was like an open, gaping wound inside Saban's soul.

"I didn't meet her until the day you came to the house to find me there," he told Claxton, striving for patience. "Until that day, Natalie had never so much as breathed air that I had passed through. How could I have harmed her or damaged your marriage?"

Claxton shook his head. "They saw you."

"Did they have pictures? Video?"

The other man continued to shake his head.

"The Council records everything, Claxton. Every investigation, every move they make, one way or the other, is recorded. If they had no proof, then it didn't happen."

"You drugged her," he bit out, his voice rising as he glared at Saban. "She divorced me."

"You cheated on her with her assistant teacher," Saban said cruelly. "You broke trust with her. You betrayed her. You refused to allow her to make her own decisions, to be herself, because you were too frightened she would learn the truth. And when she did, you blamed her."

Saban had had the investigation done. His sister, Chimera, had sent the information via the eLink, carefully organized, brutally concise, days before.

"She would have forgiven me." Claxton swallowed tightly, but his demeanor shifted slightly, lost the aggression and became pathetic rather than furious. "Eventually, she would have forgiven me."

Saban shook his head. "Would you ever forgive her?"

The other man blinked back tears and looked down, shaking his head.

"You nearly died here today, Claxton." Saban stared at the Council soldiers who had lost their lives instead. "But what would have happened to Natalie is beyond your worst nightmares. They would have cut her, studied her, and dissected her . . . while she lived. The horror she would have endured would have been more agony than you could ever imagine."

He shook his head desperately. "They have a cure. You did something to her. She can't even bear my touch."

"Nothing is wrong with her," Saban snarled, flashing his canines. "She was my woman, my lover. Why would she want the touch of one who had betrayed her? One who had fucked her assistant in her own bed? Why would she wish for your touch?"

Claxton flinched at each question, hunching his shoulders against the truth Saban laid at his feet.

"You didn't just break the law today in your attempt to aid in her kidnapping, but you broke Breed law, Claxton." He gave that a second to sink in, and as Mike's face paled, he went on. "Attempting to kidnap the woman of a Breed is punishable by death. Your trial would be a Breed tribunal, not a jury of your peers. You don't even have to be there." He leaned forward. "Justice would be horrifying. Death by the most excruciating pain we could devise. The Council taught us how to cause pain, my friend. Pain like you cannot even imagine."

Claxton's face was white now.

"I wanted to save her."

"You wanted to fucking own her," Saban snarled. "Now, here is what you are going to do. You are going to your hotel, you will pack, and you will leave before night falls. If at any time you are found to be in Buffalo Gap or if you attempt to contact Natalie without her permission, then Breed law will come down on you."

Surprise reflected on Claxton's face. "You're going to let me go?"

"I have never killed over a woman, Claxton." Saban let a growl enter his voice for effect. "But over Natalie, I will rip your guts from your navel and strangle you with them. Do you understand me?"

Claxton nodded slowly. Saban held his gaze, staring back at him, letting him see the savagery, the need for blood rising inside him.

"Why are you letting me go?" Claxton asked timidly, almost hopefully.

"You heaped enough guilt on her head during your marriage." Saban rose to his feet and stared down at him coldly. "I won't let you guilt her with your death."

The hope left his eyes. Claxton nodded again then dragged himself to his feet and stared at the dead soldiers now being bagged, the disabled van that would have taken Natalie away.

"I was trying to help her," he finally said roughly. "I thought . . . I thought she was in danger."

"As long as I live she will be safe," Saban snapped. "Can we say the same for you?" Saban looked at the bloody scene again and then back to Mike.

Mike didn't say another word. He limped across the street to his car and dragged himself slowly inside it. The bloody battle, the knowledge that his death had been so close, and that Saban would do more than kill him, did what nothing else could have. Right now, in shock, Claxton had taken in the truth of what had happened. He had nearly destroyed Natalie rather than saving her, and whether he had known it before or not, right now, he knew this was his last chance to live.

"We weren't trained to have mercy, Brother."

Saban turned to meet eyes identical to his own in a face so delicate, so sweetly curved that at times he couldn't believe she was one
of the highly trained, merciless Breed Enforcers the Bureau of Breed
Affairs prized so highly.

Long, black hair was braided into a thick plait and fell to the middle of her back, while her slender, doelike body radiated confidence
and strength.

"We weren't trained to have it, yet we do." He shrugged carelessly.

"I'll keep an eye on him for a while. Make sure he gets home safe.
We'd hate for him to have an accident between here and there." Her
smile was cold, hard, her eyes like chips of green ice.

"I gave him his life; take it at your own risk, Chimera," he
warned her.

"You're going to spoil her," she stated.

Saban shrugged again.

No, he wasn't spoiling her, he was letting her go. She would keep
the job; that had nothing to do with him. Whether she stayed, left, or
allowed Claxton back into her life was her choice.

"Tell Jonas to have Natalie escorted home and assign her a new
bodyguard," he told his sister as he fought the pain building in his
chest. "I'll follow up with the scientist we captured and see to his
transport to Sanctuary."

He had to force the words past his lips.

"And if he sends a male with her?" Chimera asked.

Saban just shook his head and moved away from her, knowing
she would do exactly as he asked. She had never failed him, not once,
not before their escape, not after. And if, as she asked, Jonas sent
another male to guard his mate?

God, such pain shouldn't be possible without an open wound.
How could his heart still beat in his chest when it felt as though it
were ripped from his body?

Love. God, he had waited for this, dreamed of it, from the moment he had learned that Breeds mated, that their one and only would be their natural one and only, he had waited and he had hoped.

And this was what he had hoped for? A woman who, though she may care for him, loved another.

He had to force himself not to look back at the mall, to the doors where he had left her. He had to force himself to the van where the scientist was confined, restrained and awaiting transport.

Saban stepped to the opened back doors and smiled. A slow, cold smile that showed his canines and bore little resemblance to a civilized being. He didn't feel so civilized right now.

"Well now, Dr. Amburg." He greeted the aging scientist with a growl. "How nice to see you here today. I trust you're doing well?"

Beldon Amburg. He had tortured, murdered, experimented on, and destroyed more lives than Saban could count. His file was extensive; the proof of the atrocities committed at the lab he headed was stored in boxes rather than files.

"You've forgotten who your masters are, animal," Amburg sneered. "One day, you'll bow before us again, and we'll know no mercy."

"Oh, you knew mercy before?" Saban widened his eyes in surprise. "Well now, you'll have to jus' tell me 'bout dat lil' thing," he announced sarcastically as he stepped into the van and wrapped his fingers brutally around the thin neck of the scientist known as Bloody Amburg. "Right this way, Doctor. We have a nice little cell just waiting for you."

The scientist gasped for air, but he put up little struggle. Saban dragged him from the bullet-ridden van to the secured security van that pulled up alongside it.

The back doors opened, revealing two Breeds, weapons held ready. The restraints locked into the floor of the van were lifted by a third Breed. And that one, Saban knew, would never leave Amburg alive if he had the chance. Mercury had more reason than most to see this particular scientist dead.

"Mercury, ride up front." Saban pulled his captive in and took the ends of the restraints himself. Snapping them on, he felt the Breed behind him move to the side.

"I'll let him live." The voice was a demon's growl, causing Amburg to collapse onto the wide metal seat bolted to the wall behind him.

"I'm just going to make sure." Saban shook his head. "Ride up front. I'll ride back here with Lawe and Rule."

He took his seat, another metal bench facing Amburg.

Mercury snarled but moved from the van, allowing the other two Breeds to jump inside before securing the doors.

"We have two escorts front and back to Sanctuary," Lawe announced. "Seems there's a report there could be more Council soldiers in the vicinity. Jonas is expecting trouble."

Saban kept his eyes on Amburg. "If they attack, put a bullet in his head. He's not worth dying for."

Amburg swallowed tightly, terror flashing in his cold, pale blue eyes.

Terror was a good thing, Saban thought, because right now, he was just enraged enough to kill for the simple hell of it. His mate was back at the mall, alone, without him, without the ex-husband she had risked her life to save.

And here he was, guarding a fucking Council doctor. Hell, today just sucked.

As Lawe moved to close the doors to the van, Saban looked out, his gaze moving instinctively to where he left Natalie. There, between the entrances to the mall she stood, one hand pressed to the glass door, her cheeks wet with tears. Her eyes were dark, too dark in her pale face, anguished, filled with pain. With sorrow.

As he watched, her lips moved, whispered his name, and he felt his soul shatter.

Lawe slammed the doors closed and secured, but nothing could erase the sight of her pain from his soul.

How the fuck could he ever live without her?

Saban sat outside the little brick house, outside Buffalo Gap, outside
period.

Natalie's bedroom light was on. She'd left the curtains cracked
just the slightest bit, and he'd warned her about that. Warned her to
the point that he had started closing them at night himself, just to
make certain they were secure.

Well, maybe not just to make certain they were secure. Her bedroom was like this hive of scents. Everywhere he turned there was
another subtle tease of a scent that made up Natalie. Her perfume,
the smell of her soap and shampoo mingling, the scent of passion on
her sheets, of frustration on her pillows. The smell of the feminine
struggle against the male dominant force. Her unconscious, wary
battle to hold back her own needs, her hungers, even as the scent of
those needs and hungers reached out to him.

Hell. He rubbed his hand over his face in frustration. How could
he have been so wrong? Dammit, Natalie wasn't a fickle woman.
Fickle had a scent, just as deceit, dishonesty, and depravity had a
scent. There was nothing fickle in what he smelled from his mate.

Stubborn. Eh, she had vast quantities of stubborn. Distrust, she
had a fairly healthy dose of that as well. But her character was strong,
pure.

He leaned his head back against the seat with a rough growl. He
remembered clearly his rage when he realized what she had done.

She had risked her life, risked the life they could have together, and her own soul with the horror she would have faced if Amburg had managed to take her. All to save the worthless hide of an ex-husband.

But hadn't she also nearly wrecked the vehicle Callan had given her that first week to avoid a lame dog in the middle of the road that couldn't move quick enough? Then, sweet *mercy*, what had that female done? She had gotten out of the car and approached it, despite its terrified growls and dazed eyes.

She had risked herself then as well. And him. He still carried the mark of that mangy mutt's teeth in his leg where it had bitten him. All because molasses-brown eyes had been filled with tears, and his mate's soft heart had decided the bastard deserved to live.

It could have rabies, yet, there he had been, risking his neck for a wounded, enraged animal so she wouldn't risk hers.

Could Mike be no more than a stray that she feared he would euthanize?

Or was he attempting to make excuses for himself and the woman who owned his soul?

He inhaled warily, looked at the digital time displayed on the dashboard of his truck, and grimaced. It was nearly three in the morning. Natalie was still awake; he had seen her shadow pass the slit in the curtains. He knew the enforcers, Shiloh Gage and Mercury Warrant, were still awake.

Two of the most contrary Breeds ever born were Shiloh and Mercury. No doubt they were in different rooms, in opposite corners waiting, like a cat on a mouse, for the unwary.

No wonder Natalie was pacing the floors. When those two were on guard duty, conversation was in very short supply.

Damn. He'd sat out here in the dark feeling fucking sorry for himself long enough. He wasn't going to have the answers he needed until he confronted her, until he asked her why she risked herself for her ex-husband. And he would have his answers.

He was man enough to accept that she had loved before, but he'd be damned if he was man enough to accept that those emotions could still remain for another man.

Pushing the truck door open, he moved from the vehicle, closing and locking it with a flick of the security button on the key before heading to the house.

The front door opened before he stepped to the porch, and Shiloh stepped outside, quietly closing the door behind her before leaning against the doorframe.

Dressed in black, her long, dark hair pulled back tight from her face, her dark gold eyes gleaming in the moonlight, she looked exactly as she was: a powerful predator, a force to be reckoned with.

She was considered the brat of Sanctuary, a bit spoiled, definitely a shade arrogant, but she had a kind heart. And from her expression, she had managed to find a bit of sympathy for Natalie.

"Shiloh." He stepped onto the porch.

"Broussard." She smiled, but it wasn't pleasant.

Shiloh wasn't known for her even temperament, but she was known for her ability to hurt a man. In ways he was sure even the Council wouldn't have approved of.

He stopped and stared back at her evenly. "Are you gonna let me into that house, Shi?"

She looked out into the night before bringing her gaze back to him.

"She's cried most of the evening." There was a hint of a hiss in her voice. "Since when is it okay to make your mate miserable, Saban? This damned place reeks of her misery."

"I'll take care of her," he assured the enforcer. "You have your own things to take care of. I thank you for coming here and taking care of her for me."

She sniffed at the gratitude but moved away from the door before opening it and heading for the steps.

Mercury moved from the darkness beyond, nodding easily to Saban before he followed the other enforcer and disappeared into the night.

Saban stepped into the house, locked the door, and checked the security system before heading for the stairs.

Strangely, it wasn't misery that the house reeked of, it was anger. Hot, brilliant, and definitely female.

He moved up the stairs, slid into the hallway, and approached her closed door. Beyond that door lay ecstasy. The bed he had shared with his mate, the scent of their passion, the knowledge, complete and overwhelming, that this woman belonged to him, no matter the evidence to the contrary.

This insanity where she thought she could save the world and those hapless males drawn to trouble because of their own stupidity was going to have to stop though.

He clenched his teeth as the scent of anger grew sharper here, firing the hormone-laced adrenaline, pounding in his head with a primal urge to show her, to enforce his dominance over her. To ensure this never happened again.

Never, ever, would she take another's side against him. If he felt blood needed to be shed, then he would shed it. He didn't need her standing between him and danger or between him and his own conscience.

She had no idea the blood he had already shed in his fight to survive. Standing between him and one weak-kneed, paranoid little son of a bitch wasn't going to make a difference, and she needed to learn that right quick.

He gripped the doorknob, pushed the door open, and with a quick widening of his eyes ducked to avoid whatever heavy object was sailing through the air toward his head.

"Dammit, Natalie!" He ducked again and quickly sidestepped another projectile. Some kind of white ceramic creature he guessed as it shattered against the doorframe as the door slammed closed. "That's enough."

"I'll show you enough!" The bedside clock flew at his head and struck his shoulder with a resounding whack. The pain was minimal, but he didn't have to give her a chance to perfect her aim. He jumped for her.

She was fast, but she wasn't fast enough. Hooking his arm around her waist, he tossed her to the bed, coming down on her quickly. He straddled her thighs, gripped her wrists in one hand, and held her securely to the bed.

The short robe she wore had worked to her thighs, the loosely belted front slipped open, revealing hard little nipples and swollen, flushed breasts.

The pert mounds bounced as she struggled against him and had his cock straining against his zipper, desperate to be free. The scent of anger and desire filled the room. The heat of it flushed her cheeks and made her eyes darker.

And the scent of pain. It was carefully masked beneath the anger, but he could smell her hurt, sense it in the air around them.

"You dirty bastard, get off me," she screamed. "Get off me, and get out of my house. Go back to wherever the hell you came from. I don't want you here."

Those were tears glittering in her eyes, the damp sheen making her eyes more luminous, darker, sweeter than ever.

Leaning toward her, he let the low, warning rumble in his chest free. The rough, primal sound only had her eyes narrowing, her face flushing deeper.

"That growling thing is not working on me," she snapped. "You left. You left me with Breeds that wouldn't even speak to me. But even worse, moron, you left me hurting!"

He had a feeling she wasn't talking about arousal or mating heat.

"And how, mate, did I leave you hurting?" He snarled. "By not trusting you? By deceiving you and placing my life deliberately in danger? Deliberately choosing another over my mate! Did I do this?"

"What you did was so much worse," she panted, her voice rasping. "You left me, Saban. You left when you swore you would never leave me." A single tear caressed her cheek. "You lied to me."

Yes, he had. He wiped the tear from her cheek with his thumb, feeling the guilt that rode inside him.

"I came back." He wasn't going to be swayed by tear-filled eyes.

"At three o'clock in the morning," she sneered.

Saban almost smiled. She sounded like a wife, and the knowledge filled him with a sense of excitement rather than anger. She could keep a time card on him whenever she pleased.

"Why did you go to him?" He asked the question, hating himself for it, hating the anger that filled him because of it. "I nearly lost you, Natalie. I would have lost my soul if anything had happened to you. Why? Why would you fucking take that risk? Is he so important to you?"

"You're that important to me." She jerked, raising her head until they were nearly nose to nose, flames flickering in her dark eyes. "I wanted him gone. I wanted him to leave, and I didn't want you to have to kill him to achieve it."

Saban shook his head in confusion. The way this woman's mind worked, he would never figure her out.

"What made you think you could make him leave? Even if the Council soldiers hadn't been involved, Natalie. What in God's name made you think he would listen to you?"

She breathed out heavily and glared back at him.

"Tell me." He snarled.

Her gaze became cutting, furious. "Because he knows me, Saban. I threw him out of our house; I divorced him despite his pleas. Once he knew, beyond a shadow of a doubt, that he didn't have a chance, he would have left. He would have hated me, and that was fine, but he would have left."

"And what could you have said to convince him of it when fear of me didn't?" He growled. "For God's sake, Natalie, there's nothing you could have said."

"I could have told him I love you!" she cried, shocking him to silence. "I could have told him that if he didn't leave, then I'd not stand between him and your fists ever again. Damn you. I could have made him see reason."

"Why would you want to?" He shook his head. She had said she loved him, and she meant it. He could see it in her eyes, in her face, he could smell the sweet, burning scent of it now. She loved him.

"Because I can't stand to see animals or fools bloody and dying. Geez, Saban, letting you loose on him would be like letting an alligator free in a chicken house. Complete annihilation."

"You were protecting him," he growled.

She rolled her eyes! Right there, staring right at him, she rolled her eyes at him as though he were an idiot. It shouldn't have pleased him, but it filled him with pride.

"No, asshole, I was protecting you from defending yourself against a murder charge," she snapped back. "If you haven't noticed, you're not exactly rational where he's concerned."

"Because he's consorting with Council scientists," he yelled impatiently, glowering down at her. "For God's sake, Natalie—"

"Well, I didn't know he was that stupid," she muttered. "Intense, yes; paranoid, sure; that's Mike Claxton, but he didn't used to be incredibly stupid."

He shook his head, amazement filling him. "You're serious." He couldn't believe it. "You expected me to be rational when he was clearly violent toward you—"

"He's never hit me."

"No, he would just turn you over to monsters." His voice was rising. "Trust me, you'd have preferred that he try to hit you."

"That's not the point."

"Not the point?" He was going to pull his own hair out.

"The point is," her voice softened, "I love you, Saban. I'd have done just about anything, said anything to get him out of our lives. I thought Mike was smarter than he was. I was wrong. I was wrong, and it will never happen again." Her voice hitched as her eyes filled with tears again. "But it won't change the fact that you left me, that you couldn't even look at me or find out for yourself why I felt I had to do it. Nothing will change that."

"That, mate, is where you are wrong."

Natalie would always remember the sight of Saban jumping into the van with that nasty little scientist, refusing to look at her, refusing to give her a chance to explain. It didn't matter that she had realized she had made a mistake even before Mike had attempted to kidnap her. What mattered was his refusal to even ask her why. She would have asked him why. She would have demanded to know why.

Shaking her head, she struggled against him, jerking at her wrists as he held her easily, staring down at her with those brilliant eyes, spiking her heartbeat with the look in them.

Possessive, dominant, everything she thought she would abhor and was now finding herself drawn to.

She stilled beneath him, watching him from under her lashes, growing angrier by the moment. Fine, he was the big, bad, strong Breed, but she hadn't been raised with her brother for nothing.

The minute she stopped struggling, his hold loosened on her wrists, just the slightest bit, but enough for her to jerk her upper torso up and to bring her lips to his. Where she bit him. A sharp little nip to that delicious lower lip before she was back, writhing, twisting beneath him.

"You little hellion." His voice was filled with wonder as a small bead of blood formed on his lip. "That was no love nip."

"How would you know?" she panted. "Maybe you're not the only one who likes to bite."

She managed to free one wrist, and before he could grab it again, she reached out, locked her fingers into the muscle of his chest, right around his nipple, and twisted.

He jerked back with a muttered curse, releasing her wrists, giving her the room she needed to twist away from him.

"I don't need a man who doesn't trust my love," she yelled furiously as she freed herself.

"You need a man to paddle your delectable little behind for being so damned stubborn," he snarled, rubbing at his chest as he stared back at her almost wonderingly.

"Or a man who isn't so damned filled with pride he can't even wait around for a reasonable explanation." She managed to roll to the side of the bed and jump out of his reach.

She had a feeling he let her, though.

"The explanation would have to be reasonable first," he growled. "Yours wasn't."

"So spank me," she retorted, her voice mocking. "At least I didn't run away from the problem."

She stood on one side of the bed breathing hard as he glowered at her from the other side of the bed.

"I intend to get to that, *cher*, real soon," he drawled, his expression tightening not in anger but in arousal. "And I didn't run far, did I *bébé*? I came right back here to be the one to deliver the spanking."

Natalie felt her ass clench at the tone of his voice. He sounded serious. Maybe he sounded a little bit too serious.

"You wouldn't dare," she gasped, her eyes widening as he stripped off his shirt.

"Watch me." His eyes narrowed on her as her gaze flicked to where he was quickly releasing the closures on his jeans.

"You are not undressing," she snapped.

She couldn't believe it. Did he think this could be fixed with sex?

"Watch me," he repeated.

He sat down on the small, fussy chair beside her bed, unlaced and removed his boots, then stood and shucked his pants.

Oh Lord, she was in so much trouble. He was furiously aroused, his erection standing out from his body, thick and heavy, the ridged veins throbbing with subtle power.

"You can take those clothes off, or I'm going to rip them off you." He moved around the bottom of the bed, each shift of muscle, each flex of his long, corded body sending a flare of heated lust to ignite in the center of her womb.

God, the man was just gorgeous. Maybe just a little bit pissed if the heated flare of emotion in his eyes was anything to go by.

"I'm not fucking you while you're angry," she informed him coolly, or at least, she tried for cool; there might have been the slightest tremor of arousal in her voice. Because he was really turning her on.

"I'm not angry." A flash of strong white teeth in a confident, anticipatory smile. "I've decided something about you, *cher*. As stubborn and independent as you are, you're coming to believe that the reason you do things is not so important as the fact that you be allowed to do them. That the control streak you're adopting be given free rein."

"So?" She watched him warily, backing up as, naked, aroused, and dominating, he stalked toward her.

"Tonight, love, you learn, in matters of your safety, this will not be allowed. First lesson begins now."

Natalie shrieked as she watched the muscles in his chest bunch, but by the time she saw it, it was too late to run. And it was too late to save the robe she had dressed in after her shower.

The material tore and slipped to the floor as the sleeves ripped and the tatters of cloth were tossed away a second later. Natalie stared down at her bare breasts in amazement then up to Saban's narrowed gaze.

"That was just so wrong," she muttered.

"Ah, but was it as wrong as defying me, slipping away from me, and nearly getting yourself kidnapped?" He shook a finger at her before he struck again.

Before Natalie could consider running, she found herself on her back, the light cotton pajama bottoms flying through the air as Saban tossed them over his shoulder.

She was naked now. Naked and hot and wet, and she was damned if she going to let him get away with this.

She jerked to rise from the bed, only to find herself pushed back, rolled to her stomach, and a hard male weight straddling her thighs as one broad, calloused palm pressed between her shoulder blades, holding her to the bed despite her struggles.

"I said I was sorry," she bit out. "What more do you want? I won't do it again."

The opposite hand stroked over the curve of her butt as his fingertips pressed lightly against the narrow crease.

"Saban, I love you. You know I love you. I swear, I learned my lesson already." Okay, she was caving, but she had been wrong, she was big enough to admit to it. "You shouldn't have walked away like that. You shouldn't have left me."

"I'll never leave you again, *cher*." The words whispered over the small of her back a second before his lips grazed the flesh. "Should you ever be so foolish again, I'll spank you where you stand."

His hand landed lightly on the curve of her ass.

Natalie froze, her eyes jerking wide at the incredible streak of burning pleasure that tore through the nerve endings there.

"Saban." Was that weak, whimpering sound actually coming from her lips? She sounded like a sex vamp begging for more.

"You'll be a good girl in the future, will you no, *cher*?" The accent slipped out, cutting words and sounding so incredibly sexy she almost climaxed from the sound of it alone.

"This is ridiculous," she cried out as another firm slap landed on her rear, sending those curling fingers of heat and pleasure to wrap around her already swollen clit.

His hand landed again, again. Oh God, she could feel her flesh heating, blushing, and she knew she should be outraged, furious; instead, she was burning alive with arousal.

She could feel the dampness between her thighs, coating her pussy, spreading along her clit and increasing its sensitivity.

"I'll not walk away again, mate." He leaned forward, his lips pressing between her shoulders, his teeth rasping over her spine. "I'll love you until you know nothing exists in this life for me but you. I'll protect you, sometimes, from yourself." He nipped at her shoulder. "But never will I leave you again."

His hand slipped between their bodies, found the juices gathering along the swollen folds there, and he growled in hungry demand.

His touch was like a flame. She could feel the pleasure burning inside her, her body begging for more. She should be fighting him, but she couldn't find the will to deny herself, let alone him, what she knew he could give her.

What she knew they both needed.

"Come, *cher*."

Natalie turned eagerly as he lifted his weight from her, turning her to him. Her arms twined around his neck, dragging his chest to her breasts and his lips to hers.

She wanted that kiss. She was burning for it, dying for it. When it came, it was filled with the taste of wild lust and stormy emotion. Anger and fear laced each desperate bite of passion, each sip of lips as their moans mingled, their hands caressed.

Oh God, his hands. Calloused and strong, they skimmed over her flesh as his lips moved to her neck, licked, stroked. A frenzy of sensations tore through her. She could feel the heat like lightning, searing her flesh.

"Mine!" He snarled the word against the curve of her breast. "Always mine."

She wasn't fighting it, she couldn't fight it. The hours he had left her alone had given her a chance to think, a chance to feel. She had faced the thought of life without him and found it intolerable.

"Come for me, *cher*." His fingers slipped inside her pussy, stroked with diabolic pleasure, as his lips covered the hard point of her nipple.

And she did just as he asked; she came, shuddering, arching, feeling the pleasure overtake her in gentle, consuming waves.

"Ah, *cher*." He licked her nipple, grazed his teeth over it. *"Ma cher."*

"I love you." She whispered the words against his neck as she held on tight and felt the shudder of response that rippled through his hard body. "I'll always love you."

She would never be able to walk away as she had with Mike. That knowledge was both terrifying and exhilarating, knowing he held that much of her soul.

"I treasure you." He kissed her nipple with suckling little motions of his lips. "I adore you." His head moved to her stomach. "Ah, *cher*, I love you until I feel lost without you." His lips lowered to the swollen, saturated folds of her pussy.

Pleasure became a vortex of sensation. She screamed his name as he licked, sucked, tasted, and growled into the wet heat of her sex.

His teeth tugged at the swollen folds, his tongue licked and probed and wrapped around her clit with rasping little caresses that sent her exploding into the night.

When he dragged his body over hers, his cock nudging at the entrance to her vagina, Natalie forced her eyes open, lifted her lashes, and became lost in his gaze.

"I marked you," he growled roughly. "Mine. Forever."

"Stole me with a kiss," she whimpered, arching against him. "Steal some more, Saban."

With his Jaguar kiss, with the taste of lust and the touch of a conquering warrior, he had stolen her heart and become a part of her soul.

Natalie cried out his name as he took possession of what was his. His erection pressing forward, the silk-over-steel flesh parting delicate tissue, caressing, burning with a pleasure that fired more pleasure and sent her careening into a world where nothing mattered but the pleasure, the touch, the taste of his kiss.

Strained cries echoed around her as she felt the blaze of ecstasy, the pounding strength of his cock shafting inside her forcefully, as sensation became a hunger and hunger became a demand.

She writhed beneath him, arching to him, driving him deeper until the force of the need exploded through her, brilliant, lightning hot, and filled with all the love she had kept inside, locked away, frightened of the pain of losing this man. If she lost him, how much of herself would she lose as well?

As she felt his climax tearing through him, felt the barb in all its burning pleasure extend inside her, locking him in place as his semen spurted hot and fierce into the depths of her pussy, Natalie knew she would lose all of herself.

"I love you more than life," she whispered, tears filling her eyes as she held him to her, her nails pressing into his back, her lips pressed to his shoulder. "Don't leave me, Saban. Never, never leave me."

"Even death won't tear me from you." His head lifted, his green eyes nearly black with the emotions ripping between them, soul to soul. "Even death, Natalie, could not tear my soul from yours."

She lifted her hand to his face, let the tears fall, and let him shelter her in the strength of his arms, in an embrace as freeing as it was protective.

It would never be easy, but right here, sheltered by her Jaguar, loved, protected, held, she knew it was definitely worth fighting for.

And together, one heart, one soul, they whispered, "I love you."